The

Sidney Sawyer

Missouri Yankees

David M. Smeltz

Other books by
David M. Smeltz

The Ace of Hearts

Mark Twain's rascals
come of age while the nation
races toward Civil War

The Adventures of Sidney Sawyer
The River War

Sawyer battles along southern rivers
to Shiloh and a midnight
reckoning at Bloody Pond

The Adventures of Sidney Sawyer:
The Year of Jubilee

Sawyer joins Lincoln's grand plan
for emancipation, climaxing in the
fires of bloody Antietam

The Adventures of Sidney Sawyer
The Father of Waters

The Union and *Confederate Armys'*
greatest scalawag battles his way
down the Father of Waters to
ransom the river for Father Abraham.

Civil War Creative Workshop
www.civilwarcw.com

Dedicated to the heroes
of the United States
Colored Troops
&
to my wife, Nina,
&
to my sons,
Ted & Andy

Men of Color
To Arms! To Arms!
Now or Never

Three Years Service!
Fail now and our Race is Doomed
Are Freemen less Brave than Slaves?

(From a recruiting poster for the
United States Colored Troops)

Foreword
Fifth packet of the Sawyer Memoirs

It is my prerogative as editor of the notorious memoirs of General Sidney Thomas Sawyer to name each packet as it is presented for publication. At first I considered christening this packet *The Adventures of Sidney Sawyer: The Ace of Spades.* This was the nickname given to then Colonel Sawyer during the siege of Charleston in 1863 by the soldiers of his regiment, the 94th Missouri USCT. (United States Colored Troops) It was meant to honor Sawyer, who was beloved by his regiment. It was a play on his West Point nickname, "The Ace of Hearts." In that less racially sensitive age his fellow officers perverted his noble nom de guerre into a term of derision. Command of Colored troops during the Civil War was considered by many to be a disgrace and a professional dead end. It may be of interest to note that another great American soldier, and a future acquaintance of Sawyer's, General of the Armies, John J. Pershing, also acquired a nickname rooted in his service with a colored regiment. His command was the 10th Cavalry– the original "Buffalo Soldiers." He was universally called "Black Jack." As with Sawyer, these names were not meant to be complimentary. On the advice of my proofreaders I decided that *The Ace of Spades* could be construed as racist even though this was the opposite of the original intent of his African American troops. As Colonel Sawyer and his regiment of United States Colored Troops were all Missouri men, I named this edition of the Sawyer Memoirs *Missouri Yankees*. This is how the men of the 94th Infantry referred to themselves.

This packet of Sawyer's memoirs was written after the outbreak of World War I, in the fall and winter of 1914-1915, when the old general and his wife returned to their home in Buffalo, New York after touring England.

I came into possession of these papers through my great-grandfather, John Martin, who rode in the 7th Cavalry with Sawyer during the Sioux Wars in the 1870's. My grandmother, Mrs. Matilda Martin, was the only soul before me to have read General Sawyer's memoirs. My Nana could not abide vulgar language and, being a lady ahead of her time, would not tolerate the racist n-word in her presence. As she read the old soldier's story she blackened out his cussing and his casual use of this racial slur. She left in the word "darkie," which in her generation was considered a polite form of address. Other than occasionally correcting punctuation or the misspelling of a proper name I left Sawyer's narrative alone. I did however keep in my grandmother's gentle editing of the reprehensible n-word. I also cannot tolerate that racial slur.

Yes, this is *the* Sidney Sawyer, Tom Sawyer's younger half-brother, described in a most unflattering way in Mark Twain's classic book, *The Adventures of Tom Sawyer*. This fifth packet of the Sawyer memoirs sheds fascinating light on the subsequent lives of Brother Tom, freed slave Jim Watson, his deaf daughter Lizabeth, beloved Aunt Polly, and Amy Lawrence, who became Mrs. Sidney Sawyer. New light is also shed on African American regiments in the Civil War, and the personalities of Secretary of War, Edwin Stanton and Generals Henry Halleck, Quincy Gillmore, U.S. Grant, William T. Sherman, George Thomas and Nathanial Banks. Finally, historically significant firsthand accounts are narrated of the Siege of Charleston and Battery Wagner, the opening of the famous Cracker Line to Chattanooga, the relief of the Army of the Cumberland and the Red River Campaign.

As with the first four packets of the Sawyer papers my contributions as editor are modest. I added footnotes to explain period terms or references that may not be clear to a modern reader. I included an appendix to illuminate events or personalities referred to by Sawyer, and I also organized his notes into chapters.

During the Civil War, Colonel Sidney Thomas Sawyer was, and remained all of his life, a scoundrel and a racist who never once considered the brotherhood of man. However, he wrote his memoirs with an honesty that is astounding. His story includes shame, shirking, fraudulent glory, and shocking behavior. He was an officer, but no gentleman. Despite his indifference to the plight of Negroes he was loved as a hero to many African Americans, including Jim Watson and Frederick Douglas. It is in honor of the 8,000 African Americans from Missouri who served in the USCT that I titled this packet of his memoirs, *The Adventures of Sidney Sawyer: Missouri Yankees*.

The Adventures of Sidney Sawyer

Missouri Yankees

Part I
England

Chapter 1

Aye, the curse is on me again like the sweats and there's nothing for it but to scribble. Damnation in the tall corn, but I've already got a thousand sheets of my foolishness stacked in the gun cabinet waiting for whoever is daft enough to read it. The only soul who will *never* read it is my Amy. And why should she? We've been married since before I chiseled my way into West Point. If she's never met her real husband it's because I've always cared enough to lie to her. The *real* Sidney Sawyer is in these pages but she'll never get to meet him. I'm never too foxed to forget to snap home the big brass Yale lock on the cabinet door, and I hide the key in the jolly boat on my model of the old *Carondelet* on the mantle. The grand old barge is so ugly she'd never cotton to give it a glance.[1]

The curse first started when cousin Sam Clemens gave up his ghost and rode off to glory on the tail of Halley's Comet back in aught-ten. You all know the story of how "Saint" Twain was born in the year of the Comet and seventy-six years later went out on its coattails. He dragged my reputation through the gumbo in his damn book about my half-brother Tom, and then again with his nonsense about Sergeant Major Finn back when Huckleberry was still a feral brat sleeping in a hogshead along the big river back in the '40s. Everybody's read his books since. The blasted things are assigned in schools– as if Sam's rubbish was Milton or Hawthorne or bloody Shakespeare.[a]

It isn't enough to make me weep, but it is enough to make me grind my molars and punish the brandy, especially after the way he pegged me in his books. Little Siddy Sawyer, the crybaby snitch, the pantywaist, the sissy. By grapes, I was never a sissy! And now the whole nation loves Brother Tom. Tom Sawyer, the loveable curly-haired rascal who's lighthearted pranks delighted generations of American tykes. Lighthearted pranks my arse. Let him and his gang of brats bullyrag you from here to breakfast, whip rocks at your legs, make your childhood a torment, and see how you like it! And he wound up a congressman– from Nevada no less! How's that for a recommendation to his character? I wanted to set the record straight ever since the mob began to look at me cross-eyed because of Clemens' slander. When he died four years ago it set the curse on me like the malaria sweats and I set Amy's Irish spoon-polisher Mairead, to the task of keeping my pencils sharp and my snifter charged. (Or is it Margaret? I can never keep 'em straight. The Hibernian help's as interchangeable as one of Mr. Ford's fenders.)[b] Then I set to writing my *own* story. Every time I reckon I'm good and done some damn fool thing happens to set the curse on me yet again. Now, where's Mairead? I've just started and an empty glass is a useless thing.

* * *

---

[a] Samuel Clemens was born with the 1835 appearance of Halley's Comet and died during its next visit in 1910. *The Adventures of Tom Sawyer* was published in 1876. *The Adventures of Huckleberry Finn* was published in 1885.

[b] In 1908 the first Model T Fords rolled off the line at the Piquette Plant in Detroit.

Most of my follies are my own foolish fault, but they usually jump up and infect me in a fashion that's timely enough for me to reckon it justice. What set this present curse on me was a folly from two score and twelve years ago that sprang up and bit me like a viper in the grass. It damned near killed me just as dead as any cottonmouth or diamond-back. We were in Europe, Amy and me, to do a last Grand Tour before we were too knackered to enjoy the ride. We had the coin and I had a letter of introduction from Bob Taft that opened all doors. Fat Bob didn't much care for the likes of me but Amy was kind to his wife Helen after her stroke, and he would have given me the credentials anyway just to get me out of the country. In any event, through the spring of '14 we traveled in style, dined with royalty, rubbed elbows with gentry at the finest spas and were finishing up our travels in England being passed from the hospitality of one noble family to the next.

The billiard room of a grand country house in the sunny downs of an English estate may seem like a damned odd place to rekindle a feud from a long ago lost cause, but people plant mischief where they reckon it will sprout. The atmosphere in the game room was as raw as any I've struck in Dakota mining hells or waterfront dives in Manila or Batavia. The tension was thick, but politely hidden under a rigid mask of proper manners. The topic of the hour was war. Europe hadn't had a general dust-up in ninety-nine years and none of the fools about the table were afraid of it. Well, I was. Now the entire continent was rushing toward it as if to the arms of a lover.

You may know the type of establishment. Or if you're an American maybe you don't. My home in Buffalo, on Delaware Avenue, is one of the grander piles in the city. Thirty rooms, with a quarter-ton chandelier above the table, Tiffany glass about the door, flub-dubs and doilies on every surface, a carriage-house with a Thomas motor-car as big as a barge, and three water-closets for family and one for the help. But compared to English country homes it just don't consider. On our side of the Atlantic we simply don't have anything like these giant mansions or abbeys or *houses*! But they ain't houses. They're more like castles, but they ain't castles either. Castles have ramparts, and redoubts, and moats to keep out enemy invaders and mobs of disaffected locals that now and again storm the walls to plunder the wealth of the resident gentry. The country homes of the British nobility don't need the stout walls that are as necessary as plumbing in the rest of Europe. The Limeys are peaceful folk and do their slaughter on Hindoos, Zulus, East African n—rs, and other simple souls who never had the grace to wear shoes. At home the British mind their manners and no walls or moats are required. These homes can ramble to hundreds of rooms, from grand ballrooms to cubbies. They have acres of roofs, miles of fields and pasture, stables of horses, and packs of blooded hounds. The surrounding villages supply swarms of groveling servants. You can find the like here and there in America, at Newport or out on Long Island, but the houses ain't as big, American domestics don't grovel, and Yankee moneybags don't have the style. The grand antebellum plantation homes in the old cotton South weren't in the same league.

I don't often find a cause that rates the effort of argument but Colonel Ballentine-Blythe waxing on the therapeutic Darwinian benefits of war was positively causing the billiard cue to spasm in my paw.

"A good blood-letting is just what England needs, what do you say? You Yanks had your fun when you were a lad– Gettysburg, Fredericksburg, *Bull* Run! I envy you General Sawyer."

The snide bastard didn't envy me anything. He certainly didn't like me. He'd been picking at my nerves since he showed up unannounced this morning in a motorcar as big as a hearse, scattering the gravel and startling the help.

"My service was mostly in the West. I missed those fiascos, but the ones I was in weren't fun by a long drop. Shiloh– Vicksburg– Battery Wagner– Chattanooga– Red River! Save your envy!"

I might have saved my breath. He was a boor out to make a point. The other half-dozen gentlemen about the table nodded like a Greek chorus of puffins. Other than a kilted Scot poor relation, Ballentine-Blythe was the only one present that wasn't in proper dress with bib and tucker. He was in full regimental fig, tight crimson cherry-picker style pants, blue tunic buttoned tight to his neck, frogged epaulets shining on each shoulder, and swarms of golden embroidery up and down his breast and about his sleeves. His tin-ware from India service and that Boer nonsense glittered on his trim chest like broaches on a dowager's bosom. His hair was pomaded in a pompadour and his whiskers were as grand as mine. His were still ginger, damn him, while mine were white as snow.

"Of course I saw my share of battle along the Khyber Frontier and in the late war– Paardeberg, and riding to the relief of Ladysmith. Ah, but it was nothing like your grand killing contests. More's the pity."[c]

"If you're talking that Darwin nonsense about finches' beaks and horses' arses you're off the mark by a long pitch."

"I believe Mr. Darwin wrote about horses necks," piped in a young wiseacre whose pimples hadn't yet cleared up. "Stretching their *necks* generation after generation to browse the higher foliage. Not the portion of the animal's anatomy you referenced."

"I read his damn book, too, sonny!"[2]

---

[c] Warfare was *and still is* constant along the Northern Frontiers of the Subcontinent and Afghanistan. During the Boer War the Battle of Paardeberg and the Relief of Ladysmith, (February, 1900) although British victories, were actually mismanaged shambles. It is almost impossible for Colonel Ballentine-Blythe to have participated in both.

I hadn't, but you couldn't help but to know the general outline of his moonshine. It had been argued, damned, and defended from parlor to parliament to pulpit for the last fifty years. Now a certain class of idiots was grafting this "survival of the fittest" drivel onto a suffering humanity, as if having a monkey for an uncle wasn't bad enough. Besides, I enjoyed calling a British peer "sonny" and seeing him flush under his whiteheads.

"And it ain't horses straining their necks to become giraffes or flocks of blasted birds pecking about in the bushes, this one for seeds and that one for bugs, that's the subject. It's war. And war ain't survival of the fittest."

"Why, of course it is, General Sawyer! Your own Mr. Roosevelt would agree. War is a racial imperative. Few races are fit to rule, and even they must be culled to promote the health of the whole with a healthy blood purge every generation or so."

I knew they'd throw that four-eyed cowboy at me. Back home Teddy was in as much of a lather for war as Colonel Ballentine-Blythe. Any war! They roll out Roosevelt like a howitzer and blast him at any argument for peace.

"See here, Colonel, war don't cull out the weak. You cull deer when there's too many of 'em in the park and they're nibbling the shrubbery. In war the first to die are the good'uns, the brave, and the strong, the true believers who love God and country more than life. They run like colts into the enemy line and are mowed down by the numbers with canister and lead and steel. It's just the opposite of TR's entire silly idea. It's your best that die in the ditches. It's the craven and the shirkers that go home to mother."

I should know. I've limped home from more wars than I care to count while better men than me fed the local worms and wigglies. But I was on my soapbox now. I'm an American and used to bourbon liquor. These Limeys drink Scotch whiskey– nasty stuff. That must have been the reason. The billiards were silent and the gentlemen swirled the whiskey in their snifters as I ranted on.

"War *revitalizes* the race? Why, by spring of '65 the trenches before Petersburg were manned by rabble. The best of the race was dead before Mary's Heights, or Cemetery Ridge, the Vicksburg Bluffs, or the Chattanooga trenches. Any infantry left was Dagos or Micks, swept into the ranks fresh off the docks as their boats braced their bowlines to the piers in the Bowery. At *least* the Irish could speak English after a fashion. Or the troops were bounty-jumping rascals that the provost swept up from the riverfront saloons on the Ohio or the canal docks of Buffalo. The very best troops in the line were the n—rs. They at *least* had a dog in the hunt!"

"Come now, *Mister* Sawyer!" sneered Ballentine-Blythe.

"It's General Sawyer to the likes of you!" I blustered.

He ploughed on as if I hadn't interrupted. "I've seen the glory of war. The test of combat! The measure of man against steel! Why, it's the greatest game on Earth."

"Hear-hear!" cried the pimple-faced peer.

The Colonel continued. "My mother is American– from North Carolina. I was brought up on the glory of the Southern cause, the valor of the Southern race."

"Besides, Kaiser Wilhelm has set the bit in his teeth," piped in a fellow with a gut fat as a mortar that I remembered was in Manchester woolens.

"The Frogs are in! Aye, an' if the Hun smashes into Belgium, by Jingo, we shall be in, too, and a damned good thing!" this from the poor relation from the highlands. He was almost as old as me, ridiculous in formal kilt and Braemar-cuffed doublet. He was out of his regiment I'd wager, and too old to muster back in.

"Still, I don't like it."

All eyes in the billiard room turned to the son of our host. He was a stout young fellow, about twenty. Foursquare and keen eyed– the type of youth I'd seen in uniform from the camps about Cairo[d] in my early days to the Powder River Country to Tampa to Manila. Social Darwinism my foot! He was a damned fine boy and knew the risk. He was a peer too, but I liked him. He had asked me to call him Jimmy.

"I have friends in Germany," Jimmy said quietly. "Fine fellows, and in France and Austria, too. Uncle Nicky's in the Russian Navy. Uncle Lutz is in the Kaiserliche Marine. Cousin Kaspar is in the Uhlans.[e] We are all the same race. Damned if we are not all relatives. How can half of us killing off the other half make the race stronger?"

Colonel Ballentine-Blythe snorted. Pimple face sniffed. The wool-peddler bit back a slur. After all, he wasn't a peer.

"Well said, Jimmy," I agreed. "All of Europe is in a sweat to hear the opening gun– the Germans, French, Austrians, Russians. Those Balkan bastards who started this mess, are marching already. Right now across the continent brass bands are blaring, bouquets are being thrown, and belles are hoisting their skirts for a last goodbye."

"Really, General!" boomed a scandalized Ballentine-Blythe. He was willing to send a generation to the guns but couldn't truck soldier talk.

"Yeah, *really*, Colonel! It ain't gonna be like plinking at the Pathans up in the Khyber country or galloping after Afghans with lance and long knife in the defiles. Sabash! Yeah, I was there too, back in the '80's

---

[d] Cairo, (pronounced kar'o) is where the Ohio River joins the Mississippi. There, in 1861, General Grant marshaled the Union Army for its drive up the Tennessee to Shiloh.

[e] Kaiserliche Marine was the German Imperial Navy, disbanded in 1919. Uhlans were the glamorous regiments of Prussian light dragoons. Cavalry was obsolete by The Great War and they fought as infantry in the trenches. They were also disbanded after the War.

and I know the sport as well as you. And it ain't gonna be like that Bore business either, where a few thousand professionals stood the line and the rest stayed home. Everyone will go to this picnic, every man and boy–millions!"

"And then we shall win!" shouted pimple-faced peer. "We shall never give in."

"Victory or death!" added wool-peddler who would never have to go.

"Hear-hear and amen!" rumbled the rest.

"Amen and a bulldog," I agreed. "You *will* never give in. The Confederates said the same thing and meant it. It must be in the race. And that's just what they are saying now in Berlin and Paris and Vienna and St. Petersburg and Buda-Pest. Never give in! Fight to the last man in the last ditch! And it'll come to the last ditch. You all have heard of the great forts the Belgians have at Liége?"

"Magnificent!" piped in Ballentine-Blythe.

"Impregnable!" agreed pimple-face peer.

"The Huns 'ud niver dare!" thundered the beet-faced Scott who sloshed the whiskey from his snifter.

"Then why the argument if you don't reckon they'd dare? They'll dare, and in the end the Fortress at Liége won't matter a damn. All of Europe will be a fortress. Every inch of Europe will be a fort. Every battalion with a wagon full of shovels can build their own fort faster than you can say "Jack Robinson" and then cry, 'Come and get us if you can!' But you can't."

"Of course we can!" blustered the Colonel. "The art of war has progressed by leaps and bounds since your War Between the States. And we have the Fleet."

The Greek chorus of puffins nodded on cue. I wanted the shake the silly buggers by their snowy, starched tuckers. They reminded me of McClellan's staff.

"The Fleet ain't gonna win the war. Your Dreadnaughts won't fit up the Rhine. An' war ain't an art. It's blunders an' blood. An' your 'leaps and bounds' will make it worse. In '63 and '64 it was only one hundred miles from Washington to Richmond. It was only a different hundred miles from Chattanooga to Atlanta. Those hundred miles took a full year and Grant and Sherman had the best armies in the world. Regiments as fine as your 20th Punjabis, Colonel, and they were white boys to a man.[f] All the Rebels had was the arrogance of race and one hundred miles of ridges, rivers, and woodland. And along every ridge was a fort and along every riverbank was ten miles of rifle-pits that they threw up in a twinkling. When we marched to their flank they'd shift to the next rise of land and dig another fort. At Chattanooga Sherman assaulted their works on Tunnel Hill head on and they slaughtered his men by the regiment. *White* men all of 'em, of the same heritage and race! And all the Johnnys had was muzzle-loading miniés, brass Napoleons, and shovels. Now you have bolt-action rifles and the Frogs have their new 75 mm field piece that can shoot twenty aimed rounds a minute of fused shrapnel."

Colonel Ballentine-Blythe gave me the look reserved for blithering old soldiers whose memories have gone a' glimmering. "The French have a word for it, General Sawyer, ''Elan!' We call it guts. That will turn the trick."

"And the Johnny Rebs had an answer for it, "ditches!" We Yankees called them trenches. 'Elan and guts can't take 'em. Human flesh can't take 'em. Ditch *or* trench!"

"Than how can we win? How can they win?" This from Jimmy. He was the only one in the billiard room who didn't look at me as if I'd just escaped from Bedlam.

"Lord James," I replied formally, "the only way to win is to stay out."

---

[f] Colonel Ballentine-Blythe's regiment, the 20th Punjabi Infantry, (the Duke of Cambridge's Own) was organized during the Great Mutiny and served through WW II. It was staffed by Pathans and Sikhs, and officered by British regulars.

Colonel Ballentine-Blythe's whiskers quivered. He drew himself up to his full military height and stuck out his chest like poultry. "Nonsense! Why, we shall take Berlin, and Vienna too, like ... well, like your Grant took Richmond."

I may as well have been talking to real poultry. These British aristocrats didn't get it and couldn't get it. They were like the Virginia and Carolina tidewater gentry before our War. *"Why, one Southern gentleman can defeat ten Yankee clerks!"* No, they couldn't. Not if the clerk was in a rifle-pit with forty dead men in his cartridge box and a Springfield rifle in his hand.[g] It couldn't be done. I'd lost the argument but the booze was making me bull-headed.

I took a long gulp of their damned Scottish poison and tried again. "Colonel, taking a city, even a capital city, won't settle it. I was there on the Red River when Banks's bummers torched Alexandria. I was with Sherman when we marched into the ruin of Atlanta. In '65 I saw what was left of Richmond and it was damned little. It was the Rebs who burned their *own* cities to deny the rails and rooming to us Yankees. By God, do you reckon the Frogs would do less with Paris if the Huns were at the Seine, or the Germans with Berlin if the Russians were swarming Unter den Linden?"

"General Sawyer's right my friends," Jimmy put in quietly. "If the Hun did cross the Channel we would scorch the earth before him. It would be like Bonaparte before Moscow, but it would be London burning."

Maybe I'd win the argument after all. "By God, gentlemen, Belgium ain't worth it!"

"We know it isn't, General," Jimmy gently broke into my tirade, "but it's more than that. And it certainly

---

[g] Forty dead men was Civil War slang for the forty rounds of ammunition issued to infantry.

isn't any nonsense about purifying the race. Your pardon, Colonel."

Ballentine-Blythe's eyes stormed over his whiskers.

"You see, General Sawyer, we are *England*. We will never suffer a Napoleon or a Kaiser Billy, or any other power on the Channel. That was the entire purpose of creating a Belgium to begin with. This war, if it comes and God spare us it does not, will not be about jingo or sport or race or the Kaiser's bad manners. It's not about *Entente Cordiale* or a Dead Archduke. Gentlemen, it will not even be about honor. It is about survival. The Germans are building a High Seas Fleet that can only have one purpose. And we cannot suffer legions of Prussian blue on the Channel. After all it is the *English* Channel. What we possess, they covet and mean to have. And there it is."[3]

And there it was. Jimmy had stripped away all of the other drivel about war. In the end there is no other reason to fight. None. A people fights to save itself when the enemy is massing at the gates set on conquest, plunder, slavery, and rape. There is no other reason that is worth a damn. Sam Clemens pegged me as a crybaby and a sissy in his damn books, but he pegged me wrong. I ain't a sissy. I'll fight like any rat if I'm cornered, and when my back is to the wall I'm one dangerous son of a bitch. That last week in July, England reckoned itself cornered. The British nation and its wide Empire was buckling on its sword, gritting its teeth and growling a defiant "grrrrrr!" Jimmy was right. The only reason to wage war is survival. It sure ain't good for the race.

The next week the Germans swarmed into Belgium. That same day England declared war and Jimmy rejoined his regiment.[h] In three weeks he was dead in the

---

[h] England entered the Great War on August 4, 1914. Sawyer most probably began this packet of his memoirs in the autumn of 1914.

Belgian mud defending Mons. The rest of England's tiny professional army was killed by the end of September. And now every British man and boy, from Scotland to Canada, from Liverpool and Leeds to Australia, from farms and slums, and the great houses of the nobility, are on their way to the trenches.

* * *

The argument was over and I lost, as if an ancient American general could have prevented the winds of war from blowing across Europe with only a bellyful of dreadful Scotch liquor and a blithering tongue. A butler slithered into the billiard room like a reptile and announced that the ladies were waiting in the drawing room for the gentlemen to escort them to the dining room. That mess-call had a sight more class than when my Auntie Polly would fetch me and Brother Tom to supper by bashing two pots together with a cry of "Come an' git it! Root hog er die!" But I was only ten then. Now I'm pushing eighty. I shot my sleeves and gave my magnificent whiskers a fluff. It wouldn't do to embarrass my Amy with any rough barracks ways in front of our British hosts. I was half foxed but I'd pass the wine and mind the port. Amy always brought out my best. She had a year on me, but was still a damn fine figure of a woman, and at the G.A.R. reunions could still fetch a whistle, and turn heads among the Brahmins of Buffalo who reckon themselves quality.

I strolled into the drawing room with the other fellows. Amy took my arm, regal in her gold tiara. It was studded with pearls that gleamed like quick silver. Centered in a nest of white diamonds was a great yellow diamond that caught the light and threw it back in your eyes like fire. It was the equal to any of the other gems and jewels that cascaded from the necks and ears of the noble English ladies. The tiara was one of Amy's few sinful vanities. Together we stepped happily toward the hall when I stopped in my tracks from a shock that almost stopped my old heart in my ribs.

If I drink, you may wonder why! It is shocks like this that make my old paw reach for the brandy. I'm swilling it now as I write and it may as well be fruit punch. Stepping from the gaggle of ladies was a tiny, frail woman in a dated black gown, clutching her fan in one claw like a stiletto and reaching for the arm of Colonel Ballentine-Blythe with the other. Her hair was iron gray and pulled back ferociously under a severe net of white lace.

"Marmy, dearest," cooed her son, the Colonel.

How sweet. What could possibly be the alarm– a lady on the arm of her doting son? So why was my mind reeling with the memory the shot-torn Confederate ensign waving like a curse above the shattered walls of Fort Sumter while a long line of ugly Yankee monitors boomed away at the defiant flag? Or why did my thoughts turn to colored infantry, sweat slicking their black faces, tearing cartridges from their kits, while they double-timed through deep sand towards the Rebel guns? And why was I seeing doomed soldiers sweeping up Missionary Ridge behind the candy cane flutter of regimental flags while Rebel shot tore ragged holes in their lines? As far as my eye could see and as far as my memory could remember, those wedges of blue infantry, like the great Vs of migrating geese kept climbing into the cannon that couldn't miss in a charge that was suicide and glory and legend. And then I felt the heat and smelled the stink as the bayou city of Alexandria burned again. In the billiard room I had chatted about that doomed city, but now I smelled the reek of smoke choking the breath from me. I felt the walls of flame singeing my whiskers while jayhawker incendiaries and Yankee stragglers raced through the streets with tins of kerosene, friction matches and faces running with soot and snot and tears. I saw Banks's defeated infantry slouching down Front Street to the long road that would take them back to the Mississippi, and they tore the heart out of Louisiana along their march. Instead of the British ladies in the latest fashion with hair swept up and pinned with jeweled barrettes and tiaras, I saw the hollow eyes of slack-faced refugees forced off the lanes by legions of marching men in faded blue. They stood in the red dust, ragged, hopeless and thin from a month of occupation, toting whatever rubbish they could salvage from their shattered lives packed in sacks and bundles.

There was danger in the drawing room amongst the silk drapes, fantasy oils in gilt frames and fine furniture upholstered in pastels to suit the tastes of high bred ladies. There was deadly danger and it radiated from the tiny lady in black on the arm of Ballentine-Blythe like venom spitting from a cobra.

A pinch to the back of my arm brought me back sharp. Amy had pinched me before, usually when I'm in the sauce and threatening to snooze in the soup bowl, but this time it wasn't the booze. It was the lady in black and her son. They were looking at me as spiders contemplate a wasp in their web. No wonder Ballentine-Blythe hurried to join our party in his huge motorcar. No wonder he seemed to dislike me. He hated me! He was the son of Hazel Brassard-Ballentine-Blythe. She was the sister of the most sinister monster I ever struck. His name was Captain Calhoun Hayne Brassard and I had sent him to Hell from the heights above Harpers Ferry back in '62.

The Adventures of Sidney Sawyer
Missouri Yankees

Chapter 2

I kept my peace at supper and nobody noticed my distress but Amy. When she lifted an eyebrow of concern from across the vast table I gave a weak smile, rubbed my guts and gave a shrug. It's easier to explain a bellyache than a guilty conscience and a yellow liver. The table was as big as a Conestoga wagon and there were a score of people sitting at supper with at least another twenty servants bustling about making nuisances of themselves. To my right was the wife of the Scot poor relation, who spoke in a burr so thick I couldn't understand a word of her drivel and didn't bother to try. To my left was the wool merchant's daughter wearing a tacky nouveau riche gown that showed a half-acre of powdered bosom. I'm new money myself, and usually the lass would be just my type of mutton, but for once I didn't even try to fetch an ogle down her udders. My attention was on Ballentine-Blythe seated next to Jimmy and his tiny marmee perched across the linen like a crow two places down from Amy.

By God, they were a pair, mother and son. He glanced at me now and again over the silver service and flowers piled on the table between the glowing candles. The dining room was gas-lit, not yet fitted for the electricity like the billiard or drawing rooms, but there was enough light to see that his hooded eyes gave nothing away. Marmee Hazel's eyes gave away everything! They glinted with pure malice, but something else was there, too. I believe it was triumph. She was happy to see me, but not exactly for my company. She was happy to see her hour of vengeance at hand just across the table. We were in the safest of civilized companies in an English country house. There were starched napkins on our laps and the crystal brimmed with the finest of wines that I didn't dare touch. We were surrounded by peers of the realm and liveried footmen with formalized manners that would have made Huckleberry Finn scratch through his shirt. Where could danger lie? Why my notions of revenge and peril?

Hazel Ballentine-Blythe-Calhoun had good reason to want to see my blood. The bitch had tried to spill it on three different occasions. If it was still sloshing through my old veins it wasn't because of her lack of effort. You see we had something of a family feud, the Sawyers and the Calhouns. The bad blood began back in '56 when as plebes in West Point I put a dueling pistol's ball through her brother Calhoun's skinny puss. Cadet Brassard was my master with sword or pistol, but a challenge was made, and as a cadet I was honor-bound to accept. Thank God, for me honor is negotiable. I cheated like a riverboat spiv and my shot took out his left eye, most of his dental tackle, a cheekbone and half his face. He may have sparked the South Carolina belles before he met me, but not after.[i]

During the War, after the Fort Donelson surrender, Confederate Captain Calhoun Brassard tried to settle accounts. With his commander, that swine Nathan Bedford Forrest, he kidnapped me under a flag of truce, chained me like a n—r on the block, and set out to finish our duel– this time with sabers at dawn. In the wee hours, with the help of a slave wench who had a crush on me, I managed to escape to, of all places, Miss Becky Thatcher's knock-shop. Miss Becky had as good a cause to hate all Sawyers as the Brassard clan. Brother Tom had put her in a family way and then abandoned her like worn boots to the tender

---

[i] For the story of the Sawyer-Brassard duel refer to the first packet of the Sawyer Memoirs published as *The Adventures of Sidney Sawyer: The Ace of Hearts*.

care of her pappy, the judge. Daddy Thatcher tossed her out for a strumpet, and a strumpet she became. Little sunny, pigtailed Becky became the flint-hearted madam of the finest house of questionable repute along the Cumberland. I *will* own that she ran a first class establishment and her whores were all top shelf and center cut. Becky Thatcher, the cat-house queen, joined forces with the noble Brassard family and together they almost took my pills for a prize.[j]

The Brassards were deep blue Carolina aristocrats and honor was their North Star. They were bound to kill me for my unforgivable crimes against the culture of the South and the honor of their family. I was a slave state Missouri boy who sided with the Yankees– in other words I was a n—r lover. I had shot off half of Brother Calhoun's face. I'd fled like a cur from a second reckoning with Captain Calhoun. They were as tenacious as Missouri ticks, the Brassards, and in the summer of '62 they came at me as a brother and sister act. I was in Richmond in Abe Lincoln's political service, which is a polite way to say I was a spy. Sister Hazel, the Widow Ballentine, (her husband was killed in the Shenandoah Valley fighting in Jackson's command) hunted me down and nailed my shoes to the floor of the American Hotel while she sent for Brother Calhoun and Miss Becky to come and join in the fun of my slaughter. She was simply Mrs. Ballantine to me. How was I to know she was sister to my worst nightmare? She kept me happily in Richmond for five weeks by letting me bull her all over the shop, and a dandy little vixen she was, lashing my arse with her hairbrush for greater effort and snarling in my face. It was only through the undeserved grace of a careless God that I slithered

---

[j] For the tale of the Siege of Fort Donelson, Nathan Forrest in Nashville, and Becky Thatcher's bordello, refer to the second packet of memoirs, *The Adventures of Sidney Sawyer: The River War*.

away when Brassard came to call with Sister Hazel and their chum Becky Thatcher.

Brother Calhoun is gone now and good riddance. He came after me one time too many and I put his lights out once and for all on the heights above Harpers Ferry while the ruins of the Yankee garrison below were still smoldering from Stonewall Jackson's raid. I was none the worse for wear except for a clout on the head that had me flitting at fairies, a pistol ball through my armpit and the scare of my life. That same day I also killed her brother-in-law Raleigh, but that fool went to glory so easily he hardly counted.[k]

How I kept my hand off the wine glass through dinner I can't reckon. There she sat with her great arrogant lout of a son, a Limey colonel no less, and me armed with a three-tined dinner fork. She couldn't have actually known I had killed her brother, but she *knew*. If I was still alive it was because Calhoun was dead, and I had killed him. There could be no other answer for it. And she had tried to settle my hash twice more, once in Charleston in '63, and again in Alexandria in '64.

Aye, it will probably take all winter for me to scribble those memories on the foolscap and lock them in the gun cabinet with the rest. But there's really nothing else to do in Buffalo when my only comforts are my slippered feet to the fire and a decanter of Shovel-labor Sunshine to warm my liver when the blizzards scream in off the lake and the curse to write is on me.

* * *

Amy's a good girl, and even though she had a million questions she kept them to herself until we were

---

[k] The events in wartime Richmond and the reckoning with Brassard are related in the third packet of General Sawyer's memoirs published as *The Adventures of Sidney Sawyer: The Year of Jubilee*.

barricaded in our chamber. After dinner, a blasted affair that I thought would never end, (the courses kept rolling out, at least fourteen of them, from soup to sherbet,) I grabbed Amy's elbow and made my apologies to Jimmy and the host.

"Your grub's too rich for this old soldier, your Lordship. Must have been the quail. Us Yanks are used to chicken. My guts are all in a twist."

This was enough for my clever girl to know that something was up. Oh, she's seen me act the boor in the company of quality before, but only when I'm wallpapered, and she knew I was sober now.

We climbed the grand staircase to the west wing where the guests had their chambers and like a fool I glanced over the banister back down to the hall. They were *there*, her tiny in black, and him tall in scarlet and blue, staring up at us. I made a chirp of fright but managed to slow walk Amy arm–in-arm down the corridor and into our room. When the door was locked, a chair wedged beneath the knob, the window checked for possible entry or fast escape, (there was none) and I had armed myself with the poker, I sat my wife down and told her a tale.

She, of course, had known about the duel with Brassard but none of the rest. After all, how could she miss the ugly bullet scar over my heart that won me the glorious nickname, "Ace of Hearts?" I never talked to her about my action in the Civil War or any other war. She'd seen the nicks and scabs I brought home from my follies, damn few of them in the front, but I never tattled and she never asked. Now I had to tell her about the Brassards and Ballentines, and why we had to bolt from this grand country house, and be damn quick about it. I left out the tacky bits about cheating in the duel, Miss Becky's bordello, rogering Hazel Ballentine all over Richmond, and a half-dozen murders along the way. I didn't know how Amy would react to all this but I didn't expect her to throw her arms about my shoulders and give me a kiss laced with passion, right on the lips.

"Oh, my brave beau, my sugar-baby! Oh, my gallant soldier! Oh, my true husband!" and she kissed me again. "Honeychile!"

What the deuce?

"I know you could never be untrue. But what was I to think? That terrible summer between Shiloh and Antietam with never a word from my Sidney– never a note from my sugar-baby. I thought you were among the dead, *or worse.*"

Or worse? What the hell could be worse than being dead? Of course she meant the marriage vows– didn't she? But now she was kissing me again, and by grapes I was kissing her back. At seventy-five there are long droughts between bouts of romance but little Sidney seemed to be game and my old girl was positively panting with passion. Splendid, except for the formal wear and gown. Amy's dozens of buttons and snaps had me practically spent before we were stripped for Adam's action. Dim gaslight hides a lot of wrinkles and she looked grand as I was about to pile into her with all the lust my creaking knees and elbows would allow. But she stopped me with a finger to my lips.

"Sidney, my brave little honeychile. Why, oh why, did you keep this from me for all this time? From Washington City to Rebel Richmond, your political work, that dreadful Captain Brassard, his wicked sister?"

It had been three months since our last thrash in the bedding and *now* she asks me? Little Sidney was wavering.

"It was Lincoln, blast him. He ordered me to keep mum– and I did!"

"Oh Sidney, you are true!" and she kissed me again.

I'm glad I stuck the chair under the knob. It doesn't just work against homicidal widows and their avenging sons. It works on lady's maids and housekeepers, too. They're all blasted busybodies.

* * *

We set Amy's Big Ben for four o'clock in the morning.[1] I'm soldier enough to know that the half of the art of war is to get there early. I climbed into my traveling tweeds with twenty gold eagles sewed into my belt and my Bulldog in my pocket. Since my Academy days I've never left home without my boodle of gold coins stitched into my tackle. Gold's a handy bribe or a deadly weapon or a comfort or a club. It's saved my bacon a score of times and without it I feel naked as a jaybird in July. The Bulldog was a different type of comfort, and when Amy saw me jam it into my coat she gave a gasp and her eyes went wide.4

I gave her a grin of false confidence and whispered, "Remember what Auntie Polly always said?"

Amy, trim in her traveling fig gave a game giggle and whispered back, "You never know!"

With that we were out the chamber door and down the corridor at as much of a trot as my rheumatism would abide. Behind us was a note of thanks, but no explanations to our host, and our Buffalo address to forward my traps and Amy's trunks. They were a competent crew so I had no worries, but I'd have chucked the lot for a clean getaway. We turned from the grand areas of the house towards the door to the narrow servant's stair and down to the business end of the mansion. There was an absolute roar of activity coming from what must have been the kitchen, punctuated by the bash of pots and the rattle of dishes being hauled in by the tray. We didn't belong here in the servants world, and some of the help let us know with looks of outraged propriety, but my wind was up too much to care. I pinched a lass in tick cap and twill apron, girls are easier to bully, and demanded she fetch us to a

---

[1] Big Ben alarm clocks were a phenomenon when first marketed in 1909 by the Western Clock Manufacturing Company (Today's Westclox).

groom and be smart about it. She led us pronto through three or four more twists of narrow halls, out a back door, and across the graveled yard to the carriage house.

"Mr. Hager!" she squeaked. "Mr. Hager, a lady and gentleman."

Hager was a husky fellow in corduroy with tweed cap who looked like he knew his business. Well, I knew mine too and knew how to handle the Hagers of this world. Act as if what you're doing is as normal as biscuits, even if it ain't, and let them see your cash.

"Thank you young lady," I patted the wide-eyed maid on her cap and let Hager see the shilling I placed in her pink hand. "Now git back to the kitchens like a good gal."

"Hager, a gig if ya please– an' make it snappy. Gotta git ta Tonbridge ta catch the milk train." I flipped him a half-crown and let him hear my Missouri accent. Being an American would answer any questions he may have about just what the hell I was about. To the English, all Americans are queer.

Hager was stable master. He whistled up a groom to harness a tall chestnut trotter to a Victoria, but I brought him up sharp and demanded a gig. I'd do my own driving if you please and leave the rig at the village livery. Even the stable boy was aghast! Drive *yourself*– without a proper groom or footman? Well, my nose was as big as a Red Indian's. Maybe they thought I was an American savage.[m] I gave the groom a shilling for lifting Amy aboard and climbed into the seat with my knees creaking like cheap furniture after last night's geriatric gymnastics. I made sure to mention the Tonbridge milk train again and whipped up the chestnut. At the end of the long gravel drive we turned south, *away* from Tonbridge and toward

---

[m] A Victoria was a popular buggy for the upper classes. It required a driver who was perched in a tall seat. A gig was a two-wheeled, two-seat rig that you drove yourself.

the market town of Royal Tunbridge. I'm a past master at sloping away from a house where the hospitality's worn thin. Usually it was scampering from outraged daddies or husbands, but those days were past. Now I was running in the early morning gloaming from a shriveled Confederate widow in a black gown and lace. I reckoned laying the false trail to Tonbridge would buy enough time for a clean escape. I reckoned wrong.

I didn't know the lay of the land and Royal Tunbridge was twice as far as I figured. It was two hours after dawn when we trotted up to the train station with the chestnut shaking in its harness with fatigue. We missed the milk train by a mile. Like a fool I wasted another quarter-hour seeing to a yokel at the local livery to give the horse a good curry and fetch him some oats. I didn't care a stale cracker for the nag, but I did for Amy's opinion. She wouldn't tolerate abuse to livestock. And that is why we missed the next market train to London. And we were damn glad we did.

When we left the narrow lane between the livery and the station, the street was busy with the morning bustle of a country market town. If Amy ever really wondered about the seriousness of our danger, the sight of the big touring automobile parked in the street settled it. Ballentine-Blythe was nowhere to be seen but his automobile hogging the lane proved the fact of our pursuit. The brute must be in the station right now stalking us. Where else *would we be* but the station? Certainly not bothering to livery the damn horse! He'd be quizzing the tellers and stationmaster if they'd seen a handsome elderly American couple, and where the devil did they go? I knew what must have happened as clearly as if I'd ridden along in the back seat. At breakfast over tea our absence would have been noticed. Ballentine-Blythe whistled up his automobile in a twinkling with no time wasted harnessing a trotter. After a word with Hager he'd have been off, full-throttle, north to the station at Tonbridge to beat the milk train. With no sign of the Sawyers he would have known he was hoodwinked, but the road only ran north and south so he must have raced like a maniac back past the country house, and on to Royal Tunbridge. God help any sheep or rabbits on the road between here and there.

The train was out of the question now, with Colonel B-B patrolling the station. It was back to the livery. We'd hire a fresh horse, lay another false trail and lose ourselves in the countryside. With Amy gripping my arm like a vice we turned on our heels back into the lane, left the morning traffic behind us, and stopped dead as a tiny figure straight from a child's night terrors stepped from a nook into the middle of the lane.

* * *

As soon as I saw the motorcar I should have gripped the Bulldog in my pocket. Now I had no more chance of reaching it than if it was back on my dresser in Buffalo. The surprise was complete and the ambush perfect. The blood drained from my face with the shock, and Amy's purse slipped from her shoulder to hang heavy from the strap in her delicate old hand.

Hazel Brassard-Ballentine-Blythe was dressed in a tan duster that covered her in one garment from neck to wrists to boots. It was buttoned to the throat, with its wide collar turned up to meet her cap of the same tan linen, which was pulled down tight to cover her ears and forehead. Pulled up over the visor of the cap were huge dusty goggles that gave her the look of a giant insect instead of a tiny lady. She would have been ridiculous if not for the look of triumphant hate on her elfin face and the silver pistol that sparkled in her claw.

"I would like to wait for my son, but I'll shoot you down now if you even twitch."

Amy squeezed my poor arm tighter still and squeaked, "Mrs. Ballentine-Blythe, what is this? A pistol? My goodness, have I given offense?"

If I wasn't already stunned, Amy's squeak would have done it. I knew my old girl had sand and I'd certainly never heard her squeak before. During that Boxer business fifteen years ago she had helped organize the diplomatic ladies into a damned effective auxiliary. And one terrible day, when the Chinamen were swarming the Tartar Wall, she almost stopped my heart by taking up a Mauser and joining the Marines on the fire-step. But Amy was only sixty then.[5]

"It's *Lady* Ballentine-Blythe. My second husband was a knight of the realm," sneered the arrogant Southern snob. "And you *have* given offense. Ya married a n—r lover, a traitor, a coward, an' a murderer."

Amy squeaked again.

"The Ace of Hearts! It's really the Ace of Spades now isn't it? Yeah, I know all about you leadin' your n—r soldiers against your own kind. And disfiguring my poor brother! I know you cheated in the duel. He told me so. Tell me how. *Now*– tell me! How'd you do it?"

I cheated all right, but I wouldn't tell her because Amy could never know, especially now. But I had to tell her something, anything to keep her talking– anything to get her rattled. Her son would be along in a moment. Getting her careless was our only chance.

"I should have killed Calhoun in that duel, but I didn't. I killed him in another duel on the heights above Harpers Ferry. He brought your brother-in-law along as a second. You know, the big dumb one, Raleigh."

Hazel's face went cold and Amy's grip became fierce.

"This time it was sabers, not pistols. Brother Raleigh was a proper Southern gentleman when he handed me my blade. I wasn't quite as proper when I backhanded it across his throat. Had to jump sharp to avoid his blood. Spurted by the bucket. Little Calhoun was quite put out. Called me a cheater."

Hazel snarled. Amy squeaked.

"Liar! You didn't kill Raleigh. He died at Sharpsburg. He died with honor."

"He died when I slit his fat throat like a carp!"

She pointed her pistol like a spear. "You could never have defeated Calhoun Brassard with a blade. He was a master swordsman. He was your master in every way!"

By God she was working up a lather of hatred. It was now or never! I'd give her one more dig and then go for the Bulldog. I was sick because I knew in my yellow soul that I'd never make it. I could already feel her bullet going through my heart. She would finish what her brother began above the Hudson sixty years ago. And then she'd kill my Amy, my girl. Oh, Jesus! The revolver was as heavy as lead in my pocket.

I snarled through gritted teeth, "Calhoun didn't look too masterful when I grabbed him by the seat of his pants and heaved his skinny arse over the cliff into the Shenandoah. Screamed all the way down to the rocks. Screamed like a school girl with a..."

She was going to pull the trigger. Right then and no escape, and we'd die at the hand of an ancient Confederate widow, when Amy did something remarkable. If I tried it we'd both be dead, but Amy did it, and it was as unexpected as a meteor from heaven. She gaped past Hazel's right shoulder, her eyes bulged in surprise, and she gave another sharp squeak. Hazel Brassard-Ballentine-Blythe was as cold as a reptile, but she wouldn't have been human if she didn't at least flinch in that direction, and the barrel of her pistol flinched with it. I couldn't even begin to reach for my pocket when Amy's purse flew up by its strap in an arc and slammed into Lady Hazel's temple with a heavy smack. The tiny bitch went down in a heap of tan linen.

I've had some shocks in my misspent life, but seeing Amy cold-cocking Lady Hazel had me paralyzed. She didn't hesitate. She stooped to snatch up the wicked little silver pistol, snapped open her purse and dropped it in with a clang. What the deuce?

She had just saved both of our giblets, but gave me an embarrassed smile and a peek into her bag. Next to Lady Hazel's tiny pistol was a much bigger one, a .38 by the look of it. No wonder the purse put out Hazel's lights.

"You remember what Auntie Polly always said," she said in a voice with no hint of a squeak.

"Yes I do." My voice had a decided squeak, "You never know!"

* * *

Amy stole the Colonel's motorcar. I didn't know how to drive. When we were out and about along the shore of Lake Erie it was our daughter Suzanne who drove our Thomas Flyer. Suzanne was a modern woman who never minded scandalizing the local gentry with her independent ways. I always sat in the back like the King of Siam and ignored the greasy mechanical details. When my girls and Amy had their pretty heads together I always reckoned they were trading recipes and gossip. Evidently they were discussing internal-combustion, magnetos, and power linkage.

With one hand on the .38 in her purse she pushed and pulled switches and levers in fine grease-ape style. With one hand in my pocket on the Bulldog, I fit the crank and on my wife's order, gave it a weak spin. It almost broke my wrist but the motor caught instantly. I scurried up to the high seat and we were off in a blue cloud of exhaust with no cry of "stop thief" behind us. We left Lady Hazel behind the dustbins and Colonel Ballentine-Blythe waiting in ambush in the station. At twenty-five miles an hour we were into open country in two minutes. Watching my old girl high on the seat gripping the wheel and pulling at the great gear lever gave my heart a squeeze. To think that I ever thought she would squeak in fright.

In less than half an hour we abandoned the motorcar and boarded a train in the village of Hailsham. Thank God for a belt packed with gold eagles. By noon we were in Brighton where my eagles bought two railway tickets for Southhampton and I wired ahead to our banker to have funds and tickets meet us there.

We were away to New York on the morning tide aboard the liner *Olympic*. We didn't worry about a pinched automobile or an old lady taking a nap amongst the dustbins. That day Germany, Russia, France, and the Austrians went to war.[n] There were bigger fish to fry in Europe than two American fugitives. *Olympic* took a day to Queenstown, the ugly Irish city in Cork Cove where we picked up a few score more passengers, mostly Mick labor who would probably wind up in South Buffalo, damn 'em. Then we were off into the wide Atlantic. Two days later *Olympic* steamed past the spot where her sister ship *Titanic* had gone down four years ago. As I strolled the deck with Amy on my arm, I touched each lifeboat for luck. It wasn't an idle gesture. We may have need of them. Everyone aboard had heard of the sinister German undersea boats that could sink any ship from a watery ambush. That day, England declared war on Germany.[o]

* * *

Now, the whole world's eyes are on this new horror– but *my* rheumy eyes are looking back to an old horror, a war from fifty years ago when blue and butternut tore the country apart and brought terror and grief to every hearth in the land. It was a war that set me sweating and

---

[n] August 1, 1914.

[o] The date was August 4, 1914. The *Olympic*, sister ship of *Titanic*, was retrofitted with adequate lifeboats. It is interesting that Sawyer mentioned U-boats. The year after he finished this packet of memoirs the *Olympic* won glory for ramming and sinking a German U-boat.

bleeding in the swamps and sands about Charleston Harbor with eight hundred Colored men at my back and Confederate die-hards before us with double shotted guns. They were Southern men burning with outrage and hate in their souls at the reality of their own n—rs coming at them over cold steel with rifled muskets led by a Missouri Yankee. It was a war that sent me into bombarded Charleston, where I was at the cold mercy of a Confederate widow with a heart full of spite and a gift for malice. It marched me up a mountain in Tennessee with flame and death pouring from the heights and nowhere to hide from the guns. It sent me shivering with fear and cold down the Tennessee River with grim men pulling muffled oars and Rebel watch fires glowing along the banks tended by killers who couldn't miss. It set me floundering up the Red River with legions of Napoleon P. Banks's sullen looters into the furnace of Alexandria as the city burned over our heads. But it wasn't all horror and blood. There was the warm glow of the campfire as the Colored troops of the 94th sang their spirituals of hope in the company of their brothers, men breathing the air of freedom that their race had been denied in this land of the free. It was the sound of Africa offered to the Christian's Jesus, and the sound of it drifting up to heaven amongst the sparks was an offering fit for any god. There was the lovely black face of the woman-child who grew up before my eyes, who I didn't have the wit to recognize. I remembered her thin naked body swimming above me in the crystal water, sunlight framing her form like a halo while I held my breath in wonder. The soft brown fingers pressing to my lips, shushing me with a scent of honeysuckle and the quiet laughter close to my ear. Aye, there are some memories that can still warm me through the wee hours of a freezing Buffalo night, but most of it was violence and fear and hate and the evil stink of death. And the reckoning came in a wall of flame with a monster and a crew of devils fit to populate hell.

The Adventures of Sidney Sawyer
Missouri Yankees

Part II: Charleston

Chapter 3

Nobody remembers them anymore, and why the hell should they, but the Colored troops who fought in Union blue during the Civil War were every inch the equal to the white soldiers from the northern hamlets and villages where nary a black hide was to be found. They proved it by stopping lead and canister every bit as well as the white troops– those same white troops that welcomed them into the Army with hoots of, "Git a shovel, Sambo! Ya can't dig our slit-trench privies with them bayonets!"

But then the African soldiers of the 54th Massachusetts shut them up by leading the attack on Battery Wagner. They were men with a point to prove and they stepped off in grand style, drummer boys to the rear, flags to the front, gear polished to a sparkle, and a mighty roar as they presented their latrine-digging bayonets toward the Rebel ramparts. The white veterans came to understand that every black hide punctured by Confederate shot meant that a white hide wasn't. The white troops began to tolerate the USCT even if they never loved them.[6]

I wasn't there then– thank God. The gallant charge of the Colored troopers of the 54th occurred only two weeks after Vicksburg fell. I was still convalescing from my sabbatical as a guest of the Vicksburg garrison. I had been captured in the fiasco of Sherman's second assault on the Johnny works and spent the spring lapping

Confederate gruel and rotting in a dungeon. During the siege, after the Rebels cooked Vicksburg's last mule, mutt, and mouser, the city was starving. There was damned little left to feed us Yankee prisoners. On the glorious Fourth of July of '63, when Pemberton finally surrendered the garrison to Grant, I was a skeletal wreck. The Army sent me home to Amy and Auntie to pile on the weight and recover my snap.

About the time the Confederates were slamming the door on my hoosegow, Gideon Welles got a bee in his bonnet to chastise the wicked city of Charleston and haul down the Bonny Blue Flag waving over Fort Sumter.[p] To do that, General Quincy Gillmore, the Union warlord in the Carolinas, had to sight his big guns on the fort and the city. He could do that conveniently from the north end of a sun-punished thumb of sand at the entrance to Charleston Harbor called Morris Island. Inconveniently, that strutting Rebel Creole, P.G.T. Beauregard knew this, built a battery guarded by stout redoubts on that exact spot and named it Fort Wagner. Battery Wagner would simply *have* to be taken. The 54th had the honor to lead the assault.

They were slaughtered, of course. Human flesh, no matter what colored skin it was wrapped in, could simply not stand up to the fire from those ramparts. The next dawn found the sand covered with Union dead piled in windrows where the following white troops fell on the corpses of the colored men in the first wave. Under the South Carolina summer sun the bodies had to be buried quickly, and no time to waste. The fort's Rebel garrison made a poor job of it– hundreds of bodies putrefied, the ugly island stunk like a Cincinnati tannery, the water fouled to the threat of cholera, and the Johnny gunners at last had to abandon their works because of the stench. The Colored men of the 54th accomplished dead what they couldn't in life. Thank God for me the Rebels had such

---

[p] Gideon Welles was Lincoln's Secretary of the Navy.

contempt for the n—r soldiers of the 54th that they didn't bury them proper.

So, what the dickens was I doing seven weeks later at the vanguard of my own colored regiment counting down the seconds before assaulting the same works? I had a whistle clenched between my chapped lips, crotch rot setting my plums aflame, my arse was blistered with Greek fire and I was basting in a private's wool uniform better suited to a Buffalo winter than a Carolina summer. How in hell did I find myself in this fix, swatting away at sand chiggers, wiping sweat from my whiskers and cursing Liberty, the darkie drummer boy, for fetching water in my canteen bottle instead of whiskey– didn't the child have a brain in his woolly head?

This was all Tom Sawyer's fault, of course. When he was still a brat and I was just a tyke along the Mississippi back in the '40s, he and his gang used to flick my ears, cuff me elbow and knee, and bullyrag me to tears. It was kid stuff, although it still sizzled my arse, but I was two years younger so what was there for me to do but snitch and tattle? In '63 I was a colonel of cavalry, late of the staffs of Generals John C. Frémont, George Brinton McClellan, and U.S. Grant. I was a hero, a stalwart six foot four in boots and spurs, and the bastard was still causing me mischief.

*   *   *

I had only seen my half-brother Tom once since my wedding day back in '56. My marriage was a scandal. We Sawyers seem to attract scandal like sows attract stink. It was a proper shotgun marriage complete with the double-barrel leaning on the pew next to my tight-lipped new daddy, Auntie Polly soaking through hankies and the congregation happily whispering the gossip fit to drown out the vows. I didn't love my Amy– then. I only mumbled the "I do's" to keep the Lawrence clan from stringing me up or shooting me down, but I love my girl now. It took me nine months of matrimony to reach that happy conclusion. Marriage to Amy is the joy of my life, but *lying* to her is a *way of life*. God forbid she ever meets her real husband.

But Tom's scandal made my wedding seem like an ethical paragon. The very day Amy and I returned from our honeymoon in the great river port of St. Louis, Tom Sawyer, the famous scamp of Mark Twain's lying books, pulled a fast one that set Lewis County on its ear. You all know Mark Twain. Stupid name! He was Sam Clemens along *our* run of the River, and Cousin Sam to Tom and me. And of course you've read his rubbish, although you would have spent your time better reading *Mother Goose*. At the end of his book that crowned Tom with the laurels of a boyhood Lancelot, Cousin Sam wrote that St. Petersburg's local big cheese, Judge Thatcher, resolved to send Tom Sawyer to West Point. And he did– after a fashion. On the day my newly respectable bride and I returned from St. Louis, the glorious appointment came through. It was also the same day that Becky Thatcher announced that Tom had rendered her in a family way. And on that day Mark Twain's loveable scamp, Tom Sawyler, packed his grips with all the plunder he could swipe and lit off down river leaving Becky abandoned, Judge Thatcher fit to do murder, Aunt Polly soaking more hankies, the town a' buzz, and me snorting up my sleeve.

I didn't snort up my sleeve for long. The Judge was bound to send a Sawyer to West Point and I was the only Sawyer left in town. Under the name Sidney *Thomas* Sawyer I was sent to the Hudson and was glad to go. Remember, in those early days I didn't yet love Amy. I was a young buck in a dull town and the Academy fit me like hands-in-pockets. And other than the occasional rigged duel, or duty that I couldn't dodge, Army life has been just the nuts to me. If you're an officer with a propensity to bully, a talent for dereliction, and a nose for graft, it's the best life for any man. I was born for the service.

In the summer of that bloody year of 1863 Lee was reeling back from disaster and defeat at Gettysburg. Grant was sucking his cigars after capturing an entire Rebel army at Vicksburg and squinting at his maps to decide which way to jump next. Rosecrans was shooing Bragg's Confederates out of Tennessee like a farm wife with a broom and I was home stuffing myself with pie. My furlough papers were *bona fide* for a change and valid until such time as my convalescence was complete and I could resume my duties in the full competence of health and vigor. Health and vigor indeed! If I couldn't stretch out that leave until the last shot had been fired and the Union was saved or scuppered, I'd be one of Mr. Darwin's monkey's uncles. I'd had my bellyful of gore and battle, sleeping in bloody snow, choking on dust in blinding heat, grinding my molars on sheet-iron crackers, gagging down rancid salt-horse, swilling water fouled with mule piss and dead horses, and generals who were criminal in their folly. I was home now, with credit as a hero and papers that could make the provost whistle Dixie. It would take an act of congress to dragoon me back into active service.

Well, it didn't take an act of congress after all. It was a presidential command signed by Father Abraham himself and instigated as a prank by my brother, Tom Sawyer.

* * *

When Auntie Polly saw it was Tom Sawyer at the door she drooped to her knees in surprise and filled her ever-ready hanky with tears of pure joy. Why she always loved that bastard best was beyond me, but then I ain't an old lady. Back during the War, I still lived in her house with Amy and my boy Grant. He was still a fat infant soiling napkins at a rate that had our colored maid, Scotland, boiling fresh linen from breakfast to noon. But it wasn't *really* Auntie's house anymore. I had shoveled enough money into the old homestead, raising the roof, porching in the front, adding a new kitchen and building a dandy new cedar outhouse, until it was almost as grand as the Thatcher mansion. I'd bought up the clap-board shanties on either side and ripped them down to give us a wide expanse of lawn complete with roses, hyacinths, peonies, and shrubs of hydrangea and lilac. The whole yard was surrounded with a picket fence (painted, not whitewashed) and tended by a codger from Darktown.

From my post on staff I had been able to steer a bundle of Army business to Temple & Son and they kicked back enough plunder to make my Army pay only pin money. If you want to call it graft then go ahead, but the government was spending money as fast as it could print greenbacks and nobody noticed or cared. If you can't make money in wartime you should stay home.

Tom walked in like *he* owned the place, tossed his beaver and carpetbag to Scotland, and lifted Aunt Polly from her knees with a hug and a twirl. He grabbed my paw with both of his little hands like he owned me too, and giggled his greetings as if it hadn't been a full eight years since he had disappeared in disgrace and scandal. Amy hurried out onto the veranda at the commotion, but at the sight of Tom she froze with a knuckle to her lips. She had no reason to love Tom Sawyer. As children she and Tom had been schoolyard sweethearts, before he met Becky Thatcher and dumped her like cold coffee. That ended any affection she may have had for the boy, but what killed all respect for the man was the way he abandoned Becky, his own baby, the appointment to West Point and poor Aunt Polly without a thought or a fair-thee-well. When he saw Amy, the swine dropped my hand and had the cheek to pull her knuckle from her lips to his and with a bow, began to nibble her hand like a pork chop. I can't blame him. Amy was the most beautiful woman in Missouri with a figure to set men to bumping into doors and stepping in buckets. In her summer frock of white batiste with a green belt cinching her narrow waist and bosoms ripe from nursing little Ranty, she was a sight to tempt a papist from his beads.

Before Tom could work his way up her arm I threw *my* arm around his narrow shoulders and steered him into the parlor. When we were lads he manhandled me at will, but I had six inches on him now and he came along as if he wanted to. He was still pretty, with his brown curls and dimpled cheeks, but he had the face of a man now, not a boy. His eyes though, were full of the same mischief as when he was a brat. And he was as cocky as the last time I had seen him under completely different circumstances, terrible circumstances, over a year ago. He wasn't a welcome sight at my door, but he did save my life that night, so even though Amy would have liked me to toss him back into the lane, I couldn't. Anyway, Aunt Polly wouldn't have let me. She loved him best, you see.[q]

Tom Sawyer was on his way from Nevada Territory to Washington City and he decided to stop off home to brag.

"I'm in politics now, Auntie! Tried the Army and it didn't fit. Joined up with Cousin Sam in Virginia City. He's scribbling in newspapers and other such trifles. Don't pay him much, but he ain't there to get rich like them other fools who scrape in the muck for silver. He's there to cut capers, and don't we just!"

That was Tom Sawyer's life in a thimble. He tried the Army and it didn't fit. He had joined the Confederate Army for a lark and at Shiloh found out it wasn't quite like the games of adventure he played as a boy. He didn't cotton to the bad grub, camp fevers, hard work, blood, and especially the boredom of camp life. He deserted his regiment with no more thought than he deserted Becky and Auntie– but everybody loves Tom.

---

[q] For Sid and Tom's adventures in the spring of 1862, refer to the second packet of the Sawyer Memoirs published as *The Adventures of Sidney Sawyer: The River War*.

Auntie demanded, and got, a blow-by-blow of Tom's health, (it was grand,) Cousin Sam's health, (he was fine,) the weather in the wilderness of Nevada, (just ducky,) the Indian menace, (small beer,) and what house of worship did he attended in the metropolis of Virginia City?

"Don't live in Virginia City, Auntie. Live in Carson City. I'm a government man an' it's the capital."

"But Tom, you do go to divine service now– don't you?"

Here Tom's eyes twinkled like they did when he was a kid caught in the jam-pot and he was about to tell a stretcher.

"Why, Aunt Polly, you know I'm a good Baptist. I go to the First Baptist Church of the Comstock. The preacher is a man-o'-God by the name of the Reverend Mark Twain. His sermons can run right through the afternoon into the night and we lean into every word. Nobody can spin a tale like the Reverend Twain."

I didn't get his damn joke until '76 when I was rudely introduced to the lying book, *The Adventures of Tom Sawyer*. Mark Twain, my arse! Tom must have thought it great wit to tell Auntie that he worshipped in the temple of Mark Twain. Worshipped in a clapboard saloon with Cousin Sam, a bottle of tangle-foot and a pox-ridden floozy, more like it.[r]

"Nevada's gonna be a state soon– two senators and a congressman. We're gonna need our own governor and a cabinet and a state legislature and sheriffs and all the rest. The Union needs our silver an' Lincoln needs our votes. Gonna be a state, just like Missouri, an' I'm right in the middle of it. Lincoln sent Mr. J. W. Nye to be our governor, and J. W. sent a committee to Washington to see Lincoln about statehood, and I'm on the committee!" He

---

[r] It was in February of 1863, in Virginia City, Nevada, that Samuel Clemens first used the *nom de plume*, "Mark Twain."

was practically crowing. "I'm movin' up in the world, Auntie!"

Dinner was a trial, with Amy as cool as pickle preserves, Auntie almost swooning with love and Tom giving a sarcastic blessing that fetched him a kick under the table from Amy, but went quite over Aunt Polly's head. Me, I tried to get a word in edge-wise between Tom's bragging and lying. After our cobbler and coffee I steered Tom out onto the porch for cigars and whiskey. I usually went to Lizabeth Watson's kitchen behind Temple & Son's office after supper for my smoke and libation, but Mr. Temple and Alfred would be there. So would Lizabeth's pappy, Big Jim. They were on my very short list of true friends and I didn't want to inflict Brother Tom on them. If you don't know why they wouldn't want any truck with the likes of Tom Sawyer, you can read Sam Clemens's blasted books.

"Why'd Governor Nye send you, Tom? How'd you get to be such a bull-frog out in Nevada?"

"Simple as eggs, Siddy. It's a snap to be a big frog if the pond's small enough, an' Nevada's a damned small pond. I'm in the House of Representatives now. 'Course it's only a territorial legislature, an' there's only thirteen other frogs in that particular pond, but there's money to be made in the government, any government, and it beats grubbin' in that damned blue stuff by a long drop."

I knew what he meant. 'That damned blue stuff' was the famous slimy mud that the gold miners had cursed as it gummed up their sluices and gear before some miner with a hunch packed a sack of it to San Francisco to be assayed. That blue clay was the richest silver ore the world had ever seen, and it set off a silver stampede to the Sierra Nevadas that swept Tom and Sam from the Confederate service to the silver fields.[s] As for making money from the

---

[s] Sam Clemens also deserted the Secessionist Army and moved first to Nevada and then San Francisco.

government, just take a peek at Auntie's new china or the crisp linens Amy had packed away in her cedar chest. Or consider my growing nest egg courtesy of speculation, cotton jobbing and Temple & Sons gouging the Army for shoddy Union blue and cardboard booties.

"But government don't seem to be your style, Tom. You were always into fun and pranks. Where's the adventure of government work? Where's the fun?"

"Fun? Why, Siddy, government ain't nothin' *but* fun! And as for pranks?"

Tom's eyes lit up like they did when he was suckering his chums to whitewash Aunt Polly's fence or when he was leading his gang of brats off on a childhood 'pirate raid' to Jackson Island.

"Pranks! Here's a prank for you." He sucked his Carolina stinker to a fierce red glow and took a mighty slurp of the whiskey. Then a deck of cards appeared in his mitt as if by magic, and he spread them, one-handed, into a full fan that would have done a Baton Rouge riverboat flash-gambler proud. But of course Tom Sawyer *was* a riverboat flash-gambler.

"Guess what was the first law we passed out in Nevada? Gold flakes and silver slugs are the currency out on the frontier. Men will kill each other over a cross word or takin' a whore out of turn. Eggs cost a dollar each, *in gold*, and a pig will sell for a hundred bucks. There's Chinamen, Dagos, Micks and Welsh shovel-labor. There's Union an' Reb deserters, and busted miners willin' to break your skull for two bits. We're buryin' 'em three deep up on Boot Hill, and that's in *Carson City*. Up in Virginia City it's worse, or better, dependin' on your point of view. There ain't enough lumber for coffins, every stick goes to the mines. The brothels, saloon's an' gambling hells are under canvas an' ankle deep in mud, and the mud's that damned blue stuff. The men are desperate, the whores are poxey, the mutts are all hydrophobic, the whiskey is poisoned with snake-spit an' there ain't an honest game of stud in the whole Washoe Range."

It must have been some prank. His cheeks around his dimples were pink with forty-rod and mischief. He was still just an over-grown boy.

He gave his high-pitched hee-hee and sang out, "We outlawed gambling!"

It was so outlandish that I just sat there in the wicker rocker like an ass.

"But… What?

"We outlawed gambling! Made it illegal to turn a card or toss the bones. What do ya think a' that, Siddy!"

"Why?"

"Why the hell not, Siddy? We're the government. We can do whatever the hell we want. An' if you want more of something, then tell 'em they can't do it."

He gave his cards a fast shuffle and flipped one ace after the other onto my lap.

"If I can't make money out of a law like that, then bury me, I've been dead for five days! Hee-hee! Besides, it was fun!"[7]

The Adventures of Sidney Sawyer
Missouri Yankees

Chapter 4

The last time Tom and I talked through the night was between Yank and Reb lines after the first terrible day at Shiloh. Our conversation was lit by tumbling shells from Grant's gunboats with fuses spinning through their arc like sinister fireflies. This night was sparked by *real* fireflies as the level of the sippin' whiskey dropped in the bottle. It was one of those rare summer nights when millions of the tiny creatures rose up from the bushes and turned the evening into a fairyland. If it was Amy, or any *other* woman on that porch, the magic would have had *us* behind those bushes, but since it was Brother Tom the only fairies came from the bottle. And those fairies were as full of mischief as Tom Sawyer himself. They set me to bragging. After all, Tom's story was a dandy and it gave me a hanker to out-brag the curly-headed little fancy-man. When will I ever learn to shut my trap? That bragging paved my own personal highway to Charleston and Chattanooga and copper colored waters of the Red River as surely as if I set the cobblestones with my own hands.

And what did I brag about? The blasted railroad! It ain't every Missouri boy who can steal a locomotive and race it through Virginia with the Confederate Army highballing after it at a mile-a-minute with sparks exploding from the stack in the rush of wind with rifles blazing from the coaches and cab. It's a grand yarn even if it did get Tom's boyhood chum Ben Rogers gut-shot and abandoned on the tracks to the mercies of Johnny horse troopers. Of course, the tale I spun to Tom made me out a ring-tailed hero. The real story, warts, scabs and cankers, is somewhere locked up in my gun cabinet with my other memoirs. If you ever read it, I'm dead and don't care. It's a damned good story even if the truth would have had me run out of St. Petersburg.[t]

Tom seemed impressed with my high-iron adventure, which kept me to bragging. What younger brother don't want the approval of his older brother? Between the tangle-foot and the attention, old Tom's company didn't seem as disagreeable as I remembered– silly me. That railroad yarn led me to other stories about the *other* railroad I had traveled on since we last met– the Underground Railroad. I wrote those stories down too, and they're also locked up with my other scribbles in the gun cabinet. You see, while shirking duty and fleeing from my own follies I happened to hook up with two separate bands of runaway slaves, once in Virginia and again in Mississippi. I didn't give a stale biscuit if the darkies made it to the Jubilee or not, but since we were running in the same direction I teamed up with them. Odd Africans are handy company to have when you're on the run. Traveling with a white man they didn't seem to be runaways at all, and with a string of 'slaves' in tow I had a reason to be on the Southern roads. I knew Tom didn't give a damn for anyone but himself and that he had a nothing but contempt for all n—rs, property or not. To twist his britches, I laid on that I was a conductor on the Underground Railroad for the noblest of motives and that my passengers looked to me as a Missouri Moses. It would give him the sizzles and he'd never know that I was just along for the ride. Besides, I didn't hate all darkies on principle like Tom and his Confederate pals did. You see, I don't *have* many principles. I finished my tale in grand style, with my dusky

---

[t] Sidney Sawyer's great locomotive chase is recorded in *The Adventures of Sidney Sawyer: The Year of Jubilee*.

charges floundering from the swamps, one foot ahead of a posse of vicious slave catchers with guns, ropes, whips and dogs, and winning to safety in the noble arms of the bluebelly army.

It was a blue-ribbon tale and Tom slapped my knee, struck a lucifer to a fresh cheroot, recharged his tumbler from the bottle and called me a n—r-lover. Just then, with the worst of timing, big Jim Watson appeared at the foot of the porch steps with half of a pie wrapped I cheesecloth and a friendly, "How do, Sidney."

Tom was a smallish man, sitting in the shadows and half-swallowed in our huge wicker furniture. Jim didn't see him until the words were out of his big lips. Jim knew his place like every other darkie who didn't want to entertain a hemp noose over the crook of a stout branch, but he was one of my few true friends and his place with me *was* up the front stairs with a 'how do.'

But Tom Sawyer was a true son of Missouri and he came out of his seat with a snarl.

"Sidney? 'How do, Sidney?' Git your black arse off this porch, boy, an' it's *Misto* Sidney to you, you black bastard!"

Jim's jaw dropped at the sudden attack and then his eyes bulged when he recognized Tom Sawyer. Bless him for a good boy, he didn't drop the pie.

"Misto Tom!" In an instant Jim adopted the attitude of a good Missouri darkie, eyes down, neck bent and a backward shuffle. "Didn't see you sittin' dere, suh. My 'pologies, Misto Tom. Just bringin' some o' Lizabeth's pie fo' Misto Sidney an' Miss Amy."

"Why, you're old Jim, ain't you?" Tom piped.

"Yes, sah. Sho' am. It be fine to see you again, Misto Tom. Ain't seen you since you was a pup."

"I ain't a pup no more, so mind your tongue, boy. You're free now, ain't you?

"Yes, sah, I is."

"Then remember your place, boy. Don't go presuming. You know where the back door is. Git!"

Well this was raw. Tom knew old Jim well from when he was a brat. He had spent enough time tormenting Jim with his boyhood pranks to qualify him as a chum, if not a friend. But Jim *was* my friend, even if he was as black as your boot and had hands like farm tools. And it was *my* porch and *my* pie, and Tom had just called me a n––r-lover, so I figured, what the hell?

"Jim don't have to go around the back, Tom. He's company, just like you. Come on up to the porch there, Jim."

But Jim was Missouri-bred and born a slave. And Tom Sawyer was a river-bred, Missouri-born white man, and old Jim knew the score. He bowed, shucked, grinned and passed over the pie.

"Gots to git back to work now, Misto Sidney. Mighty fine seein' you again, Misto Tom. 'Evenin' gentlemens." Jim hurried back up the lane towards Lizabeth's kitchen.

Tom thought it was the funniest thing since the Nevada legislature. He finished the liquor straight from the bottle, tossed it into Amy's peonies, thumped my back and giggled, "Damnation in a hat box, Brother Siddy. If you ain't just a n—r-lovin' Missouri Yankee? Hee-hee-hee!"

He wasn't a big man and with the amount of liquor he had aboard Tom was well foxed. After a trip to our new cedar-paneled two-holer outhouse I helped him up the stairs to the back bedchamber. He giggled and 'n—r-lovered' me all the way. He was already snoring as I yanked off his boots and tossed the quilt over him. Tom was out like a wet wick and I reckoned in the morning he wouldn't have a notion what we gassed about over the whiskey. I hoped he would though. To my brother I was a n—r-lover. To his type of man that's one of the worst insults you can smear on a fellow. I knew he would get a case of the sizzles just recalling it, but I didn't think he would. Well, he did.

The next morning we saw Tom Sawyer off on the cross-river steam-packet that would take him to the railroad line at Quincy. Auntie soaked through another hankie. Amy waved a cool goodbye. I shouted 'good luck' and was glad to see his back. Tom waved and his pretty grin puckered the dimples in his cheeks. I hoped to never see him again.

Ten days later I got orders from the General in Chief of the United States Army, Henry Wager Halleck, to report to Washington City– *immediately*.

* * *

Immediately? Why the devil Old Brains Halleck would want *anything* immediately, let alone me, was a puzzle for the Sphinx of Egypt. Halleck was the General in Chief of the entire United States Army, but his only claim to leadership was that he worshipped every scrape of paper generated by the American war-machine. He lived to know where it came from, where it went, what it wanted, how much it would cost and where the damned thing was on file. He was a clerk, maybe the best clerk in the world, but he wasn't a leader of men by a long-drop. His lone dabble in wartime generaling was to diddle away the summer of '62 after Grant won the Battle of Shiloh and let the Rebels catch their breath, brace their britches and lick their wounds. He never did anything immediately. For all his bulk he probably never had a hot meal in his life. His grub would chill on the plate while he blithered over which fork to use.

I had to leave, and that was flat. The orders canceled my furlough and there was no room to wiggle. I *had* recovered from the scrapes and bruises and starvation inflicted on me by Southern hospitality in the Vicksburg lock-up, but the General in Chief couldn't have known that– and why would he give a snap? After a month of home cookin' I had piled back on the weight that fighting vermin and Ohio Democrats for rations of pone, sawdust and sewer-water had burned off of me. I'd never recover from the fright and fear and horror, but those were wounds that a counterfeit glory-hound like me could never let show. Aye, I've got memories to twist my liver, but why the dickens would Old Brains care?

I loitered about for a week. If it was Grant or Sherman's 'immediately,' I would have been gone with the morning mail-packet, but I reckoned Halleck's 'immediately' had some cushion to it. In the end I was right, and I'm glad I took the time. No wife on the river knew how to say a fair-thee-well to her soldier boy like my Amy. I'd taught her all the tricks I'd learned from a long ledger of dolly-mops, lonely widows, eager farmers' daughters, a parson's wife and most lately, a Creole *fille de joie* whose boat tied up at the levee one afternoon to bunker cordwood. My lass was innocent enough to reckon we'd conjured up all those finer points of fornication by ourselves, sort of on the spur of the moment. But she was woman enough to take to any new technique with the enthusiasm of a New Orleans mattress galloper. We called our love-making 'riverboat games.' Whenever she was eager to play she'd give me a slow smile that would scandalize her winter sewing circle, pantomime a pull on a river queen's whistle and give me a 'toot-toot!' She always had the grace to blush and still does after almost sixty years of matrimony. Come to think of it, our last frolic was in old England on the night of our skedaddle from the Widow Ballentine. We ain't as frisky as we used to be–but you know… it ain't that late, I ain't drunk yet, the Irish help is scrubbing pots in the kitchen and I can hear my old girl humming in the front parlor. Toot-toot!

* * *

On the fourth of August of '63 I waved fair-thee-well to my dear ones at the wharf of Temple & Son's from the aft deck of the packet that would take me to Quincy and the Great Western.[u] From there it was four days jarring over wartime railroads to Washington. I hate that city– always have. It's more Africa than America with darkies swarming at all the tasks that aren't fit for a white man. The canal stunk as bad as it did on my last visit the summer before, the hogs still rooted in the mud off the boardwalks, the heat still pressed down on a body like a boiled rag, and after a brief but raging thunderstorm the traffic churned the avenues into a fine gumbo of horse dung and mule piss. But it wasn't just the stink of the place. It was the attitude of the city that twisted my gizzard. The walkways, saloons and boarding houses were thick with wire-pullers, jobbers, sharps and shoulder-hitters on the make. They strutted in their tight pants, belted high on their bellies under their vulgar vests with their fourteen-inch beavers tilted on three hairs and cigars clamped between their lips as they chirped lies at a mile-a-minute. They gave no more regard to the soldier boys bivouacked around the stump of the Washington Memorial or on the Capital Hill Common than a shark has for herring. They were predators and the prey was the greenbacks in the pockets of the soldiers and the wealth of a republic at war. The city was still thick with troops coming and going in formation along the avenues or drilling on the greens but they didn't swarm like my last visit after Second Manassas. Then the Army was a mob of whipped infantry sulking in muddy uniforms with weapons and gear slung slipshod over slouching shoulders. Now the soldiers were mostly fresh fish, learning the mysteries of march and countermarch to the cadence yodeled by sergeants who had the look of veterans. Most of the Army was south along the Rappahannock with Meade having a timid slap-fight with Bobby Lee's boys

---

[u] This was the Great Western of Illinois Railroad. Sawyer must have had at least six transfers before he boarded the Baltimore and Ohio Railroad (B&O) that went through to Washington.

who had been savaged the month before at Gettysburg. By God, there's a fight I'm damn glad I missed, but I was at Vicksburg the very same day George Pickett sent his division up Cemetery Ridge and had troubles of my own.

And there was something new in the Capital that summer. Not just new in the American Capital– new in the world. I knew it was coming but when I saw it with my own eyes it gave me a jolt like I had been struck by lightning. It's six city blocks down C Street from the B&O Terminal to Pennsylvania Avenue, then another three to the 'rooming house' where I intended to perch, and another two or three farther on to the Presidential Mansion. Despite the stink, after the press of passengers in the cars, it was a pleasure to walk, but the sight when I turned onto Pennsylvania Avenue stopped me in my tracks like I'd been electrified.

Swinging toward me was a company of men, obviously recruits, but marching in good order. Their uniforms were new denim of crisp Union blue with booties that squeaked in the rhythm of their stride. Their kepis were squared on their heads and the patented leather brims were stiff and straight. Cartridge belts, bayonet sheaths and haversacks glowed with soft-soap and rifles were held stiffly on broad shoulders. The barrels sparkled in the sun and the stocks shone with polish. Leading them on a tall mare was a lieutenant in full regimentals, sword, sash and Hardee hat. Along side of the company strutted a sergeant, red in the face and blowing wind from shouting encouragement and instruction to the pie-eaters– a Mick from the sound of him, the Army's lousy with them.

"Your feet! Mind your feet, ye ignorant apes. Jaysus, Mary an' Joseph, who told ye ye could march? Match your mate's step. Skip a step to catch up. Skip a step!" He ranted like he knew his business and quick-stepped besides a recruit who was sweating like a field hand. "Ye think you'll make a soldier, boy-o? I think not!" and he kicked the boy's ankle to make him stumble in step with the company. He roughly straightened the musket to the proper angle on the boy's shoulder and gave the back of his head a slap that knocked his cap over his ear. "Tain't a hoe you're totin' now, blacky! Look sharp, ye black bastard, your betters are watchin'!"

And they were. It wasn't just me that was frozen in my spot to stare at the troops marching past up the hill towards the Capital Building of the United States of America. Everyone on the Avenue had stopped to stare. We were looking at a new world. The company of troops– kitted, booted, uniformed and marching under arms, were colored.

Here was the rebellion. Oh, the Johnnys considered themselves to be the rebels– up in arms against the Old Flag, but here, marching up Pennsylvania Avenue in a column of fours were the true revolutionaries– black men in Union blue with rifles at shoulder arms. I knew this day would come, but Christopher Columbus on a crutch, to see it was a jolt. As early as Shiloh I knew it had to come. In those early days the War was a simple notion. We'd lick the Southern boys in one or two big fights and show them we meant business. They'd get over their mope, sulk back to their plantations and the Union would be restored just as it was. A country philosopher named Sergeant Major Huckleberry Finn of the 3rd Iowa poured cold water all over that simple notion. On his boyhood drift down the Mississippi River on a lumber raft with Jim Watson, Huckleberry grew to love the old black man like a father. He loved Jim's high-yaller deaf daughter Lizabeth like a wife and he hated slavery to the death. Finn spent the '50s as a Jayhawker with old John Brown and his 'Angels' fighting the ugly war in Bleeding Kansas. He knew from the first shot that the War wasn't a gentlemen's quarrel over state's rights, tariffs and the balance of votes in the Senate. It was a revolution and the Yankees, not the 'Rebels' would be the real radicals.

Sergeant Finn explained the truth of it to me after Shiloh while I lay recovering from my ingloriously won wounds. It was a harsh truth and I slurped my bedside bourbon like it was cider as I listened. After all, when I mended I'd have to fight Huckleberry Finn's revolutionary war. If the Africans could be enslaved then any man anywhere could be enslaved. Through all of history men had made slaves of other men. Black slavery in our land of the free was the bottom of the pit. It was hereditary and hopeless and a man's own skin marked him and his as chattel forever. If these black slaves could be free then *all* men everywhere could be free and all men *should* be free. The War couldn't end, and *shouldn't* end until the very notion of slavery was killed, and if the *notion* couldn't be killed then the men who had the notion *must* be killed. All of them! It had to be done or no man anywhere could reckon his own freedom as a right. If it *was* done here in America, than every man, everywhere, could count their own freedom as a right, and Huckleberry's revolution would go on until every chain was broken and every man free– everywhere! The South would fight against this revolution to the last ditch and we would have to kill them in that ditch and to do it we needed the slaves themselves to put on the blue suit, study war and go after Marse over the bayonet.

This was an ugly reality and despite the Emancipation Proclamation and the endless roll of the dead, most Americans didn't believe it– yet. But Lincoln did and Stanton did and Huckleberry Finn did and those black soldiers marching up the avenue did. And I did because Huck told me.

The Adventures of Sidney Sawyer
Missouri Yankees

Chapter 5

After bouncing on bad rails and horsehair seats through four states,[v] chewing on cold beef, stale bread and cheese for four days and having the shock of watching darkies marching as men-o-war, I wasn't ready to report to Old Brains Halleck quite yet. It's a grand thing for a soldier to have a home-away-from-home and I was blessed to have one in the capital city. It wasn't exactly home though. It was the fanciest knock-shop in Washington. The madam was a wonderful old trot named Missy Ruth, with udders like the top-hamper of a China clipper and enough rouge to putty her sagging face like marine caulk. I had stayed at her establishment on my last two visits in the city and was greeted at the door by the same darkie major-domo as the last time. No one in this life has a better memory than a whorehouse butler and he knew me right off the stick.

"Mr. Yonge– or is it Colonel Sawyer this afternoon, sir?"

I've had more than one *nom de guerre* in this war. The summer before I had snuck into Richmond to spy for Father Abraham. I was tarted up as Mr. Danforth Yonge, a reporter for a Canadian newspaper. It was a fool's errand that almost landed me in Libby Prison, or worse, dancing

---

[v] Sawyer is wrong here, but not by much. He traveled through five states, not four. When he arrived in Washington, *West* Virginia had been a state for less than two months.

the Virginia Reel at the end of a length of Confederate hemp. It was a name I'd sooner forget.

"It's Colonel Sawyer from now on, old timer, and don't forget it. Here's a nickel for you, boy. Now, fetch me a brown ale and my Dust Mop."

His eyes got big and he studied the carpet. "Oh, Mr. Colonel, sir. Yo Miss Dust Mop, she ain't here no more," and he gave a look of pure sorrow.

I knew that stargazing was a dicey profession, but it saddened me that my favorite trotter had come to no good. She was a frisky little bundle with nipples the size of thimbles and a mop of wild blond hair that inspired her name.

I shouldn't have asked, what was it to me really, but I did.

The old fool practically had tears in his eyes. "Why, Colonel, sir, she went an' done got married. Gentleman from Baltimore."

Well, I knew it must have been something bad but losing my little cocotte to matrimony was just damn depressing. My mood was rescued by the madam herself. Miss Ruth sailed into the foyer like a full-rigged ship, gave a squeal of pleasure at the sight of a good customer, called me 'Ducks' and pulled my face into her mammoth bosoms. While I tried to brush her dressing powder from my whiskers she dragged me into the parlor where two other officers and a sport in a flash suit were sipping flip and playing scat while trollops nibbled their ears and giggled advice on the deal.

One of the officers was a huge brute, a major in a neat uniform tailored to cover his bulk to best advantage. He must have gone over three hundred pounds. Those regimentals weren't drawn from the quartermaster. They must have cost a pension. He wore his Jeff Davis hat indoors, which was damned odd for a gentleman, and it had the wreath insignia of staff. I'm staff too, but I wore the crossed swords of the cavalry on my hat. It has more flair and the Jeff Davis was styled for horse troopers anyway.[8]

There were a half-dozen other girls of every shade and size lounging about Missy Ruth's parlor. Men like a good mix. The girl hugging the fat neck of the staff major was the tiniest one in the room. She was pretty and thin, delicate as a bird and stood on tiptoes to rest her chin on his shoulder as he sat glaring at his cards. Scat's a simple game, but there was money on the table and he wouldn't be rushed. To hell with him! It wasn't cards I was interested in.

I perused the other girls perching on establishment's fancy furniture and a dandy lot they were, bright as parrots in vulgar gowns cut to show their décolletage to the tops of their rosebuds. There wasn't another fair, thin girl to remind me of my Dust Mop so I reckoned to go in the other direction. One of the ladies was a colored gal, black as your buttons and husky. Her shocking pink gown exposed wide shoulders, strong arms and bosoms fit to frighten the French. She gave me a steamy glance, puckered her big lips and the deal was done. I love a short courtship. My brown ale was fetched by a black brat, I parked myself on an upholstered couch, pulled my new dusky friend onto my lap, felt the furniture sag under her weight and introduced myself to my new lady friend.

"How do, Miss Blacky? I'm Mister Sidney."

"An' I'm Miss Dutch. An how you doin' today, Misto Sidney?"

"You don't look Dutch to me, Missy."

She wiggled her stern quarters on my lap, devoured my ear with her soft lips and whispered, "An' you gonna be *in* Dutch, you keep sassin' me like dat, Misto Colonel, soldier-man."

By grapes, here was a lass after my own heart and I began nuzzling her bouncers with my whiskers when the mood was broken by a scream from the card table, and a crash as the tiny hooker on the staff major's shoulder went flying into the crockery.

"You little bitch!" the major roared. "Keep your poxy hands off my cards!"

Missy Ruth and the major domo rushed into the room.

"Kitten, what's the fuss? Major Middlesex– sir?

"Discipline your whores, you fat slut! She cost me the hand and twelve dollars."

Well, Missy Ruth was heavy and she was a slut, but really? Major Middlesex wasn't a gentleman, and not just because he wore his hat indoors.

Little Kitten was on the floor running with tears. Her gown was yanked down to the waist and the fingers over her breast were slick with blood. When she looked at her mutilated nipple beneath her fingers she whimpered, "He pinched me, Miss Ruth! Oh Jesus, it hurts, I'm bleeding!" and with that she turned as white as linen and tipped over into a dead faint.

"Well, that's a damned rude way to spoil a frolic," I growled at him. I tried to stand, but with Miss Dutch on my lap I was pinned to the sofa. It was good that I was. Major Middlesex stormed to his feet, sending his chair flying like a thistle and glared down at me. I was wrong about him. He wasn't huge, he was gigantic– taller than me by two hands and a hundred pounds heavier than I had reckoned. He was fat as a sow, with his smooth shaven face red with rage and his pig eyes tiny in the mass of flesh. For such a monster he was quick and towered over me as I squirmed beneath Blacky Dutch.

"What's it to you, you fancy Southern son of a bitch?" Mad as he was, he had picked up on my Missouri accent.

He shook a fist the size of a ham in my face and Miss Dutch tumbled off my lap to the floor with her crinoline hoops flipping over her head exposing her huge black backside to the room. Maidens in knock-shops don't burden themselves with unnecessaries like pantaloons and knickers.

"At least I take my pleasures white, you n—r loving scoundrel!"

This was a terrible man, a dangerous man and it wasn't just tiny whores he was fixing to abuse. His bile was focused on me. I *hate* to fight– always have especially with enraged giants. I'll gladly run, to hell with dignity, but I was cornered on a davenport before his mountain of flesh. If cornered I'll use any weapon at hand, fighting fair is the game of an idiot, but Miss Dutch had knocked over the end table with its handy ashtrays and flub-dubs that would have doubled nicely as clubs, and my Remington was checked with my traps at the door.[w]

He grabbed both my lapels in one massive mitt and hauled me up and off my feet like so much dunnage. God, he was strong! Hauling around four hundred weight of lard all his life had given him the strength of a bull. I tried to strike him in the face, left and then right, but with my feet off the ground there was no momentum in the blows. His face wasn't soft with fat, but hard as suet and he didn't even blink. And then his fist cocked back for a punch that would shatter my teeth– all of them.

The whores were screaming like panicked poultry. The card players scooped up the stakes and were stampeding to the exit. I heard reinforcements pounding up the back stairs, houses of pleasure always have a bullyboy or two on the payroll for emergencies like this, but they would be too late for my teeth.

"Got a soft spot for whores, do you? Interfere with *me* will you, you mincing pimp?"

"That's *Colonel* Pimp to you, *major*!"

But pulling rank wasn't going to work with this one. That terrible fist was coming like a locomotive,

---

[w] This would be the 1858 Remington .44 caliber, cap and ball six shot revolver.

nothing could stop it– and then Major Middlesex dropped straight to the floor like a sledged ox in a slaughterhouse.

Missy Ruth was quite out of breath when she scurried around the major's carcass. He was too big to step over. She grabbed my cheeks and clucked like Aunt Polly.

"My brave Ducks! Defendin' my gals like that, an' he's such a big brute now, ain't he. An' you're always such a gentleman, ain't you? Not like this one here!" and she gave the unconscious Middlesex a kick in his ear with her slippered toe.

She nodded to her two tardy crushers, and with the help of the butler and two big floozies they dragged his arse through the back parlor door. If he was lucky he'd wake up in an alley, pockets turned out, stripped of watch and boots, and with the other pigs chewing on his toes. *There's* a lesson to be learned, young readers. Take it to heart– never start a row in a cat shop, especially in a strange city. You can't win and you can't get even. The management pays off the local bulls and the judges are their best customers.

While the girls tended to tiny Kitten, and Dutch set right the furniture, I looked about in relief and asked Miss Ruth what the hell had just happened.

"I don't really look that fat, do I Colonel Sidney?"

"What the blazes?"

"That awful man– he called me fat. Said I was a fat slut," and she looked ready to cry.

What the deuce is wrong with women? Young, old, virgins or trollops, they're all just a little bit daft.

"Middlesex," I pointed at the empty door. "Middlesex– *he* was fat."

"But he said *I* was fat, too. Am I now, Ducks?" she whined.

Lord love a duck! "No you ain't, Miss Ruth– not at all. Not a bit of it. You're stately, like the Queen."

Maybe that wasn't the best thing to say. Queen Victoria was piling on the poundage herself, but it seemed to cheer the brothel queen up, and after all we *were* chums of a sort.

"And you ain't a slut either. You're a businesswoman, and a damned good one. And a lady, too." Lord, the things a fellow will say to keep the peace. If Amy and Auntie could have heard me…

She brightened right up and when I asked, "Now who saved me? Somebody put out his lights good and proper," she tittered like a schoolgirl.

"You have to hit them a good smack in the temple. It's a thin bone betwixt the bat an' brain and no matter how big they are they'll drop like wet laundry."

The old trot actually blushed through her rouge when she pulled a ten-inch sap from the folds of her gown. It was neatly sewn black leather and sagged with the weight of the lead that gave it its pop.

Missy Ruth giggled like a virgin as she tucked it down between the cleavage of her bosoms. The sap slid all the way down and out of sight. She settled it with a satisfying wiggle and purred, "An' a lady's gotta protect her gals *and* her friends, don't she?" and gave me a look that any man could have read like the morning post.

What the dickens? She wiggled her knockers at me and the sap didn't hinder their bounce. And then I thought, what the hell? I had just been looking for the opposite of my little Dust Mop. How different could I get? I fluffed my whiskers and gave her look right back at her. Miss Dutch stuck out her big pink tongue at me as I followed Miss Ruth's stern up the stairs. A seasoned professional like the madam would certainly know what she was doing and it's handy to have any prosperous, competent woman owing you a favor. And my bareback ride would be on the house.

* * *

Like a good trooper I reported for duty at the Winder Building Annex at the open of business on

Monday with Halleck's orders in hand. I took a hack the six blocks to 17th Street because I felt as if I had been pummeled by a pugilist– and it wasn't from my run- in with Major Middlesex either. Apparently Missy Ruth gets titillated from cold-cocking brutal giants and she took it out on me. She knew her way around a featherbed as only a lifetime of mattress galloping could teach. Her vocation was fornication and she was a willing worker. She navigated me around the mattress with all the authority of a riverboat pilot, and when she took topside my poor hips almost dislocated. I'm not complaining– her flesh was a bit past its prime but there was plenty of it and I dug in with both hands and enjoyed the ride. And then I did again, and when I was an exhausted hulk, *she* did it again. Young reader– again, let old Professor Sidney instruct you in the ways of the world. Don't dismiss an older woman out of any misplaced notion that an old trot isn't worth your time. I learned this lesson on my own tick when I was a young buck during the War and I pass it on to you free of charge. Older women are damned good fun. They know the ways of fornication like a giggling virgin couldn't imagine. There's none of the clingy romance and love nonsense that can be deuced inconvenient, and you don't have to make any false promises or even pay them. They have their own means, there are no papas with shotguns about to spoil the sport, they usually have a safe place to consummate the capital act and they're jolly. That last is important because it's supposed to be fun and Miss Ruthy and I spent half the night swilling her brandy and laughing in each other's faces. By the time she rolled off me with a satisfied snore there was damned little left of me for the Army.

I had no earthly idea why the General of the Army would want to see me. My orders were signed by Halleck himself, but I assumed my business would be handled by a lesser clerk– there were enough of them scurrying around the corridor. Lucky pups. None of these paper-collar soldiers would ever sleep in the mud or gag on salt-horse. I hoped I could join them. After presenting my papers to a pink-faced lieutenant, I expected to cool my heels for half the morning but there wasn't even a chance for a quick doze in the adjutant's office before a sergeant in crisp blues escorted me into presence of America's chief warlord.

I had met Halleck twice before. The first was when Grant visited him in Saint Louis before Fort Henry and Donalson. He treated Grant like a poor relation and didn't impress me a wit. All he did was sulk and rub his elbows. And he was damned rude. Our second meeting was when he and Lincoln visited McClellan's staff after Bull Run to give Little Mac command of the combined Armies of Virginia and the Potomac. As I recall, he wasn't at all rude to McClellan. He groveled like a Sheeny tin-ware peddler before the Young Napoleon. I still wasn't impressed. He rubbed his blasted elbows then, too. His nickname was Old Brains and looking at his drooping face again, I could see why. His massive head was all forehead, with wisps of hair combed across the top of the big dome. He tucked the rolls of his chin down to his weak chest so he perpetually looked up from bulging eyes. General Halleck looked as out of place in military traps as Auntie Polly would have in circus tights, but the nation reckoned him a military genius. Not the Alexander or Hannibal kind– the book kind. He wrote them, and at West Point I had to read them. The damn things were as dull as he was. Halleck attended the Point a generation before me, went to California to fight the war with Mexico, stayed in the Golden State and made a fortune. After Sumter, Lincoln made him a Major General. Now he was in the War Department Annex doing what he was born to do. Halleck was the best clerk in the Union Army.

I expected him to be as rude to me as he was to Grant back when he was an unknown brigadier with a reputation for the jug. Instead, when I presented myself with a snappy salute, he pulled his spectacles down from his rummy eyes, stood with a weak-chinned smile, let go of his elbows and reached out his hand like a favorite uncle.

"Colonel Sawyer, my dear fellow! How good– how good– how good of you to come."

Well, this beat the chiggers. 'Good of me to come?' I was under orders and a week late, but if he was happy, I was relieved.

"Sir!"

"Colonel Sawyer, you come with the highest of recommendations. The Republic needs men like you. Men who are true to the cause– men who will do or die."

Well, this didn't sound like staff work.

"Sir!"

"We have heard of your own personal crusade. Yes, even here in Washington, far from the fray. Your labors in the vineyards of the Lord on the Underground Railroad– in Virginia, and again in Mississippi, the dark heart of the Slave Power itself."

My God– what fool had been filling his fat head with this nonsense?

"Sir!"

"You are to be given a new and glorious commission. One fitted to your metal. Your zeal has been noted and your dedication will be rewarded."

The old fool was practically weeping. What the deuce? I reckoned to at least give it a try.

"Sir, I am overwhelmed with the confidence you place in me. I am eager and ready for any staff billet you have for me. I learned supply and procurement from Generals Frémont and McClellan. If I may say, sir, I was born for the bureaucracy."

I prayed he'd want a stalwart veteran like me around his digs to give the place a bit of military credibility, but it was no soap.

His eyes bugged out farther than usual as he made to reassure me, and he started rubbing his damned elbows again.

"My dear Colonel, nay! To waste a man of your missionary fervor on staff would be a sin– nay sir, a *crime* against the cause. You shall have a commission worthy of the struggle. I summoned you hither for the pleasure of meeting you myself. My rank allows me these vanities, but it is Stanton who has the honor of presenting you with your command."

Command? I'd avoided command like the pox. And Stanton? What did that abolitionist gravedigger want with me?

"Report to Secretary Stanton at the War Department for orders." He let go of his elbows and stood in dismissal. I gave him my best plebe salute and he returned it like he meant it. "God's speed!"

The Adventures of Sidney Sawyer
Missouri Yankees

Chapter 6

'God's speed' indeed! The War department was just across the street. It was a big barn of a building, fifty yards across, facing Pennsylvania Avenue with a portico of Ionic columns stuck on the front as an afterthought. A great flagstaff was grafted dead center of the gable with Old Glory sagging in the damp heat. Its ugly sister, the Navy Department, was next door.[x] The sentries flanking the mammoth doors didn't hinder the stampede of staff officers, wire-pullers, jobbers, contractors, draft dodgers, wishful salesmen and visiting farmers that rushed in and out on the business of the Republic. The interior was as hot as the boiler room of a pook-turtle and just as noisy as the mobs dispersed left, right and center, or stomped up and down the grand granite staircases. They all seemed to know where they were going, but I didn't. There was a civilian clerk across the foyer perched at a high desk laboring away at a nest of paperwork. He'd know.

"Stanton?"

"Here," he gestured at the door behind him with his pen. "Name?"

"Colonel Sawyer, by order of General Halleck."

The clerk scribbled this down and shouted "Boy!"

---

[x] The War and Navy Department buildings were demolished after the Civil War and replaced with the architectural monstrosity that is now called The Eisenhower Building or the Old Executive Office Building. On any visit to Washington it can't be missed. It is right next door to the White House.

A colored brat in livery snatched the paper and dodged into the room.

"In there, Colonel. Wait your turn," and he stuck his nose back in his papers.

That was damnedable news. I was already sweating like a bargee, it would break all military custom to strip off my tunic, and I'd have to wait all day for a word with Lincoln's god of war. I tucked my hat under my arm, stepped through the door and was treated to a tableau that might have been written for the stage by Harriet Beecher Stowe.

It was a large room with a well-worn carpet, dark wainscoting and prints of presidents, generals and battles adorning the walls. Spittoons and stiff chairs lined the room and a skylight centered in the high ceiling lit the scene. Half the chairs were filled with the usual run of jobbers you would expect to find waiting for their chance to swindle a nation at war. At the back of the room was a long desk of heavy oak, built for standing, not sitting, and tilted toward the back. A bulk of a man stood foursquare behind the desk, feet apart and hands behind his back in the manner of the captain of a ship at sea. He was sweating in a black wool suit complete with waistcoat, high collar and silk tie half hidden by reach-me-down whiskers that covered his breast to his third button. His upper lip was clean-shaven and beneath his high forehead were cold eyes behind tiny spectacles. There was no pity in them. He reminded me of an Old Testament prophet who was ready and willing to call down the wrath of the Almighty on any and all transgressors, doubters or slackers. This was Secretary of War Edwin Stanton and he was as different from Halleck as a wolf is from the family dog.

His cold eyes were on a family that was kneeling and keening before the big desk. They looked like a mother with three young daughters and a boy of five or six. The woman, thin from a hard life of farm labor, was dressed in what must have been her Sunday best and was twisting her bonnet in her hands. Tears soaked stringy hair that fell across her face.

"Mercy– oh mercy, sir. Their pa is dead– killed by Missouri border ruffians in '57. Please don't take my son. Don't kill their brother. Robert is all we have."

At the word 'kill' the oldest sister gave a wail and fell into a swoon face down between her sisters. They fell on her with sobs that would have melted the heart of Herod, but not Stanton whose dark eyes never blinked. The girls' shoulders shook as they swayed and howled. The boy gulped in terror and his nose ran onto his tightly buttoned shirt.

"Sir, spare our Bobby. He is only eighteen– just a boy– a good boy!"

Stanton spoke in words as cold as the grave, "A soldier, not a boy. The court has ruled. He must die."

The mother beat her breast and pressed her head to the floor. "He fell asleep, sir. He marched all day. My baby is not a coward. He is a good soldier. Spare him, sir!"

"A sentry may not sleep. Duty must be done or the cause is lost. The judgment stands."

And I stood– I jumped to my feet I couldn't help it– it was just so damned pathetic. Here a family had traveled to the capital from beyond the Missouri no less, begging mercy for a boy who took a snooze on picket duty, from a man who had no mercy in his heart. Like a fool I took a step toward the mother but was stopped when those terrible eyes shifted to me. When will I ever learn? Stanton turned on his heel and stalked through a door behind the desk.

"Oh Lord, melt his heart of flint," sobbed the woman as she gathered her daughters around her and the tiny boy broke into hysterics. "Bobby– oh my Bobby! What shall we do? We shall starve! Oh God– oh God it is so hard!"

At that the clerk and a corporal rushed in to help the destroyed woman and her brood from the room. I joined them. I have no idea why, it was none of my concern but at times I'm a simple sentimental sap and have to stick in my oar. I'd done the same thing at the whorehouse yesterday defending a stargazer from a giant major and almost lost my dental work. There was absolutely nothing I could do for them and why would I want to? Skinny farm wives in cheap gingham ain't my style and the daughters were too young to tempt. But then I had an idea, and looking back, I'm damned glad I did. I saved Bobby's life, the malingering swine. What the hell? For sleeping on the picket line he should have been bucked and gagged, not shot.

I shook the mother and gave her a slap to drag her from her grief and focus on me. "Go to Lincoln, do you hear? He's a soft touch and won't say no. Take the boy with you but leave the girls on the porch– too much noise. The boy will seal the deal. The Ancient just lost his son so he won't let them shoot yours. Go to John Hay first– not Nicolay, he's a prig. Tell Hay that Sidney Sawyer sent you. Tell him you're a cousin of Missy Ruth's over on 12th Street, but for God's sake don't mention Ruth to Lincoln."

She looked at me like I was salvation on a stick. "But where is Lincoln? How do I see him?"

"The Executive Mansion is right next door. The darkie butler will let in anybody. You can't miss it– it's a big white house. Just walk in the front door, ask for Hay. Tell 'em Sidney Sawyer sent you. Take the boy, leave the girls," and I gave her a swat on the arse to send her on her way. I have such a soft heart. John Hay was the president's secretary and controlled the flood of petitioners that infested the halls of the mansion. He and I were chums who cut some gay capers last year before Lincoln sent me to Richmond to spy on Jeff Davis and company. And he was a card who would get the joke.[y]

---

[y] John Hay rose to become Theodore Roosevelt's Secretary of State. For his escapades with Sawyer refer to Volume 3 of the *Adventures of Sidney Sawyer: The Year of Jubilee*.

* * *

No sooner did the family of sodbusters stumble away than the clerk tapped my shoulder and announced, "Colonel Sawyer, the secretary will see you now."

Damnation and small dogs, in the soup again. Why the dickens did I have to interfere with Stanton's business when his business would, of course, include sending derelict pickets to the firing squad? I followed the clerk back through the room, around the odd standing-desk and into the much smaller office where Stanton was sitting behind a normal desk. The man was sobbing. His shoulders were positively shaking. Tears ran down into his beard and he was blowing his vast nose with a huge snot-rag. I stood to attention and wondered that if between Halleck and Stanton the War wasn't being run by lunatics.

He composed himself, gave his snoot a last good blow and looked at me with his dark eyes, now red with grief. "Colonel Sawyer, I have heard, and now I know, that we are kindred spirits." He reached across with his nose-blowing hand to shake mine. "Sit."

Well, this was looking up. Maybe this gravedigger wanted me on *his* staff?

"You have been recommended to me, by the president and by more intimate sources. You are the man I have been looking for. I know that now. When you were moved to such pity by that poor mother, I knew my man."

"Sir."

"But pity is a blessing I must deny to myself. War is hard and to flinch would be disaster. Some must die to hold others faithful to duty. I shall pray for her son's soul, but my duty is as hard and as clear as crystal."

"Sir."

"It wasn't simply your valor at Shiloh and in Richmond that was your recommendation. The Republic is blessed with heroes by the legion. It was your compassion, your Christ-like devotion to the welfare of your fellow man."

I actually looked behind me. Nobody there– he *was* talking to me. I'd been misjudged before, but this took the bird.

"Sir."

"Your work on the Underground Railroad, twice I have been informed, sets you apart and above from my other abolitionist brothers. You are an abolitionist of the sword, a true soldier of the Lord."

Sweet dreams and dripping eyebrows, this wasn't sounding like staff work.

"Sir."

"Your zeal has been noted and your reward is at hand. There is a regiment, newly mustered from your home state, Missouri– The 94th USCT. They are in South Carolina off Charleston with General Gillmore. Their commander, Colonel Moog-Hess, a gallant fellow from St. Louis, is dead from the diarrhea. You, sir, will command the 94th. Your service will be a gem in the crown of the cause."

The cause? What cause? Abolition? Why the deuce would anyone reckon me an abolitionist? And what the hell was USCT? I asked and was sorry I did.

"United States Colored Troops!" Stanton said it like a prayer. "Every man a freeman. They freely volunteered, as did you, to free their brothers in bondage from the lash and the chain. Glory hallelujah!"

Glory hallelujah, my arse! I didn't volunteer anything. But somebody *had* volunteered me. I'd kill him. I'd strangle the bastard. In as calm a voice as I could muster after having my world turned on its ear, I asked the secretary, "Who?"

"The congressman from the Territory of Nevada, the honorable Thomas Sawyer. I believe he is your own brother, sir."[9]

* * *

It was six days to South Carolina on the *Isabelle Brody,* a steamer loaded with heavy ordinance, fifty cavalry mounts and a dozen assorted passengers. Off Hatteras, a summer gale churned up waves that flooded the boiler, broke the legs of a dozen nags, had the passengers and half the crew vomiting all over the companionways and held us up for two days while the ship labored under shortened sails. Thank God I'm a good sailor, but the blasted voyage gave me too much extra time to stew over Halleck and Stanton's gullibility, Brother Tom's treachery and my own rotten luck. Him and his filthy pranks! If he reckoned that outlawing gambling in a frontier territory populated by desperate miners, whores, grafters and sharps was sport, he must have roared over recommending me to Washington abolitionist society as a fellow n—r loving do-gooder. Getting me gazetted as the colonel of a darkie regiment, the likes of the one I saw tripping on parade up Pennsylvania Avenue, must have sent him over the moon. If he had been on the boat I would have kicked his backside over the rail. Black troops! I'd never live it down. I'd lose all the credit I'd won in a career of counterfeit heroics and dubious accomplishment.

I knew that since the Emancipation Proclamation the Army was recruiting every Sambo that could fill a blue suit. Most of the Army didn't expect much from the colored troops except for digging trenches, hauling firewood and other fatigues. Nobody thought n—rs could fight. Hell, didn't they squat passively on slave row for two hundred years as mute as the other livestock? I knew better, of course. I'd seen enough darkies in situations other than stoop-labor to know that if given the chance they'd pitch into the task of slaughtering ol' Massa with a will. Now they *thought* they were getting the chance, but I didn't really believe the Army would give it to them. Those colored soldiers that flabbergasted me in Washington may have been issued rifles, but it was the spade and axe for them in the ranks of a white man's army.

And all their officers *were* white. Volunteering for the blackbird regiments was a back door to promotion. A sergeant could make lieutenant, a lieutenant a colonel, but I was already a colonel, damn it! I wouldn't have volunteered for this commission for a promotion to Frog field marshal.

Colonel Sidney Sawyer, commander of the 94th Missouri, USCT! I could wring Brother Tom's skinny neck!

The *Isabelle Brody* limped into Hilton Head harbor on the seventeenth. It is one of those ugly barrier islands that the ocean throws up along the southern coast that are all sand dunes, featureless beaches, mosquitoes, bad water and hot wind. They are overrun with wild hogs, bobcats, alligators and serpents living in brush and forest so thick that Hannibal's elephants couldn't plow through, let alone a man. Some of these blasted islands run for scores of miles and when there is a gap between them there is most likely a sheltered harbor behind them. The harbors cradle cities. Forts must protect the cities, and the forts must be built on the tips of the damn barrier islands. Garrison duty in these forts, and there were a score of them along the Confederate coast, was the worst duty in the army. There is no other earthly use for these islands except for strategic location, and Hilton Head sheltered a serviceable harbor between Savannah and Charleston. Flag Officer duPont and the Navy took it from the Rebels in '61 and now it was the Army's headquarters for the Department of the South. I reported to Fort Welles on the north tip of the island to find my regiment. It wasn't there.

The island was a madhouse. There were thousands of Negroes, just none of them in blue. Runaways had been flocking to the island since the local gentry fled to Savannah at the sight of the Union Navy. How additional swarms of colored folk crossed the sound, God knows, but there were now so many of them that New England abolition societies sent down boatloads of missionary busybodies to bring them up to Yankee standards of freedom. They ginned up schools, black village councils, workshops, a hospital, churches and good luck to 'em. It still wasn't Boston by a long pitch.

The harbor was choked with shipping– warships to man the blockade, supply ships to keep them in biscuits and rum, and more ships ferrying troops to and from the siege at Charleston. Entire regiments were bivouacked in the yards and fields of idle plantations that the former slaves had grubbed from the prickers and thickets. It was too hot to drill, but it wasn't too hot for baseball. Between the dock and the fort I passed a half-dozen games with whole companies of troops lining the base paths, jeering and cheering at each pitch. Parked behind home base were sutler's wagons selling candy, pickles, cheese, beer, booze and anything else a sweaty baseballer might need between the innings. Beside the fort itself, there was an entire clapboard and tent city catering to all the sins of an army in transit and a fleet on blockade.

Fort Welles impressed me. It was laid out by Rebel engineers who knew their craft, and since we took the island our engineers improved it with earth works and rifle pits.[z] I wouldn't want to assault the damn place. I'd heard of the commandant, General Overbrook. He was a jayhawker in the 50's back in the days of Bleeding Kansas. He slouched behind his desk in a linen duster as I presented my orders. Overbrook must have reckoned it great wit that a Missouri man would be made top-kick of a colored regiment. And why wouldn't he? These jayhawkers were mostly New England abolition men who moved to Kansas ten years ago to save that territory from the slave power. They spent years fighting Missouri border ruffians in a quasi-war of barn-burnings, bush-whackings, lynchings and flat out murder.

---

[z] Rebel Fort Walker was designed by Gen. P. G. T. Beauregard. It was taken in Nov. 1861 by the largest U.S. expeditionary force up to that time (over 13,000 troops) and renamed Fort Welles.

"Colonel Sawyer, of the gallant 94th. Your regiment awaits you opposite Charleston. Why do you linger here? Ain't you all a' fire to take your n—rs in hand? You are from Missouri– perhaps you'll find some of your relatives in the ranks."

Overbrook was a card in the mold of my brother Tom. He was also typical of abolitionist meddlers who wanted to free the darkies but looked on that race with nothing but contempt. And he was mocking my boys. I hadn't met them yet, and I didn't want them to begin with, but they were mine and I'd be damned and dipped if I'd let this Kansas window-shooter poor-mouth my regiment. No soldier would.

"They ain't n—rs no more, General Overbrook. They're soldiers in the Union Army and don't forget it." I usually don't sass generals but I was about to drop a name. "Secretary Stanton was proud to tell me that every man in the regiment is a volunteer– and so am I." (A lie, but let him think Stanton and I are chums.) "General Halleck told me he looks upon the 94th as his own regiment." (Another lie, but what the hell?)

"But you are from Missouri, a slave state as I understand. How comes it that you are so soft for the Negro?"

I ain't soft for the Negro. I could care less for the general run of that race, except for the mischief they cause, this War being the best example. I *am* partial to individual darkies who I know and trust. Just these few have gotten me labeled as a n—r lover on occasion. Now I had to make up an explanation that would serve me credit with this Kansas hypocrite.

I gave the general my noble look. "My family's anti-slavery, which ain't as popular in Missouri as in Massachusetts– or as safe. At seventeen, before I entered West Point, I fought in the border wars with my friend, H. Finn."

"Finn– I recall a fellow name of Finn– a true believer who rode with John Brown's Angels. This fellow had a ridiculous name. What was it, now?"

"Huckleberry, but you call him that at your peril."[a]

"And West Point– why, you're the fellow who fought that duel with that southern scoundrel over the cause! You are the Ace of Hearts."

I was surprised he had heard of me. The Regular Army is a small village and we all know the gossip, but this character was a volunteer.

"I have that honor." Time to lay it on with a trowel. The only way to run a regimental shop was to go in with both boots. I was in and stuck with it so I may as well act the part. "And I also led two caravans of pilgrims north to the jubilee on the Underground Railroad. I ain't a dilettante, General. I ante up and the stakes are my own arse. Missouri born or not, my credentials in the cause are as good as yours." I didn't like this fellow's style and with sponsors like Stanton and Halleck I reckoned I could be abrupt. "You have my orders, send me to my regiment."

He didn't like that but he didn't like me either, so he rapped his knuckles on his desk and shouted, "Smith! Come and fetch your Colonel."

In marched a soldier, ramrod stiff and black as a backcountry bear with the chevrons of a sergeant major filling his sleeves. He was at least in his thirties, it's deuced hard to tell with darkies, was a bit shorter than me, had a barrel belly but wide shoulders and hands that looked like they could crush stone. He was proper from his squared forage cap to his britches bloused in gleaming boots. His head was a solid ebony block with wide lips and nose spread below intelligent eyes.

---

[a] For Sawyer's adventures with Huckleberry Finn in the border troubles refer to the first edition of the Sawyer Memoirs, *The Ace of Hearts*.

"Sergeant Smith, at your service, sir," and he crashed his boots and threw a regulation salute. There was more Missouri than Africa in his voice.

Behind him was a boy of about fourteen in a private's uniform cut at sleeves and trousers to fit his small frame. His britches were held up with a wide belt high on his belly. He was as black as Smith, but with his smooth face, wide eyes and ridiculous slouch hat pinned up at the front with the bugle insignia of the infantry, he was what Aunt Polly would have called a cutie. The boy's hand fluttered up in his own salute and I returned them both smartly.

"Colonel Sawyer, sir– this is private Liberty Smith, drummer boy, and my son.

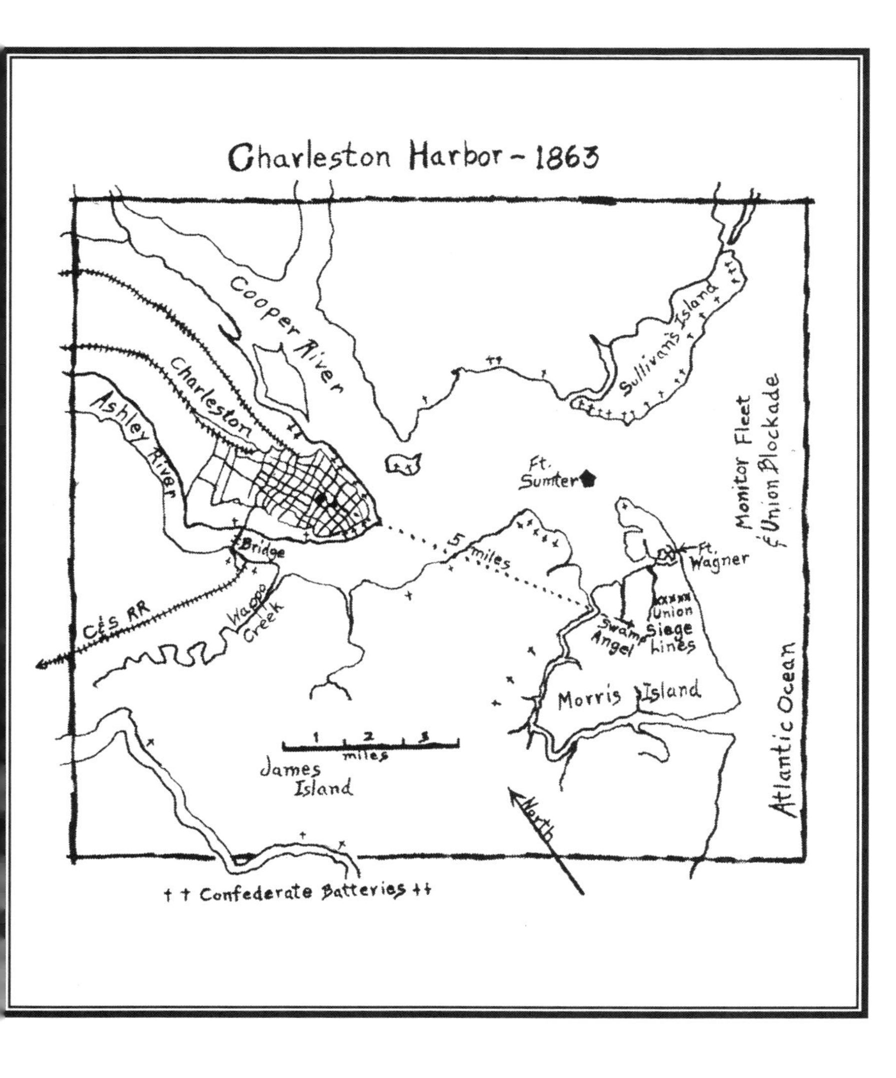
Charleston Harbor - 1863
Cooper River
Charleston
Ashley River
Bridge
C&S RR
Wappoo Creek
Sullivan's Island
Ft. Sumter
5 miles
Ft. Wagner
Union Siege Lines
Swamp Angel
Morris Island
Monitor Fleet & Union Blockade
Atlantic Ocean
1 2 3
miles
James Island
North
† † Confederate Batteries ††

The Adventures of Sidney Sawyer
Missouri Yankees

Chapter 7

The Navy had rated colored sailor-men in the fleet since John Paul Jones, so the crew of the screw steamer *USS Pocahontas* didn't bat an eye when I shipped as supercargo to Charleston with my pair of darkie troopers. The deck of a warship is a busy place so we found a rail forward of the port guns and tried not to trip any of the barefoot tars as they rushed in gangs to hoist this line or lash that rope. It was a short voyage of sixty miles north to Charleston where the *Pocahontas* would drop us off with a handful of other officers and then make its way down the coast to resume blockade duty off of the Southern Sea Islands. The other passengers spent the voyage smoking cheroots and gassing with their Naval hosts on the quarterdeck. I didn't have the time. In a few hours I would be taking over an outfit that I didn't know from a sack of buckwheat. I wasn't completely green. It's a colonel's job to command a regiment and I *had* commanded a regiment once. For a brief spell, while its commander was recovering from the Tennessee two-step, I'd run the 3rd Iowa Volunteer Infantry during the Vicksburg Campaign. I knew the drill. I didn't much like it but that didn't mean I wasn't good at it– I was. It's like running any other large establishment. Trust your subordinates with the details (but let them know you're watching), act like you give a damn in front of the rank and file, pat a few heads and kick a few backsides. And the 3rd Iowa was a crack outfit with my friend and former jayhawker, Sergeant Major Huckleberry Finn to hold my hand and wipe my nose.

Many officers wouldn't dream of gossiping with a sergeant. By grapes and by God, I was a colonel and this sergeant was as black as boot polish, but I wasn't after gossip– this was business. I had long ago learned to trust the wisdom of sergeants. A good sergeant major had a bigger hand in running a regiment than the lieutenant colonel, and despite his black hide, Smith looked like a good'un.

"Smith, I was given the honor to command the 94th less than a week ago by Secretary Stanton, but that is all he gave me– the honor. I have the commission in my pocket and nothing else."

"Sir, the 94th be a grand regiment. From de drummer boy to de officers, we are crusaders fo' a heavenly cause." At this Liberty looked up at me with worship. "Most of de ranks is freemen. I's free. Run away from marse when I's a boy. Take to blacksmithin'. Dat how I got my name, Girardeau Smith. I lives in Cape Girardeau an' I be a smith. Saved every penny an' bought my freedom from marse back in Arkansas. I be free with the papers to prove it."

Well, here was a proud one. And where did he learn about crusades?

"Who taught you to read?" It was a good guess.

"Why sir, from my wife. She passed on birthing Liberty. Be just me an' the boy since. He read, too. Lot a' men in the 94th read, an' we's teachin' the rest. 'Bout one man in four's a runaway, fresh out a' de patch."

He was proud of the regiment and his place in it, and by the time a bumboat met the *Pocahontas* off Morris Island to ferry us to shore, I had a good handle on the outfit. It was mustered in last March at Jefferson Barracks and was meant from the start to be a model regiment. It was sponsored by abolition societies in Kansas. Liberty wasn't the only trooper in the regiment to have a saucy black slouch hat. The ladies of free Kansas donated them and also presented the 94th with its colors in a ceremony that had all ranks wiping their noses on their new blue sleeves. Give 'em hell, 94th! Show 'em what colored troops can do!

All of the soldiers were to be freemen, but Missouri didn't have enough free darkies to fill out the ranks, so runaways from Arkansas, Mississippi and Louisiana rounded out the roll.[b] There were 900 men in ten companies, all officered by white men. All the sergeants and corporals were colored. There were 35 officers, almost all of them veterans, but only a dozen were officers before joining the 94th. Being from Missouri, I just might have some problems with them. Half of them were New England-born Kansas jayhawkers who had a low opinion of any white Missouri boy. Master Sergeant Girardeau Smith learned the word crusade from them. I hope they had all heard of Huck Finn.

"Don't you worry 'bout bein' from Missouri, Colonel Sawyer. We couldn't help but hear when you an' Gen'l Ov'brook wuz talking." I gave him a look of thunder and he hurried on. "Couldn't help it, sir. De door wuz mighty thin an' we wuz right there. Heard what you done fo' de colored folk. Underground Railroad an' all. God bless you, sir!"

"Indeed." I wasn't really upset. My noble reputation would spread through the regiment in ten minutes. It wouldn't hurt me with the officers either.

Sergeant Smith also introduced me to the damnedest nonsense I'd ever heard, and I'd been in the Army since I was seventeen. It seems the entire regiment, black troops in the ranks and officers in the mess, weren't drawing their pay. The Army figured that colored soldiers should be happy enough with steady rations and shoes so

---

[b] In 1863, slaves in Missouri were still slaves and couldn't enlist in the service. The Emancipation Proclamation only freed slaves in *rebel* states. Missouri never left the Union.

they only paid them ten bucks a month instead of the thirteen white troops got. And they had to pony up three dollars a month from that to pay for uniforms, booties and bullets. In protest every man boycotted his pay. I was horrified! I really didn't need the two hundred dollars the service was shelling out to me in colonel's pay. I had plenty of tucker from my dealings with Temple & Son and never left home without two hundred in gold sewn into my belt, but the twenty bucks Smith was turning up his flat nose at in sergeant's pay must have hurt. What bunkum! I'd seen it before and was sick of it. As soon as you free 'em from the plantation they start to dream of equality. Let the camel get his nose under the flap and he'll want the whole damn tent. And there was nothing I could do. I'd have to go along, fanatical abolitionist that I was to them. If I didn't want to poison my command before I took it, I'd have to grin and give up my pay as well. It was only two hundred in greenbacks, but that ain't cabbage.[10]

It was that blasted little snot Liberty that piped up and gave me my regimental nickname.

"Outrageous!" I blustered. "Ten bucks a head? Why the scruffiest Mick, drunk in the ranks, gets thirteen. And the whole regiment rejects this injustice– including the quartermaster? Splendid! I shall toss my voucher back in their faces and see if they like it. Hurrah the 94th!"

It was then that Liberty looked up at me with awe on his pretty face and chirped, "Mister Colonel, sir, you are my hero." The boy's voice was musical with Missouri in his accent and precious little slave row. "We heard what the general called you, the Ace of Hearts. You come to lead us. You have risked all for us. You give up your pay for us. To me you are not the Ace of Hearts. You are my Ace of Spades."

The Ace of Spades, damn the brat! That name spread through the regiment by the end of the day and through the Army in a week. I was hung with that tag until the end of the war. I had come to lead them, eh? Risked all for them, gave up my pay for them, eh? There's no end to the mischief of a good reputation. And as for the pay, I kept my vouchers and cashed them in as soon as I was shot from this folly. I invested the lot in a Lehigh Valley foundry that sold shoddy iron plate to the Navy. I made a bundle.[c]

* * *

I reported to General Gillmore in the Union bivouac that had a look of permanence to it. A permanent camp means an army ain't moving and from Grant I learned that an army that ain't moving, ain't winning. He was a tall fellow with a widow's peak and short beard. He wore his Hardee hat with the brim down, wide-awake style, pulled low to shade his eyes. He took a pointer to a map and explained the situation to me in simple words that implied he thought me an idiot. I was a regular army colonel taking command of a Colored regiment. Of course he reckoned me an idiot.[11]

Morris Island was a worse hellhole than Hilton Head. There was only a wedge of firm land up from the beach, a couple of miles long and a few hundred yards wide. The rest was swamp and scrub fit for nothing except night creatures and bugs. There were almost a dozen regiments in bivouac along that narrow strip. The sun was merciless and the wind up the beach tore at every tent and awning. That hot relentless wind blew from the south everyday from dawn to dark and was fit to send the men mad.

Off and away in the ocean, across the shallow-water bar, the fleet endlessly sailed on station to intercept blockade-runners bringing tucker to defiant Charleston.

---

[c] 'Spade' did not come into racist usage until fifty years after the Civil War. In Sawyer's time it was a shovel, or as used here, a black suit in a deck of cards.

Any soldiers tempted to curse their lot could look out to sea and thank their stars they weren't sailormen on a blockade voyage that would only end with the War.

Here was Gilmore's plan and if you think it a sorry scheme, well, squint at a map and see if you could do better. Charleston sits on a peninsula between the Cooper and Ashley Rivers inside a harbor that is six miles long and two and a half miles wide. You can't attack it from the land side because the land ain't land at all but marsh and swamp and thicket. We tried it twice through James Island, but it was no soap. The only other way was straight in through the harbor, but again, squint at the map. The Confederates rimmed both sides with batteries of heavy artillery, and smack in the middle like a troll on a bridge, squats Fort Sumter. These guns would slaughter any ships that made the attempt. Also, the harbor was shallow, and shipping could only enter through narrow channels. The Rebels pulled the channel buoys to confound the Yankees, strung nets and other rubbish to foul the propellers of Union warships and salted the entire horror with torpedoes.[d] Finally, gunnery ranges to where the Yankee fleet would have to sail were sited in, measured to the inch and marked with buoys. They couldn't miss– and they didn't.

Of course, the Navy *had* to give it a go. The new ironclad monitors that were being turned out at great expense would be just the ticket to bull through the Confederate gauntlet and humble the viper of secession in its nest. In April, Admiral Du Pont steamed his mighty fleet of nine monitors and the gigantic battle ship *New Ironsides* into the harbor between Sumter and Sullivan's Island. They'd go through the Rebels like worms through a goat and we could all go home for parade and mother.

---

[d] Civil War era marine mines were called torpedoes. They were anchored to the bottom of the channel and had no propulsion.

The monitors were mauled. Each ship took scores of hits that made the armor ring fit to burst the ears of the crews. Rivets that held the armor flew through the turrets like bullets, and steel bent and buckled. Every exposed fitting on every ship, flagstaffs, boats, anchors and railings were swept away by shot. The monitors blasted back mightily, but their shot merely chipped some of the masonry from Sumter or buried itself into the sand parapets protecting the Johnny shore batteries. After a few hours of this nonsense Du Pont turned the fleet right about and sailed back outside the bar. The next day one of his ironclad monsters turned turtle and sank. He never had the sand to try again.

In July Du Pont was replaced by men with both the sand and the plan– General Quincy Gilmore commanding an army of 13,000 men and Admiral John Dahlgren, the inventor of the bottle-shaped artillery of that name, would command the fleet. Here was their logic– to win the War, Charleston must fall. To blast it into submission, Fort Sumter had to be taken. To take Sumter, guns would have to be placed at the northern tip of Morris Island. The Confederates had placed a battery there to prevent the Yankees from reaching that very point and named it Fort Wagner. So, to win the War, Fort Wagner had to fall. Gilmore launched a bold assault that took all of Morris Island except for the narrow beach that led to Battery Wagner. The next day he sent in an attack that the Rebels knocked back on its pins. Not to worry. Wagner *would* be taken, Sumter *would* be smashed, Charleston *would* fall and the War *would* be won.

The next week the Army threw up parapets and hauled in two score heavy siege guns. On July 18 they opened fire on the Rebel works and the Navy steamed its monitor fleet close ashore to stick in their trident from the sea. At dusk, after seven hours of fire and shell, the guns fell silent and the assault force led by another model Colored regiment, the 54th Massachusetts, stormed the enemy parapets. They were gloriously slaughtered along with their white officers and that's the way it stood until I showed up a month later to take command of my own ten companies of blackbirds.

* * *

With General Gillmore at my elbow and Sergeant Smith a step behind I went through the formalities of assuming command. The officers welcomed me with some skepticism; they didn't know yet that I was the noble Ace of Spades. My second was Lieutenant Colonel Gould Florissant. He was one of those fore-square chaps who accomplish their tasks with all the imagination of a Lowell power loom but at least did them with similar precision. I liked him right away because I reckoned I could foist off most of my routine tasks onto his broad shoulders. I liked him more when I discovered he drank. The adjutant was a likely youngster, Major La Badie. He came from old New England money, which meant that grandpa most likely was a slave trader. Both would become chums once my nobility was manifest. Gould unbent after a few swallows of bark-juice, and 'Baddy' was a pisser. He reminded me of that strutter, Georgie Custer. The other officers were the usual rabble you would find at the head of a troop, but in general they were a competent lot.

The regiment was paraded to give me a look at the men and to have them get a look at me. I was relieved at what I saw. They marched as well as the Corps of Cadets, but with a sassy rhythm to their gaits that I've never seen with white troops. Kits were neat and square and weapons gleamed. Sergeant Major Smith knew his business. I spent the rest of the day inspecting the bivouac by the company with Smith at my elbow and Liberty in tow, and could find damned little fault. If they were white troops, I'd have had a crack regiment.

Crack regiment or not, the next day it was back to shovel duty for my black boys. They couldn't really resent it. The entire force, white and black, was busy with pick and shovel in swarms that looked to me like the Hwang Ho River coolies I'd see forty years later during that Boxer foolishness in Peking. Along with a New Hampshire outfit we were set to another bit of foolishness the Yankee boys called a 'mud lark.'[e] The rest of the Army called it the Swamp Angel. Gilmore was in a snit that he couldn't bombard Charleston until we took Sumter, so he studied his maps, did his ciphers, and lit on a way to do the impossible. He reckoned there was a spot on Morris Island that was far enough away from Confederate batteries on James Island to be relatively secure, but only 8,000 yards from St. Michael's Church steeple in the middle of Charleston. That's five miles to you and me. The problem was, this location was in the middle of a bottomless swamp. The soldiers built a boardwalk 1,700 yards long from the beach to the spot. That's almost a mile. Piles were driven deep into the gumbo and two layers of logs were bolted into a grill on the pilings. The 94th had the honor of filling thousands of sandbags and piling them on the grill to make a parapet that floated above the swamp waters. Behind this parapet the men flattened the grasses and bushes, covered the space with canvas, piled God knows how much sand on the canvas until it was above the level of the water and covered the result with lumber. The whole platform sort of floated on the semi-liquid sand that was held in place by the canvas.

They had been working on this folly for weeks before I arrived and it was almost done. I simply *had* to walk the boardwalk to the parapet to see the fuss and I was sorry I did. It got me blown up.

There, behind a triangle of sandbags was installed a steel gun carriage that must have weighed four tons. A score of men, stripped to the waist, sweating like field hands and swearing like teamsters were struggling with block and tackle inching a huge parrott gun over the

---

[e] The 94th New Hampshire Volunteer Infantry Regiment.

carriage. Swamp Angel indeed! The bloody thing was greasy black with two thick steel bands around its thick breach to keep it from exploding when it fired its massive charge. It was an eight inch rifled gun and I knew the blasted thing weighed over eight tons.

As I watched the fun I edged up to two other officers taking their ease in shirtsleeves and cracked wise. I'll never learn. "Why, the entire damn battery looks like bullshit on stilts. If it don't sink when they set the gun, it sure as hell will when they fire that monster. And how do you aim it? You can't even see Charleston from here."

"Compass!" the younger one said with a look that would freeze gin. "I shall aim it on a compass bearing, sir. I am Lieutenant Sellmer, sir, at your service. That is my shit being placed on my bull, and it was Colonel Serrell," he nodded to the other officer, "who built the stilts. Who might you be, sir? Are you a tourist?"

Damnation in the high grass. Sometimes I can wear out a welcome faster than a Papist at a camp meeting. "I beg your pardon gentlemen. I am Colonel Sidney Sawyer of the 94th Infantry. Just arrived from Hilton Head. This is a singular battery and I am sure it will–"

"It will!" Serrell sneered. "Sawyer, the new commander of the n—r soldiers. The Ace of Spades– good name. Your boys did yeoman's work filling these sandbags. I am sure you are proud. There are 13,000 of them. Count them if you like. The glorious 94th."

Well, I did gore his ox, but this was the limit. If I let this engineer disparage my regiment I'd never hear the end of it. "The 94th is a crack regiment, all picked men, freemen and volunteers, sir. They'll do their share with a spade, and with a willing heart, but they are men-o-war and don't forget it." What the hell did I know?

As I finished my brag, the Swamp Angel settled in its carriage. The men cheered, the gun platform sagged, but didn't sink and after stiff pleasantries I made my humiliated way back down the planks to the beach. In three days the Swamp Angel revenged itself for my insult

and in three more my brag almost got me killed on a stage
of blood and sand lit by the light of a calcium sun.

The Adventures of Sidney Sawyer
Missouri Yankees

Chapter 8

With the Swamp Angel's 13,000 sandbags stuffed and stacked, the 94th moved on to other shovel work. Again I couldn't fault the command for sticking my Africans in the ditch just because they were born to it. The entire Army was burrowing itself closer and closer to the parapets of Fort Wagner. You couldn't approach it above ground and live. That was flat. Any movement brought a response from the Rebels and as often as not that response was a shower of shrapnel from one of their big guns. Our own guns were never silent. Day and night artillery pounded Battery Wagner. If it had been a masonry work like Sumter it would have been a shambles. The new rifled artillery shredded stone and brick fortifications like rocks through windows. Out in the harbor the Rebels were learning that the rubble that *was* Fort Sumter made a better fortress than the original fort. Battery Wagner was an earthwork and most of our shot had as much effect as tossing peach pits at mashed potatoes. The Navy stuck in its oars by steaming their monitors close ashore in relays and letting fly with massive eleven and fifteen inch Dahlgren smoothbores, but the rubble and palmetto ramparts sucked in the shot with hardly a splash of sand. If the Swamp Angel ever *did* manage to fire on Charleston we couldn't have heard it above the din.

The 94th was officially part of Gillmore's 'Grand Guard.' Grand Guard my arse! It was ditch digging at its filthiest– soldier-work as old as war itself, digging parallel siege works closer and ever closer to the walls of the fort.

When one trench was complete, spanning the width of beach between tide line and the swamps, new ditches were dug toward the fort for another fifty yards and from there a second trench was dug parallel to the first and then another and another until the distance was close enough to allow an assault that wouldn't be simple suicide. Gillmore's Army had been hard at it for the past five weeks while the 94th had been humping sandbags. Fresh regiments were rotated in when the others were spent. This was Gillmore's 'Grand Guard,' and now we were rotated into the trench.

At night the men labored under the harsh glare of a wonder new in warfare– calcium lights. The engineers lit the battlefield with blinding beams of pure light that kept the Johnnys in their ditches while we extended our parallels to no more than a hundred yards from their parapets and less than half that from their rifle pits.[f]

The work was a horror! Every day I had to zig-zag my way to the head of the trench with Sergeant Smith and young Liberty duck-walking behind, to let my blackbirds know I was on the job. Thank God's teeth that the rest of my day was paper work and detail. It wasn't simply that if you stuck your ears above the ditch a Southern boy with a grudge would shoot them off, but sand is a deuced cruel thing to dig. Every inch of the walls had to be bucked up with timber or sandbags and the bottom of the ditch was a gumbo of wretched mud. It stunk fit to make your ears bleed. What made the mud so wretched was that the closer we dug to Battery Wagner the more often we dug into the corpses of the men who had made the first two assaults on the Battery. The Rebels did a poor job of burial detail and we'd find the moldering bodies in clumps at the bottom of their shallow graves. Aye, this was no work for a white

---

[f] Limelights, burning oxide of calcium, lit theatrical performances from the 1830's until their replacement with electricity in the 1890's. Calcium lights were a brighter improvement on the original.

man, especially because most of the corpses could still be recognized as colored infantry.

After three days and nights we were rotated to the rear where I set the men to boiling every stitch of clothing they fouled in the Grand Guard. A busy regiment is a happy regiment and I had my white officers sprinting from company to company to see to housekeeping, cooking and nitpicking. More soldiers die of camp diseases than enemy fire and I wanted my darkies fit and happy. And they were.

All soldiers sing. Lonely, drunk, happy, hungry, scared, or any combination will move a soldier to song. The voices of the Negro troops, with rhythms that could only have been born in Africa, tore at my heart with a melancholy no white man could fathom. This music was the only possession the slavers couldn't strip from them and it was their treasure. The first evening away from the ditches I stood aside in the darkness with Gould and Baddy, smoking and sipping from our flasks while the headquarters platoon squatted around their fire of pine cones and driftwood. They sang in a way white troops could not hope to match or even understand. Smith sat on a biscuit box and kept time by drumming it between his legs while he sang a low tune without words to the rhythm of his drumming. The men quietly tapped sticks, clapped or rasped their rough hands together making a music that stood the hairs up on the backs of our white necks and lifted the flasks to our lips. Then each of the men sang in his turn, making up verse to the beat, as casually as if the wild poetry of their song was an every day trifle and not a testimonial of racial genius.

A big private, who was too shy to even ask for his rations in the presence of any white officer, took his cap in his hands, looked heavenward through the sparks and sang in the deepest basso profondo–

Dem guns, they soundin' through the night,
dey don' fill my heart with fear.

We's doin' yo work o' Jesus my Lord,
an' it good to feels ya standin' so near.

Dem boys we dig up in de ditch today,
a molderin' in de sand.

Sweet Jesus, we's know you keepin' de faith,
ain't no chains in de Promised Land.

The men hummed the tune, Smith gave a soft 'amen,' Gould wiped his nose and I took another swig. Then Liberty clapped his hands loudly to a faster beat and piped in with a boy's soprano that was as sweet as honey. It was *Kingdom Coming*, a hysterical tune that I didn't cotton to before, but afterwards found myself singing whenever I got a skin full of oh-be-joyful.

Say, darkies have you seen de massa,
with de muffstash on his face,

Go long de road some time dis mornin',
like he gwain to leave de place?

He seen a smoke way up de river,
where de Linkum gunboats lay.

He took his hat and left right sudden,
and I 'spect he run away![g]

The men howled with joy, Liberty danced, his daddy beat the time, and us white officers kept well outside the circle of light so as not to break the spell. With the music, the ocean breeze cooling the camp and the

---

[g] *Kingdom Coming* or *The Year of Jubilo* was written before the Emancipation Proclamation by Henry C. Work in 1862.

whiskey warming my belly I remembered why I loved the Army. By God, it's the life for any man!

De massa run, Ha-Ha! De darkie stay, Ho-Ho!
It must be now de Kingdom Coming,
an' de year of Jubilo!

And then the brat did something that I reckoned damned queer. He made up the last chorus and while he sang, stared into the darkness toward where I stood slouching against a pine.

The Ninety-fourth, Ha-Ha! I'll love you all my days!
Missouri Yankees, on parade,
an' I love de Ace of Spades!

And then the boy gave me a cute little bow. Like I said, damned queer.[h] Before Baddy could dig me with a sassy take on my new name a lieutenant with a down-east accent as flat as a skillet appeared at my shoulder.

"Couldn't find ye, Colonel Sawyer. Had a' ask the coons." He pulled a dispatch from his sleeve and handed it over like their black had rubbed off on me. "Compliments of Colonel Serrell and Lieutenant Sellmer."

He stood at insolent attention while I read the note. It was an invitation to the Marsh Battery to visit the Swamp Angel. It would seem that I had picked a scab and these officers wanted to show me a thing or two.

* * *

I didn't have to go. Serrell couldn't issue me an order, I was a colonel too, by grapes, but I wanted to see

[h] During the Civil War, and in 1914 when Sawyer wrote this packet of his memoirs, 'queer' meant odd or out of alignment. It had no sexual context.

the show. I took Smith in tow and we followed the down-east Lieutenant up the beach to the boardwalk and strolled our way into the swamp.

Great balls of fire! The entire swamp lit up in a– well, a great ball of fire that filled half of the sky. A rolling explosion reached me seconds later. No gun could do that! Were the Rebels attacking the battery? No, there were no other shots or flairs. We were still a half-mile from the parapet and crept along the boards ready to take to the swamp at the first hint of threat, and damn the leaches. As we neared the battery I heard curses from the gunners, the reedy voice of Sellmer snapping orders, and saw shadows dance in the light of lanterns. It was not a happy crew. I paused to eavesdrop for a moment and was glad I did. The battery went silent for a three-count followed by a sharp command. Then the world exploded in blinding fire and noise. The Swamp Angel must have blown its breach, but no– when we stepped into the dim light the huge cannon sat on its carriage with men swarming around it with soaking sponges, fresh shot, powder and ramrod.

Sellmer was before the gun, swearing at the gunners in language usually reserved for shovel labor on the Buffalo canal docks. Serrell was beside the parapet looking thunder at a smoldering wall of sandbags.

"Thank you for the invitation, Colonel. I see you're giving Charleston hell on a lumber raft." I was in the mood to be cheeky.

"If it isn't the Ace of Spades and his entourage? Yes, we are giving them hell," he sneered. "And it ain't on a lumber raft. It's a raft of fire– Greek fire. The city's burning as sure as we stand here. Greek fire, do you hear."[12]

I knew the problem in a second. Several of the shells, loaded with some sort of incendiary brew, had exploded in the barrel– not over Charleston.

"The only fire I've seen is in the muzzle of your angel. You can't fire this monster again. Did you check the breech bands? You'll blow yourself–" I remembered Liberty's song, "to Kingdom Coming!"

Sergeant Smith stifled a laugh with a snort, but Serrell didn't get the joke. Good man Smith, I think I'll call him Smitty.

"Of course we check the breech bands, and what the devil does a colonel of darkie infantry know about artillery?"

"West Point, '59, sir. And I had the honor to serve on the *Cincinnati* before Fort Henry. I saw action at Donelson, Shiloh, South Mountain, Antietam and Champion's Hill. I ran the batteries at Vicksburg with Porter's brown water fleet. I was staff with Frémont, Grant and McClellan, sir. I know my craft, sir. And I'm *cavalry*, by God."

If he was impressed he didn't show it. Instead he pointed and said, "Look there!"

A gunner took a ten-pound hammer and gave the breach band a bash. Instead of a solid gong it gave a sickening clang.

"Loose as a hooker's corselet!" Sellmer shouted with a curse.

And well might he curse. Breach bands were massive bands of iron snugged around the breach of a Parrot gun to prevent the massive charge of powder from blowing it and the gun crew to porridge. It didn't stop them from finishing the load. The shell with its brew of Greek fire was placed in the swabbed out barrel like it was grandma's crystal. Sellmer himself set the carriage along its compass bearing, placed the cap and rigged a double length of lanyard. Then all hands were ordered to the *outside* of the parapet, which ain't standard gunnery at all. Smitty and I joined them in the marsh with water flooding my boots.

13,000 sandbags between me and the Swamp Angel or not, when Sellmer shouted "Stations!" I squatted, covered my ears and shut my eyes. At "Fire!" the concussion almost took off my scalp, but it was normal shot. The Angel had sent another load of Greek fire on its way to Charleston.

"Shiloh? Antietam? Cavalry, you say?" Colonel Serrell sneered as I came out of my squat. "Come on, man," he thumped my back as if I was his little sissy brother. "No one's shooting at you here." But of course they were. Confederate shot from James Island sent up splashes of gumbo every five minutes as they searched for the Angel. "Enjoy the show. You considered this battery a folly. Now, watch how it's done."

And I watched, this time without squatting with my fingers in my ears. Every fifteen minutes or so, after delicate loading, the gun crew blasted another round of fire into the distant city. Serrell and Sellmer had proved their point. I was tuckered, my feet were wet and I was sick of it. Time to swallow my pride, give them an attaboy and retire back down the boardwalk, but Lieutenant Sellmer, damn him, stepped up with a dare I couldn't refuse.

"Colonel Sawyer, do you have the time?" In the dim light of the work lanterns I couldn't see my blasted watch and neither could he. "The gun is as sound as a dollar, sir. I'll have no more of this dodging behind the parapet. *We* will fire from beside the gun. You and I can read our watches in the glare of the shot."

He was mad as a hatter. This gun should be pushed into the marsh and a new piece mounted. It was fatally weakened and he knew it, but it was a challenge I couldn't refuse. If I did, the tale would be around the Army before morning mess. The 94th Colored Infantry wasn't commanded by the Ace of Spades, but by the *Queen* of Spades.

With a smirk he added, "And you, sir will have the honor of firing the Angel."

What could I do? The rest of the gun crew was filing out of the parapet while Sellmer set a standard lanyard on the cap. I was in his chicken coop now, and there was damned all I could do except order Smitty out with the rest of the troops. I looked him in the eye, stuck out my noble chest and lied, "Honored, sir!"

After this shot I'd give him my compliments and head back down the boardwalk for a drink and dry boots.

I barked, "Fire!" and pulled the cursed string.

I was blown out of my boots, ankles over ears, thirty yards into the swamp. My britches were tatters and the burns on my backside blistered in the swamp-slime. All around me Greek fire was floating on *top* of the water, flaming and hissing like nests of reptiles, throwing shadows that Dante would recognize from his blasted poems. How I wasn't killed was a miracle. How I was only knocked *half* out of my wits was another miracle. My ears rang like a steam whistle and when I tried to flounder to my feet in the hip-deep muck, I kept falling back on my arse. My vision was cockeyed. It *must* have been! On *top* of the parapet was the Swamp Angel, pointed at me, glowing a satanic red. It was an eight-ton Parrot gun! Who could have set it there like a child's pick-up stick? Was I losing my mind? And then I knew that I was. There, in the swamp, lumbering toward me like a darkie haunt, back-lit by fire, was a swamp creature– a giant. It reached down to me with mammoth hands.

I screamed the scream of a child in terror, "*Aunt Polly!*"

And I was lifted like a child and carried like one back to the wreck of the battery. The Swamp Angel had exploded and tossed Lieutenant Sellmer and me into the soup like rag-dolls. But what was this swamp creature that loomed from the wreckage and plucked me from the muck? When we reached the light it looked down at me with a face like a sow and spoke.

"I should have left you for the crawfish, you n—r loving son of a bitch– but I've got plans."

I'd last seen this giant, laid out cold as a cod, being dragged through the back door of Miss Ruthy's knock-shop in Washington City.

Major Middlesex dropped me on the scorched boards of the gun platform like so much rubbish.

"I've got grand plans for you, n—r lover!"[13]

The Adventures of Sidney Sawyer
Missouri Yankees

Chapter 9

Aside from blisters where the Swamp Angel splashed Greek fire on my arse, and a wicked splinter in the same location jammed home when Middlesex dropped me onto the wreckage of the battery, I came through the explosion in one piece. (Even the vile sludge of the tidal swamp didn't smother the chemical flames.) Flying through the ether like a trapeze dancer frightened me out of my senses, but add to it Middlesex popping up in the muck like a sinister genie, and I was ready to baste myself in the oil-of-gladness. To the roar of Middlesex laughing like Jack's giant, I hobbled back down the plank path with Sergeant Smitty propping me up under one arm and a down-east webfoot from the 11th Maine under the other. The fat bastard may as well have been singing "Fee Fi Fo Fum!"

I set the bivouac a' buzz when I limped in before morning drums with my trousers in shreds looking like a dog's breakfast. The regimental quack plied his pliers on the splinter, smeared a mustard salve that stunk like old newsprint on the blisters, and pronounced me damn lucky. Aye, lucky like the three-legged, one-eyed, wormy mutt of the same name. Smitty positively tut-tuted while the medico stitched up my backside. Liberty wept like a girl. I damned his eyes for a sissy and sent him running for my flask. In fifteen minutes I was out cold on my cot with a pint of sutler's shine to kill any dreams.

I slept like a babe through the morning cannonade against Wagner, and slept on when the Navy steamed its monitors past the fort in line-of-battle adding their huge smooth-bores to the tumult, but I couldn't sleep through Liberty's piping voice shouting while he pummeled and rocked my shoulders . "Mr. Colonel, sir! Wake up! Wake up! Mr. Colonel Sawyer, sir, the gen'l wants ya. Wake up, sir. Gen'l Gillmore, he wants ya!"

And he did. As I rolled out of my rack Major La Badie barged into my tent without so much as a tap on the pole and recited a dispatch ordering me to headquarters, "at your earliest convenience."

Baddy grinned like a coot when I grabbed the thunder bucket and tossed up the morning whiskey along with a pint of marsh sludge. This was nothing new. For a peace-loving fellow I seem to get knocked senseless more than most. As often as not I spew like puss with a hairball after I come back to my senses.[i] Most men sleep in their drawers– thank God my Amy broke me of that silly convention. I must have been a rare sight kneeling by the cot with my head in the commode, and my bare arse covered with stitches and smeared with yellow muck. Aye, the dignity of rank. Before Smitty yanked him out by the scruff of his neck, Liberty stared at me with slack-jaw and empty head as I pulled fresh britches over my poor suffering backside. Hadn't the brat ever seen a white man's courting tackle before?

"At your earliest convenience," means right bloody now, but there was no way on God's green earth I could mount a horse. I limped the mile to Army headquarters with Baddy and Smitty on each side to catch me if I foundered. It was at Lighthouse Point where a pretty channel separates Morris Island from Folly Island to the south. Set in a pleasant glade, it must have been the only decent bivouac on the Carolina coast.

I wasn't at my best.

---

[i] Vomiting after a blow to the head is a symptom of a concussion.

"Sawyer!" Gillmore snapped. "Just because you command n—r troops doesn't mean that you have to comport yourself like one. You look like a Black River stevedore! And you're late."

I gave him the steadiest salute I could manage, which wasn't all that steady because looming behind the general in the middle of a mob of disapproving staff ticks was Major Middlesex. Fee Fi Fo Fum!

* * *

I may have looked like liver on toast but at least my companions did the regiment proud. Sergeant Major Smith looked like a black Mars in polished boots, green cummerbund, (which for some reason was the regimental color, as if we were Black *Irish* for God's sake), gleaming buttons, blocked and brushed Jeff Davis and crisp uniform. How he managed it in this heat after a mile hike through the sand I couldn't credit. But he was only a sergeant and a darkie to boot so he carried no weight. Major La Badie was turned out like a barracks spiv. He was flash in his tailored blues, napoleon beard trimmed to a turn, leather gleaming with his mother of pearl colt horse pistol peeking from his belly holster and green polka dot neckerchief tied at the throat. He wore his kepi on three hairs and the smirk on his handsome face was only an inch on the subordinate side of insolent. I told you he was a pisser.

He realized I was too foxed to speak for myself, clever lad. He explained to the general in the most respectful manner that I had been on duty all night, had recently been blown up by the Swamp Angel and had a reason to be a tad worse for wear.

The general glowered.

I tried to help my cause by explaining the condition of my hindquarters as to why I walked instead of rode.

A colonel with mutton-chop whiskers snorted.

I tried to suck in my belly and stick out my noble chest but all I succeeded in doing was floating an air-biscuit marinated in cheap whiskey that had Gillmore slapping at his nose.

The assembled staff recoiled.

My reputation in this Army was shot, and there was nothing for it, when I was saved by an unlikely angel– or should I say genie?

"Sir, with respect, I myself saw Colonel Sawyer man the lanyard at the Marsh Battery. It was he who fired the last glorious shot into treason's bosom-city, ignoring all peril and regardless of personal security."

Well, this was fine, but why was Major Middlesex singing *my* praises?

"Blown from the battery, sir– painfully wounded with the incendiary Greek fire on his buttocks."

This was helpful but what the deuce was this brute's game?

"General Gillmore, sir, Sawyer's papers have come across my desk. He is highly recommended by General Halleck, Secretary Stanton and even President Lincoln. He commands the 94th because he is true blue to the cause. I'm sure that there are mitigations for his current– state."

"Have you met?" Gillmore asked in surprise.

"Briefly, sir, in a Washington parlor, but only for a word." He smiled with yellow horse teeth and held out his hand. "Major Melrose Middlesex, Massachusetts, at your service, sir."

I took his paw and he took care not to crush my hand– very white of him.

It didn't take me long to find out just what the bastard's game was. He meant me mischief and no error. Middlesex was only a major of staff, but a general only knows what his staff feeds him and my fat friend was feeding him cabbage about how anxious the late Colonel Moog-Hess was to prove his colored troops in battle. It was the same nonsense Gillmore had heard from Shaw, the commander of the 54th Massachusetts back in July. The man had been in such a lather to show the world what black soldiers could do that he begged to have his blackbirds lead the assault. He did prove what they could do. They could serve every bit as good for target practice as white troops. Only four days ago we'd been digging them up in clusters.

There was an assault planned for dusk the next night. The Johnnys had dug rifle pits outside Fort Wagner's moat to make life miserable for the sappers of the Grand Guard. For the final parallels to be completed these ditches had to be taken. Middlesex had volunteered the 94th for the honor of the assault. By grapes, there's a grudge for you. It was Missy Ruth who cold-cocked the swine, not me, and for good reason. He had abused a perfectly good whore, but I couldn't very well explain that to him in present company.

Thank God for my morning spew. We were tardy, so Gillmore passed that honor to a regiment from New York.[j] They were welcome to it, but Smitty and Baddy were positively crestfallen that their precious 94th wouldn't get the chance to prove its mettle.

* * *

Well, we did get a chance to prove our mettle and damn all malicious busybodies. The next night the New York regiment went after the Confederate trenches like rat terriers. They took the trenches in high style but the works were built to protect from the *front*. When the Reb defenders scampered back to the moat, the guns in the fort couldn't miss. To stay in those earthworks was suicide so the New York boys did their own scampering and in an hour the Johnnys were back in their ditches crowing insults at the defeated Yankees.

---

[j] 100th New York Infantry commanded by Colonel Dandy.

Gillmore wasn't done by a long drop. The very next night he was bound to try again, and egged on by my new champion, Melrose Middlesex, the 94th was chosen for the assault.

I'd always hitched my wagon to the staff for a reason. I had led assaults on prepared enemy works before and had no stomach for the task. It's a damned sight harder to get killed a mile behind the firing line, sipping rio and tut-tuting over maps, than it is gripping a sword, squaring your shoulders, giving the command and knowing that as soon as your battalion clears the line of sight a thousand Confederate killers are going to fire by the volley at the first bluebelly officer in their sights.

When word reached the ranks that we were the chosen ones, some of the men actually wept with joy. They would finally get a fair chance to prove their manhood by striking a blow at the slave power. Damn– nothing will get you killed faster than the company of brave men. We would go in with a white regiment, the 24th Massachusetts Infantry, which seemed to be a competent lot. Their colonel was down with the sweats but I got on well with his second, a Colonel Larkin if I recall. We had our powwow and laid our plans, but other than some details there weren't that many plans to make. The New England boys would attack from the right or ocean side of the parallel and us Missouri Yankees would go in from the left or the marsh side. We'd go in without packs. Kits would just get in the way. Besides rifles and bayonets each man would take two water bottles, extra cartridges stuffed into pockets and a secret weapon. Logan suggested, and I agreed, that if we didn't want to repeat the defeat of the Knickerbocker regiment we had better get creative.

I made my own personal preparations. I'd carry a carbine and wear a private soldier's uniform and forage cap with only a sidearm and my own white face to peg me as an officer. Before the attack I'd smear that with mud. My rank was tacked to my shoulders but I'd muddy the shoulder boards too. Gould, Baddy and the other officers were the ones all a' lather to slaughter Rebels. Let them wear their best regimentals with braid, sash, brass and plumes. I'd blend in with the darkie mass and duck.

We filed into the parallels an hour before dusk and made our way through the stench to relieve the Grand Guard in the last parallel. The daft bastards actually cheered us.

"Huzzah! Give 'em hell, 94th!"

"Show 'em cold steel! Don't count the cost! Hurrah for the 94th."

Sulking bastards were just happy that they weren't making the assault– and thank you for letting the Johnnys know we were coming. The last parallel was less than a hundred yards from the rifle pits and those were only a hundred yards before the fort. I didn't risk a peek above the ditch, but I knew from hogging a telescope that morning that Fort Wagner was showing the effects of the constant cannonade. The ramparts had lost their shape and were now only mounds of sand and smashed palmetto logs. I didn't see any guns in action, but I knew they were there with their crews tucked away in bombproof shelters ready to swarm out and man the battery at the first sign of Union movement. I squatted in the middle of the line, slurping from my flask, while the company captains bothered me every five minutes reporting that the men were well in order, in good spirits and eager to begin. But we wouldn't begin– not until full dark.

Night came too soon for me but not for the men. They were like virgins at the altar and couldn't wait to get on with it. I had been up and down the length of the parallel with Smitty, who was in full fig including his black-Irish cummerbund. He and the men in the ranks completely misunderstood my mud-blackened face. The Ace of Spades was one of *them*. They blessed me and touched me as I slouched by. I believe the brutes loved me. A good reputation is a damned difficult thing to live down. Even the officers missed my true motive and mud appeared on white cheeks along the line. One infant

Lieutenant in C Company broke down before the nobility of it all and wept when he grasped my hand. Leadership is a damned queer thing.

But then the sky was black, and the cannonade suddenly sounded like the crack of doom, lobbing shells over us into the enemy ditches. They shrieked like banshees close above our heads with their fuses glowing and spinning like shooting stars before they exploded raining shrapnel on the Confederate works. The calcium lights flared on with a brightness that punished our eyes illuminating targets and blinding the Rebel defenders. Between the smashes of artillery, an odd crash sounded and in seconds sounded again and yet again. It was a new horror of war. To keep Confederate heads below the rims of their ditches a Regua Battery was spraying bullets into their works like water jetting from a hose. And then, under the glare of the lights, the guns stopped with a silence that sounded like the rim of hell.[k]

This was our signal to begin the assault. Off to the right I heard the Massachusetts men give a hurrah as they began their attack. Beside me the color-bearer shook out the green regimental flag. I stood up, waved my Remington, and let out a croak that may have been "Charge!"

Down the parallel the officers blew on their whistles, the men gave a roar of tension and hate, and the 94th clawed up the wall of the trench and charged after the colors. I, of course, slipped on the fire-step. I wouldn't be the first one out of that ditch for a pension.

I limped after the men bellowing my battle cry, "Go get 'em you black bastards! Oh, get 'em boys."

---

[k] A Billinghurst Regua Battery was an early machine gun. Its 25 rifle barrels, mounted xylophone style on a cart were serviced with a preloaded clip of cartridges. It could be reloaded in under ten seconds and fire up to 175 rounds a minute.

And then Liberty was at my side screaming, "Go get 'em you black bastards!" and pulling me along by my sleeve.

What the deuce was he doing here? We sent the drummer boys to the rear before the regiment entered the parallels. His pappy would kill him if the Rebels didn't kill him first. And where the devil was his drum? Now the Rebels were up on their fire steps firing by the volley with cruel effect as the men swarmed towards their works. It seemed every third man in the first rank was shot down, but the rest lowered their bayonets with a roar and ran on over them like a black landslide. Above the din of musketry I finally heard the real battle cry of the 94th and it almost stopped me in my tracks.

"Missouri Yankees and the Ace of Spades!"

Liberty thought I'd been shot and pulled at my blouse with horror in his eyes.

"Mr. Colonel, sir! Is you? Is you?"

No I wasn't! This was no time to fall into a swoon. Confederate shot was blasting chunks of red-hot metal into the sand all about. To my right three colored troops were caught under an exploding shell and were thrown into the bracken like they were smashed by the hand of a furious god. Around me men screamed in the agony of wounds that ran with black blood in the ghastly glare of the calcium lights. I was only halfway to the Rebel works and this brat was slowing me down. Ahead of me soldiers halted by the company to fire at Southern heads popping up from the ditches. Damn, these were good troops, but they'd have no time to reload. The issue would be decided with the bayonet, man-to-man, black against white.

We had to reach the enemy rifle pits and go at them with polished steel or we'd be slaughtered like mutton in the open sand.

"Missouri Yankees and..." Oh, damn it to hell. I picked up Liberty, flung him over my shoulder fireman style and finished the battle cry– "Meeee!"

That seems droll to me now, especially since I've just emptied the decanter. You know I drink when I write. I know that Amy's carpet-pounder, Mairead, will fetch me another relay of brandy. She's a good girl and Irish. That race has a sixth sense for when liquor is needed and why. It's needed now. I must have been mad, racing with a mob of armed n—rs into the muzzles of Confederate guns, across a battlefield lit like a circle of hell by lights brighter than the sun, with a colored brat over my shoulder shouting a battle cry straight from a show-boat minstrel skit. I'd been in fights before. This was only a sizable skirmish besides the slaughters of Donalson, Shiloh, Antietam or Vicksburg, but it was big enough for the men, white and black who struggled over that ditch. I ran past what shrapnel had left of the infant lieutenant from C Company. His mother wouldn't care about the size of the battle that laid her darling low.

I trotted as fast as my blistered arse would let me, waving my pistol and bellowing nonsense. Twenty yards ahead of me the first of the men had reached the Rebel works and stood on the rim of the pits shooting into the mass of Confederate riflemen. They were blown back from the edge by fire from below, but in an instant swarms of avengers in blue were thick before the ditches. They fired down into the Rebels, pointed their terrible bayonets low and disappeared into the trench like a waterfall of men. It was over in minutes. The Confederates were only defending a ditch. The 94th Missouri USCT was proving a point– that black men could be men-o-war, and none of the Johnnys in the ditch, tossing down their weapons and throwing up their hands before the steel wielded by these colored troops had any doubts. If their defeat had an extra measure of gall because it was at the black hands of Missouri Yankees, they could go to hell. Every man in the ranks knew that if it was they who were defeated, the Rebels would have given no quarter. It would be death or slavery. White officers would be killed out of hand.[14]

The officers were bringing order to chaos in the bloody ditches. Corpses of both races were manhandled up and out. Prisoners were hustled back to the parallel before the prick of bayonets wielded by Africans with a grudge. I knew it was time to deploy our secret weapon.

"Smith!" I bellowed. I needn't have shouted. He was right there, gray with sorrow. He must have seen me dump Liberty into the ditch and reckoned he was dead. I pointed to the child squatting amid the carnage at the bottom of the trench and shouted, "Tend to your brat later. See to your duty. Runners up and down the works. You know the order– dig!"

And the men dug with a will. Each man had *two* spades strapped to his back. The guns from the fort had already begun shelling us and we had only minutes to pile dirt up on the north side of the ditch or we'd be thrown back like the New York troops the night before. The sand and mud was literally flying. The men of the 94th were mostly free men, but by buckwheat and butter, they could dig like delta plantation field hands when they needed to. Now confederate riflemen opened fire on the ditch, but a rampart was forming before my eyes, growing taller by the spade full. And the men began to sing. They'd won and knew it. The sand flew and they sang with fierce joy.

The Ninety-fourth, Ha-Ha! I'll love you all my days!
Missouri Yankees, on parade,
an' I love de Ace of Spades!

If you wonder why each man had *two* spades, well, as Aunt Polly always said, you never know.[1]

---

[1] The assault on the Fort Wagner rifle pits was on August, 26, 1863. The Confederate defenders were the 61st North Carolina Infantry, most of who surrendered.

The Adventures of Sidney Sawyer
Missouri Yankees

Chapter 10

Twenty killed, double that wounded and none unaccounted for, which ain't bad for a frontal assault over an open hundred yards into the teeth of entrenchments. The 24th Massachusetts paid about the same bill to the butcher and Gillmore and staff were well pleased with the night's work. Well, not all. Melrose Middlesex wasn't overly pleased that I'd survived but I reckoned there was damned little mischief the swine could do to me now. If I'd only known, I would have slit his fat throat while he slept.

Of course Fort Wagner was still in business but at least it wasn't *our* business. The 94th filed out of the captured ditches, white troops filed in to relieve us and we returned to bivouac. And a happy batch of darkies we– they were. Aye, there were holes in the ranks that saddened the men, but they had advanced under fire, won the day and the euphoria of victory salved the sorrow. And the rum ration I footed for the regiment helped spread the salve. If a daily dollop of rum was good enough for the blockade squadron bluejackets it was good enough for my blackbirds and I had the tin. They'd earned their frolic. Quartermasters are reasonable coves and for an honest bribe a detail delivered three barrels of Dominican tangle-foot to Smitty. He doled it out to the platoon sergeants who watered it down into proper grog and dippered it out to the men who got properly toasted– but not too toasted. A well-run regiment is a joy to behold.

My officers filled their glasses with a better order of liquor and drank to the young lieutenant from C Company killed in the assault. His name was George Holly from St Louis. It was the first time I had to write one of those ghastly letters to kin to trump up the glory of, and inflate the nobility of, the sacrifice that Mother offered on the altar of the cause. At least I didn't have to fib when I assured the Holly clan that young George never felt a thing. I can still remember the crash of the shell and the sickening slap of iron into flesh as he was minced by Confederate shrapnel. Life left him before all the bits had hit the ground.

After bagging sand, toiling like moles in the Grand Guard and the night assault, the regiment was rewarded with light duty. This included guarding the Rebel prisoners. The men reveled in it.

"Bottom rail on top now, ain't it, Johnny Reb?"

"De view ain't too good from behind de wire, is it white boy?"

"Lincum dun freed us an' dun unfreed you."

G Company's mascot was a razorback mutt the size of an over-grown rat named Archie. Its bottom teeth were out at the gums and the beast's tongue hung out like a bloated tadpole. It was the sorriest creature that ever waddled on the face of the earth and the men of G Company loved it beyond credit. G Company guards took to strutting past the wire penning the sullen Southern cavaliers with Archie on a string.

"Y'all wants ta turn rabbit, y'all go ahead. Us colored men, we's gots our own hound now. Archie be half bloodhound an' half gator. Track you white trash here ta St. Louie. Chew up yo white ass."

The prisoners cursed them for a pack of uppity n––rs, Archie chased his mangy tail and tangled his arse in the string and the colored soldiers of the 94th hooted the laughter of free men.

Other than camp chores we were on a picnic, which was fine with me, but of course it couldn't last. Two days after the battle I was summoned again to headquarters. This time I didn't look like a trunk-line railroad bum. In full uniform with whipcord britches, boots, spurs and bonnet, I looked damn fine. With my whiskers fluffed, I looked even better. The HQ platoon had my tackle polished to a shimmer, my nag was curried to a luster, with her mane and tail braided like a French tart, and my backside was healed enough to suffer the mile trot to Lighthouse Point. I wanted to make a good impression. I needn't have bothered.

Other than the usual dogrobbers, slouchers and contraband rabble there was no one of note before the awnings pitched about headquarters. Under the shade and out of the glare however, was one figure that couldn't be missed. Middlesex leaned on a pole with a weight that flexed the oak. He could only be waiting for me. I'd had quite enough of this nonsense. This was the nerve center of a siege army and not a Capital City brothel. Bold as a Polack goose, I strode up to have it out. But not too close!

"See here, major, what's the quarrel? You seem out to do me mischief– and for what, a few cross words in a knock-shop?"

"You interfered with my business. I'll take that from no man."

His accent was a flat New England drawl that can only come from old money.

"It was you that upset the deal, and pinching off that poor star-gazer's nipple interfered with *my* business– monkey business. And it was damned rude too."

"You give lessons on etiquette, now?" he snarled. "I understood that all you Missouri swine could do was club a man unawares, turn out his pockets, steal his boots and watch, and roll him in a ditch between the hogs."

He was building up a fine head of steam and I looked in vain for other officers beneath the awnings. We were quite alone. I couldn't let this monster come to grips with me. I'd reason with him.

"That wasn't me." I whined. "You were half wallpapered and about to put out my lights and take out my teeth. It was the lady of the house, Miss Ruth. She slapped you a good smack with her sap and you went down like a side of bacon."

"I want my watch. Give it here!"

"I don't have your damn watch! It was Ruth's crushers and a half dozen of her whores who dragged you out and stole your grips. And what the devil would I do with your boots? Haul coal?"

"My watch– now!"

Reason wasn't working.

"I don't have your blasted watch!" I said with some heat and dug my own from my britches to show him.

He snatched it from my fingers and held it between his own, which were as big as German sausages. I heard a pop and gave a squeak as I realized he was crushing it like a beetle between two coins. Tiny pieces dropped into the sand and he tossed the rest into the sun.

By God, he *was* a monster and this was the limit. "You forget that I'm a colonel, *major*, and you've spit in my gumbo one time too many. I've got friends in high places. The highest! I'll have the provost after you! I'll see you in the stockade! I'll see you drummed from the service! I'll ......"

"What you'll do is get me my watch, not your cheap piece of dross! I know all about your affairs and you'll do nothing."

He took a step toward me and I took two back and snapped open my holster.

He roared a laugh that sent his spit flying past my ears. "My family is in textiles– cotton textiles. We have contacts up and down the Ohio and Mississippi, from Cincinnati to Memphis. *Cincinnati to Memphis*, do you understand? I sent feelers out about you, Colonel Sidney Thomas Sawyer of St. Petersburg, Missouri, to merchants and brokers and lawyers up and down the rivers. Know your enemies! And I know you, Sawyer. And I know about the Temples and their shoddy boats and jobber prices. I know your military record too. Interesting reading, do you think? I know that you steered Army business to the Temples at bounties that would disgrace the Jews. You will do nothing except fetch me my property or I'll expose you for the grafter and scoundrel that you are. And you ain't the only one with friends in high places. I'll break you like your cheap watch!"

Damnation in a dogcart, he was insane! If he took another step I'd draw down and shoot. I'd rather face court martial than let this mastodon get his mitts on me again, but then he smiled a charming smile, touched his brim with a casual salute and whispered "Smile you Missouri son of a bitch, here's Gillmore."[m]

*　*　*

Liberty was dressed in disreputable castoffs with the knees out of his ancient twill britches and a linen blouse straight from a ragbag. It was vast about his thin body and buttoned up to its tattered collar. His moccasins had the stitching out at the toes and he had my carpetbag slung around his neck. It was just the ensemble for a pickaninny slave boy tagging after his wounded master limping on his cane down Meeting Street to the South Battery in the insurrectionist city of Charleston. I was dressed in a borrowed butternut uniform from a lieutenant of the 61st North Carolina. It fit well enough, was brushed to respectability and the pockets were stuffed with Confederate currency. My boots were buffed as well as the scuffs permitted and my slouch hat sported a rakish crease down the center. I tipped it to a trio of Southern ladies and gave them a brave grin through my fraudulent pain. They gave me a smile and tittered at Liberty's Union Army kepi

---

[m] Mastodon remains were discovered in America over 150 years before the Civil War. Sawyer may have known that the name means "nipple tooth."

that covered his head down past his ears. The kepi was a touch of brilliance and answered all questions in an armed camp that had provost snoops guarding every country crossroad, wagon stop, train station and wharf into and out of the city. I had been wounded in the defense of Charleston. A dead Yankee's cap crowned my servant. How dashing! I was a Southern hero. What else could I be?

What else I could be was a Yankee spy in the very heart of the Southern beast. It was Major Middlesex's mischief and there wasn't a damned thing I could do about it. He had bragged he knew all about me and curse him, he did. The fat villain had greased my skids into Charleston with Gillmore before I had even arrived at Lighthouse Inlet. Only a handful of men knew that last spring Lincoln had sent me to Richmond to deliver a private message to Jeff Davis, president to president. I spent the rest of the summer sweating, spying and running for my life.[n] It must have been that Scottish bounder, Major Allen, or one of his intelligencers who snitched to Middlesex. They were a rum lot and would sell out their brothers for a bottle of that vile venom the Scots call whiskey.[o] He knew chapter and verse of my reluctant Virginia exploits and sung them to Gillmore's staff making me sound like the second coming of Nathan Hale or Natty bloody Bumpo. The swine even knew about the great railroad chase when I highballed through Virginia on a stolen locomotive with the Confederate Army after me like hounds after a runaway darkie. Even I had helped his cause by bragging how I'd *twice* dared Southern power leading lost souls to jubilee on

---

[n] For Sawyer's adventures as Lincoln's spy refer to the third packet of the Sawyer Memoirs published as *The Adventures of Sidney Sawyer: The Year of Jubilee*.

[o] Major Allen was the Civil War nom de guerre of Allen Pinkerton, the founder of the U.S. Secret Service and the Pinkerton Detective Agency.

the Underground Railroad? When will I ever learn to keep my trap shut?

General Gillmore reckoned he needed a snoop to spy on Charleston, and I was Johnny-on-the-spot. Middlesex saw to that. The Swamp Angel had bombarded the city with fire– our pickets heard the alarm bells and the blockade Jacks saw the flames. Were the citizens of Charleston ready to give up the game? It was one thing for the troops ringing the harbor to face Yankee guns, but civilians? A town cruelly shelled, set to burning, homes and churches up in smoke– surely the town fathers would demand that Beauregard evacuate the city. Gillmore *had* to know and there was only one way. Send in a spy.

I tried to demure– manly modesty, that was my line, but it was no soap. The General needed an intelligencer and he had his man. I wanted to tell the ass that it was a fool's errand. I'd been at Vicksburg and the Confederate patriots of that city lived under Yankee guns for two months without a notion to surrender. They slept in their cellars and dined in caves to escape the bombardment that rained iron on their dwellings night and day. When the grub ran out they ate their pets and roasted rats on sticks. Pemberton only gave up when his troops were reduced to eating the nits plucked from their rags in the trenches. And Charleston wasn't starving. The harbor was corked, but trains, barges and wagons poured in tucker for the population, and shot and powder for the garrison. Charleston would no more surrender than pigs could fly. They'd no more surrender than Lincoln or Grant or Huckleberry Finn would surrender. It took only five minutes on Meeting Street watching the city's work-a-day bustle to tell me that.

Getting into the city was a fine point of espionage. I'd sulked about enemy territory before, in Virginia, Tennessee and Mississippi where I had picked up some pointers. I'd learned that a darkie is a damned handy item to have along when you're on the dodge in a Confederacy dedicated to holding on to its n—rs. Liberty was a likely lad– he'd do. His pappy almost threw a mutiny when I ordered the boy to kit himself in slave duds and I had to speak to him damn sharp. Uppity rascal! He had his chevrons, but they don't come issued with an opinion. At any rate, Liberty was keen to go and in the gloom of the moonless night of the twenty-ninth we were perched amidships in a black whaleboat pulled by eight hardies from the fleet and commanded by an ensign who looked to be younger than Liberty. The bluejackets were armed with pistol, carbine and cutlass like Black Beard's buccaneers. We left from the same slough that Colonel Serrell used two weeks before to barge the Swamp Angel to the Marsh Battery. The oars were muffled and the oarsmen minded the splashes as we entered the harbor. To our right Sumter loomed, and to our left lay the low coast of James Island. It was lined with rebel batteries sighted to interfere with just the kind of caper the sailors were rowing me into. We were simply a darker hole in the blackness of the night and knew we'd be invisible to any sentries along the batteries. We weren't the only Yankees abroad on the harbor. As we left the slough a steam launch ghosted past with only a whisper of mechanical noise. A low voice gave us the watchword and our ensign squeaked the countersign. Our biggest dread was encountering a Confederate boat like our own. In the dark of every night they supplied Sumter and the harbor defenses with fresh troops, supplies and dispatches. We hadn't a notion of the Rebel passwords and any challenge would have to be answered with fire. After two hours that had me chewing my nails to the knuckles Sumter was at our stern, the harbor opened wide around us and the watch lights of the city were dead ahead.

I had just begun to suck easier breath when the ensign hissed, "Ship oars! Sharp on the starboard bow– torpedo!"

How he saw the infernal machine, awash in the black water, I can't credit, but there it was. The Rebels had salted the harbor with the evil things. They stuffed iron or oak casks with explosives and fused them to blow the water line out of any ship unlucky enough to blunder into one. They anchored them in the shipping channels where any Yankee gunboats would simply have to go. The cheating dogs! It was a hell of a way to fight a war. Despite the sailor's slow quiet pull through the harbor it looked as if we were racing toward it. The ensign hauled the tiller hard a' port and we were clear but in the next instant, I and one of the bluejackets spotted another. It was bobbing toward our port side and would strike in a second. I gave a squeak of warning and the idiot sailor dropped his blasted oar on it with a clanging that almost sent me over the side. It was four feet long, black, shimmering with harbor slime, and tapering to points at either end. The oar didn't set it off but being rammed by a whaleboat would do the trick.

I swear it will be my liver that kills me. If my poor heart hasn't given up its pumping with the shocks its suffered along the way nothing will kill it. Liberty saved us. He sprawled across my lap and practically dove onto the torpedo as it was about to bash into the side of our craft. He wrapped his thin arms around the filthy thing and hung on for dear life, keeping it away from the boat as we drifted past. His belly balanced on the gunnel and his arse and legs hung in the boat. As the boat moved past the floating horror I passed his arse and legs back to the sailor behind me and he passed his arse along to the ensign at the stern. Then, Liberty let it go, and with a hiss of passing water the evil machine disappeared in the night. The tars let out their collective breaths and I looked back at Liberty with awe. As the ensign pulled his shoulders aboard the two boys came together breast to breast with the snotty's arms around the colored boy. He kept them there for a long count of ten before I brought him back into the Navy with a ship's biscuit off his forehead and whispered threat.

"Pull yourself together, boy. This is no time to be frozen with fear! Tend to business or I'll toss you in after the blasted torpedo."

That brought him up sharp but I soon learned that it wasn't fear that had paralyzed the brat.

The rest of pull to the Ashley River was long but uneventful. We drifted up Wappo Creek where it entered the river and silently grounded the boat at the high tide line on the north bank. The lights of Charleston flickered to our right, and before us was a sleeping battery placed to defend the Ashley River Bridge. We were now far enough from any Yankee threat for the Reb sentries to risk a snooze. Once we crept past the pickets, the depot to the C&S Railroad was only a ten-minute stroll.[p] I leaned on my cane and remembered to limp. I didn't lean on it too hard. It had a wicked eighteen-inch blade tucked inside, just in case. We crossed the tracks as if we had every right to be where we were and be doing what we were doing. I was a confederate officer, by God– and wounded! See me limp? I settled onto a bench with Liberty squatting at my feet and waited for a train.

We didn't have long to wait. The C&S terminated at the depot. Cargo was unloaded and barged across the Ashley or hauled over the bridge. Passengers were either met with carriages, hitched a ride on a wagon or walked. Within the hour, as the sky was lightening, a train pulled to the platform and out swarmed farm wives, soldiers bound for the garrison, gentlemen in their stovepipe beavers with their ladies in dated fashion, and here and there, wounded soldiers on the mend. I joined them and from the Ashley River Drawbridge we watched the sun come up over distant Fort Sumter.

---

[p] Charleston and Savannah Railroad.

The Adventures of Sidney Sawyer
Missouri Yankees
Chapter 11

We scouted the city on streets that marched us back and forth at neat right angles. Our stroll took us past St. Michael's just as service was dismissed. It was the Swamp Angel's aiming point but we evidently missed. It's a damned handsome church with a steeple like a wedding cake. I reckoned it would be a shame for the War to claim it, but I also reckoned that if the Union red straps used it to range their shots it was the safest place in Charleston. As a matter of fact I hadn't seen any evidence of the bombardment all morning.

I'd never given it a thought, but today was Sunday, not that I *ever* give that a thought. I mingled with the mob of sanctified Confederates filing out of church and joined their promenade down to South Battery. St. Michael's is Episcopal, which meant its parishioners were the cream of South Carolina's tidewater gentry. Us Sawyers are Baptists, which means the woodwork in our churches don't measure up, the windows are ordinary glass and our preachers tend to be a bit shrill. And *we* only have services. Episcopal bluebloods attend a Papist style mass with incense, bells and all the trimmings. I ain't a spy for nothing. I held up my chin, straightened my spine and limped with resolution. I made sure Liberty was the approved three paces behind and pasted a look of Carolina arrogance on my face. It worked like a charm. In the space of the three block walk to the battery I wound up arm in arm with an old cove in a frock coat, twelve-inch beaver and belly like John Bull. His missus, fanning herself against the heat, was all a' fluster with holy outrage over the depredations of the wicked Yankees, and if fine young soldiers like me didn't smite them dead than the Lord surely would. Behind them, dressed in livery, was their slave girl toting the lady's bag and their Books of Common Prayer.

I introduced myself as Samuel Clemens, a name I'd borrowed before, from Brunswick County, North Carolina. It was a region I knew well enough to pass if I wasn't questioned too closely about Wilmington gentry. After chatting about how grand the service was after making due with the rough prayer meetings on bivouac, the conversation turned to the War.

"It chased me from my own bed! My own bed, do you hear?" the lady worked her fan with fury. "Those cowardly Yankees, too afraid to face our gallant army–raining death upon a defenseless city!"

Defenseless my foot! This wasn't called the South Battery for nothing. Guns were mounted and manned the length of the waterfront with ammunition stacked neat as cobbler and ready to hand. And anchored in the harbor, only a cable's length away, were the *Palmetto State* and the *Chicora*. They were two of the ugliest ironclad monsters in the register, cut for four guns each and flying the Confederate naval ensign with its St Andrew's cross on a field of red.[15]

"Why Samuel, my n—rs was as frantic as a bunch a' chickens. Miss Molly here, may as well of cooked breakfast herself. Them bombs set a few fires, disturbed the peace, didn't kill nobody, but was damned pesky nonetheless. Pardon my cursin', Molly dear."

"Remember yourself, Radcliffe," Molly scolded, but with a smile behind her fan. "Lieutenant Clemens will think we are as vulgar as the Yankees. We are honored to be in your company, sir. Our own boys, Tradd and Wentworth, are in Virginia with General Lee. We are proud, but anxiety is our closest companion."

"Vulgar, never, Miss Molly. I am proud to make the acquaintance of such a charming couple as yourself and blah-blah-blah."

To paraphrase the conversation, I learned that there was no chance in hell of the city of Charleston showing the white feather with citizens like Marse Radcliffe and Miss Molly strolling the battery. I learned that instead of overawing the population with Greek fire, Gillmore's abbreviated bombardment only fired them up to the point where they would rather see the whole city in ashes before giving up the embers to the hated Yankees. I learned that they lived in a sizable townhouse a block up Legare Street from the Battery and were solid members of the gentry with a fortune in indigo, rice and blackbirds. They were maintained by a household of a half-dozen slaves, supper was at six and would I be kind enough to join them? My uniform would be acceptable dress, being wartime and whatnot, and bring my boy along to help in the pantry.

I loafed around the city taking in the sights for the rest of the day. After all, that's what we had come for. Charleston is a damned fine city. In from the fashionable promenade along the battery is a neat grid of cobbled streets lined with well-tended shade trees and handsome townhouses. Along the Cooper River are at least two-dozen wharves that were all but deserted. They wouldn't come alive until after dark when bateaus and fast steam packets scudded out to victual the batteries. The blockade was having its effect on shipping, but the SC Depot[q] on Morris Street was booming with traffic, and two blocks west on Elliot, wagons were thundering over the Ashley Drawbridge as fast as freight from the C&S could be unloaded. We might eventually burn Charleston, but it wouldn't starve.

---

[q] South Carolina Railroad.

The city seemed to be going about its business despite the booming of the distant guns bombarding Sumter and Wagner five miles away. Along the East Battery there was even a skinny artist squeezing his tubes of pigment onto his pallet and laboring away on a harbor scene that included the ugly Rebel ironclads with Fort Sumter in the distance. Amy and Auntie Polly would have enjoyed the view. Art always gives a feeling of civilization to any scene, even if the artist is a scruffy Johnny soldier with chevrons stitched on his sleeves. Why the Confederate Army would let him waste his time was beyond credit.[16]

At six we presented ourselves at Molly and Radcliffe's mansion on Legare. The darkie butler regaled in black livery was dignity personified. He ushered me into the parlor like I was Beauregard himself. Liberty was escorted to the kitchen by the same little colored gal from church. She giggled at the sight of the oversized kepi down over his ears. Dinner was first rate– no blockade on Legare Street. The only concessions to the War were Radcliffe apologizing that he was out of brandy, but had a damned good port, and Molly having a little weep in the pudding that her boys Tradd and Wentworth weren't home to meet their new friend, Samuel. After the pudding, us men retired to the veranda to enjoy our port and cigars in the cool of the evening. My espionage in Richmond last summer wasn't as pleasant as this by a long pitch. I could get used to this. I do believe that old Radcliffe was about to invite me to stay the night when his little house n—r pulled at my sleeve and dipped in a curtsey.

"Marse Clemens, sir. Yo boy, he say to remind you dat you gots to be down at de wharf come full dark to git de boat back to James Island."

What the devil was this nonsense? My host was quite put out.

"Samuel, you never said– you never hinted that you were reportin' for duty tonight."

Well, old timer, that's because I didn't know myself, and the stupid look on my face must have shown that as clear as gin to the little colored wench. She was a quick study and ploughed on before I said something fatal.

"Marse Clemens, yo boy be out back with yo grips." She looked straight at me, bulged her eyes and made a face. "He *know* you gonna be in a *hurry* to kitch yo boat."

For a count of three I sat there like a stooge with Radcliffe's cigar sagging between my lips. Then it hit me in a rush of panic that out of nowhere I was suddenly in deadly danger. Think fast you fool!

"Radcliffe, my new dear friend, duty is harsh but it calls. Indeed, I did not choose to spoil Miss Molly's evenin' with talk of duty, but my wounds are all but healed and my regiment awaits."

He wasn't pleased, but at least he didn't smell a rat. I didn't smell one either but Liberty must have and sent this girl to fetch me out back. As sure as lard for breakfast we weren't taking any boat to James Island. Radcliffe was put out but polite. After apologies, promises to write, invitations to visit, backslaps and a hug from Miss Molly, I was limping up Legare Street to fetch Liberty. It wasn't quite full dark, but there was no whale oil for the street lamps and people out for the evening air were hidden in gloom. I reached the end of the block but Liberty was nowhere to be seen. Blast! Where was the brat? Why the dickens did I have to insult my host, abandon my port and find my own lodgings when I could be tucked into a featherbed with a belly full of decent liquor? I was about to shout for him, damn the tranquility of the night, when a colored girl with a satchel, trim in gingham and slippers, and pretty beneath her bonnet rushed up and pulled me by the hand into the shadows behind an azalea bush. Well, this could be pleasant, but it wasn't exactly the time and where the blazes *was* Liberty?

The girl was a stargazer of course. She was dressed a damn sight better than the usual run of n—rs so what else could she be? Offering horizontal refreshments to handsome Southern soldiers was a dandy sideline for a slave wench to pick up a little spare coin, and it *was* after all, a garrison town. But whores are a dime a dozen and they ain't my usual style– and anyway, I wasn't in the mood. In the mood or not, this darkie filled her gingham damned well and I had to be polite.

"Sorry my little black-eyed Susan," I smiled giving her hindquarters a friendly two-handed knead. By grapes, she was prime mutton. "I have to be off on unfinished business." I felt her stiffen beneath my paws. "By the way have you seen a boy, 'bout your height, wearin' a Yankee cap?"

The whore looked up to fix me with her eyes and I almost barked in incredulity.

"Mr. Colonel Sawyer, sir," Liberty whispered to me from under his bonnet. "We got to go– got to git. We are undone. We are betrayed!"

The Adventures of Sidney Sawyer
Missouri Yankees

Chapter 12

I've been flabbergasted before, but never like this. I ain't no sodomite. I'm an Army man! It's the Navy that's overrun with the perverted rascals and they can have 'em. I yanked my mitts of off Liberty's arse like it was a red-hot stove. *Liberty's* arse?

"What...what...what?" I've always had a clever tongue. This wasn't my finest hour. "What...what?"

"Mr. Colonel Sawyer, dey knows about us. Dey's been told we's here! Dey lookin' fo' a tall North Carolina lieutenant travelin' with a slave boy in a Yankee topper. That's us! We gotta git! We gotta hide!"

"Who knows about us? How? Who betrayed us? What the blazes are you doing in a frock? You're a boy, ain't you?"

Liberty answered my questions in the order I asked them.

"The provost knows 'bout us, de whole city knows, and dey's lookin'. It was the fat man. He come to Charleston all de time. Sellin' medicine– calomel an' quinine an' such. An' I'm wearin' dis dress 'cause dey's lookin' fo' a boy." And then Liberty gave me a look that proved I wasn't a sodomite and answered my last question. "An' no, Mr. Colonel, sir, I ain't no boy!"

Well, feeling his– her arse should have told me that, but behind an azalea bush in an aroused city wasn't the best place to discuss it.

"Here Mr. Colonel, sir," She pushed her satchel into my hands. "Put on these duds. I got 'em from Mazy."

"Who?"

"Marse Radcliffe's house girl. Put 'em on. They's Marse Wentworth's– the old master's son. They ought a' fit. They lookin' for *you*, not a gentleman!"

Well, that was harsh. A glance up and down the lane told me the coast was clear. The azalea would be a decent enough fitting room. But then an odd thing happened. When I made to strip off my britches the sight of Liberty beside me in his trim frock gave me a start. His? He'd– she'd already seen me bare-arsed and doubled over, tossing my biscuits into the thunder-bucket after my adventure with the Swamp Angel. I still remember the look of stupefaction on his– her face. Maybe she never *had* seen a white man's courting tackle before! And why in hell was I modest now? And now I knew why that brat of an ensign didn't want to let Liberty go in the whaleboat. For a drummer boy he had a fine arse!

She gave me a sharp 'sssst' that set me back to the task at hand. My belt with the gold eagles sewn in the stitching went around my waist. The Remington was holstered snug on my belly over a vest and under a stylish moleskin jacket. My boots would have to do since she didn't bring any, but she did bring a wide planter's hat with a maroon band and a wide silk tie that I bowed at the neck to finish the effect. I kept my cane and hoped I wouldn't need it. The butternut uniform went behind the bush and we stepped around the corner onto Broad Street liked we belonged there.

A darkie had no business walking beside a gentleman, but it was dark and Liberty was respectable in her bonnet. We avoided close scrutiny, kept our heads together and talked. I had a million questions but stuck to essentials.

"How did you know this? Who told you? Can you trust them?"

"Mazy told me. Dishes was done an' she went out to smoke her pipe. Come back in ten minutes with her eyes as big as buckles. She heard about us from the n—rs next door. News is all over town, 'bout a Union spy, sneakin' around the city with a colored boy in a big Yankee hat. Mazy wants to be free. Wants de blue soldiers to win. She say that if it was Wraggs, de house n—r butler that knew, he'd a' called the provost faster than you can spit."

God in heaven, if we hadn't gone to an early supper with Molly and Radcliffe the crushers would have scooped us up on the street before dark. And Mazy, bless her, warned Liberty. The 'girls' put their heads together, disguised Liberty as what she really was and pinched the young master's traps for me. If young Marse Wintworth was up north with Marse Robert he'd probably never need them again. Thank God I didn't have to limp any more.[r]

"Who's this fat man? You said we were betrayed by a fat man."

"Mazy say there's a giant Yankee, a big fat Yankee, must be ten feet tall that comes to Charleston by night in a boat stuffed with medicine an' such. He snitches to that Beauregard what the blue soldiers is up to. He does it for silver. He ain't just a spy, he's worse."

Yes he is– much worse Miss Liberty, but you don't know just how much worse. Major Melrose Middlesex! The fat swine didn't simply mutilate nipples, smash pocket watches and hold grudges, he was a jobber *and* a spy. The sheer cold-bloodedness of his plot set me to shake. He had trumped me up as the greatest spy since Joshua, sent me off to Charleston like a hog to a pig-roast and than hurried ahead to inform to his Confederate chums. Talk about mixing business with pleasure. He must be making a fortune selling the Rebels medicine that they

[r] A word of explanation may be in order. Slaves called their masters, 'marse,' never massa. Marse Robert was the Confederate Army's affectionate nickname for General Robert E. Lee.

could never sneak in through the blockade. Liberty mentioned calomel and quinine, but chloroform and morphine would be worth more than their weight in silver to the Rebels. The villain! Oh, I'd dealt in Southern cotton. Who didn't? Even General Grant's own daddy was tied up with a ring of Cincinnati cotton jobbers to the point where the general had to toss his own father from the Western Department, but there really wasn't any shame in jobbing cotton. Everybody winked at it from New Orleans to New England, and if you couldn't make a bundle in cotton, than shame on you– but jobbing medicine? A boatload of those goods could net you a fortune.

Boatload! By grapes, it must have been the fat bastard's own steam launch that passed us in the bayou last night. He must have been laughing his sagging stern quarters off when he called out the password. Mixing business with pleasure indeed.

"You're spot on, Miss Liberty. He is much worse."

I reminded her of the boat that passed us on our way into Charleston Harbor.

"That was him, sure as eggs and I know who he is. When we get back we'll see him hung."

"He as fat as Mazy say, we gonna need two ropes," and she smiled up at me.

Damnation in July, but little Liberty was pretty. No, not pretty, she was beautiful, and she wasn't all that little for a girl. And with a start, I realized that she was no girl. She was a young woman, a damned sight older than the fourteen or fifteen that I reckoned her– him to be. As a boy I reckoned that Liberty was just a sissified brat that an Adam's apple and eventual whiskers would set to rights. I ain't blind and I ain't stupid, so I guess that I saw what I expected to see.

I grinned back at her. "We'll borrow an anchor cable from the fleet and put the 94th on the line to haul him up. And I can't call you Liberty anymore. It's a damned odd name for a slave girl. I'll call you Libby."

Was I just flirting? Easy there, Sidney. You're a Colonel and *she's* a drummer boy. No fraternization with the ranks and no time to get frisky. Wouldn't this just be a damn fine point of military etiquette to present to the faculty dons at West Point? I yanked myself back down to earth.

"The provost are looking for two people who don't exist anymore, a Confederate officer and a colored boy in a funny hat. I'm a gentleman now and you are my servant, Libby. We will blend in."

She stood at attention, which was deuced distracting with her breasts testing the gingham and asked, "Where we gonna go, sir? What we gonna do to get out a' town?"

"To start, don't act like a damned soldier! Slouch, shuffle, keep your eyes down and hang your head. You're a slave now and if you don't act like one it'll be us at the end of a rope."

It was only two blocks to Meeting Street and to our right there was St. Michael's again. The sidewalks were filling with couples strolling arm in arm. Behind us a couple was laughing in anticipation of the Sunday Hop at the Social Hall. A hop, what a grand place to hide in plain sight. I hissed to Liberty-Libby to keep three paces back and followed the crowd. The South Carolina Social Hall was beside the church and at the door I stuck my finger in Libby's face like I would with any other slave.

"I'm going in to see what's what. You blend in with the other n—rs and learn what you can. Slaves have a better grapevine than the signal corps and they'll know anything that's worth knowing."

She started to draw herself to attention again and I snarled, "And remember, you're a blasted slave! Act like one!" I straightened my sombrero and joined the other Carolina bucks in the queue to drop a coin in the plate and enter the dance.

There was a colored band on a low stage at the end of the hall playing lively airs as a double line of dancers did a reel down the center of the wide room. Along the far wall was a sideboard set with cookies, fruit and punch tended by squad of slave women. The rest of the room was packed with Carolina's finest– Rebel officers in full regimental fig, gentleman of the gentry in frock coats, peg pants and spats, dowagers fanning themselves in the heat, chaperoning the belles dressed in their frilliest frocks, showing off as much of their bosoms as fashion allowed. The atmosphere was gay but a bit shabby. After two years of blockade the men's cuffs and collars were frayed and their beavers were scuffed. The officer's uniforms were clean and brushed, but all of them showed signs of hard wear. One captain of Georgia infantry twirled down the line of prancing dancers with a butternut patch stitched across the arse of his uniform gray britches. The lace on the ladies' gowns was limp, there was mending at the hems of their skirts and saddest of all, when they raised their arms to their partners in the reel, their armpits were stained with two summers worth of sweat that their mammy's labors on washday could never scrub away. Sherman wouldn't say it for another year, but "War is hell!"

I wasn't there to dance. I drifted around the edges of conversations to glean any useful gossip. You never know when an odd bit of information will come in handy to a spy. If my civilian duds were questioned I'd already dreamed up a line that should deflect any but the closest inspection. I was glad I did.

"Medicine is what we need! After Gettysburg the medicos was amputatin' arms an' legs without no chloroform. Just a slug o' whiskey and a bullet betwixt the teeth to keep the boys from swallowin' their own tongues. A disgrace gentlemen– just a disgrace."

A trio of gentlemen gave their amens to the speaker, a thin gamecock of a man with a dark face, a flamboyant mane of white hair and a tight suit. "We get some in through the blockaders but it's never enough."

Another gent spoke up, "We mine our own lead, manufacture our own powder, dead Yankees provide us with muskets, but we have to bring in opium through the blockade. It's beginnin' to pinch."

Well, this was interesting. Middlesex was running opium, and I *was* a spy.

"Gentlemen, I couldn't help but overhear. I understood that just this morning a shipment of medicines and opiates arrived in the city."

They looked me up and down and the gamecock sneered.

"Excuse me gentlemen, allow me to introduce myself. I am Major Murat Jackson Ives, of Demopolis, Alabama."

My roommate during my plebe year at West Point was Murat Jackson Ives. We called him Billy. He was out west fighting the war against Grant. If Billy Ives was bagged with the garrison of Vicksburg he was out of the War and wouldn't mind my borrowing his name. Once, as cadets, we had to gin up maps of our hometowns as a punishment drill, so I knew enough of Demopolis to pass for an Alabama boy.

"Mr. Ives?" He spoke the name as if he doubted my pedigree. "This is a private conversation– between gentlemen."

"And I sir, am an officer *and* a gentleman, and procuring medicine for my country is my commission. My country is Alabama, sir, and we take second place to no state in our resistance to Northern aggression– including the gallant state of South Carolina." I touched the brim of my hat and gave a bow.

A second chap, one with a face as red as an snapper and a dome as bald as a boar's buttocks poked his cigar at my chest, "Why don't you'uns ship it in through Mobile?"

"It embarrasses me to admit this, gentlemen, but the Yankee blockade of Mobile is absolute. And since Vicksburg fell, any goods from Mexico through Texas have been choked off. Governor Watts has commissioned me to visit y'all here in fair Charleston to investigate procurement of medical comestibles."

"And you bring your commission to a hop?" the gamecock sneered, looking down his nose. It was a good trick looking down his nose at me when I was eight inches taller than he was, but he was South Carolina tidewater gentry and pulled it off with style. The little swine gave me the sizzles. Where had I seen that look before? I'd approached these wirepullers when I had overheard the word 'medicine.' I had hoped they could give me more information to use against Middlesex. I decided to plough on.

"It is Sunday, sir. I'll make my official inquiries in the morning. But unofficially, I have heard of a Massachusetts Yankee who runs mercury, opium and quinine to us through the blockade. I have only heard him called the Fat Man."

I was hoping for a reaction and I got one. The gamecock gave a start and snapped, "If you will excuse us gentlemen?" to his companions. He steered me by the arm straight through the mob of dancers into a door behind the darkies ladling up punch, through the kitchens and into a short hall by the side door. The hall was crowded with crates of produce and an open barrel of pickles. Mops, buckets, brooms and aprons hung from pegs. We were quite alone.

He rounded on me like a terrier and blustered, "That is privileged information sir! Privileged! How came you to know of this– this Fat Man? It is a secret, sir! An important lifeline of goods comes through that gentleman and must be maintained."

This was dandy. I'd wanted enough information to hang Middlesex and Mr. Bluster here might give it to me.

"Sir, I learned of it from the n—rs. It's all over Charleston. I've been in town only a day and my wench told me of this fat fellow not an hour ago."

"Fetch her! I must know where she learned this startling rumor."

"At your service, sir."

Just out of the side door were a score of darkie servants loafing while their masters danced. Liberty seemed to be the center of attention with the bucks clustered around her– blasted little flirt. With a sharp word from me she came running. I hoped she wouldn't stand to attention and salute.

"Now, Libby, this gentleman wants to ask you some questions about the fat man that the darkies *waiting at St. Michael's* told you about. You pay heed to Mister… sir, I beg your pardon but you have the advantage of me."

The gamecock gave a click of his heels and answered, "I am Colonel Brassard, Colonel Hayne Brassard of Colleton County, South Carolina. At your service, sir."

Do you wonder why I drink? With the shocks that life has jolted me with it's a wonder I ain't pickled like a Hibernian gandy dancer. It's only the booze that's carried me this far along in my misspent path and thank God the decanter is charged and my tumbler is topped. Colonel Hayne Brassard of Colleton County! Colonel my foot– the swine was probably a corporal in the War of 1812. If this old whip of a man knew he was talking to Cadet Sidney Thomas Sawyer, West Point class of '59 he would have been at my neck with both hands.

If any Southern clan, bloated with brittle tidewater honor, had cause to hate, the Brassards had cause to hate the Ace of Hearts. They had earned that right when Hayne's son, Cadet Calhoun and I commenced a feud in our plebe year at the Academy. I was, of course, blameless, but Papa Hayne wouldn't be interested in that detail. And with another start I realized that this old bastard would have heard about the real Billy Ives from his son. We were all roommates. And his vicious daughter, Hazel, had tried to ambush me last summer to avenge her disfigured brother, using her own malignant fornication as bait. I had to get out of here before he put two and two together and got Sawyer.

"Now gal, y'all told your master 'bout a fat gentleman that was bringin' medicines here into Charleston. Where did you hear this?" Brassard senior was ferocious. "Who told you?"

Liberty's eyes grew huge and she turned her face to me. Brassard gave her a slap and roughly took her cheeks in his hands pursing out her lips. "You talkin' to me, bitch, not him. Who told you about the Fat Man?"

If I needed a reminder as to why I hated that family, this was it. The little swine was hurting Liberty. I had to defend her. I was gallant.

"Get your hands off my n—r! I won't gore your ox– you don't molest my stock!"

He let her go, but glared bullets at me.

"Are Alabama men so tender with their n—s?"

"We hold our property dear and don't abuse without cause."

He gave Liberty a slow up and down leer and turned back to me with a greasy smirk, "I see– you gentlemen from Alabama certainly do hold *some* of your darkies dear."

By God, he was as rotten as his son, Calhoun and his randy daughter Hazel, but let him suspect what he wanted as long as he didn't suspect the truth.

"See here Brassard, I want information on the Fat Man to secure medicals for my chiefs. You seem to want information from my girl. Libby, tell Marse Hayne how you came to know this rumor while I was at divine service."

And she did. In fine slave style she shuffled and ducked and told the little gamecock a whopper about gossip with the other house n—rs while Marse Sidney was at church just up the street at St. Michaels. She took to my hints like a trout but I almost reached for my Remington when she called me Marse Sidney. Like an ass I never shared my notion to be Billy Ives, but Brassard didn't seem to notice. He didn't *need* to notice.

"Daddy, you are missed. Why on earth are you secluded in this dark side hall?" I started like I was stung by hornets and whirled to face this new voice. "Bring your companion up to the light."

Thank Jehovah that the hall was cloaked in gloom. And thank him again that I'd already had my share of shocks today so this one didn't paralyze me. Standing framed in light from the kitchen was a small woman in a brazen purple gown, her dairy tackle squeezed up and out in a startling display of milk-white skin and black hair spilling over her shoulders in ringlets. Miss Hazel was not at all like I remembered her from Richmond. Last summer she was in widow's weeds with her hair pulled back in a severe bun. Her tits were the same.

"We talking business, darlin'. Major Ives, this is my daughter, Mrs. Hazel Ballentine."

I gave a bow with my planter's hat covering my face. When I bobbed back up the blade in my cane came up with me. I grabbed Father Brassard's necktie and held him fast while I pressed the tip into his narrow face.

"We've met! Hello, Mrs. Ballentine."

Her recognition was instant and in that instant I had never seen such a look of pure malice on any human face. She took a step toward me and I shoved the blade through the tight skin of Papa Brassard's puss.

"A inch farther and I'll put out your daddy's eye too!"

And then he got it. "Sidney! Your n—r called you Marse Sidney!" and he took on the same look I had learned to loath on his miserable son.

"Sawyer!"

If Hazel had simply screamed, Southern chivalry would have swarmed from the hop to the rescue, but she was too full of hate for that.

"You hog! You dog! You n—r lover! Where is Calhoun? We have had no word. What have you done?"

She advanced another step and I twisted the needle in Brassard's cheek sending a run of blood down his face.

"Stand where you are!"

"You won't, you coward! You would have to kill me too. You don't have the courage!" By grapes, she was going to do it. She was going to set at me with nails and teeth and I'd be forced to cut. The screams would draw a crowd of Southern heroes. We would be taken.

Hazel gave a last snarl, "You don't have the balls!"

"He sure *do* got the balls!" It was Liberty. She had a nasty flick-knife pressed tight against Hazel Brassard-Ballentine's throat. "I seen 'em!"

The Adventures of Sidney Sawyer
Missouri Yankees

Chapter 13

We stood frozen like four statues in that narrow hall. Gay music from the hop filtered through the kitchen. From outside, carefree voices of the colored servants softly drifted in from the alley. It couldn't last and it didn't. Either Liberty and I would slaughter them where they stood or the Brassards, father and daughter, would screw up their hate and force the issue. But neither happened. I had butted in on Brassard's conversation and his three companions finally decided to see what was the fuss. They barged into the narrow hall led by the red-faced bald one. Behind, to the right, followed the younger taller one with the older fatter one to the left. And there we stood– me with a long blade in their chum's face and Liberty with a knife to a lady's throat!

Hell broke loose in a narrow corridor!

The three Charleston burgers charged us, reaching for pistols and knives as they came. True Confederates never go unarmed! I would have driven my rapier through Daddy Brassard's head but they'd have swarmed me before I could have withdrawn the blade. God, how I hate to fight, but when I'm cornered I'm a cornered rat, and this hall with it's pickle barrel, cartons, crates and mops was as narrow a corner as I'd ever struck. I whipped the tip of the blade from Brassard's cheek, pulled him sharply toward me by his tie, and drove the butt of the handle so hard into his teeth that one of his molars stuck in the grip. I'm hell on Brassard family dental work. This brought the blade high to my left, perfect for a full-blooded backhand lash at red-face. I caught him full in the neck. A saber! If I'd had a saber I'd have taken off his fat head but my light blade struck his spine and flexed with a spring that sent it spinning from my hand. Both Brassard and red-face fell like slaughtered hogs, red-face spraying gore like a fountain.

Liberty and Miss Hazel were showered with blood. The colored girl cringed in revulsion, but the Lady Ballentine was a Carolina slave mistress and blood didn't repel. Quick as a snake she gripped Liberty's knife-hand and they struggled over the blade slipping in the gore and going down in a tumble of purple taffeta smeared with deeper crimson.

From the dance floor the band struck up "Dixie." The crowd gave a cheer, stomped their feet and sang the Southern anthem with a roar. With a different kind of roar the two Carolina bucks came at me in a rush with the younger, taller fellow leading the way with a Bowie held before him like a lance. Disarmed before the big knife I was dead mutton when three things saved me. I backed and tripped over the arms and legs of the two fallen Southern gentlemen. Younger-taller took a stumble of his own when his boots tangled in Hazel's petticoats. At that same instant, Liberty freed her arm from Hazel's grip, and took a wild stab at her with the knife, but only managed to slash open my attacker's knee above his boot. Down he came on top of me but with his Bowie in an *underhanded* grip. Damned ineffective for stabbing *down* at a fellow and before he could recover I had a mop handle between this blade and my throat. His older fatter friend loomed over his shoulder and pointed down at me with a pistol. It was one of those nasty pocket guns, small one-shot affairs, but with a bore as wide as a colt horse pistol. I was on my back with a Bowie at my neck and an avenging killer drawing a bead on my head. I gave a scream of pure fear and kicked out with my boots at anything they could reach. They reached a shin at the same instant the pistol went off in my face.

The mob in the social hall bellowed

*"I wish I was in Dixie! **Hurrah-Hurrah**!*
In Dixieland I'll take my stand
to live and die in Dixie!"

Burning powder singed my whiskers, the searing wad hit me in the cheek but my desperate kicks upset the aim and the bullet went through younger-taller's wrist, smashing the bone to splinters. Before he could even howl I fetched him a sharp rap to the bridge of his nose with the hickory mop handle and snatched up the knife. From flat on my back I stuck it straight up at older-fatter and slashed his thigh through to the bone. He gave a high-pitched scream and with a twist that slipped the bloody handle from my hand, he fell onto the pile of dead gentlemen.

*"Away, away, away down **Soooouth** in Dixie!"*

Curse the Confederates for having a short anthem but the cheering that followed nicely drowned out the screeches of Hazel and Liberty as they clung and fought in blood that seemed to be flooding the floor. Younger-taller was my size if he was an inch, but with a slit knee, only one good arm and a broken nose he couldn't prevent me from finding my feet. Grabbing him by the ears, I pulled him from the floor and plunged him backwards into the barrel of pickles up to his shoulders. He struggled like a madman but had no leverage as I let go of his ears and shoved his face with both hands, pushing him deeper until the pickles bobbed about my elbows.

A quick glance told me Liberty was in trouble. Hazel was tiny, but strong as a panther. I had found that out last summer in Richmond when the tart tried to kill me with fornication. Plantation life and abusing slaves made her hard and cruel and the only thing soft about her was her bouncers. She was astride Liberty with her bloody hands digging for the girl's eyes. Her gown was pulled down to her waist and those bouncers were a sight from hell, smeared with blood that I could only hope didn't come from Liberty.

With his head upside down and backwards in the brine the Carolina buck was at enough of a disadvantage that I could spare a quick kick at Miss Hazel. The tip of my boot found her ribs with a satisfying crack and I turned back to the business at hand, which was murder. I could actually feel when younger-taller took in his last deep breath that sucked the brine deep into his lungs. With a final convulsion he was limp and dead.

Older-fatter! Was he behind me with the Bowie? A slash in the leg wouldn't stop him. He was a Confederate and they take a world of killing. I released the drowned hero who flopped out and down into the blood and whirled to meet the threat, but there was no danger. He was on his back, face as white as death, with the last of his life-blood pulsing weakly from the gash in his thigh. I'd slashed the big veins in his leg and he was bleeding to death even as he dropped. No wonder the floor was flooded with gore.

And then from the end of the hall at the kitchen there was a scream that sounded above the din of the patriotic Rebels at the hop. A darkie kitchen wench stood at the door with the back of her hand to her mouth, which was wide open in a shriek fit to raise the dead. She turned and ran screaming through the kitchen. Time to go.

If I'd have had the Bowie I would have taken Miss Hazel's head off, but it was somewhere in the mess on the floor and the mob would be on us in seconds. I picked her up by her ankles, she was light as a feather, and dunked her head first into the pickles. Drown you wicked bitch! Her skirts sagged around the top of the barrel in a reeking sodden mass and her legs kicked straight up in their silly ankle-length pantaloons.

Liberty was drenched in blood and almost hysterical. I was neither and knew just what to do. I dipped my handy mop into the barrel besides Hazel's kicking legs and swabbed Liberty up and down with the dill brine. Pickles would be a world easier to explain than blood. I gave her another slosh for good luck, snatched a bib apron from a peg, yanked out my Remington and pulled her out of the side door just as the citizens of Charleston swarmed in from the kitchen.

The darkies waiting in the alley took one look at us and scattered like ducks. That is all but one, a high-yaller boy who looked at Liberty and froze. He must have been one of the bucks flirting with her when I called her in, what was it– five minutes ago?

Liberty was recovering fast. It must have been the mop of cold pickle juice in her face. She ran to the boy and whispered fiercely in his ear. Without hesitation he turned toward the docks and pointed with his arm out like a railway signal. We ran the other way and were out of the alley onto Meeting Street when we heard the first shouts of the avenging dancers. I hoped they'd follow the pointing boy instead of our footprints of blood and brine.

* * *

We had to stay ahead of pursuit. We were a step ahead now and had to stay that way. I slipped the apron over Liberty's head and hissed at her to say three paces back. It was late enough for most good citizens to be indoors and with the blockade there were no lamps lit along the street. Charleston's streets are in a grid, thank heaven, and even though I didn't know every block I knew the general lay of the city. And without a boat there was only one way off the blasted peninsula, the way we came, over the Ashley River Bridge. It was at least a mile and a half, maybe two and we'd have to make tracks to reach it ahead of the cry "bloody murder!" I dodged left at the first side street and then right at the next and then another left and right. We were heading uptown, away from the Cooper River docks where the high yaller boy, bless his heart, had steered the mob. How long it would take them to scour the wharves for us was an open question. Please, Lord, don't let some busybody follow the trail of pickle juice.

I'd been a spy long enough to know that the best way to sulk through a hostile camp is not to sulk at all. Hide in plain sight, that's the ticket and I'd done it more than once. I learned it from a Scotch sergeant at West Point named MacTavish who had a burr that could strip the barnacles off of a bateau. Draw just enough attention to yourself, he taught, that you simply couldn't be what you really were– a snake in the grass. Within the first two blocks we overtook a quartet of Confederate officers strolling along as if *they* weren't fleeing from the scene of a crime.

"Damn it, Libby! Hurry along there. Mother's a' waitin'!" I turned and snapped at poor Liberty as we passed the four men at a half trot. She must have thought I had gone daft. "You tell her where I been, I'll tan your black arse! Hurry along there!"

The soldiers har-har-hared at me for a hen-pecked puppy and I tipped my hat as we hurried past. What they made of Liberty dunked in brine I couldn't say. For the next half-hour I used this dodge a half-dozen times and Liberty, like a good'un picked up on the ploy and helped me along.

"I comin' along as fast as I can, Marse Sidney. I don't say notin' to Miss Molly when we git home. I be a good gal!" And passersby laughed and smirked and left us alone.

At any rate I knew that at Spring Street– or was it Elliot Street we'd turn left to the bridge and have to bluff our way over. It was guarded with a squad of infantry at each end, led by an officer who may or may not know his business. We were out late, blowing like nags on the home stretch and reeking of dill pickles. Only an ass would give us the road.

We took a wrong turn, wound up blocked by a blasted pond and had to double back two streets which set me to swearing fit to give Liberty the shakes and sniffles. I took myself in hand, gave her a pat on the cheek to calm her down, wiped her nose with my snot-rag and tied it around her briny hair mammy-style. She was on her last legs, up all night wrestling torpedoes in the harbor, marching through a hostile city all day where any false move would send us to the gallows and knife-fighting a raging Confederate widow in a lake of blood. What a woman!

This was not a fashionable section of the city. It was deserted and the shabby houses on the lane were dark and quiet. There was no one about to disapprove of a white gentleman embracing his n—r and so I did. She gave a sob and molded her body to mine. Damnation in July, but she was first-rate and center-cut. I was as tired as she was and had been frightened out of my wits a score of times, but still Little Sidney insisted on making an appearance. She was only a darkie drummer boy, sticky with dill, and it was all I could do to keep my paws from roaming up and down her wet gingham. I gritted my teeth and gave her a brotherly and comforting, "There-there."

What a woman!

We hurried along for another two blocks and blundered onto Elliot Street. The bridge, lit with watch-lights, was only two hundred yards to our left. Streaming past the lights in our direction was traffic, which told me that a C&S train was unloading at the depot on the south side. If we were still ahead of any alarm and could make that train we would have a chance, but courage was fleeing and we approached the sentries like we were heading to the dock. My hands flustered to my face in anxiety. We could never win across the bridge. And then I smelled Libby's pickle brine on my fingers.

Come on, Sidney! Gather your guts. *She's* only a girl but *she* went to war. She advanced with her regiment against enemy works when she could have stayed safe with the other brats in the rear. She warned me about the Fat Man and saved my hide. Pull up your socks, Sawyer. You can do this. They're still lookin' for a Johnny officer with a colored boy in tow. You know what to do– hide in plain sight!

I turned to Libby and gave her a grin that I may have actually felt. "Play along, girl. Us Missouri Yankees are gonna confound them yet. I'm the Ace of Spades and you're the lady drummer boy of the Colored 94th. We're both play actors. This is gonna be fun!"

And it was, sort of.

"I've seen some dizzy darkies, but she's beyond all credit!" I stormed at the sergeant of the guard who was lounging on his rifle at the edge of the watch light. He seemed a no-nonsense type of soldier– the armies of the world are lousy with them. We couldn't have our wars without them. I would have preferred an officer. Sergeants have sense. Most lieutenants are idiots. He squared his Enfield at port arms and stood foursquare in the road. Behind him his detail came on the alert.

"Look at her! Look! Or better yet, smell her!"

He looked at me as if I had a slate loose.

"Go on! Go on– smell her."

And he did. The sergeant wouldn't have been human if he didn't step over and have a sniff at Liberty.

"Pickles?"

"*Dill* Pickles! I could see if it was sweet gherkins. Every n—r in Carolina has a sweet tooth, but dills?"

Liberty joined into the spirit of the thing. "Marse Sidney, I's sorry. Didn't mean to spill the whole jar down on my head. Just wanted one."

"Well you got the whole lot! Never been so embarrassed in my days."

She wrung her hands, rolled her eyes and went down on her knees. A crowd was gathering from the pedestrians off the train.

"But Marse Sidney, I thought dey was sweet pickles, the little kind. It's just these was big."

The sergeant rolled his eyes too and the crowd gave a giggle at the pickle clowns.

"Big gherkins? Miss Molly's gonna switch your silly behind when we get home, that is *if* we git home. Way you reek, they ain't a' gonna let us on the train. Gonna put you in the cattle car."

Liberty started to moan and the crowd tittered.

I took a page from Papa Brassard's book and blustered, "An' I suppose none of y'all have never had n—r trouble. None o' y'all ever had a darkie smelled like cucumbers at brine time."

This was too much for the sergeant. The thoroughfare was clogging with hoi polloi blocking wagon traffic and Liberty's sobs were become irritating.

"Where you headed, Mister?" the sergeant demanded.

"Tain't Mister. T'is Captain– Captain Dillard of Pocotaligo." Pocotaligo was fifty miles down the C&S line. Let them hunt for us there since we were getting off in Jacksonboro.

"*Dill*ard?"

"Yeah, Dillard, an' if y'all make a pickle joke I'll call you out!"

This time the sergeant laughed along with the mob and ordered us to move along and stop blocking the traffic. He wouldn't think it so funny when found out he was bamboozled by two smelly Yankee fugitives from a blood bath.

As we hurried across the bridge our eyes were drawn to the eastern sky. The horizon was lit with flashes from the Union artillery's perpetual shelling of Sumter and Wagner. We wouldn't be safe until we sheltered under the muzzles of those guns.

The Adventures of Sidney Sawyer
Missouri Yankees

Chapter 14

We made the train with a half hour to spare and paid our passage to Pocotaligo with Johnny treasury notes looted from the prisoners taken in the rifle pits. They'd lost half their value since Gettysburg and Vicksburg. Paper money is like love and religion. It's value floats on faith and faith is easily broken.

I rode in the coach and Liberty rode in the baggage car with the rest of the property. Our plan had been to leave Charleston the way we went in. After two days of scouting the city and dodging our duty we were to meet the whaleboat in the wee hours at the same high-tide line on Wappo Creek. I had seen enough well laid plans go belly-up not to prepare for the worst. I'd made bloody sure I knew every road and rail out of Charleston by heart. The sentry on the Ashley River Bridge was told we were on our way to Pocotaligo, the fourth stop from Charleston. We'd steal off the train at Jacksonboro on the Edisto River, twenty-five miles short of where I hoped they'd be searching.

And they would be searching. Even if they didn't put Samuel Clemens, the Yankee spy traveling with a colored *boy*, together with Sidney Sawyer, the murderer traveling with a colored *girl*, we were still in Dutch. I know I hadn't killed Papa Brassard, rot his boots. There just wasn't enough time. When he regained his senses he'd be tattling through his broken teeth to every lawman in the city. If Hazel didn't drown in the brine, and they'd have fished her out before she did, she'd tell them to just follow the pickles. Union spies or bloody murderers, South Carolina wanted us dead. And we would be if anyone had thought to telegraph ahead to Jacksonboro.

Leaving Charleston, the cars were mostly empty and after two hours of jolting along the Confederate Railroad I stole off the coach at Jacksonboro leaving only a faint odor of dill. It was late and no one but the brakeman was up to see me fetch Libby from the rest of the baggage. We disappeared into the Southern night.

There was damn little to disappear into. The land about was flat as a skillet. North of the tracks was pine swamp and plantation country. South of the rail line was the same order of tidal-marsh and wasteland that graced the Swamp Angel Battery. This wasteland was our highway to safety. Through it flowed the Edisto River. Actually 'flowed' was too strong a word. It was a meandering, stagnant tidal slough, but it twisted to the ocean and there was always a Yankee frigate on station across the bar. We needed a boat.

I only knew Jacksonboro as a dot on the Army ordinance map, but standing in the gloom of the open shed that passed for the station I realized that it wasn't even a town. It was just a spot where a lane crossed the tracks. The telegraph wires ran beside the rails without a break. There was no telegraph station! Any news of fugitives would have to arrive overland and when it arrived there was nobody to tell. Glory hallelujah, we had time.

I knew the lay of the land. A mile or so to the north on firmer ground ran the Savanna Road. I reckoned to hike there, turn right to the Edisto River and see to stealing a boat. That could take all night and God knows how we'd explain ourselves to any patrols.

I was looking north. It was the only way to look. To the south the crossing lane could only end in the marsh.

"Mr. Colonel Sawyer, Sir." Libby was tugging my sleeve. "What's that down the road?"

That was nothing. There was nothing down that road except swamp grass and brackish water but she ran down the lane and called to me from the dark.

"It's a sign– and a trail."

And it was. I had to pick her up at her hips to read the sign, which was damned distracting. To make out the letters one by one she had to squint from a distance of two inches. Lucky me– not only did little Liberty have first-rate stern quarters but she was probably the only darkie in Carolina who could read.

"PURVIS LANDING"

A landing! And a landing meant boats! Didn't I tell you Negroes were handy traveling companions? I'd have never seen the sign. How Libby did was beyond credit. Maybe traveling with the baggage her eyes were used to the dark.

* * *

In the end we had to buy the damn boat. It was a skiff, dandy for the swamps and bayous, but open water would be a trial. It came equipped with two oars mounted on pegs, a spare paddle, tin cups for drinking and bailing, tin plates, a basket stuffed with simple grub, fishing line, sticks and canvas to rig an awning, a rag quilt and a jug of raw farm liquor.

We were only halfway down the lane when a quartet of mutts set up a bark and howl fit to arouse the establishment. We couldn't sneak up, so what the hell?

"Purvis Landing, ahoy! Hello the house. Ahoy!"

The establishment was two ancient brothers with matching chest whiskers, overalls and brown teeth, who came out of their shack with lantern held high and shotguns held low. I couldn't fault the scatterguns, I was a stranger and it was after midnight, but the old goats became civil after I spun my lie and they saw my money.

Nobody had met my train and that was damn inconvenient. We needed a boat to get upriver. How far?

Well, that's my business, aint' it? They asked no more questions.

They were watermen and didn't care beans nor biscuits about the war– it wern't none of their business. Their business was the marsh and they were slicker than okra soaking in the sink. At the landing, which was a considerable pier with four boats bobbing from their painters, we haggled over the price of the skiff, food and gear. In the end the two old crooks took me for every dollar of my confederate script plus two gold eagles. When I dug them from my belt I kept my belly gun visible in case the two thieves decided they wanted more. All watermen are thieves.

I bundled Libby in the stern to call directions, set the oars and pulled us up-stream. It was the wrong way, but the only way. I'm a river boy and don't know crackers about the tide but I do know you can't paddle against it. The ocean was at least fifteen miles downstream, but the tide was oozing the dark water up the Edisto and we went with it. But we didn't go with it far. In fifty yards we were swallowed by the dark and in fifty more were beyond sound. I tied the skiff to a stump and waited on the tide.

It was cloudless and chilly on the water and there was only one quilt. I wanted to spoon with Libby for warmth (and to try my paws under her gingham) and I wanted to ask my little drummer boy a dozen obvious questions. But most of all I wanted to stay awake for the turning of the tide, so I tossed her the quilt, gnawed on a butt of greasy jerky, (it's a stretch easier to keep awake when you're eating) and waited for the Edisto tides.

Of course I went to sleep. The river's bullfrogs boomed back and forth with a monotony that would etherize a caged squirrel. Libby woke me up with a hand on my cheek and the aroma of dill. It was cold as Satan's liver and as dark as his soul with only the earliest hint of dawn in the east. The tide had turned and the skiff was trailing at the end of its painter, eager to float with the current to the sea. We slipped the line off the stump and with me steering with the paddle the Edisto did the work. In two minutes we were past the pier at Purvis Landing without arousing the mutts or the proprietors and on our way to the Atlantic.

We drifted with the tide through a wilderness of rushes and grasses. The noises of beasts and birds were a lullaby. I woke up again with the rising sun in my face and Libby in my arms beneath the quilt. The dawn was too pretty and I was too tuckered to be tempted by the black bundle in my arms. We drifted around a bend and before us the river spread out a half-mile wide. Both river banks were deserted, the marsh came down to the water's edge and inland were groves of pine and palm. When the tide turned again we tied up near the bank in the shade of a pretty grove and I could finally ask what I was bound to ask.

"Liberty," and I looked her up and down, "what the hell?"

"Mr. Colonel, sir, I had a' be a boy. My daddy was gone for the Army and he couldn't keep me back home. Missouri be full a' peril these days. 'Specially for a woman– 'specially for a Negro woman in Girardeau."

Well, this I knew. And did she just refer to herself as a woman instead of a girl? I asked an insipid question. "How old are you?"

"I was seventeen on the Fourth of July. That why my mommy name me Liberty."

"There was no one to take you in? No one at home?"

"Ain't no home left. Arkansas raiders come through Girardeau last March and burn daddy's shop. Ain't nothing left but the anvil. Union white folks blame the n—rs for the War. Confederate white folks want to own us or kill us. Daddy had a' go for the Army. The other free colored folk look up to him. That why he the sergeant major. Men just want a' follow him. I follow him too."

"But you as a *boy*?" I must have looked at her like a fool. She agreed.

“Fool you! Short hair, baggy britches, big shirt and floppy hat– who say I ain’t a boy. Play the drum better than any other drummer boy in the 94th, too.”

“How do you stand it? Army life is hard, crude, vulgar… ”

“I got my daddy and nine hundred big brothers.” Then she gave me a look that set me to sweat and make my little Bengal Lancer forget that the rest of me was up most of the night. “An’ I got you, Mr. Colonel Sawyer, sir. Now, if you don’t mind, I smell of pickles.”[17]

Liberty, the drummer boy stood up in the skiff, pulled her gingham over her head, kicked off her cotton underpants and with a hop, jumped feet first in the Edisto River.

* * *

I usually wouldn’t have gone bathing in a tidal river for a pension. There were gators in those waters, not to mention cottonmouths and leaches, but there was also a naked colored girl in the Edisto with flawless skin the color of anthracite, a beautiful African face, and seventeen or not, a body like the Queen of Sheba. In two shakes I shucked my duds, impressed my drummer boy with a neat dive that almost upset the skiff and found to my delight that the Edisto only looked muddy from the top. In my boyhood on the Mississippi I learned to swim like an eel. I had to with Brother Tom Sawyer and his gang of bullies dunking me every time we went river-balling. It was only a lark for them but I had to learn to swim with my eyes open to avoid their ambushes. Now, those hard lessons paid off in spades and trumps. I could see for a good fifteen feet and what I saw was something few men ever do. How many men do you know that can hold their breath for two minutes and swim with open eyes?

Libby floated above me with a dog paddle that flexed her legs and pointed her little toes. Water magnifies what you see. Her slim legs looked muscled and strong, her narrow hips seemed wide and her arse cheeks, with just a hint of an African jut, looked like a chipmunk with its cheeks stuffed with sunflower seeds. But *you* know I'm a tit man. Have been since Professor Roseasharen gave me my first tutorial in love back when I was a brat. I love to watch 'em bounce but in the water they don't bounce. They float, weightless, straight out and the chill of the Edisto had Libby's tiny nipples at full military attention, pure black against her deep brown skin. If I ever see Brother Tom again, I'll thank him for the swimming lessons.

I had been under for at least a minute and Libby must have thought the snappers got me. She was swiveling about in the water looking this way and that for any sign of me, a bubble or a toe. Her floundering was the damn prettiest aquatic dance you could imagine, her obvious concern was poignant and her distress was touching– so I hung below her for an extra half minute taking in the view and in a rush of bubbles popped up before her face with an evil grin. She shrieked, fetched me a roundhouse clout on my temple, set up a splash that blinded me and wrapped her arms around my neck like a panicked monkey. If she *had* thought I'd drowned, she almost finished the job. Libby was trying to help, I know she was, but we both went under like ballast. Water shot up my nose and filled my head to the eyes. I was already out of breath and if I hadn't pried her arms from around my throat with the last of my strength we'd have both been feeding the Edisto catfish.

I believe that if I hadn't been such a swine, taking underwater liberties with Liberty, I'd have had her doing the Edisto River marsh polka in the bottom of the boat right then, but nothing kills romance like blowing pints of phlegm from your snot-locker and vomiting up quarts of brackish river water over the side of a skiff. She hadn't swallowed as much water as I did and recovered quicker. While she washed out her britches and frock in the river she dressed me down like no drummer boy had ever dressed down a colonel. I was gagging too much to pull rank or even ogle her properly as she wiggled back into her dress. Duty in the Intelligencer Corps is a pup.

When the tide turned we turned with it and made good time with me manning the oars and Liberty steering with the paddle. The river widened with each twist and turn. A bayou entered to the east and I knew that the land on our left must be Edisto Island. I expected it to be just another waste of marsh and swamp like Morris Island but instead we passed oak and pine forest with cleared land between the groves and here and there plantation docks with glimpses of fine houses up from the river. But we never heard a dog bark or any other sound, and if there was a living soul on Edisto Island, they never showed themselves along the water's edge.

* * *

Edisto Island was a ghost island. The plantations along the left bank were abandoned and as I rowed with the tide past the docks and landings not a soul showed, not a human sound echoed. It was late afternoon when the tide turned again, but we had reached the point where the river met the Atlantic. The flat-bottomed skiff the Purvis Brothers skinned me for in the wee hours last night could take us no farther. To the north the ocean rollers were breaking in long lovely curls of the purest, bluest water and the Edisto was becoming a millrace of incoming tide. We landed on the flooding sandbar of Edisto beach which stretched away and out of sight, clean and deserted for as far as we could see and dragged our craft well out of the reach of the incoming tide. Out in the ocean there was a thin smudge of smoke on the horizon. It was a cutter from the blockade squadron but we may as well have been Robinson Caruso and his girl Friday for all the safety that distant line of stack gas promised us.

It's the fashion now to pack up the family and travel to the beach for a summertime frolic. My introduction to the charms of the wide ocean beaches was during my third spring at the Academy when I traveled with some Yankee chums to Cape Cod for a lark. It was April, the ocean was an ugly gray and frigid gales sent waves thundering onto the beach like hungry monsters. If my cadet host from Provincetown didn't whistle up some mischief-minded maidens the whole visit would have been a frost. As it was the girls cleaned cod in a local plant and their hands stunk of fish guts and scales. My only other experience on a beach was Morris Island with the 94th and I've already written about that chapter and verse.

My holiday on the Edisto Beach with Libby was an adventure of a different sort altogether. Since that diamond perfect evening I've loved beaches as few other places. There's no better refuge on earth for a man than to sprawl on a canvas lounge swilling tonic and gin, reading cheap fiction and watching the women dancing through the surf with their wet bathing costumes plastered tight to their bodies. Amy and I have a cottage at Sturgeon Point above the bluffs on Lake Erie where the beach runs for miles and shallow waters extend out for a hundred yards. Our grandchildren can splash and play up to their chests in the sweet water and there's nothing in the Lake that will bite them. I love the beach!

We made a picnic of it. Libby kept on her frock, but I stripped down to my underbritches. What the deuce, she'd seen me in my birthday best twice before. Now that I think about it, both times I was gagging up a dog's breakfast. I turned the skiff over for shelter, propped it up with the paddle, set a driftwood fire to blaze and we were home. We waded into the surf with the fishing lines provided by Purvis and Company, and fish that I couldn't name literally jumped onto our hooks. Nobody can clean a fish faster than a river-bred boy and as a fat three-quarter moon rose from the Atlantic we feasted on fillets and pone cooked in grease. The fish was the finest I ever ate. Under that Carolina moon, beneath the stars, on soft sand before the black ocean, which creamed white foam before our camp, the pure white meat from the fillets broke off in smooth delicious flakes. But it wasn't white meat that was on my mind. There was prime dark meat beside me at the fire and she was licking her fingers with her full lips and shockingly pink tongue. Liberty's gingham, still wet from the surf, clung to her like a second skin and the chill of the salt air had her nipples poking at the thin fabric like berries. The memory of her treading water in the Edisto, while I ogled up at her had me panting like a hound after a corndodger. By grapes, I hadn't had a woman since my elephantine romp with Missy Ruth before Brother Tom got me dragooned into the 94th. Here was a handy little goer across the fire on a deserted beach after a meal fit for a duchess who I knew had a candle lit for me.

But she was only a girl– seventeen, and I was a colonel in the United States Army. I was *her* colonel! She was in *my* command– a drummer boy no less. There was no way I could just command her to strip off her dress and present herself for inspection and night maneuvers. Even I had my limits. And Liberty might not be keen on advances from the likes of me. She was really just a girl, certainly a virgin. Jumping bare-naked into the river to rinse off the pickle juice wasn't the act of seasoned bareback rider but only the innocent lark of a child. I'd be a swine to simply reach over, grab her and break into a chorus of *Drink Puppy Drink.* And I was, after all, a white man.

No, my usual Sidney style with this chaste child wouldn't do. So I got out the Purvis Brother's farm liquor and filled up her cup.

Fifteen minutes later Libby was singing to me in a jolly voice punctuated with happy giggles.

De massa run, Ha-Ha! De darkie stay, Ho-Ho!
It must be now de Kingdom Coming,
an' de year of Jubilo!

Ten minutes later I topped off her mug, swigged myself a long snort straight from the jug and sang along.

The Ninety-fourth, Ha-Ha! I'll love you all my days!
Missouri Yankees, on parade,
an' I love de Ace of Spades!

Five minutes later she was snuggled in my arms gazing into my eyes with love and trust as I fondled her bouncers with both hands.

Two minutes later I was humming with lust as I edged the hem of her gingham up over her thighs.

Two seconds later a bayonet flitted out of the black night held by two blacker hands and pricked the base of my throat above my collarbone hard enough to draw blood.

From a face as ugly as a burned boot a gravel voice growled, "Hol' fast, buckruh. Yo trespassum' in da Republic o' da Edisto. Give o' die!"

The Adventures of Sidney Sawyer
Missouri Yankees

Chapter 15

Edisto Island wasn't deserted after all. There were a half dozen of the brutes, barefoot and dressed in tatters, but armed to the teeth with spears, knives, and clubs. One of them waved a navy-style cutlass, another gripped an Indian tomahawk in each hand and the buck with the bayonet at my throat sported a gigantic tri-corner hat with tiny pink scallop shells stitched around the brim and a cockade of cock feathers.

I croaked out, "Give!"

Libby giggled, "Gosh!"

The giant with the bayoneted musket glowered with huge eyes and impossibly white teeth. He was the only one who talked and was the only one with a firearm so I assumed he was the leader of this posse. The others were a rabble of husky darkies holding their weapons with aggression but without grace. Tri-corner was worth another look. He was huge, not tall, but huge with a barrel of a gut jutting naked from a Federal blue uniform jacket that was two sizes too small for him. His belly was slick with sweat and grease and was crisscrossed with ugly scars that could only have been put there with a whip. The sleeves were cut off at the elbow and his forearms looked ox-strong.

"What yo Carolina buckruh do wi n—a she she on de big bay?"

What?

"Jimo-Jim, tay 'em op!"

What the hell?

"Who are you boys? Are you runaways? I can help. Who are you, big boy? I'm a Union ......"

The one with the club yanked Libby off my lap like a rag-doll. Another one, Jimo-Jim no doubt, booted me onto my belly and trussed my arms behind me like poultry, all the while with tri-corner's long knife at my neck.

"Boys, there's no need for this," I whined with sand up my nose and terror in my liver. "I'm an officer– a Yankee! Help us off this island. Who are you? What do you want?"

I was answered with a sharp slap to the back of my head and a shout of outrage from Liberty.

"Leave him alone you ignorant Sea Island Gullah! He's my colonel. He's the Ace of Spades!" She was sobering up fast. "He's my hero! He's......"

"He be Carolina buckruh who wan eenjy push-push wid n—a gal. Dat who! I be King Wadmalaw, da bos o' Pont o' Pons. I tarrygate yo yuh. Yo no tarrygate me yuh."[s]

By grapes, I was in the soup and my only paddle was useless. That paddle was my glib tongue. Libby called this black monster a Sea Island Gullah and she was right. We could only talk our way out of this peril but the Gullah's had a language of their own that was half African, part English and God knows what wild mix of other heathen tongues. The Carolina Coast slaves had been isolated on Sea Island cotton hells for generations. The only conversations between master and slave were spoken with the lash and a pidgin English that belonged more on the coast of Guinea than the coast of America.[18]

---

[s] An approximate translation from Gullo is, "He is a Carolina White Man who wants to enjoy sex with a Black Girl. That's who! I am King Wadmalaw, the boss of Point of Pines. I will interrogate you. You will not interrogate me." (Wadmalaw is the main bayou flowing through Edisto Island.)

They kicked out the fire, helped themselves to our rations and liquor, booted me to my feet with their horny bare toes and we set off north, up the beach. King Wadmalaw draped my holstered Remington around his fat neck, the gun belt would never fit around his belly, and perched my beaver on Jimo-Jim's wooly skull. They were a merry crew of black pirates and jabbered nonstop as they frog-marched us along the endless beach. After an hour of listening to their savage language I began to recognize a rhythm to their tongue and pick out more and more tortured English words from the jumble. There is no way on earth that I can reproduce the pidgin Creole of those African marauders, but here is what I heard as near as I can translate and what I heard turned my knees to pudding.

Jimo-Jim– "King Wadmalaw, sir. The girl is quite attractive and will make a fine addition to our community, however this buckruh (white man) does present us with a dilemma."

Tomahawks– "Jimo-Jim is correct, Your Majesty. We simply have no place for this fellow. What shall we do with him? By the way, my friend, your new hat sets off your rakish style quite nicely."

King Wadmalaw– "Gentlemen, you are correct. White men are such a bother. As I see it there are only three possibilities. We can keep him, let him go or kill him."

Jimo-Jim– "It would be very inconvenient to keep this buckruh. We have no facilities at Point of Pines for incarceration. Also, his presence would upset the tranquility of your kingdom."

Tomahawks– "Well, we certainly can't let him go. He will report our island's insurrectionist Negro community to the authorities on the mainland. The South Carolinians will come in force to exterminate us."

King Wadmalaw– "I am aware of this. After all, am I not the sovereign of Edisto? He will have to die, but first we must question him."

Cutlass– “But he will surely lie. He has already said he is a Yankee officer. This buckruh must think all of us Gullah Black Men are addled.”

Me– being dragged along by the brute with the club, “I *am* a Yankee officer you ignorant black villains! Take a boat out to the blockader. They’ll pay you handsomely. Money, rum, guns! Tell ’em I’m Colonel Sidney Sawyer. Tell ’em……” I got the butt of the club in my kidney for my trouble.

Libby– (being roughly held by one of the bucks with a spear.) “You let him be! You let us go. You men in big trouble now! We gonna bring the Army down on ya!”

Jimo-Jim– “This young woman must be a house n—r.”

King Wadmalaw– “I agree. Isn’t it a shame when slaves confuse their loyalties and side with the Rebel Army against their own people? This fellow is almost certainly a Confederate deserter. We will have to kill him.”

Tomahawks– “Burn him!”

Libby– “No!”

Me– “No!”

King Wadmalaw– “No! That is not our way. We are not savages, although if caught by the buckruh they would surely savage us. We will not take delight in tormenting our enemies.”

Me– “Well thank God!”

King Wadmalaw– We will drown him in the bayou behind Seabrook Beach.”

* * *

They all agreed it was a dandy idea to dunk the inconvenient buckruh in Seabrook Bayou. It was on their way home, it would solve any messy disposal problems and even though it wouldn’t be as much fun as burning me, it would get the job done. And there was the bayou before us, a narrow inlet dividing our stretch of beach from the next, with King Wadmalaw’s royal barge secured above the tide line. It was a flat-bottomed bateau built to haul cotton bales to the wharf, twenty feet long and ten abeam and surprisingly shipshape considering the crew. Wadmalaw's subjects manhandled the boat into the bayou and Liberty almost swooned as they dragged her aboard. Me, they tumbled in, barking my shins cruelly. They used the paddles as poles, pushing us through the narrow bayou for fifty yards where it widened into a proper stream. Then, two to a side, with Jimo-Jim covering me with a cutlass and the King steering, they paddled between two banks dark with jungle. Presently King Wadmalaw hauled the tiller to starboard and we entered a river with tropical jungle to the right and cleared fields to the left. The water was deep and black.

"This is the deepest part of the Seabrook, gentlemen. This will do nicely. Lash that line around his neck. He may as well go in Seabrook Bayou headfirst. After all my subjects, the quality of mercy is not strain'd. It is twice blessed. It blesses him that gives and him that takes. This cracker will die faster and thank us for it."

With the damnedest sense of deja vu I began to blither my prayers. I don't know why I bother. The Almighty only hears from the likes of me when I'm about to be thrown into the gumbo, this time literally. Although this happens often enough that the Lord and I are solid acquaintances, if not friends.

The King heard my prayer and gave a low laugh that sounded like church music in the quiet of the bayou.

"Therefore, cracker, though justice is your plea, consider this, that in the course of justice we do pray for mercy and that same prayer teaches us all to render the deeds of mercy."

"Oh, don't kill me boss! I ain't no Johnny deserter. I'm a Yankee officer. We're on the same side. Oh, let me go! Let me go! Aunt Polllly!"

The black boys snickered, Libby groaned and the King thundered, "Don't you dare go into the Seabrook and eternity with a lie on your heathen lips. My mercy will be that you will die quickly and without wound. It is the Lord's mercy you must seek now! Jimo-Jim, tie off that line right short to the anchor stone."

The swine looped the line about my neck through the iron ring fixed to the anchor stone, yanked my face six inches from the filthy thing and lashed it fast. He hoisted the rock that must have weighed two score pounds and rested it on the gunwale awaiting the execution order from his lord and master.

I had almost drowned once before, not the snootful of brackish water I snorted when I was ogling Libby floating in the Edisto the day before, but actually drowned to the point of death. It was in the Potomac Rapids in '62 when Virginia slave catchers and provost bulls chased me into the current. The whitewater sent me through the boulders and drops like a rat through a sewer. It was horrible beyond all sanity and the pain of water flooding my nose and throat and lungs was torture beyond telling. Now these black monsters were going to drown me headfirst as an act of mercy? When the anchor stone hit the water, I'd follow like a puppy on a leash and the black water would fill my head and the pain would explode in my soul and my last intake of breath would be the heavy water that would… I screamed!

"Die like a man buckruh. Make your peace with the lord and the Seabrook!"

He raised his hand like Henry VIII set to dispatch a bride. Jimo-Jim tilted the stone to outboard. I set to scream out my last breath. And then Liberty said, "Seabrook? I know the Seabrooks! There be Ishmael and Isaac Seabrook and Peter and James."

King Wadmalaw's hand never came down with the order to send me into the river but the anchor stone had a life of its own. It slipped off the gunwale of its own weight and jerked my poor neck along with it. My head hit the filthy water as I screamed my last air and in came the black water through my nose and throat and in that terrible second Jimo-Jim's hand reached below my wild eyes and seized the line. His arm was roped with muscle as only a field hand's could be and he hauled the forty weight of stone and me back aboard like a bullhead on a hook. I lay on my back, hands bound behind, spewing like Hibernian shovel labor on bark juice with the noose of rope strangling me at every gag. A knife flashed before my eyes, but only to cut the noose, strong hands hauled me upright and rough fists pounded my back until the Seabrook Bayou emptied from my lungs. And only two hours before I had been sipping farm liquor and sliding my paw up little Libby's frock.[t]

* * *

The noose was off my neck but my hands were still bound behind me and it was a misery to lay belly down on the rough planking of the bateau with my eyes streaming and my lungs pumping like the village forge.

The king spoke gently to Libby. "Girl, what do you know of these Seabrook men– Ishmael and Isaac? Speak truly or your buckruh or Yankee or liar or lover goes back into the bayou."

I had no notion of what the hell had just happened other than I was still breathing the breezy stuff and was on the dry side of the black water. Before this Seabrook nonsense they had been interested in nothing we had to say. Now, what Liberty had to say saved me from feeding the mullet.

"Me an' Colonel Sawyer are in the 94th Colored Infantry Regiment. We truly be Missouri Yankees. He be our colonel an' the Ace of Spades. He a hero an' my daddy's friend an' my friend. He a Underground Railroad man an' a champion o' the colored man. He know Father

---

[t] For Sawyer's previous drowning experience, refer to the third packet of his memoirs, *The Adventures of Sidney Sawyer: The Year of Jubilee*.

Abraham an' lead us against the rifles of the slave power an' he…"

By grapes, but the girl was worked up.

King Wadmalaw took her in hand, literally. He grabbed both her thin shoulders with his big mitts and spoke to her almost as an uncle. "Slow down child. Tell me about the Seabrooks. How do you know about the Seabrooks?"

"The Seabrooks is famous. Everybody in the Colored Army heard of the Seabrook boys. Last May, seven brothers signed up with Captain Sharp of the 2nd South Carolina Colored Regiment. All on the same day! There was Isaac Seabrook, an' Ishmael Seabrook, an' Peter an' James Seabrook, and Eddie an' Jeffries…"

"There was one more brother. Think child, you say you are Yankees with the blue army. Who was the last Seabrook man?"

If I wasn't hog tied, belly down with a black foot on the back of my neck I would have shaken her. Remember the name you silly black baggage! Who *was* that last blackbird in the 2nd SCCT? I had no notion just what this was about, but my life seemed to hang on the outcome. *Who was he?*

"Prince! He was Prince. You be the King. Are you his daddy? His name was Prince Seabrook!"[19]

"I am not his father, but I would be proud to claim that honor. You may indeed be who you claim, but one thing rings false. You say you are a soldier in a Northern regiment. You are too young, too small and we have noticed that you are a girl. The blue army has no women in its ranks."

Libby lit up with a proud smile. "I ain't no woman. I'm a drummer boy."

God in heaven, they were going to kill me for sure! But they didn't. Instead the King's boatmen rowed the barge a mile farther up the bayou to a fine landing with a stout wharf before a plantation house that loomed like a Roman temple in the moonlight. The mansion had the beat of anything my home state of Missouri could claim. It was at the head of one hundred yards of crushed shell drive with a broad oval before a portico that sported six columns below the second and third stories. Off in the overgrown lawn were grottos and gazebos and pools set to reflect groves of fruit trees and hedges. The drive was flanked with classical statuary and in the middle of the oval was a marble fountain that was layered like a wedding cake. The fountain had no water, the windows no light and the establishment no sound except the King and his court chattering away with Liberty, who was rapidly increasing in familiarity with their Sea Island Creole. The topic was the heroic Seabrook boys who had anted up on the same glorious day to join the ranks of Marse Lincom's slave army to smite ol' master hip and thigh. The idea that Libby was a soldier was too ridiculous for even these rogue slaves to credit.

I wasn't dead but I wasn't trusted. My hands stayed bound and we set out on a hike down a fine road past the ghostly mansion. The moon hanging in a cloudless sky lit the way and as we marched I was amazed. I was amazed by the wealth of Edisto Island. We walked for well over an hour, first inland to the northwest and then right to the northeast. The stars were my guides, but my captives wouldn't have needed them. The route was a fine road between cotton fields gone to seed and we passed other plantation houses at least as fine as the one at the landing. Damned if these Sea Island cotton barons didn't do well for themselves– but where were they?

I shut up and sulked along behind the King, trying to pick up as much of their lingo as I could. My mouth has always been my best weapon but it wouldn't wash with these blackbirds. Libby chatted away with them like a magpie and seemed to grow in understanding with each step. The men teased her as a card, drummer boy indeed, but along the way she began to ask some of the same questions that were troubling me.

"Your Majesty, where are all the white men? There set their houses and playgrounds and lanes, but where they be?"

"Why Miss Liberty, they are gone. Two years ago, they left. They left us Negroes and the cotton standing in the fields and left. Some of the buckruh burned their cotton and slaughtered their cattle and sheep to rot in the yards, but most simply bundled up mother's silver and master's traps and skedaddled."

"But what happened to the colored folks? These fields, an' these houses, and all this…" Libby gestured round-about flapping her hands like a bird in flight, "There must a' been thousands of you black folk to do all this work. I know the white folk didn't do none of it."

"You are right, child. We slaves were left to our own devices. We couldn't eat the cotton burned in the fields, but we had our gardens and the smokehouses were full where the buckruh abandoned them without burning. The bayou and ocean are bottomless larders of fish, crab, oysters and bounty. There were hogs and cattle running wild in the woods and ducks and geese were thick on the ponds. We ran our own affairs like free men. Our preachers proclaimed the word, baptized our babies, buried our dead and married our maids to our bucks. We judged our own justice. There were one thousand of us and in the months of our freedom we were joined by an equal number of runaways who dared their master's wrath and the currents of the bayous to join us in our Republic of Edisto."

"Then, where is everybody?"

"The Yankees came. Soldiers in blue, from two Yankee lands, came to Point of Pines.[u] They hired the black folk to return to the fields and plant cotton. They brought teachers and preachers and told us what to do. They did not bring the lash or the block, but our day of freedom was over."

---

[u] 47th New York and the 55th Pennsylvania Infantry.

I had to interrupt, "Then where the devil is everyone, blast you! If there are Yankee busybodies about then bring me to them. And why did you feed me to the turtles when you could have sent me to the Union bivouac and been rewarded for your troubles?"

I was getting my sass back. They didn't seem bent to do me more mischief and now that the black bayou water had drained from my sinus and belly I was beginning to feel damned put out. These bastards had interrupted my beach party where I was about to board a tipsy but willing black stunner. I had just escaped from the net cast by that fat traitorous swine Melrose Middlesex, the Brassard clan, and the Carolina provost. We were in sight of the blockade squadron and salvation when these Gullah louts with their tri-corner caps, tomahawks and clubs interfered. They ate my grub, swilled my liquor and scared me from here to Hannibal.

"Where the dickens is everybody? This island is a ghost land of shadows and haunts. Take me to Union camp. Now damn it, or it will be the worse for you!"

What on earth is wrong with me? I wouldn't have spoken to Frémont in St. Louis or Grant in Memphis or McClellan on the road to Sharpsburg like that. This black king was every bit the lord and master of his domain as those commanders were in their theaters of war. And King Wadmalaw *was* at war– a war with no quarter for insurrectionist slaves, and any error in judgment, such as mercy for a loudmouth white man, could result in extermination. What did I expect for my tantrum? What I got was a calloused hand at my throat that lifted me to the tips of my toes and for the second time that night I began to choke.

"There is no Union camp, you buckruh fool! They are gone. The Carolina men came in the night and defeated them. Your men in blue ran like chickens. They ran like geese. Then your men of big affairs sent more regiments and still more until Edisto was a vast camp of your blue Yankee soldiers."

My eyes were popping and my ears sang with blood. My hands bound fast behind my back were useless to save me. My vision darkened and then exploded with stars and lights.

"Your Majesty, you said '*your* men in blue!' You said '*your* Yankee soldiers!' You know he be a Union man." Libby begged, "Don't kill him just because he a buckruh fool."

Wadmalaw sneered, "But your Yankee soldiers are gone– all of them! In Virginia the South defeated the North and Master Lincoln called all of his soldiers home. They left and took the colored folk with them. They are all gone! There is nothing left!"

With that I found myself on my arse in the crushed shell lane trying to gag my tongue back into my mouth while a darkie pirate with a dirk sawed away the bonds at my wrists and Libby sobbed at my neck, damn her, I was trying to breathe.

"Only we are left. We would not go. We are the last men left on Edisto Island, but we *are men* and we are *free*."[20]

The Adventures of Sidney Sawyer
Missouri Yankees

Chapter 16

I never heard a drummer boy rap out the taps to beat Liberty as she fanned the air to a blur on the overturned hull of an ancient jolly boat with sticks improvised from the hickory spokes of a shattered wheel. I never saw a drummer boy to beat the vision of Libby either as she arched her back in the joy of her craft, cotton damp with sweat clinging to her thin figure, silhouetted by the sparks of a driftwood blaze flaming into the heavens. By grapes, it was a command performance fit for any king.

We had reached the seat of the King Wadmalaw's government, a landing called Point of Pines. It had a good dock that reached into the North Edisto River for thirty yards and was graced with a tavern and a pretty chapel with stain-glass windows lit by lantern from within. Next to the chapel was a slave block with a thick iron ring set deep into the stone where Africans were shackled while the bidding commenced. The chapel window above the block was of Moses lugging the Ten Commandments carved in stone. Didn't Father Moses lead a slave insurrection back in Holy times? It seemed a damned odd theme of worship for a civilization built on the backs of slaves. In testimony to the War were the charred ruins of two substantial warehouses, no doubt torched by the Edisto Confederates when they abandoned the island.

As we trooped into Point of Pines we were joined by forty-five or fifty jolly darkies that seemed to be the entire population of King Wadmalaw's realm. They looked at me with surprise and fear. I was, after all, a buckruh, but when the King pounded my back, rolled his cow-eyes in a mock and introduced me to his subjects as a Yankee king, they roared. When he lifted Libby by her narrow waist high above the mob and declared her a Union drummer boy, they howled. I had the good sense to keep mum but Liberty rounded on him, hands on hips like a tiny fury.

"You tease Colonel Sawyer at your peril, you ignorant Gullah field hand. But you tease me an' I'll show you what I can do on your thick head with my drum sticks. Fetch me a drum! Git me a drum and I show you what a drummer boy from the Colored 94th can do."

And so the party moved down past the chapel to a narrow shelving beach where a jolly boat with a shattered bow was turtled. The children of the realm fetched drift wood to built the watch fire into a blaze and chirped like crickets until a buck thrust two oak spokes into Liberty's hands. They shut up in astonishment as she clicked her sticks to tempo, beat a long drum roll on the hull that sounded like Judgment Day, and let loose with a half-dozen commands from "Assembly" to "Advance at the Double Time." And then she did something queer. Libby tapped out the same commands again, but she didn't play them Regular Army-style. She trumped them up or pumped them up and played the beat faster and more lively and… and different! There ain't a word for how she played but she had the children bouncing around in the firelight, the grown ups shouting and clapping fit to move your soul and even the likes of me grinning and pounding my hands together to the rhythm.[v] Banjos and a fiddle appeared, a fat mammy set to a washboard with thimbles on her fingers and two bucks bellied up to the boat with their own sticks. Different measures of the jolly boat made different sounds and the King kept his own time by slapping his vast belly with both hands. It made a damned odd counterpoint to Libby's percussion.

---

[v] There *is* a word for this music– jazz.

As if by magic, jugs appeared and were passed. When I took a pull the raw liquor ripped at my throat from the inside every bit as painfully as King Wadmalaw's paws did from the outside. When a buck tried to take the jug for his turn at the nipple I pushed his mitt away and slugged down another five swallows. Damn the burn– I'd had a bad two weeks and this was mother's milk. The vile n—r shine hit me like a howitzer.

It was the middle of the night, but Libby and I were an event. The impromptu party roared on into the wee hours. Some of the black wenches prancing before the fire in their thin frocks were damned handsome women. On any other night I might have been tempted to tease one of them into the long grass, but not tonight. I had committed murder on three Southern dancers, relieved Daddy Brassard of his front teeth, dunked delicate Hazel into the pickles, fled through an aroused city and almost drowned peeping at Libby's brown behind floating in the Edisto. I was marooned on a deserted beach to be kidnapped by black pirates led by a king from a riverboat minstrel show. I was bullied and bound and drowned again in the bayou with an anchor as a choker, frog marched through a landscape of ghosts, and choked again. Now, I was surrounded by frolicking fugitive slaves and getting wallpapered on raw corn liquor that I wouldn't have inflicted on contraband dogrobbers. And besides all that, Libby was watching and it wouldn't do for her to notice the heroic Ace of Spades waltzing a wench into the bushes for a bounce and tickle. The Edisto bucks might take exception too.

I was sniffling when the jug passed my way again and when another one came my way I was positively weeping. I don't mope into a crying jag often, but do you blame me? Five weeks ago I was happily at home in the bosom of Amy and Auntie. Then that swine Tom Sawyer came home to piss in my pudding. Now, here I was squatting in the sand on a Godforsaken island watching black savages pound wild rhythms on a wrecked boat. For the time being I was safe from the Confederate crushers but my chances of getting out to the blockade fleet and true salvation were slim. My head swam, my eyes ran, my squat collapsed into a sit and my sit degenerated into a drunken recline. An obliging darkie spread a sack over me, wedged another wadded-up sack under my head and I fell into a slumber as a man falls of a cliff.

* * *

"Git up Mr. Colonel sir– Git up! They's here! It de Federal bluejacket Navy men. dey comin' 'round the Point!"

Opening my eyes was a chore. The lids were gummed together and the low morning sun stung my brain like a lance. The fire was wisping smoke, the jolly boat was still turtled in its place, but of the King and his court there was no sign. I would have told the brat to go to the dickens but I was laid out in the sun and there would be no more rest until I dragged my sorry arse into the shade.

"See 'em, Colonel Sawyer sir? We's saved! It's de Navy! Hurrah!" and she ran past the jolly boat to the river waving her arms and shouting like a girl demented.

I flopped myself onto a patch of sweet grass below a live oak and was ready to damn her eyes for a barking goose when it hit me like a slap– the Navy! Who's Navy? By God our ruckus the night before must have alerted Johnny pickets and they were on the way. That must be why every darkie on the premises had vanished into the backcountry. And there was that blasted girl waving like a whore at a troopship to hurry them along. I was up like a scalded hen running for the high bracken along the bayou and let the bastards try and find me. Libby was on her own. The silly trot invited her own disaster waving the Confederate provost to our very spot thinking the Union Navy would just happen to be cruising the North Edisto. If she couldn't tell blockade tars from Rebel raiders than too bad for her. They wouldn't kill her, she was just a girl, but she'd be peeling spuds or warming bellies for the Confederate Army for the rest of the War.

I was in the clear. I'm a fast man over broken country when the bullies are on my heels and thanks to Liberty's foolishness I'd had a good start. I was just breaking stride to let my pounding head catch up to my laboring lungs when not ten feet before me was Jimo-Jim with my tall beaver cocked on his wooly black skull and my own Remington pointed low at my belly.

I was caught between two fires and paralyzed with fear and funk. What did this African scoundrel want with me? Was he going to turn me over to the Rebels for some reward or favor? Wouldn't they take him, too? Was he just going to gun me down in the path, taking his own revenge against any and all buckruh? Oh, I didn't deserve this! Of course I had just abandoned little Libby to her fate, but that was different. I was white and an officer and by God, I deserved better!

Jimo-Jim's ugly face broke into a wide smile and his eyes lit like he'd just won a pie at the picnic. "Colonel buckruh, sir. So glad I found you before the Yankees arrived."

I knew I was understanding Gullah better, but what the hell did he say?

"King Wadmalaw wishes you a good journey and wants to thank both you and Drummer Boy Liberty for a charming evening."

He was still pointing my hog-leg at my belly but it was waving around like a bird on a branch as he talked. I'd have to keep him talking.

"What is it you want from me?"

"Why colonel, I want to give you back your hat."

What the deuce?

"King's orders." And with that he flipped off the tile and held it out to me with a bow.

I've come up with snappier responses.

"Say what?"

"Your hat sir– and your pistol." He held that out to me too and from a sack dragged out my snap-flap holster. "If you were a Carolinian, that would be different. You'd be sunk head-first in the Seabrook, but we are on the same side and we do not steal from our comrades in arms."

"But where did you all go? Why did you clear out? Those *are* Yankees in the boat? Are you hiding from them?"

"Of course we hide from them, Colonel sir. We are free on our island but we are free only as long as we are free of buckruh, all white men, North and South. One side wants to enslave us and drive us back to the fields. The other side wants to civilize us, but still set us back into the fields. It cannot last. One side or the other must win, but until that day we are free."

And they were. Those Gullah Sea Island darkies were free men and women living under their own king in their own land and eating the daily bread earned by their own sweat. They owed neither loyalty nor labor to any other men. Around their island a vast war thundered and flamed but in this tiny place, isolated by marsh, bayou and ocean, for this time, these few score colored folk had found their kingdom. It was exactly like Liberty's song…

De massa run, Ha-Ha! De darkie stay, Ho-Ho!
It must be now de Kingdom Coming,
an' de year of Jubilo!

I belted my Remington on my hip but paused when I made to perch the beaver back on my head. What the hell, I handed it to Jimo-Jim with a bow of my own. He was a gentleman after all, if only of the Gullah variety. He grinned like a coot and jammed the tall hat back on his crown. After all, it wasn't my hat. It belonged to young Marse Wintworth of Charleston, currently serving in the CSA. I wouldn't need it anymore. Once I was back in the Army I'd never take off my Jeff Davis again.

I sprinted back to the beach and almost got shot for my enthusiasm. The cutter was only fifty yards from the beach with the bluejackets rowing like the Yale crew and I came charging from the bracken dressed as a Carolina dandy with a pistol holstered at my belly. An officer in the bow barked a command, three marines snapped carbines to their shoulders and I dug in my heels, tossed up my hands and screamed in a falsetto note I didn't know I could reach.

"Union! I'm Union! I'm Union, you silly bastards!"

I believe they might have shot anyway if Libby hadn't sprung on me and clung with arms and legs. At another barked order the carbines returned to port arms as the boat ground ashore before the wreckage of the jolly boat. I almost wept with relief. Stitched to the ribbons around the straw hats of the tars manning the oars was '*USS Pocahontas*.'

* * *

I was under guard and under suspicion when I was presented to the Captain of the *Pocahontas*, a heart of oak sailor man with the dramatic name of Hazzard. I didn't remember him or any of his crew from my brief voyage from Hilton Head to Morris Island and none of them remembered me. It was only three weeks ago, but I had my head together with Sergeant Smith and we were out of the way forward of the port battery. I identified myself and explained my situation but my tale was so improbable that it actually had me blushing. I knew it would all be straightened out in time, but I didn't want to spend that time in irons cooped in the rope-locker while the *Pocahontas* spent the next month patrolling the coast looking for blockade runners and Rebel raiders.

"Why, I'm Colonel Sawyer, 94th USCT. Damn glad you happened along. I was only a step ahead of the Carolina provost.

"Not at all! I ain't an escaped prisoner. I'm a spy.

"Not a Rebel spy, damn it! Sent by Gillmore to see what's what in Charleston.

"It's a *Missouri* accent and what's wrong with that? Missouri's still in the Union and my regiment's the Missouri 94th.

"Her? She's my servant. Tell these gentlemen, Libby.

"Drummer boy? Ha-ha, where do these darkies get such notions? I took *her* along (harsh glare at Liberty) for local color, you see. Pappy's in the regiment.

"How came I to Edisto? Why, we took the train."

This wasn't working. Captain Hazzard stood before me with a face like a Baptist in a brewery. The jacks were elbowing each other and grinning beneath their straw bonnets, and the bo'sun and a skinny Lieutenant were looking at me like I was something scrapped off a shoe.

"See here, men, I'm Colonel Sidney Sawyer. Really! In the Army everyone knows me, Grant, Sherman, Little Mac, Halleck... even Stanton... and Lincoln." I was babbling like a biddy in the cooking sherry but my head was pounding from last night's rotgut and my throat was raw from abuse. I'd had precious little sleep since Middlesex Shanghaied me to spy on Charleston and the thought of Navy irons bruising my wrists and ankles had me shaking with palsy.

"Everyone in the Army has heard of me. I'm the Ace of Spades... *Hearts*! Oh God!"

I was cooked and knew it. but then the skinny Lieutenant spoke up.

"I know him. Or of him."

I almost swooned.

Hazzard lifted a bushy eyebrow, "You know this... gentleman, Lieutenant Mahan?"

And he did. It was one of those incredible coincidences that could only happen in the middle of a War.

"My father, Colonel Mahan, who holds the Engineering Chair at West Point knows this gentleman well. He is a bully and a duelist. I was away at Annapolis at the time, but I know of the affair. He crippled a fine young cadet in a duel– a duel he provoked. I believe it had something to do with his love of Negroes." And he shifted his arrogant gaze from me to Libby.

Of course! This young officer was his father's son, the same thin face and bland eyes– the same bored voice. By gizzards and guts, he *would* know of me. I had used his daddy's own guns in the duel with Cadet Brassard back in '56. They were .50 smooth bores, a French-made matching set with checkered grips. Papa had provided them for the duel hoping that they'd be used to slaughter *me*! The ball I put through Brassard's face was the foundation for all my future credit in the Army.

I was too fagged to stop him when he pulled my filthy blouse apart to show the scar on my breast from Brassard's own pistol ball. It would have killed me if I hadn't rigged the duel like the bluejackets rigged the fore and aft masts of the *Pocahontas*.

"There is your Ace of Hearts, gentlemen," Mahan sneered, "and the Army may have him back."[21]

The Adventures of Sidney Sawyer
Missouri Yankees

Chapter 17

It was Liberty's performance on the jolly boat that had brought the Navy to Point of Pines. Sailorman or not, Hazzard recognized Army drumming when he heard it. The ship was patrolling close off the point of Botany Bay Beach, which is where the Little Edisto joins the ocean. The booming of the big sticks on the boat could be heard all the way to the Atlantic. Hazzard waited for dawn and sent a cutter to investigate. Damn lucky for me he was so nosy! After a quick meal of Navy rations that included a dollop of watery rum, I demanded a decent set of duds for Libby. Her calico was shredded to the point of indecency. I didn't mind looking, but the jacks were tripping over their swabs and stubbing toes on the bow chaser. A colored powder monkey fetched her a set of Navy ducks with a blue jumper.[w] When she appeared on deck, tiny in her baggy togs beneath a bonny straw bonnet with its *Pocahontas* ribbon, she was a dress-up doll come to life. Amy and Auntie would have eaten her with a spoon. I didn't. I found a coil of hemp, curled up on it like a cat, and was dead to the world. While I slept like puss in Nanny's yarn, Captain Hazzard piled on steam. He set the top hamper, driving the *Pocahontas* to her rails to deposit his unexpected supercargo back into Army country as fast

---

[w] Powder monkeys were boys, some as young as twelve, who fetched gunpowder from the magazines to the guns during naval combat. They also served at any task afloat from cabin boy to objects of sodomy.

as ever he could without blowing the boiler. He didn't seem to like me.

Thank God for the grub, the grog and the nap. I was a going concern, when just after noon the cutter fetched me back to Light House Point on Morris Island. And thank God for Liberty's new duds. The sailors *knew* she was a girl, but in that rig she could pass in the Army as a boy, at least until her pa got her… *him* back into *his* regimental blues. No more Libby. It was drummer boy Liberty Smith again, and no error.

If you plunder Army Archives for a written report of my shenanigans in Charleston as Gillmore's spy, you won't find them. I reported to headquarters straight away to give my report and snitch on that fat traitor Major Melrose Middlesex. I'd had enough time to block out the particulars in my mind and I'd deliver it in my usual Sawyer style. I'd inflate the little actual information I had gathered and give a modest, "oh shucks" to the dicey parts. You know me.

'Seems the city is low on wine, medicals and taffeta for the ladies. Rebs won't cry uncle over that. The bombardment is just a bagatelle. We're gonna have to get serious and level the city. Wrath of God, and a measure of brimstone ought a' do the trick. Went to a church hop to sniff the wind. Some Confederate rascals got nosy and cornered me in the pantry. Killed three of them– hand-to-hand– bad business. Had to rough up an old gentleman and abuse a lady though. That will tell on my conscience. Oh, and by the way, it seems we have a traitor here in our bosom. Fat rascal, selling medicals, sundries and information to the Johnny's. Why, there he is now! Middlesex, ain't it? Fetch a rope, dig a grave, ready a coffin, or better yet a piano case. Hang the scoundrel straight away, or shoot him, or let me shoot him. Am I too late for lunch? The intelligence corps is hungry work.'

Aye, I had my story straight and memorized. It would fetch me credit as a hero who don't count the cost and fetch Middlesex straight to a rope. Well, that's what I reckoned.

When the cutter touched the dock I sent drummer boy Liberty straight back to daddy. She'd only get in my way and I was a man on a mission. The cutter backed away from the landing without salute or farewell, spiteful swabs, and I set off for Gillmore's headquarters with the stride of the just.

Gillmore wasn't there and neither were half of the staff loafers that hang about any army command post like ticks. A headquarters battalion sergeant sat me down under a corporal's guard to cool my heels until I could be vouched for. After all, I was dressed as a Carolina dandy. I watched the increasing activity and it told me something was up with the Army– something big. If I'd have known what it was I would have run the guard and swum back to the *Pocahontas*.

The afternoon was warm, the breeze was a lullaby, the ache behind my eyes had receded to a bother and a soldier knows when to catch a nap. I was awakened with a gentle hand on my shoulder and a soft voice in my ear.

"Colonel Sawyer, how good to see you safely home. I thought you would be dead by now. Welcome!"

I opened my eyes and there before me, blotting out the sun, was the bulk of Major Melrose Middlesex. He was smiling like a Dutch uncle, but there was nothing welcoming in his eyes that held all the emotion of a carp. I made to spring away but his gentle hand turned into a talon that dug fingers deep into my collarbone and the pain brought my hind quarters back to the bench and tears to my eyes. The corporal's guard was gone.

"Let me go, you fat swine! I know your game. You're a traitor and a spy for the Rebels and a villain and I'm gonna see you hang."

"You will see *me* hang? How interesting. Tell me more, Sawyer."

"I met your chum Brassard in Charleston! You didn't count on that now, did you? I found out that you run medicals through the blockade to the Rebels. And that ain't all! You sell 'em information– intelligence on your own army. And you informed on me! Me, damn your eyes!"

Gillmore and the staff had returned while I was napping. There were enough fellows within sight and earshot that I knew Middlesex couldn't simply throttle me and say I tripped. That gave me the sand to let my natural insolence boil out. "They knew I was coming. The whole city was aroused. You didn't expect to see me again, did you, you bloated bastard? You traitorous dog!"

Middlesex was as cool as a bull gator and just as ugly. "Yes, nothing is worse than a traitorous dog. *All* of them should hang"

The malevolent confidence in his voice kept me on the bench and stilled the shout in my throat that was set to bring the guard.

"I told you before you fool, that I had contacts up and down the rivers from Cincinnati to Memphis. I do business with the Adara brothers, Asher and Aharon, and with Mr. Jessie Grant too. I know of *your* treason, chapter and verse!"

"It weren't treason, neither!" By God, the brute had me! "It was business, plain and simple. I was buying cotton– legal cotton. And Jessie Grant, the general's own papa, was my partner. General Grant himself will stick up for me. And where's this treason then?"

I was cooked. The previous winter Jessie Grant and the Temples, father and son, had suckered me into a scheme to buy Rebel cotton and sell it to New England mills for a dollar a pound. The reptilian Adara brothers of Cincinnati were at the center of the cabal. Cotton was white gold and Yankee moneybags like, well, like Middlesex and his clan, could make a fellow rich with the booty from just one riverboat loaded with the snowy stuff. My little expedition to Memphis was a fiasco that damned near got me killed but it was nothing like the raw treason of Major Middlesex.

"Where's the treason, Colonel Sawyer? Are you not the commander of the 94th Missouri? I have heard however, that you rode with another Missouri regiment last winter. Not as its Colonel– that would be Colonel Robert McCulloch, and you were only a simple trooper. The regiment was the 2nd Missouri."

My jaw sagged open and my face must have bleached to ivory.

"But isn't the 2nd Missouri a Confederate regiment? Isn't riding with the enemy against your own Army– treason?"

Middlesex leaned close enough that I smelled the leeks on his wet breath. "Who is the treasonous dog now, Private Samuel Clemens?"

I was dead! I'd hang for sure. Last Christmas in General Earl Van Dorn's infamous raid on Holly Springs, I was captured with a trainload of contraband cotton. To save my skin I joined the Johnny cavalry with the nom de guerre of Sam Clemens. How did the swine know? Could he prove it? Of course he could. It was true!

"And Sawyer, I want my watch back."[x]

* * *

My report to Gillmore was short, sweet and verbal. Nothing was written down to bite me on the arse later and nothing was mentioned about slaughtering Southern dancers, swimming with female drummer boys, black kingdoms in the Sea Islands, treasonous staff majors or turncoat commanders of colored regiments.

I was back with the 94th before evening mess and welcomed like Lazarus stumbling from his tomb. The whole regiment knew I'd been to Charleston, so much for

---

[x] For the scandalous story of Sawyer's time in the Confederate cavalry refer to the fourth packet of his memoirs published as *The Adventures of Sidney Sawyer: The Father of Waters*.

any *secret* agent nonsense, and nobody expected to see me again until Liberty skipped into the bivouac looking like Cracker Jack to herald our return. It was handshakes, backslaps, and pass the bottle as Gould Florissant and Major LaBadie held court in the command tent. The white company officers filed in to share the booze and have a squint at the 94th's own Lazarus raised from the dead. Colored troops gathered outside to have a peep at me like I was the Second Coming.

Despite demands for all the daring details I kept the story of our excursion into Charleston to the bare essentials. Navy whaleboat to Wappo Creek, Ashley Bridge to the city, two days of snooping, the C&S night train to Jacksonboro, skiff to Edisto Island and the *Pocahontas* home. I'd have dearly loved to spice it up with the tale of our battle among the pickles and our little beach party with King Wadmalaw, but that was no soap. It would open up cans of worms I'd rather keep closed, and LaBadie would probably stitch a pickle on the regimental flag. About my neck were bruises from rope and Wadmalaw's big mitts and the officers could draw their own conclusions from my natty civilian duds with the knees out and the stitching popped at the shoulders. And there was one more thing that would set the regiment's curiosity to a boil.

I snapped at a corporal standing easy guard at the tent, "Fetch Sergeant Smith, and be quick about it!"

I knew he would be quick, I could see him standing with the troops, not fifty feet away. He came on at the double, crashed his boots to attention and flung me a great salute.

"Sergeant Major Smith, reporting as ordered, Colonel."

He was positively beaming until I looked past him in surprise, "What's this Sergeant Major? Where's Sergeant Smith? I'm not gone a week and the regiment falls to rats and mice. Corporal!" I boomed. "Fetch me

Sergeant Smith– Sergeant Liberty Smith, and no error this time."

The officers looked at me like I'd gone daft and the expression on Smitty's face was downright comical. Liberty ran in and thank God she was back in her usual baggy drummer boy get-up.

"Soldier, you're out of uniform. Sergeant *Major* Smith, see to it that *Sergeant* Smith sews two more stripes on… (sweet Fanny Adams, I almost said 'her') his sleeves by supper."

And I reached out to shake Liberty's little hand just as if she were a man and just as if she was white. It was a proud and happy regiment that settled down to their coffee, beans and biscuits that Friday night of September 4, 1863. They were prouder and happier when orders arrived from General Gillmore in the morning that we would have the honor to lead the final assault on Fort Wagner in the predawn gloom of the seventh. That hound Middlesex was at his mischief again.[y]

* * *

It was the assault on the rifle pits all over again, but this time without spades strapped to backs and with only half the chance of victory, or even survival. By God, this had been tried before, twice, with nothing to show but the moldering corpses dug up by the sappers of the Grand Guard as they inched the parallels ever closer to the savaged walls of the fort.

The 94th duck-walked into the rifle pits in the middle of the line. These trenches were dug immediately in front of our fifth and final parallel. We were less than one hundred yards from the fort and could feel the Rebel

---

[y] This was not unheard of. Drummer boy John Clem became the youngest sergeant in American history for heroics in the Battle of Chickamauga. He retired as a major general in 1915 as the longest serving Civil War veteran.

ramparts loom above us in the night. The stars were blotted out by the flashes of thousands of shells crashing into and bursting above the battery. The bombardment had begun over forty hours before. It pounded all through the night of the fifth, all through the next day and continued through this night as the regiment wound its way through the trenches. We reached our jumping off point at midnight. The bombardment seemed to redouble as I squinted at the hands of my borrowed watch. There were hundreds of officers, ashore and afloat, minding their timepieces tonight. General Gillmore's batteries of artillery and Regua guns, and Commodore Dahlgren's ironclads would cease-fire at the same instant. That instant would be my moment of glory. I'd jam a whistle between my lips and blow the signal for the men of the 94th to charge from the trench, roar their battle cry, hoist their scaling ladders and do or die. They'd probably die. The Rebels knew we were coming. The instant the bombardment stopped they'd swarm out of their bombproofs like wasps to man the rifle steps and serve their preshotted guns. The glare of the calcium lamps would blind them in the first moments, but would silhouette us all the way to the walls. We were flanked by white regiments, but the 94th would be first onto the east parapet where the guns would rake us from front and left like rats in a ditch.

I'd taken my precautions, private's uniform and mud-smeared face, but it would be one hundred yards of hell, and then up the ladders in the face of Confederate killers driven to white heat by the sight of the regiment's black faces, and then into the battery where it would be hand-to-hand and no hope of quarter. Baddy was grinning on my left with drawn saber and colt. Smitty stood silent to my right with his uniform as immaculate as the Queen's own guard. The men up and down the trench were wound like springs and stripped for the fight– no packs or rations, only extra rounds and bellies warm with Army rum. And then the hands of my watch raced to the fatal hour, the bombardment from the monitors ended with a final avalanche of sound, the Army's guns dwindled to the ripping crash of the Regua batteries, whistles sounded from right and left and in the terrible glare the Colored 94th was out of the trenches with a roar!

"Missouri Yankees and the Ace of Spades!"

It takes but half minute for a body of men to run a hundred yards over blasted earth through deep sand. In that thirty seconds I died the thousand deaths of a coward, blithered my prayers and almost had my knees give out when Baddy measured his length in the sea grass. His pistol and sword flew from his hands before his body and I stumbled with gorge filling my throat. It had started! The Rebel defenders had swarmed to their fire steps and the slaughter would begin. These colored heroes would be swept into hell like their brothers from the 54th Massachusetts last July. But Baddy sprung up like an India rubber ball and with a curse and a laugh snatched his weapons from the sand and sprinted toward the parapet like a man possessed. The men threw their ladders at the ramparts, screamed like animals and scrambled up like apes. A roar of victory filled the night and in the harsh calcium light the green regimental flag waved from the redoubt. As a dozen strong hands pushed my arse up a ladder our banner was joined by the Stars and Stripes. The fort was ours!

The soldiers of the 94th USCT capered, danced, sang and wept. Battery Wagner was abandoned. During the bombardment Beauregard had evacuated the fort, taking with him powder, rations and his own damn flag. Our victory won us the shattered ruin of a hollow fort. Its guns were spiked, sitting askew on blasted carriages. The walls were mounds of unrecognizable rubble. The air stank of water fouled by the putrefying bodies of the 54th Massachusetts whose stench had seeped through the sand to poison the well.

The Adventures of Sidney Sawyer
Missouri Yankees

Part III: Chattanooga

Chapter 18

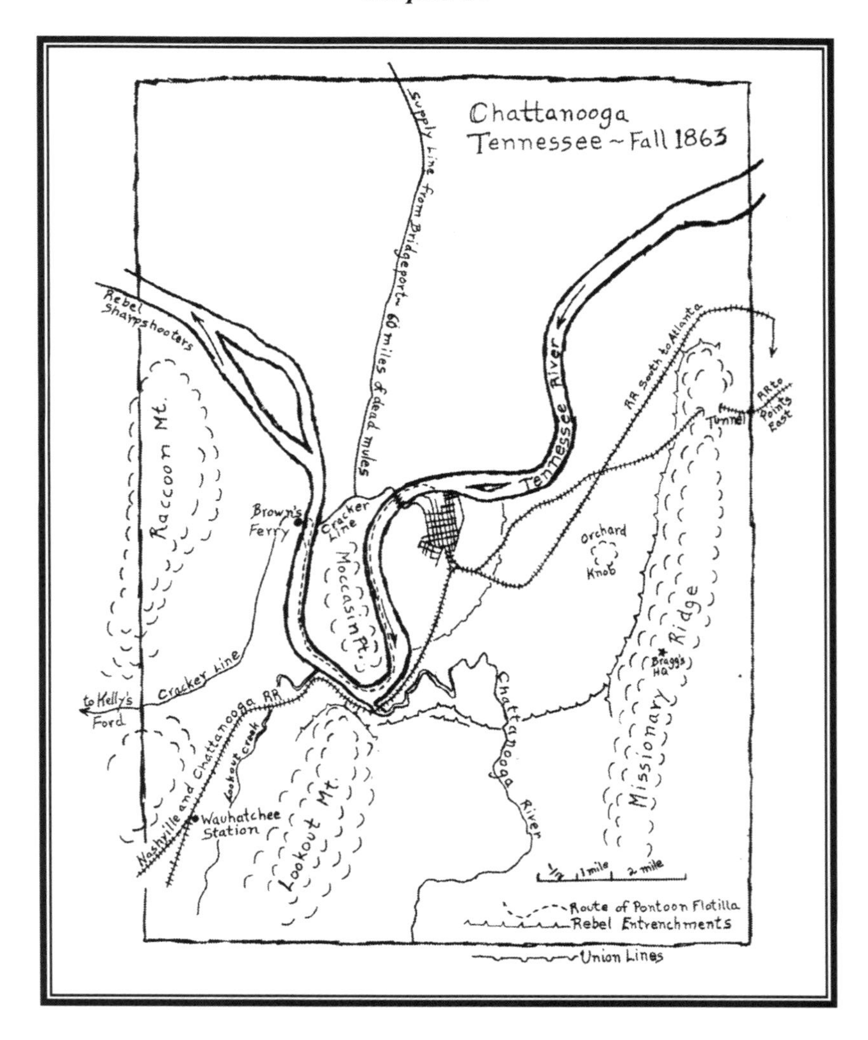

Sweet dreams and dripping eyebrows, it's Stanton! And he ain't weeping now! And what the hell was he doing in Indianapolis, storming up the platform after Grant's train that a yard-monkey had just flagged to a halt as it began pulling away from the station? The last time I'd seen the grim bargee was in Washington when he was dripping tears into his beard after sending a sleepy soldier boy to the firing squad for dozing on duty. That was the day the swine had sent me to Carolina with a 'Glory, Glory Hallelujah' to command the Colored 94th! I was so surprised to see the Secretary of War himself in the grubby Hoosier capital that I made a blunder a pie-eating recruit would have avoided. I let him see me! That blunder set me on a starving horse through sixty miles of dead mules and squatting in a pontoon drifting past batteries of Confederate killers as surely as if the hairy warlord had placed me there with his own hand. I live and learn, but sometimes the lessons are hard.

I was on my way from Charleston to Grant's command at Vicksburg, and good riddance to my regiment of Colored hero-worshippers. With Battery Wagner taken it finally became obvious to even engineers like Gillmore that taking the bloody fort hadn't been worth the effort. Now he could sight his batteries of smooth-bore Dahlgrens directly at Fort Sumter and his big Parrot rifles could punish Charleston at will. So what? All the Dahlgrens could do was to make the rubble that *had been* Fort Sumter bounce. By day the shot would shred the Rebel ensign and by night the Johnnys would stitch it up again and haul it back up the staff. As for Charleston surrendering to bombardment– well, you could ask Squire Radcliffe and Miss Molly about that. In the end the city was burned to rubble with never a thought of surrender. It wasn't until Sherman's frolicking bummers cut Charleston off at the roots that the city fell, but that wasn't until '65.

Regiments of battle-tested darkies were no longer needed in the Department of the South. That made it a dandy time for ambitious staff colonels to transfer back to the one general that would make promotion a buckled cinch– U.S. Grant. I reckoned that Grant's success would make him safe. Generals that lead divisions and even corps could, now and again, blunder into harm's way. And hadn't I seen that often enough? I had been there in Maryland exactly one year ago when a trio of generals, Reno, Mansfield and Rodman were blown to glory.[z] Wouldn't a general of the *Armies* simply *have* to stay safely out of range? Grant in glory would tend to telegraph flimsies, logistics, maps and nosy politicians– ain't that what General Halleck did? Any staff rabble that hitched themselves to Grant's wagon would dine on chicken and gravy, sleep in feather beds and be safe as houses for the duration. I was off to find Grant– but not too fast. I'd take my sweet time reporting for duty– maybe stopping off home to freshen my Amy, bounce my boy Ranty on my knee and fatten up on Auntie Polly's home cooking. I'd take a route far to the north of any Confederate mischief, up through Pennsylvania and Ohio, and maybe through Indianapolis.

I left my command of loyal darkies six weeks after our assault on the abandoned works of Battery Wagner and a damned uncomfortable six weeks it was. When dawn broke over the shattered works of Wagner, above the stench of the rotting black warriors of the 54th Massachusetts, the black warriors of the 94th Missouri could only smell glory as they capered through the Rebel ramparts and bomb-proofs. They dragged anything and everything that could be considered a trophy of war into the rising sun and waved their green regimental banner along with abandoned Confederate rags and relics. Across the water the monitor fleet steamed close ashore, decks

---

[z] General Jesse Reno (a Nevada city bears his name) died at the Battle of South Mountain. Killed at Antietam, General Joseph Mansfield's name lives on in the Middletown Mansfield's baseball team. Isaac Peace Rodman, also killed at Antietam, is all but forgotten. His grave lies neglected beside a gravel pit.

packed with cheering bluejackets and every horn, whistle and siren was blaring Billy-be-damned in salute. The white troops cheered us to a turn and we cheered them back three times three. Aye, it was glory in a sandpit and it lasted until noon. Then we were ordered to occupy Cummings Point a mile and a half farther up the beach and off we went at a trot. The Point was the very northern tip of Morris Island where the Rebels had a stout battery that supported Fort Sumter across the narrow channel. They had abandoned it along with Wagner. Now General Gillmore was in a lather to mount our own battery there to have a slash at Sumter. The 94th was Johnny-on-the-spot and was sent to the soldier's work of filling sandbags. It was fatigue work and we were eight hundred handy field hands. It was the pick and shovel for the regiment from then on. Heaven knows there was no more fighting to do.[a]

While the regiment dug, I played every card in my deck to get the hell out of the African Army and back with Grant. I wrote my congressman, both of Missouri's senators and every other politico and wirepuller in the register. I wrote to Lincoln's secretaries John Hay and John Nicolay. I pestered Generals Gillmore, Halleck, Sherman and Jimmy McPherson. I did *not* go whining to Grant himself, however. He hates a shirker and wouldn't have given a goober pea anyway. I even sent a pathetic epistle to Old Man Temple, and that's what did the trick. As my pal Alfred Temple's daddy taught us when we were brats, 'money speaks– bullshit squeaks.' In my present circumstance there was no way for me to steer Army contracts, jobs and freight to Temple and Son. In the first two years of the War my position on staff allowed me to funnel a king's ransom in government plunder through Temple boats, wharves and warehouses. The old scoundrel made a fortune and the loot he kicked back to me put the Sawyers in the ranks of the local gentry. He and Alfred

---

[a] This was Battery Gregg. The Federals rechristened it Fort Putman.

wanted me back on staff as badly as I did. He pulled a few strings, spread around some cash and my orders came through just in time to save my giblets.

* * *

Except for the boredom of garrison life you may wonder from what direction my giblets could be threatened. It wasn't from any possible Confederate action. There was no way they could come to grips with us anymore than we could engage them. Other than long-range bombardment by the Army and blockade duty by the Navy, the War had passed Charleston Harbor by. And that fat traitor Major Melrose Middlesex was gone, and good riddance. With the campaign winding down his prospects for treachery and larceny narrowed so that within the week he was gone for greener pastures. With his connections, that swine had no problem ginning up a transfer.

So where was my peril? It was in the person of a certain drummer boy with wonderfully budded breasts, an arse that would start a brawl at a Baptist camp meeting and the face of an angel. She– *he* was modestly disguised again in baggy britches and blouse, but I knew that under the Union blue was prime mutton. And the girl– boy had a crush on me that was plain to any trooper in headquarters company, including her daddy. Darkie or not, Sergeant Smith senior wouldn't truck any shenanigans with Sergeant Smith the junior. And if I didn't look sharp young Sergeant Smith's mooning cow-eyes could get me pegged as a blasted sodomite with the officers. Now, that would be a dandy addendum to my reputation along with n—r lover and the Ace of Spades.

And Liberty was always there, *right there*. Drummer boys were exempt from the pick and shovel brigades of the soldiers of the line. They were more like cabin boys on ships at sea, running errands, fetching grub and gear and making nuisances of themselves. And Liberty *was* a nuisance. With perfect timing, she'd pop up with my morning coffee when I was yanking on my summer cotton underbritches. I couldn't toss her out. She was one of the boys– wasn't she? This was the Army– wasn't it? No modest privacy here– was there? As often as not Baddy or one of the company captains was present seeing to some detail of regimental beeswax and they'd snort in their rio when my knickers grew a bulge as I turned away hopping into my trousers. She'd deliver my breakfast, dip her fingers into my oatmeal as bold as a pantry cat and suck her fingers one by one with a look that had me grinding my molars. She'd stand behind her pappy licking her lips while he reported on the trivia of blue mass or the regimental dairy goats.

Aye, the lass had her cap set for Colonel Sidney and no error. Other than her pappy, I was the only soul outside of Girardeau, Missouri who knew her true gender. It must have been the feast on Edisto Beach before King Wadmalaw and his apes interrupted our randy amusements by the fire. She'd seen the goods when I was stripped down in the surf casting for our dinner and she wasn't *that* drunk when I was pawing under her calico before we were rudely interrupted. And she didn't know that I was ready to toss her to the sharks when I reckoned the Confederate Navy was landing at Point of Pines. To Liberty Smith, I was an abused hero, a champion of her race, a compassionate commander, and my shoulders and whiskers didn't hurt my cause. But I couldn't simply clear the staff rabble from my tent, strip her down and mount her with a chorus of Boots and Saddles. There was more traffic through regimental headquarters than through Washington Junction. Her daddy was always about, knew the score and watched me like a bulldog. And she was colored and a boy to boot. It would be all over the Army in a flash that the Ace of Hearts was a pillow fighter. It would be the Queen of Hearts and call me Nancy!

The regiment labored through September, filling in the parallels from the month's long siege. They barged the artillery from the old lines to the new batteries at Cummings Point. They dug bombproofs and built parapets and extended piers. They sweated through the month at honest soldier labor while I sweated through the month trying to hold my dirty water. Ah, the heavy mantle of command. And then on the first cool evening since May I decided to take a stroll.

The Swamp Angel was long gone, but the boardwalk Colonel Serrell built to the Marsh Battery was still there and I reckoned it would be a pleasant walk. I stuffed a hat with cheroots, topped off a pint with the good stuff, and reckoned a little solitude in the marsh at sunset would be grand. Us soldiers are a sentimental lot. It was damn pleasant strolling above the swamp. Great herons ignored me as they stood still as statues, necks cocked and tense, waiting for movement below the stagnant water that would signal suppertime. Red-winged blackbirds perched on every cattail that grew above the black grasses that waved in the fresh breeze from the Atlantic. I took a swig of the good stuff and the sweet nectar of the booze drew a pair of hummingbirds. They orbited my head and the low sun turned their ruby throats into a dazzle of scarlet. After the stench of the bivouac the clean air smelled of salt and honeysuckle and I didn't reckon that this Carolina evening could get finer– and then it did.

Sergeant Liberty Smith was waiting for me at the abandoned battery. But it wasn't Liberty this evening. It was Libby. She was in her white duck sailor's bellbottoms from our short voyage on the *Pocahontas*, with her thin cotton jumper unlaced down to her belly. Her breasts were covered, but barely and she stood next to a satchel, barefoot and bare-headed, with hand on hip and lip in a pout and how anyone could ever mistake this panther of a woman for a boy was beyond credit. She had seen me fumbling for my cigars and topping my flask. That was all she needed to reason that I was off for a walk– clever wench. How she divined my destination was beyond me and she must have hustled to beat me to the boardwalk.

But there she was, looking like a soldier boy's dream in the only place on Morris Island where a man and a maid could hope to be alone.

Our courting had been accomplished in Charleston. We wooed on Edisto Beach and all questions were asked and answered one fine morning when she fetched me the post. For a change the tent was empty of the usual rabble that infest any headquarters, and at the same second we both glanced towards the tent flap, and for the same reason. In that second she was in my arms and our hands were exploring each other like Marco Polo on bark juice. I ran my hand along the inside of her thigh up to her whisker-biscuit and gave my fingers a wiggle. Shame on me for a lecher, but the girl moaned and leaned into it. We were brought up short when some lout tripped over the tent's guide rope and we pulled apart before we were caught out, but *there* was my peril. You know me! I can't help myself. Liberty would be exposed as a boy and expelled from the only home she had. Sergeant Major Smith would kill me, and hang for it. If he didn't kill me, Amy would. The scandal would break Aunt Polly's heart. The 94th would be a laughing stock. Colored soldiers everywhere would be disgraced. Tom Sawyer would giggle with glee. But I'd do it, and we'd get caught out sure as gravy on grits. The regiment has no secrets. You know me!

Now, here *we* were, alone in the one place where we *couldn't* get caught. And there *she* was standing besides the burst Swamp Angel, which rested upside-down on the parapet's 13,000 sandbags, looking lovely and innocent and unsure of what to do now that she was ready to do it. Well, I knew what to do! I've perfected my technique on a score of women, from farmer's daughters to dowager aunts. I call it the Sawyer sally. Walk up to the lass as bold as a Polack goose, no time for chit-chat– left hand on her right arse cheek and pull her close– right paw to the left bosom and bounce it like you mean it– lips pressed tight to her lips to quiet any untimely protestations and to get immediate response on their level of enthusiasm. This is a dandy way to start a romance and it positions a hand, both fore and aft, to deal with any buttons, laces, hooks or ribbons that may hinder groping from that direction. With Libby I didn't have to bother over much with buttons or hooks or level of enthusiasm. The way she chewed my lips and pulled my face to her with both hands told me all I needed to know. A tug on the drawstring and her bellbottoms slid down without a whisper. The neck of her jumper was so wide I slid it off her shoulders and she stepped out of it as she stepped out of her bellbottoms.

What a sight and what a woman! The setting sun set her black skin to shine like copper, her teeth showed white enough to startle and her eyes sparkled with light. I was over dressed and kicked out of my boots and britches in the time it takes to tell. I was in a hurry, but long practice makes for good habits and I always place my boots together and my duds piled neatly on top. Most of my fornication is the unlicensed variety and it don't do to be searching for your boots under beds and cupboards when husbands or daddies are pounding up the stairs with pistols and grudges. But there were no busybodies to interfere with our pleasures that twilight at the Marsh Battery– were there?

I also learned as a lad not to be a hound, especially with an eager but untutored virgin. Rutting like a bull in season will make a shambles out of what should be a tender moment. Acting beastly could put any girl off the pleasures of lovemaking for a lifetime, which would scotch any chance for a remount– and it's just bad manners. Also, it ain't as much fun as drawing the act out for as long as possible to milk all the joy out of the moment as possible. And it's supposed to be a joy, complete with laughter, breaks to pull a swill from a handy flask, tutorials to the novice on the many naughty fine points of fornication, and lies about love, tomorrow and destiny.

We began with Libby aloft to let her find her own seat at her own speed. An aroused Sidney is a sight to awe most women but with only a soft "Ooohh" the walls were breached and Libby was all over me like a– well, like a panther. My last labor in the vineyards of Venus was with Missy Ruth and when she took topside her bulk almost dislocated my hips. Libby was as light as a dove and I could spin her every which way and back as the moment took us. Her satchel was packed with her drummer boy uniform and we spread out our jackets on the rough planks and thundered away stern wheel fashion. For a time I hoisted her by her arse cheeks and strutted her around the battery horse artillery style. By grapes, but the girl was a dandy tumble, tiny, but strong, jolly and eager but willing to let Colonel Sidney command the maneuvers. I sing when I'm happy and I got through three verses of "Drink Puppy Drink" before we finished with the sunset painting fire across the western sky, a sand bag under her bottom for elevation and my boots back on my feet for better traction on the pine boards.

It was a cool night, but not cold and we lay naked on our jackets as the night closed around us. We laughed, recalling how we hoodwinked the guard at Ashley Bridge with our ridiculous pickle story. She poked me in the ribs when I reminded her how she almost drowned me in the Edisto when I popped up beside her after my underwater ogle. She giggled remembering the sight of my face when I realized that he was a she back in Charleston. We cuddled like turtledoves at the memory of our picnic on the beach with the moon shining over the ocean breakers and the fire and the liquor warming our hearts. (I'm damn glad she remembered it *that* way!) And then our lips were together and Little Sidney was rallying for another round but as we pulled back to gaze in each other's eyes a feeling of danger swept over me like a wave of cold water.

She loved me. Even in the gloaming light I could see it in her eyes as clear as gin. Oh, we could do the capital deed here, tonight and who was to know, but now that we had at each other, we'd want to keep having at each other and we'd be caught out as sure as lard on toast. And love? I was fond of the child– damn fond, but I was in love with my Amy. A soldier's life is a lonely one and what the wife don't know won't hurt *me*– but love? I've made it the law of a lifetime to fuel my lust with liquor, lies or cash on the barrel– but love? I want my dollies to like me, not love me. Love can tie a noose tight enough to pitch a hangman into a fit of envy. It complicates the simple, spoils the game and ruins the fun. But the look of love in Libby's beautiful brown eyes wasn't the only thing that washed me with ice water and sent Little Sidney back into his thimble. There was also the soft sound of muffled oars and the low tone of a Southern voice coming from the bayou.

"There she be, boys. Tis the infernal Federal fire battery. No guns unless it's your life. Kill if you must, but quiet like, with the blade. It's prisoners we're after, not blood. We take only officers."

* * *

As the Rebels swarmed from their bateau on the west side of the battery, we scrambled for our traps and rolled under the railing into the marsh on the east side. They left a corporal's guard to watch the boat and we were left in the slimy gumbo of the swamp for the four hours it took the swine to return. The Rebel raiders arrived on the same bayou that Serrell used to barge the Swamp Angel and its carriage to the Marsh Battery. They were looking to snag an officer to fetch back to Beauregard. They'd sweat Federal intentions from the poor bastard and then send him to Libby Prison in Richmond to rot out the rest of the War with a thousand other unlucky Union officers. God help me if they ever took a peek under the boardwalk. They'd find a naked Yankee colonel, covered with leeches and skeeter bites, and a drummer boy brazenly out of uniform. If I was reckless in the face of danger, which I ain't, I might have tried to sneak away to spread the alarm. I may have attempted to overcome the guard, there were only two of the brutes, and be a hero. I could save the day, but of course I only saved my arse.

About midnight, the raiders returned in a sulk, empty-handed. Well, not exactly. They weren't empty-footed. When they arrived they soft-footed up the boardwalk in bare feet. There was only one set of booted feet and they must have belonged to the officer in charge. Now, as they piled into their boat the thump and squeaking of new Yankee booties drowned out the marsh peepers. The shirking scoundrels were ordered by their chiefs to fetch Federal brass and they settled for Union brogans while we shriveled in the swamp. We waited another ten minutes in the chilly water for whoever might be chasing them but there was no one. We crawled from the gumbo looking like drowned dogs and spent the next half hour feeling for leeches and dousing them with splashes of the good stuff to pry them off. Leeches don't seem to like whiskey as much as I do and after the booze stung their slimy hides they came off without leaving their jaws in our skins. If I was prone to have any randy thoughts inspecting Libby's bottom for the loathsome little bloodsuckers, the leech she pried from my tally-whacker killed the notion.

The Adventures of Sidney Sawyer
Missouri Yankees

Chapter 19

The next morning I got my orders to report to Grant at Vicksburg by quickest transport and to give over command of the 94th to Gould Florissant and good luck to him. And just in time. I knew that when the leech's sucker bite on my lizard was healed I'd be all over Libby like a reptile. We'd be caught out as sure as fifes and swords and disgrace would rain down on the regiment like vinegar. I sent for Gould to give him the joyous news but instead of my second in command, I got as ugly a surprise as I was ever served for breakfast.

Liberty, dressed in her full sergeant's fig, knocked on my tent post like a military orderly instead of a brat. She pulled back the flap and drew her– himself to ridged attention. What the deuce?

There outside the tent was a big man in a white cotton suit over a ruffled linen blouse, patent leather shoes, maroon cravat and a tall, odd straw topper with a matching maroon band. He would have looked a flash dude but his huge hands looked fit to rip leather tackle to ribbons and his expression was as somber as an undertaker. His hair was black and wild with a white stripe of gray through the crown and his chin was bristled with a narrow beard that would have given dignity to a goat. I'd seen this worthy's likeness a score of times in the national rags and knew him in an instant, and what the devil was he doing here while I was packing my grips and scribbling a note to Amy? I wanted no part of this fellow. His powerful shoulders stretched the fabric of his light summer suit and his dark eyes fixed me like a moth caught in Gillmore's calcium lights.

He was also as black as any webfoot in the 94th USCT. What the devil was Frederick Douglass doing in my tent? He looked a hell of a fellow and reminded me of my black friend Jim Watson, but better dressed and with an uppity look about him that would set any white man's teeth on edge. At least Old Jim knew his place. I'd heard that Douglass was half white on his pappy's side, (all mixed breeds were white on their pappy's side) but he looked a full blood African to me other than a nose that jutted like the bow of a bark canoe.

Even as I stood there hoisting up my suspenders, darkies from the regiment began to crowd around the entrance of the tent. Frederick Douglass could pack swarms of adoring white folk into the churches of Rochester, Boston, and Buffalo, and he was having no trouble attracting every black hide in the Negro infantry. Before I could properly button my tunic and stick out my mitt in greeting, Baddy, Gould, and Sergeant Major Smith had piled into the tent along with half a dozen company commanders and a spiff jasper with tablet and pencil that I took to be a reporter from an abolitionist newspaper.

"Mr. Douglass, sir, you do me honor. (It was no honor, it was a damned nuisance.) "Welcome to the bivouac of the glorious 94th United States Colored Troops." (I wanted to toss his black arse out into the surf and get on with breakfast and packing.)

We warmly shook hands and the quickly assembling multitude cheered and applauded like it was a performance of *Uncle Tom's Cabin*. I've said it before a million times, nothing sticks to a soldier like a good reputation. This blackbird must have heard about the noble Ace of Spades from the likes of Stanton or Halleck or even the Ancient himself. I'd heard tell that Lincoln actually had this American-African paragon to the Executive Mansion as if he was a black Moses. But it wasn't any abolitionist politico that had shagged Frederick Douglass to my tent flap.

"My esteemed friend, if I may presume to include such a gallant paladin of emancipation among those that I treasure to include within my circle of comrades, it is with honor and joy that I finally meet you, still at the head of your regiment of colored heroes."

I said, "Hello."

"Colonel Sawyer, the distance between this encampment and the slave plantation from which I escaped is considerable, and the difficulties to be overcome in getting from the latter to the former are by no means slight. That I am here today is, to me, a matter of astonishment as well as of gratitude. You will not, therefore, be surprised, if in what I have to say I evince no elaborate preparation, nor grace my speech with any high sounding exordium. With little time, I have been able to throw my thoughts hastily and imperfectly together; and trusting to your patient and generous indulgence, I will proceed to lay them before you."[b]

Get to the point, you windy bastard.

"The eye of the reformer such as your noble self is met with angry flashes, portending disastrous times; but his heart may well beat lighter at the thought that America is young, and that she is still in the impressionable stage of her existence. May he not hope that high lessons of wisdom, of justice and of truth, will yet give direction to her destiny?"

This clown was going to make me miss my boat but the gathering mob was hanging on his every word and ohhing and ahhing whenever he took a breath.

---

[b] Frederick Douglass protested that he was only "able to throw my thoughts hastily and imperfectly together," however most of his comments related by Sawyer, were recited verbatim from his famous *The Meaning of July 4th to the Negro* address from 1852.

"America is false to the past, false to the present, and without the actions of heroes such as yourself will solemnly bind herself to be false to the future. Standing with God and the crushed and bleeding slave on this occasion, I will, in the name of humanity which is outraged, in the name of liberty which is fettered, in the name of the constitution and the Bible, which are disregarded and trampled upon, dare to call in question and to denounce, with all the emphasis I can command, everything that serves to perpetuate slavery — the great sin and shame of America!"

Well, he was preaching to the choir, after all this was a *colored* regiment and every officer in the mess was an abolitionist to his bones. What the hell did he want? And then I *knew* what he wanted. He wanted me to reject my hard earned transfer and stay with the 94th. Our noble work was only begun, he pleaded. My history with the Underground Railroad showed my mettle. My noble nom de guerre, the Ace of Spades, won at the muzzle of a pistol in a duel with a wicked son of the slave power was an inspiration. The brute went on for a full ten minutes, painting me as the greatest champion of emancipation since Joshua. My transfer, which I myself must deplore, was the greatest betrayal since Judas.

What could I say? To deny this appeal seemed impossible. It would blacken my reputation and it was already black enough. There was only one thing I could possibly do– change the subject.

"Sergeant Major Smith!" I thundered. "Turn out the regiment by the company for a review. A grand review in honor of our esteemed guest, the Most Reverend Frederick Douglass. Let each man turn out as he is. There is no need for spit and polish in a fighting regiment. Let the work details parade with shovel and pick. They are soldier's gear with all the honor of the musket and sword." I wanted this done fast and no nonsense with polish and brush that would make me miss my ship.

"Ten minutes, Sergeant Major. That will be just enough time for Mr. Douglass and the officers share a toast."

At the word 'toast' Douglass gave a start. Of course! Paragons of his stripe were temperance.

Smith the elder was off at a run to turn out the regiment. I turned to Smith the younger and snapped, "Sergeant Smith, lemonade and a dozen glasses, on the double."

At the word lemonade, Douglass relaxed his shoulders and Liberty scampered to the mess for our beverage. Lemonade– I despise the stuff.

The toasts stretched on for a half-hour but the Reverend Douglass didn't have a chance to bullyrag me again, what with a swarm of adoring officers around him like bees around our pitcher of lemonade. The review went off like clockwork. The 94th was, after all, a crack regiment. Seven of the companies were sharp in brushed blues with rifles polished and bayonets gleaming like the family silver. Three companies were pulled rudely from fatigue work and were rough in muddy britches with suspenders pulled over sweaty cotton undershirts. But they were grand with spades and picks and axes held at ridged present arms and their lines were as straight as any Frog brigade on Napoleon's birthday. By God, I was proud of that regiment, *my regiment,* that morning with Colonel Florissant foursquare and proud on my left, Frederick Douglass uppity on my right and Sergeant Major Girardeau Smith a pace behind, decked out like a black Wellington. The review ended with three cheers and a bulldog for the Republic, for Douglass and for the Ace of Spades. The men were dismissed, the officers dispersed, I sent a corporal on an errand, and Douglass and I strolled alone on the boardwalk to Lighthouse Point and the pier.

"We must defeat the intentions of what ever villain has arranged your infamous transfer away from your heart's desire."

There was my ship, a brig rigged, side-wheel steamer named *Grand View Bay*.

"Your officers idolize you. Your men worship you. You have built a regiment that is a monument to the movement to free the Negro race from the bondage that I know so well from my own youth in slavery and degradation. The 94th Colored Infantry shall answer with Southern blood every stripe drawn by the lash and every tear torn from the hearts of millions of suffering bondsmen. My own sons have taken up the sword in this cause that men like you and my humble self have so far, so nobly labored and led."

Damnation, the tide was running strong from Lighthouse Creek, the bo'sun's pipe was giving its shrill squeal and the deck apes were casting off the bowlines. It was time to go! My traps were piled on the deck where the corporal stacked them and this swine wouldn't shut his fat lips.

"Colonel Sawyer, will you reject this infamous transfer? Will you stay true to the calling of emancipation and the brotherhood of all mankind? Will you give me your hand, sir, that we may follow the North Star of truth and freedom to the jubilee where the words of our glorious Declaration of Independence, 'That all men are created equal and blessed by our creator in heaven with the inalienable rights of life, liberty and the pursuit of happiness,' be made actual and in fact?"

He held out his big hand to me but I didn't dare take it. He might not let go. Instead I grabbed him by his massive shoulders, looked him square in the eye, man-to-man, and said, "No!"

I left Frederick Douglass on the pier looking thunder, and skipped up the gang to the deck of the *Grand View Bay* just as the bluejackets shoved the plank back on the dock. The whistle shrilled, the paddle wheels churned the bayou to foam and I reached into my grips for my pint. I saluted Douglass with the flask and washed the taste of lemonade from my mouth.[22]

The Adventures of Sidney Sawyer
Missouri Yankees

Chapter 20

I knew Grant was on the train pulling out of Indianapolis station. Up and down the platform there was an excited buzz that the great man was passing through town. I was passing through too, in the opposite direction on my way to report to the very creature. I was changing trains, had my carpetbag in hand, my uniform brushed, my Jeff Davis blocked, my boots polished and to any other soldier it would have been simple common sense to hop aboard the general's cars and present myself for duty. But I ain't any other soldier. As far as I had known only an hour ago, Grant was still in Vicksburg or back in New Orleans smoking cigars by the hatful and plotting his next bloodbath. That is where I was bound, but as I said before, not right away.

It could reasonably take me another week to reach Vicksburg by train and steamboat through the chaos of the Mississippi in wartime, but I planned to stretch the journey out to at least a month. I'd go home and work out my infatuation for darkie drummer boys with good old-fashioned wholesome and sanctioned marital romping. Libby was a dandy tumble but I've never run across any woman who could hold a candle to Amy's efforts on the counterpane. It would be 'howdy-do, Aunt Polly, we'll see you at supper,' and I'd fetch Amy up fireman-style and sprint up the stairs to our bedchamber. Damn the neighborhood busybodies who will snicker and gossip over the disturbance. My girl and I make a power of noise when we make love. Furniture gets upended, laughter is howled and instructions are shouted. I'll sing *Drink Puppy Drink* or *Kingdom Coming* and Amy will finish with her fine soprano. Home! Then I'll spend time with Alfred and Big Jim Watson in Lizabeth's kitchen behind the Temple & Son's offices telling stretchers, swilling Liz's wonderful rio and stuffing myself with pie. I hadn't had a good gallop (on horseback, not the other kind) since just after Champion Hill and I hankered to ride Juno, Old Man Temple's vicious mare, across Lewis County to let everyone know the hero had returned.

The last thing I wanted to do was board Grant's train and report for duty. He was going east and I was going west. How was I supposed to know that I had just missed him? I could claim that I'd traveled from Vicksburg to Memphis to St. Louis to breakfast and kept missing the man. I could drag out my furlough until Thanksgiving or know the reason why!

And then I knew the reason why. That was when the yard ape ran out with his blasted flags waving Grant's train to a stop before it had fairly gotten started and Stanton came bustling up the platform with two clerks in tow. And that was when the brute saw me with a start of recognition that I couldn't ignore, damn him. There was nothing for it but to tag along while my plans went up in the smoke of the locomotive's barrel stack.

America's chief warlord was in a hurry and was pumping away on his short legs with sweat soaking into his beard. I only needed a stride to catch up and when I did he panted, "Sawyer, Grant sent you? You're late! Give me an elbow."

Grant hadn't sent me but I stuck out my elbow and hoisted the plump politico up onto the rear platform of the last car. His toadies tossed up his baggage and I swung aboard behind. The yard ape wig-wagged his flags, the train's whistle gave a blast, the car gave a sharp lurch, Stanton was through the door at a trot and I cursed the ill wind that blew President Lincoln's god of war across my path.

I caught up with Stanton and his entourage three cars up where he was pumping the paw of a sawbones who had a look of horror on his hairy face.

"General Grant," Stanton puffed. "How are you sir, how are you?"

General Grant? This fellow wasn't Grant. He was an army quack– couldn't Stanton savvy the insignia on his tunic?

"General Grant, I knew you on sight from your photographs."

This was going to be good. I was almost glad that I had to tag along.

"Mr. Secretary," I piped in. Stanton gave me a growl for butting in on his big moment. "I believe that General Grant is at the *end* of the car. Excuse us Doctor." I nodded to the medico who didn't look anything like Grant.

I would have *liked* to say, "Mr. Stanton, I believe that fellow in the last seat asleep with a hat over his puss and scuffed boots blocking the aisle is General Grant. At least I hope he's asleep. He may be wallpapered. Don't trip on his crutches. You see him at his martial best."[c]

That's what I would have liked to say, but of course it wouldn't do. Grant seemed to be traveling light, that is with only a half-dozen staff loafers, none of whom seemed to know who the blazes the tubby coot with the John Brown whiskers was. I saw a dandy chance to rejoin Grant's official family and I took it. I strode over to the sleeping general and plucked the hat off his face. I knew Grant didn't stand on ceremony.

"General Grant, sir! You have a visitor."

---

[c] The doctor mistaken for Grant was Edward Kittoe. Grant needed crutches due to a dislocated hip injured in a nasty fall from a horse in New Orleans on September 4.

He squinted open one eye and his recognition of me was instant. He wasn't drunk.

"Sawyer, if you're the visitor, I'm going to have you tossed off this train. I've been traveling for a week and I am fatigued." The train gave another jolt. "And where the deuce are we and where are General Rawlins and Mrs. Grant?"

Mrs. Grant? Maybe he wasn't traveling that light after all. And of *course* Rawlins was with him. And it was *General* John Rawlins now– Grant's nanny was moving up in the world. Rawlins was from Galena too and it was his holy mission to keep Grant from embarrassing the hometown. If anyone brought a jug within sniffing distance of Grant Rawlins would transfer them to New Mexico to fight the Navajo. And Rawlins was a bear for paperwork and red tape. He'd never lead men into battle but we all have our jobs to do. It was no wonder General Grant was sober. With Rawlins and cross-eyed Julia Dent around sobriety was guaranteed.

"We just pulled out of Indianapolis, sir– we're heading to Louisville. I'm sure Mrs. Grant is in the next car with the ladies, and I ain't the visitor."

Beside me Secretary Stanton was appalled. This couldn't be the famous General Ulysses Grant, the victor who had demanded and received the surrender of two great Confederate armies. His vest was unbuttoned, his hair was plastered to his head, his tunic was balled up for a pillow and before he swung his boots to the floor he bit off the end of a stinker and fired up a Lucifer.

I snapped to attention and announced, "Secretary Stanton, may I present General Grant."

Grant stuffed his crutches under his arms and labored to his feet. To his credit, he handed me his cigar to hold before he reached for Stanton's hand.

"Mr. Stanton, sir, you do me great honor. I am on my way to Louisville to receive my orders. I never expected you would come to meet me."

"The honor is mine, General. I bring you your orders and it is my privilege to present them to you in person."

With a flourish he dug a packet of papers from his suit and handed them to Grant with a bow just as Rawlins scurried into the car. They were two copies of the same order. Grant read them without comment and passed one to Rawlins and the other to me. Rawlins gave me a look that could freeze farm liquor. He didn't cotton to me–thought I was a bad influence.

By direction of the President of the United States, the Departments of the Ohio, of the Cumberland, and of the Tennessee, will constitute the Military Division of the Mississippi. Major General U. S. Grant, United States Army, is placed in command of the Military Division of the Mississippi, with his headquarters in the field.

By grapes, Lincoln was putting humble Ulysses Grant in charge of the whole shebang between the Alleghenies and the Mississippi. And three years ago he had been tending the counter in his pappy's dry-goods store in Galena, Illinois.

* * *

'Headquarters in the field!' Damnation in a chicken coop, Grant was a major general in command of a half-million men spread over a half-million square miles. His headquarters should be in the best hotel in Nashville or even back in Washington City. Crutches or no, if I knew my general that 'headquarters in the field' nonsense would put me at Grant's right hand in whatever woods or canebreak was nearest to the Confederate works. But I still wanted to keep my wagon hitched to Grant's scruffy harness. If there was any credit to be squeezed from this war it would be with the only general who seemed to be able to follow a campaign through to a decisive victory.

There were other commanders who won battles but they usually let the fruits of their victories go a' glimmer. McClellan won a draw at Antietam, but then he let Bobby Lee and the whipped Army of Northern Virginia skulk away over the Potomac to rearm, reshod, resupply and reload to slaughter Ambrose Burnside's army at Fredericksburg. That old snapping turtle G.G. Meade whipped Lee the next year at Gettysburg, but then let the Confederates limp away unmolested as if the lessons of the year before had never been taught in blood. And the Rebels were no better. At Chickamauga, Longstreet's corps smashed Rosecrans's line like a cheap teacup. When Rosecrans and his whipped Army of the Cumberland skedaddled back to Chattanooga, Bragg only tagged behind the routed Yankees to see them safely into their works along the Tennessee River. Grant seemed to be the only general on either side to go for the neck and demand and get unconditional surrender. But he belonged in Nashville with his rough fingers on the telegraph– not 'in the field.'

I'm a handy fellow to have around any headquarters and I proved it again the next day in Louisville. The two chiefs powwowed all day on the train and continued at the Galt House Hotel. Grant wanted Rosecrans out so Stanton gave Old Rosy the sack. George Thomas was put in command of the Army of the Cumberland. Sherman, of course, took Grant's place as the boss of the Army of the Tennessee. Burnside, who wasn't much of a general, would stay top rail of the Army of the Ohio, but then the Army of the Ohio wasn't much of an Army. After this was all settled, Grant and the Missus went to call on some of their Kentucky kin.

Grant was no sooner gone than a wire arrived trumpeting some fresh disaster at Chattanooga. Messengers scoured the city looking for the general who was nowhere to be found. Fingernails were chewed, dogs and furniture were kicked, Rawlins was in a tizzy, Stanton had an asthma attack and Grant still could not be found–

until I found him. It was easy. I simply asked the colored hotel help. Around midnight I ushered the general into the august presence of Secretary Stanton who was barefoot in his nightshirt and waving the fatal telegram like it was the Union's death certificate. Grant didn't even blink. Fresh telegrams were drafted and orders were sent to the besieged garrison at Chattanooga. At one in the morning I handed Grant a flimsy from the Army of the Cumberland's new commander, George Thomas.

"We will hold the town until we starve."

I was back on Grant's staff.

* * *

Staff work with Grant ain't what staff work is for most generals. Grant got his promotion to the top slot in the West on October 17. He left Louisville on the 18th. We reached Nashville on the 20th but my hopes that the little sodbuster would settle into comfortable headquarters like a proper theater commander were splashed with cold water when he left for Stevenson the next day. Stevenson, just below the Alabama line, is where the railroad south from Nashville meets the Memphis and Charleston Railroad. Forty miles farther east the M&C reaches Chattanooga. From there, the Western and Atlantic Railroad heads south to Atlanta and there you have the reason for all the fuss. This was a railroad war and a river war and where the rails went and the rivers went, so went the armies. After Braxton Bragg's Rebs licked Old Rosy at Chickamauga exactly one month ago, the Army of the Cumberland retreated to the cold comfort of Chattanooga. Actually retreated is too gentle a word. After two days of slaughter along Chickamauga Creek that killed or wounded 30,000 men, the Union battle line tore like cheap muslin. In a rout that would have disgraced the dagos, General Rosecrans outraced his own Army's wild retreat back to the

Tennessee River– fat lot of good it did him.[d] Take a squint at the map and you can see Rosecrans's problem– or maybe you can't. The Army of the Cumberland was stuck in Chattanooga like a roach in a bottle and since they left most of their baggage and biscuits for the Rebels along the road from Chickamauga they commenced to starve. Men's gums turned black from the scurvy, guards had to be posted at the stables to keep hungry soldier boys from pinching the nag's fodder, rations were cut and then cut again and the nation trembled at the specter of an entire Yankee army surrendering to the Confederates.

But how can that be? This was a railroad war and a river war and Chattanooga had both. Well, it did and it didn't. One line ran east to Virginia– no help there for the bluebelly army. Another ran south to Atlanta, but that line supplied the Confederate Army that besieged Rosecrans. The other railroad ran west to the line that fetched Grant to Stevenson and on that line the gravy train rode on biscuit wheels. But the gravy and the biscuits couldn't roll into Chattanooga. And steamboats stuffed with rations and fodder couldn't tie up at the city's wharves to supply Rosecrans's loose-toothed troops either.

South of the Tennessee River and east of the city, Missionary Ridge, one of those endless mountains that make traveling through the Appalachians such a trial, dominated the horizon from north to south. It was thick with Confederates from base to crown and Johnny red-straps had their artillery sighted in to dominate the whipped Yankees. Just west of Chattanooga the river dips south and then sharply north around a height of land called Moccasin Point. Just south of the bend, rising to the clouds was the mass of Lookout Mountain. The Tennessee ran

---

[d] There were 30,000 casualties in the two-day Battle of Chickamauga. (September, 19-20, 1863) Only the three-day slaughter at Gettysburg was worse. The Union lost 1,600 killed and 9,700 wounded. The Confederates lost 2,300 killed and 14,600 wounded.

directly beneath this massive hill with the railroad running tight along its bank. The guns Bragg placed on the height closed the river and railroad so tightly that not even a cracker could reach Rosecrans and his hungry Army of the Cumberland. Than why not use the road? Surely there must be a road! The Union Army had wagons and mules, didn't they? Why not hitch up a train of wagons and fetch in all the crackers Chattanooga could chew? Again, the map don't tell the whole story.

There *was* a road– and I rode it with Grant, but it was a road straight from the night haunts of a darkie's worst nightmare.

Grant stayed in Stevenson just long enough to meet with Rosecrans. The two disliked each other, that was as plain as porridge, but Rosy owned up to the shambles in his command like a good'un and shared a plan to relieve the siege with the man who just ash-canned him. He didn't have to do that. I was in Grant's car to witness Rosecrans's disgrace and to gloat over the two staff officers he dragged along with him. I was in crisp blues, with boots gleaming and hat brushed and blocked. They looked like routed infantry, filthy linen, muddy boots, and they stunk like shovel labor. One of the poor bastards had his pants out at the knees. Rosecrans looked like a Jew tinker imploring an angry farmwife. His plan was nonsense anyway.

When Rosecrans sulked off to his train back north we took the short ride to Bridgeport where the M&C crossed over the Tennessee and on to Chattanooga– but for us it was the end of the line. Upstream, the Rebels had both river and rails blocked below Lookout Mountain. Thomas's besieged troops weren't alone, however. Supplies for *two* armies were piled up at Bridgeport and the place swarmed with soldiers from the Army of the Potomac. Two divisions under Hooker had just arrived on the cars from Virginia. Farther west along the Tennessee, Sherman waited at Eastport with his entire corps of five divisions for his chance to pile in. But the way things stood, neither tucker nor troops could get to where they needed to be.

With an escort of cavalry in the dew of dawn, we set off on the hellish road to Chattanooga. You've heard the old joke about the city slicker who asks the bumpkin for directions. The rube pulls his whiskers, scratches his arse and replies, "You kain't git thar from here!" Well you couldn't get to Chattanooga from here either and I found out the hard way why Old Rosy's staff officers looked like bums.

The Adventures of Sidney Sawyer
Missouri Yankees

Chapter 21

I helped Grant onto his horse, no task is too menial for an ambitious staff toad, and with his crutches strapped to his saddle we made good time north to a burg called Jasper, and then east towards our destination. But we couldn't go east for long. That road would have taken us along the north bank of the Tennessee past Raccoon Mountain and on to Chattanooga– but we couldn't take it. Bragg had mounted artillery on its crest, and along the river itself platoons of sharpshooters would make a hard day for any Yankees on the trail. We detoured north along the Sequatchie River, a stream with no charm and no bridges. When we had to ford, Grant had to be hauled across bodily, like so much baggage. After twenty miles of bad roads, wet boots, and soggy britches we turned east to pick up the road south again to Chattanooga. We struck that road at Anderson's Crossroads where I smelled the worst stink I'd ever struck– and I've been in greaser hoosegows, dined on rancid dog in a Mescalero Apache lodge and sailed downwind of a Hwang Ho honeybarge.

Even before we passed through Jasper the trip had been damned unpleasant. The only possible sustenance was the grub and fodder we carried with us. The country was deserted, without house or barn or farm. Dead mules fouled the air every hundred yards and broken down wagons were tipped off the trail at all angles and attitudes of destruction, but Anderson's was a sight from the inferno. Three weeks before, my old roommate from West Point, Little Joe Wheeler, had caught a train of 400 wagons stuffed with supplies for the hungry Army of the Cumberland. Back at the Academy, Joe Wheeler had been a card and damned good chum in the mess. Now he was a Confederate general of cavalry, and besides Forrest and Mosby, the best horse commander in the War. The only Yankee galloper in his league was Phil Sheridan. He rode a raid from Muscle Shoals to Murfreesboro and on the way burned the wagon train at Anderson's Crossroads. Four hundred wagons with all their plunder, up in smoke and the thousand mules and horses that pulled them lay bloated and rotting along two miles of rustic road. Black clouds of crows prevented conversation and buzzards were almost too fat to flap away as we rode through the carrion. Above one shallow gully Wheeler's butchers must have led the mules one by one to the edge and sabered them over the edge. The creatures were piled god knows how deep, and I could actually feel the warm gasses from their rot and stink rise up past me as our column rode past. I've seen sights and smelled stinks but Anderson's took the quilt. I've heard since that over 10,000 horses and mules died on that terrible road and we saw many of them die ourselves as we passed wagon trains coming and going. A mule would simply drop straight down dead under his harness and teamsters who were too tuckered to swear stripped off their tackle and levered the carcass off the trail. Another poor nag from the string of replacements would be buckled into his place and the team would groan on up the road. And along some stretches it wasn't a road at all.

The sky was gloomy, overcast and cold. Rains had turned every low place into mud that tripped our horses and topped our boots when we led them through the worst of it. Grant had to be carried over the washouts and through the gumbo by floundering troopers while his adjutant Rawlings fussed like his grandma. Grant's crutches were useless. They would have sunk in the sludge up to his armpits. Why couldn't he have stayed in Nashville like a proper general? We were two days on that road and when we reached Chattanooga on that dismal twenty-third of October I was as shabby as the rest of the garrison.

Chattanooga wasn't much better than the trail. It was a shabby railroad town, about ten city blocks square. It stunk with the rot of a thousand horses that had starved to death from lack of fodder. And there was another stench– the odor of forty-five thousand defeated soldiers. It didn't take a major general to see the tactical situation that faced Thomas and his wretched army. Lookout Mountain loomed like a troll with its crest in the clouds. Confederate watch fires ringed its slope like a garland. To the east Missionary Ridge filled the horizon and more Rebel fires flickered for miles along the measure of its length. If the road from Bridgeport was the only way in, that meant there was sure as hell no way out for this army. They'd starve or surrender. There was nothing else they could do. Well, that's what I thought.

Grant lost no time meeting with Thomas– the grubby counter-jumper never lost *any* time, damn him. Pap Thomas had set up shop in one of the few decent establishments in the city. There was plenty of room for both staffs to pile in. I had only enough time to brush my Jeff Davis hat and comb out my whiskers but I was still muddy to my knees and didn't measure up to my usual style. And I was as hungry as a wolf. The garrison was down to quarter rations and us officers had to set an example by starving along with the men. God, but I hate to go hungry. Army rations ain't that bad, especially for an officer, but in a besieged city or on a desperate march the commissary won't answer. Thank God I hadn't nibbled through the grub I'd squirreled away in my dunnage. The escort must have reckoned me a dandy because of the care I paid to my hatbox strapped over my bedroll behind my saddle. Dandy indeed! The box *did* carry my bonnet, but it was stuffed with salted pecans wrapped in waxed paper and around the brim I had packed enough hardtack to round out my rations for at least two weeks. I couldn't let anybody see me eat them of course. Us officers have to set an example.

I had never met Pap Thomas before. He had been a cavalry instructor at West Point, but left the academy the year before I got there. The cadets called him Slow Trot Thomas because he always walked the boys through their drills. The newspapers called him 'The Rock of Chickamauga' because it was him that held his corps steady before the Confederate onslaught that sent Rosecrans and the rest of the Army swarming off the field in a rout. His own soldiers called him Pap. They loved him, you see.

Despite the siege he was fat, but his face had a sag to it from the lean rations. Sag or no, behind his short beard his puss had the no nonsense look of a true believer in the cause of Union. Thomas had better be a true believer. He was from Virginia and back home his family had turned his picture to the wall to hide the face of a traitor to the Old Dominion.[23]

With a few handshakes and not a jug to be seen, the meeting came to order. Thomas spent an hour explaining his reorganization of the Army of the Cumberland. He'd been a busy man in the week since Grant placed him in charge. He had shuffled regiments, juggled commanders, cut the number of his divisions from eleven to six and merged Rosecrans's four corps into two. General Rawlins was in his element. He lived for staff work. If Thomas expected an argument from Grant, he didn't get one. The consolidation was breathtaking, but Rawlins nodded to Grant and Grant nodded to Thomas and that was that.

Then Thomas turned the proceedings over to his chief of engineers, General W.F. Smith. I had met him before but didn't know him well enough to call him Baldy.[e]

---

[e] William Farrar Smith, (Baldy to his friends) was a West Point-trained Vermont man who served with the Union Army from First Bull Run to Petersburg.

"General Grant, the wheels are in motion and the orders are drafted." Smith was as bold as a Polack goose. "I shall relieve this siege within the week. All you have to do is say 'go'."

The presumptuous puppy actually arched an eyebrow at Grant.

"General Smith, three days ago, General Rosecrans shared with me a plan to create a serviceable supply line into this city. Is this the plan you refer to?"

"It is, sir!"

By greens and gravy, I'd heard Old Rosy pitch this plan to Grant and I had dismissed it as merely face-saving by a disgraced commander. It was lunacy!

"Please review your plan for me one more time, General Smith."

It couldn't be the same plan– could it?

It took Baldy twenty minutes to run through it again. It was!

Grant looked around the room, still no jug. He scratched a Lucifer on the bottom of the table, fired up a fresh stinker and grunted, "Go."

* * *

Grant said 'go' on Friday. At three o'clock in the black morning of the next Tuesday, I was drifting with the current down the Tennessee River, farting pecan air biscuits in the bow of a pontoon loaded with Cumberland infantry. There were sixty pontoon boats in our flotilla loaded with 1500 troops, each man with a grudge and each boat with an officer. I was the officer in boat #2. But boat is too glamorous a name for a pontoon. We were navigating the Tennessee in the cold dark wee hours, in scows hammered together to support the planking of floating bridges. They weren't built for desperate assaults against arrogant Rebels whose boots had been on their throats since Chickamauga. And what the hell was I doing here? It was Rawlins' mischief. Grant found me useful and even amusing on his staff, but Rawlins, his chief of staff had me receipted and filed as a scoundrel from the get-go. The prissy midwife was a damn good judge of character and he saw a chance to teach me manners. Last spring, I'd twice run the batteries before Vicksburg. It was my own fault. I had collected a minor wound and limped around headquarters like a hunchback, the better to dodge duty. Grant reckoned it a favor for me to avoid a march and ride in style on a transport. That was the night the brown water fleet ran the Rebel gauntlet. My boat was sunk of course, and I barely escaped with my skin. When a second flotilla, this one of unarmed transports stuffed with rations, ran past the Vicksburg guns, Rawlins again made sure I was aboard. I had experience, don't you know, and might come in handy. I didn't. I was sunk again and lost my best boots floundering through the Mississippi's mud to safety. For a time the wags in the mess were calling me "Shoeless Sawyer the Shipwrecked Sailor." Rawlins remembered all this (the swine never forgot a thing), and suggested that an officer from Grant's staff ride the pontoons– just to observe you see![f]

The night was as cold as the black water in the river and the dew and damp cut through our uniforms like we were naked to the wind. I reckoned I was as cold as a body could get, but I was wrong. I'd get colder and soon. The mist rose from the river in will-o-the-wisps that muffled the sound of the sweeps that were only used to steer our barges as close to the right bank of the river as the snags would allow. To the left, Union watch fires flared through the gloom, but we wouldn't be ghosting along the Union fires for long. We were headed due south from Chattanooga on a great bend of the Tennessee that would take us around Moccasin Point. Directly above the Point were the terrible Rebel batteries at the crest of

[f] For Sawyer's adventures running the batteries before Vicksburg refer to the fourth packet of his memoirs published as *The Adventures of Sidney Sawyer: The Father of Waters*.

Lookout Mountain. The current would then sweep us north to Brown's Ferry where a Confederate garrison guarded the road. There was no bridge at Brown's Ferry and the ferry was closed. It was that garrison along with the guns on Lookout and Raccoon Mountains that had the Army of the Cumberland bottled up and starving on short rations.

So what the devil was a battalion of Yankees doing drifting down the Tennessee River towards a Rebel wasp's nest in three score pontoons? Well, we had a plan. Unfortunately, it was the same plan that Grant grunted 'Go!' to four days before. It was based on secrecy, moving parts and perfect timing. That kind of plan looks keen on maps in the comfort of headquarters but is next to impossible to execute in real war. Grant knew this. *None* of his plans ever went according to the script. In every campaign since Forts Henry and Donalson his well-laid plans came apart like wet paper. And that ain't a criticism of Grant. Hell in a sewing basket, all plans of all generals in all wars bust at the seams the second they run up against real weather and real geography and real time before a real enemy. Grant knew this and what he thought of Baldy Smith's harebrained scheme can only be guessed. God knows his face didn't give anything away. But something *had* to be tried and this plan was the only thing *to* try. So here I was with my buttocks as cold and wet as a well-digger's, in a pontoon jammed with Kansas infantry, and bothered by a lout breathing in my ear who had supped on wild leeks. The brute's breath stunk worse than my pecan petards.

I was the captain of boat #2 and I took my duty seriously. I took the spot at the very front left of the blunt bow and squinted into the dark like my life depended on it. I leaned as far forward as I dared to get away from leek-breath. To the left was the gap between Rebel and Federal lines, where no fires glowed in the gloaming. Presently, across the stream, the Chattanooga River emptied into the Tennessee and above it was the height of Lookout Mountain. Now, the fires above were tended by Rebels, and along the bank were sentries with long guns and keen eyes and ears. Any sound would give us away. This was the time of maximum danger. The men had been ordered to sit fast, shut up and for God's sake no one was to fire up a cigar. Anyone fool enough to fall overboard would be left and we were all warned to have the patriotism to drown without making a racket.

It was as dark as the inside of a dog's belly and the only sound was the soft swish of the moving water and the steering oars. The only smell was the autumn damp and leeks– and then I saw it!

"Torpedo!" I screeched.

Two score "Shushes" answered my shout along with one hissed, "Quiet in the boat ye God-damned fool!"

"Torpedo!" This time I squeaked.

I had seen the infernal things before– in Charleston Harbor and I knew just what to do. Hadn't Liberty Smith shown me the technique? I leaned as far overboard as I could without tipping into the current and reached with both hands to shove the filthy thing away. It wasn't heroism. I ain't a hero. It was survival and I'd save the day!

My hands met it along its widest part and I shoved with all my heart. My hands slipped off the slime growing on the waterlogged stump and I was into the Tennessee headfirst. Well, in the dark it *looked* like a torpedo. The shock of the frigid water almost stopped my heart. My boots and sword and Remington cavalry pistol dragged me down. There was no help or rescue. It was I who had laid down the law to the company in my barge– "We don't stop for anything or anyone. Have the good grace to sink quietly."

I screamed like a trussed hog, "Save me! Save my you bastards!"

Water shot up my nose as I reached for the stump. "Stop! Stop you swine!" I gagged and then the steering sweep cracked me in the temple sending stars spinning before my eyes. My hands slipped from the stump, the weapons strapped to my waist carried me under and I thought it was damned unfair to die like this– I ain't even in the Army of the Cumberland.

A strong hand grabbed me by the collar and pulled me up and onto the stump. I wasn't that far gone yet. Liberty had fetched me a bigger shot of water up my snoot when she caught me peeking at her swimming bare-arsed back in the Edisto River. But it was bad enough. I coughed and gagged my lungs clear, my temple still rang where the helmsmen tagged me with his oar, the bastard must have done it on purpose to shut me up, and I was shivering like granny with the croup. I clung to the stump for my life and when my senses floated back I wondered who was the hero who had saved me from feeding the bullheads? And then I knew.

"Colonel Sawyer, sir," the stink of leeks washed over me. "Sir, are you all right? Can you breath, sir? God Almighty, sir, don't die! It will break Mother's heart."

* * *

Mother's heart? What the hell? But I couldn't ask. One by one the rest of the flotilla drifted silently past and if I didn't want to get knocked off the stump with another sweep I knew enough to be quiet. The Rebels never raised an alarm. Either they were deaf or figured that the lout shouting from the river was a clumsy Yankee picket who slipped into the drink or more likely a drunk. Leek-breath and me kicked with the current and presently our stump snagged up in the mud of the east side of the river. We staggered through the ooze and used roots and branches to scramble up the bank. Lord, but it was cold, but I was alive, thanks to this fellow who didn't want to break his mother's heart. As we made our way shivering up the riverside path I gave him a heartfelt thank you, a slug of good brandy from my hat box stash and asked him about his mother.

"Sir, my mother loves you like a son, like a savior. She's a Godly woman and you are in the Boone family prayers every night. She has written your name in our Bible alongside all of our kin, back to the first Boone to live on this side of the water back before the 1812 War. You are her hero, sir and you are my salvation."

What the dickens? Could this big lout be my son? I'd been scattering my seed up and down the Mississippi since I was thirteen years old. But no– I was only twenty-five. My oldest bastard could only be twelve. This fellow was as old as me. He didn't look like a Sawyer. His hair was corn-yellow, his teeth bucked out like a mule's and we had no kin named Boone. Who *was* this Kansas webfoot and what was I to him? And then he told me.

"They was gonna shoot me like I was a deserter or a spy or a thief. Mother went all the way to Washington City to plead. Took my sisters and little brother– went to Stanton, but he's a hard man and cruel."

"What'd you do to fetch a firing squad?"

"Sir, I'm shamed to say that I went to sleep on picket."

And then it hit me.

"You're Bobby!"

"Yes, sir, Bobby Boone. You sent Mother to see Lincoln– President Lincoln himself! He treated her like a lady. He shed a tear an' held her hand an' patted little Willy on the head."

Willy! No wonder Lincoln shed a tear. His own boy Willy had just died of the trots.

"He remembered you fondly, sir. Said you was a hero an' a friend an' you was always poppin' up an' doin' things that he couldn't credit. An' then he wrote a letter to General Rosecrans himself to spare my life. Mother still has the letter tucked in our Bible. She told Mr. Lincoln that a letter wouldn't do– I was to be shot presently, so he sent for your friend Mr. Hay to send a telegram an' he did an' I wasn't killed, just bucked and gagged."

"But how did *you* pop up at just the right second to save my life? I've heard of coincidence, but this takes the bird."

"Weren't no coincidence, sir. Heard you rode in with General Grant to save me again. Been keepin' an eye on you. Won't let nothin' happen to you while I live. When I saw you get in boat number two, I got in right behind you. I belonged in boat six and may get bucked and gagged again, but it don't consider. I was there when you needed me."

And then the big fool began to sniff and his lip quivered over his buckteeth and with a sob he drew himself up to a shivering attention and threw me a salute.

It was ridiculous, but what could I do? I returned the salute.

He sobbed, "You saved my life, Colonel Sawyer."

I shivered back at him, "And you saved mine, Corporal Boone."

"But sir, I ain't no corporal."

"You are now, soldier, and send a hello to your ma."

That's when two pickets sprang into the path like genies, leveled their muskets and demanded, "Who goes there? Yank or Reb?"[g]

---

[g] There is a record of only one man falling overboard from the pontoon flotilla. He did indeed scream but did not alert the Rebel sentries and was presumed drowned. There is no mention of Sawyer or Boone.

The Adventures of Sidney Sawyer
Missouri Yankees

Chapter 22

The sentries were Union, thank God, but their bayonets poked in our faces gave us a turn until they were able to identify me as a Yankee officer in the gloom. I dragooned one of the pickets as a guide and we hotfooted for at least another mile up the path to where I knew there was a road that crossed the narrow neck of Moccasin Point. The picket never gave a notice that we were both wet to the skin and that Boone had no musket, cartridge box or kit. I knew who was *supposed* to be waiting on that road. It was part two of Smith's grand plan– and there they were. Crouching along both sides of the lane was a brigade of Cumberland infantry, silent and waiting. I gave the picket a 'thanky' and turned left, back towards the river.[h]

And there was Baldy Smith surrounded by staff squinting at the water towards Brown's Ferry like a hopeful brat waiting for St. Nicolas to pop out of the chimney. What the hell– I may as well get some credit from my dunk.

"General Smith, Colonel Sawyer reporting. The flotilla is cracking along in fine shape. All pontoons are in order and proper and the Rebels have not detected our movement."

---

[h] General Smith had two brigades and a battalion of engineers waiting opposite Brown's Ferry on October 27, 1863.

"Sawyer? What the devil are you doing here? You were ordered to the flotilla, sir."

"General Smith, I was ordered to observe, and I did. All is well with the pontoon fleet so now I am observing here. I see that your troops are in place." Time to remind Baldy just who I was working for. "The commanding general will be pleased."

"You were on the pontoons? How came you to be here?"

"Why, isn't it obvious? I'm wet."

And then from across the Tennessee the quiet was broken by a shot and then another followed by distant shouts of command. The pontoons had arrived at the ferry. The plan was for the flotilla to surprise the Johnny garrison and secure the ferry. From the sound of only two shots it would seem that we did. Half of the barges would stay there while details of engineers began planking the pontoons from the west bank. The rest would row like thunder to Smith's side where more engineers were waiting with planks and anchors to stretch out the pontoon bridge from this side.

There was no need for secrecy now. Fires blazed along the riverbank to illuminate the labor, troops sprang to their feet with a cheer and when the pontoons pulled up to the east bank engineers who knew their jobs swarmed them. Small boats set anchors upstream, planks were secured from one scow to the next almost as fast as the boats could be fetched in line. It was a race to see if the bridge could be built before Confederate reinforcements arrived in enough strength to drive the 1500 pontoon soldiers into the river.

Heavy fire erupted from the far bank. Thank God I'd fallen in the drink or I'd be in the middle of that fight. A quick dunk in cold water ain't as deadly as a skirmish in the dark. As the flares of the guns flickered through the trees in the far woods, the engineers never stopped their labors. It was at least 5 AM when I presented my sopping self to Smith. By early light the fighting on the far bank was over and as the sun peeked over the hills on Moccasin Point the bridge was done. Four hours to bridge the Tennessee River, most of it in the dark– not a bad night's labor. Now Smith's brigade swung across the river to secure the Western side and Brown's Ferry was part of a Union road.

So what? The Confederates still had guns on Raccoon and Lookout Mountains. There *was* a road, and a damn good one, from Brown's Ferry to Kelly's Ford, but what use was it to Thomas's hungry army? The Tennessee River spent its time twisting around mountains in this neck of the rebellious state of Tennessee, and above Raccoon Mountain it twisted south again to Kelly's Ford. That was only five miles by road from Smith's brand new pontoon bridge. But again, so what?

Here's where the next part of Smith's plan came into play. Only four days after Chickamauga, in an agony of terror at the specter of an entire Union Army falling into the Confederate bag, Stanton ordered two corps from the idle Army of the Potomac to race to the rescue. Within a week, in a wonder of railroad organization, twenty thousand men, sixty guns, bag, baggage, ammunition and nags were present in Bridgeport on the Tennessee. They were led by the braggart who had disgraced himself at Chancellorsville back in May– Fighting Joe Hooker.

The day before the pontoons began their wee hour voyage Hooker was to cross the Tennessee at Bridgeport and march three divisions of Eastern troops along the M&C line to Wauhatchee Station and meet up with Smith's Cumberland boys. A military miracle happened that next morning. Hooker was right where he was supposed to be. He left one division to secure Wauhatchee. With the other two he and Smith fixed to drive the Johnnys off of Raccoon Mountain. It worked! Smith's idiot plan actually worked! Steamers could unload grub and guns at Kelly's Ford. The road to Brown's Ferry was open. The men christened it 'The Cracker Line.' Smith's pontoon bridge would feed the supplies over the short road to

Chattanooga and the Army of the Cumberland was saved. And then, it wasn't.

A chain is only as strong as its weakest link and of course that link was Joe Hooker. A Kansas politician named Geary commanded the division left to guard Wauhatchee and Hooker hung the poor bastard out for target practice like a bottle on a fence post. Geary's division was three miles from any help Hooker could send and they gazed up Lookout Mountain at a universe of Rebels. Their lines and pickets were placed with no more thought than a housewife would give to tossing her laundry into a basket. The Rebels were Longstreet's men, sent over from Lee's Army of Northern Virginia before Chickamauga. They had made a habit of licking boys from the Army of the Potomac, especially Fighting Joe Hooker's boys.

Figuring the night attack by Smith's pontoon soldiers had been a crackerjack idea, Longstreet reckoned to try one of his own. The next midnight Confederates swarmed down the mountain and lit into Geary's boys like Lucifer's own hand.

Of *course* Geary's boys would be whipped. It was their habit. As the first flashes of artillery lit the southern sky, Hooker frantically sent his other two divisions back to Wauhatchee to save the day but they got sidetracked in the dark and never showed up. Ammunition ran low, the Confederates closed in, Hooker would be forced back to the pontoon bridge with whatever force he could salvage. He would retreat back across the brand new bridge to Chattanooga and destroy it behind him. His Potomac troops would starve along with the Cumberlands. Grant would be disgraced, an army would be lost, the country would recoil in horror and, as Lincoln would have put it, "The bottom would be out of the tub."

But then the day was saved– or the night was. Geary's teamsters scattered when Rebel fire got too hot. Abandoned mules driven mad by the flashes and crashes of battle broke their tethers and stampeded through the blackness of the battle like a troop of insane Cossacks.

"Yankee cavalry! Run boys, we'ins is cut off. Git back, git back, git!"

The Johnnys stampeded with them, Geary rallied his men, Hooker's tardy rescuers showed up and the Cracker Line was safe. It was officially the Battle of Wauhatchee but the men called it the Charge of the Mule Brigade. It would have been droll if not for the 800 boys shot down in the dark or General Geary's own son who died in his daddy's arms in the dim moonlight below Lookout Mountain.

* * *

Legend has it that there were only four cases of hardtack left to feed the entire Cumberland Army when the Cracker Line opened at the end of October. Thomas's men went back on full rations, black gums turned pink, loose teeth set back solidly in jaw-bones and gaunt faces filled out with flesh. Chattanooga lost its stench as the dead horses and mules were burned or buried. With fresh fodder the few beasts left stopped dropping dead in their traces and fresh nags flooded in with cocky cavalry from Sherman's Corps. The city was saved and the four cases of hardtack became part of Grant's legend too.

Was he a drunk– a butcher– a modern day Wellington? Whatever the hell he was, he was a Union general who won battles! U. S. Grant! The name was patriotism in a bottle. Unconditional Surrender Grant– hero of Fort Donalson, Shiloh, Vicksburg and now Chattanooga. He was the man who had stumbled from one civilian failure to the next only to rise through the fires of war to become the savior of the Republic. Grant, the man who accepted the surrender of two entire Rebel armies when all the other Union generals floundered in confusion and defeat.

And I rose with him. Even John Rawlins couldn't nudge me from Grant's orbit. Once the story made the rounds of how I saw the pontoon flotilla safely around Moccasin Point and then made a midnight swim to see that Baldy Smith and his engineers were hard on the task, I was solidly back in the official family. It ain't like Grant and I were drinking chums– I never actually saw the little tipper take a swig. And except for when he introduced me to his cross-eyed Missus and his brat, Freddy, he never treated me as anything but a handy tool of war. No, I knew I was back in the club when he simply began assigning me tasks.

Looking back, I believe Grant liked me. I'm damned if I can figure out exactly why. Like Lincoln, I reckon that he saw through my act of earnest nonsense and pegged me for a kind of scoundrel. But I was a handy scoundrel and he mistook my propensity for disaster as a type of heroism. To him the circumstances of my comings and goings were droll, witness my popping up on the train when Stanton was pumping the fin of an army quack he mistook for the general. And I believe he was amused by Rawlins distaste for me, as if I'd ever spit out a cork and pass him a swig. If I were killed I do believe the little sipper would pause for a sniff and a prayer.

Supply was my bailiwick and he set me to the task of divvying up the river of tucker flowing into Chattanooga between Hooker, Thomas and Sherman. Sherman's fellows were just then setting up camp north of the town. I was glad for the work. First of all, I'm good at it. I had learned the business of rivers and railroads from Alfred Temple's pappy back when I was a pup in St. Petersburg. Other than peacetime service in the Army, that is the best vocation for any man. My biggest problem with the Chattanooga commissary was that the post was a frost. The civilian population had long since fled south and there wasn't a lass in the bivouac worth a second look. The grub was straight rations of beans, hardtack, salt-horse and coffee, that as an officer I had to pony up for from my own purse. The liquor was pure farmer's corn with the varnish on, too raw for even my taste. The work was relentless and the garrison was so isolated there was damned little opportunity for lining my pockets or steering federal money to Temple & Son to earn my rightful kickbacks. Chattanooga was a flat frost.

The last of the November foliage, glowing in the autumn sunlight in blazes of red and yellow, framed the Confederate works along Lookout Mountain and Missionary Ridge. Tiny sparkles of light reflecting off the polished brass of Confederate artillery punctuated a beauty that made you forget that soon, very soon, Grant would send his soldiers up those slopes into the fire of those sparkling guns. But I wouldn't have to do it. By God, I was a colonel of staff. I wasn't just passing along Grant's orders like I did back at Paducah in '61. Now I was drafting my own orders and sending them by the relay to all points. And I had a helper. I had transferred Bobby Boone from his regiment and dragooned him into my service as an orderly. It's damn handy to have a loyal stooge to brush your duds, tend your gear and empty your necessary bucket. The last batman I had was a colored drummer boy who was as different from Boone as silk is from silage, and thank God for that. I wouldn't be trying to shimmy into this one's britches.[i]

For the next three weeks I was busier than a one-handed nitpicker and the garrison swarmed like the gates of hell on the Reckoning Day. Three forces were coming together under the leadership of Grant. The disgraced Army of the Cumberland was camped between the Chattanooga River and the Tennessee. Hooker's corps of Eastern troops was bivouacked between the N&C Line and Raccoon Mountain. Grant's old Army of the Tennessee,

---

[i] Batman is a British term for valet or manservant. A bat horse or packhorse would carry an officer's accoutrements and his orderly or batman would tend to this gear.

now under Billy Sherman, was pouring up the Cracker Line after its long march from the Mississippi.

I knew that Grant, Thomas and Hooker were plotting a breakout but I didn't know the grand plan. This was a damned strange fix for a staff colonel in an army where secrets were as poorly kept as a Dark Town privy. It was my job to shovel bacon, beans and biscuits up the line for the troops, and oats, hay and harness for the nags. I was in and out of headquarters enough to curry an acquaintance with Fighting Joe Hooker but I picked up never a word as to the order of battle for the coming fight.

I wasn't prepared to like General Joe Hooker, and I didn't particularly, but I did spend as much time at his headquarters below Lookout Mountain as I could. His command was XI and XII Corps from the Army of the Potomac. Us Western boys fancied the Eastern troops to be paper collar soldiers, but the officers in the mess loved to drink, skylark and gossip, and Hooker let them. I was welcome as long as I didn't brag about Grant's victories, or bring up unpleasant memories of Bull Run, Fredericksburg or especially Chancellorsville. Rawlins kept Grant and Thomas's headquarters in town dry. God help any man who fetched a jug into Grant's shop! Grant didn't notice and Thomas didn't care, but I did. For cards, booze and flash talk it was Hooker's command post for the likes of me.

Hooker himself was a pompous rascal. He could even look pompous while draining a jar of oh-be-joyful while one of his girls giggled away in his tent. He was as tall as me, clean-shaven with a long nose and a weak chin that he jutted at you when he spoke. He ran a clean camp and a happy one, with decent grub and clean water for his soldiers. He was at least as good a housekeeper as McClellan and the men liked him. His name in the papers was "Fighting Joe." I reckon he could fight well enough when somebody like Little Mac was passing out his marching orders. It was when he was on his own hook that the wheels would fall off his wagon. I'd heard about his cock-up at Chancellorsville where Jackson went through his right flank like gravel through a gander and I knew that he almost spittooned the Cracker Line at Wauhatchee before he was saved by the "Charge of the Mule Brigade." He was a climber so I was politic enough to let it slip that I had served on Little Mac's staff in Maryland and knew Lincoln, Stanton and Halleck. He called me Sidney. I called him General Hooker.[24]

It was my talent for toadying up to the mighty that landed me a ringside seat at Fighting Joe Hooker's glamorous Battle Above the Clouds– and it almost fetched me the pox and got me busted through the tripes.

The Adventures of Sidney Sawyer
Missouri Yankees

Chapter 23

Along his march from the Mississippi to Chattanooga, Sherman had left one of his divisions under a driver named Dodge to patch up the destroyed tracks between Decatur, Alabama and Nashville. Johnny cavalry raiders had made a vocation of ripping up those tracks and Dodge's job was to repair the right-of-way to give Grant a second all-weather supply line back to the Cumberland River and points north. Dodge reported that he was beavering away in grand style, rebuilding trestles and culverts, but it was Grant's nature to double check. He'd been suckered by over-optimistic subordinates before and would be again.

Staff ticks gossip like dowagers so I heard that Grant was bound to send one of his officers to Decatur for a snoop. I made sure I was Johnny-on-the-spot with uniform brushed and bonnet blocked. Rawlins picked me and was glad to see my back– and I was glad to go. Garrison duty in Chattanooga was, after all, a frost. Boone and I left by way of the Cracker Line to Bridgeport, caught the cars to Decatur and followed the repaired rails to Dodge's rolling headquarters all the way up to Pulaski, Tennessee. We arrived at dusk. I quartered in a Shelby tent crowded with engineers and staff. Boone wrapped up in a blanket on the ties beneath a flatcar piled with gleaming new rails.

After a fine breakfast of beefsteak and eggs, (these railroad soldiers do damn fine for themselves) I reported to

General Grenville Mellen Dodge and gave him General Grant's respects. Dodge wasn't blowing stack gas when he reported his division was working like beavers. To reach Pulaski I had passed over a score of new trestles, each one protected by a blockhouse stuffed with infantry, and every culvert was rebuilt down to the cinders. Three of the bridges were decorated with Confederate irregulars hanging by their necks for the locals to contemplate. They were fellows who were caught with snips for cutting the wires or pry-bars for levering off the rails. From the railhead I rode with Dodge up the line where a thousand men were rebuilding the next ten miles of culvert. Squads of colored gandy-dancers were in a race, spiking in the rails to keep up with the right of way.

G. M. Dodge was hell on the Confederates, but at heart he was an engineer and a railroad man. Oh, and he was also a wirepuller, an opportunist and a crook. That's probably why we hit it off like grease in gravy. He was as tall as me but ten years older with a beard brushed tight to his face and his hat worn high on his forehead. And he was a force of nature. From dawn to dusk he was a whirlwind of motion and a bear for work, but bless him, in the evening he liked to pull a cork and bounce a hooker on his knee. I'd heard of trollops referred to as hookers since West Point but the term was new to Dodge and he thought it a great joke to call his camp followers Hooker's girls. Except for hard work and a sense of duty we had the same interests. By the end of the day we were chums. After the war, I made it a point to keep in touch with Dodge. He attracted money the way Irish infantry attracts whisky. I was with him in '69 out in Utah, at Promontory Point when the golden spike was pounded into the last tie to complete the transcontinental railroad. *That* was a party I didn't want to miss. You've all seen the picture– two locomotives nose to nose covered with drunken Mick road graders waving bottles and two gentlemen shaking hands before the mob. Those men were Dodge and me. That's Grenville on the right. I broke it off with him in '01 when the damned hypocrite investigated *me* before Congress for financial shenanigans during the War with Spain. The bloody cheek![25]

Dodge seconded me a fine gelding and we rode through the division's labors with his staff. Boone bounced along behind us on a fat mare with all the ill grace of the Kansas sodbuster that he was. Dragging him along may not have been such a good idea. Our party rode up the line past great whirlwinds of effort that looked to be all confusion, but wasn't. Locomotives backed up, pushing flatcars loaded with ties and rails to the repaired roadbed. Relays of shirtless troopers ran the iron ahead to the spikers– twelve men to a rail, two to a tie. Portable forges mounted on cars hammered away like the "Anvil Chorus" straightening rails twisted by Confederate raiders. Rolling kitchens, with mules slouching in harness served by swarms of colored dogrobbers, parked beside the tracks dishing up hot grub to lines of troopers. Cavalry rode by at the trot in both directions, while teams of sweat-flecked mules pulled loads of looted timbers from local barns and houses to build the next bridge. With the iron clang of the hammers, the shouting of the line bosses, the shriek of the locomotives and the swearing of the teamsters, Dodge reckoned it great wit to refer to his rolling kingdom as "Hell on Wheels." It was all of that. Dodge's Division wasn't with the rest of Sherman's Corps when they stormed up the north end of Missionary Ridge three days later but they did as much to insure Grant's victory with their hammers and shovels as any of their brothers did with bayonets.[j]

An officer with means can travel in style and Dodge was an officer with means. His private car was fitted out like the lobby of the Palmer House. After snapping the last orders to his staff in the setting twilight

---

[j] Sawyer must have been with Dodge on November 21, 1863. Sherman's Corps attacked Missionary Ridge on Tuesday, November 24.

we retired to his rolling boudoir and it was anything but hell on wheels. Past the grand salon was Dodge's personal cabin. It had its own private toilet chamber that sported a sink with running water. Beyond it were two smaller cabins that were divided by panels that slid aside to make one larger cabin as the situation demanded. These guest cabins sported walnut woodwork, velvet curtains, neat bunks that folded flat to the wall, and chamber pots on shelves at a handy height besides the cots. Leave it to Dodge to have his thunder-buckets crafted in the latest style. They were formed from heavy porcelain but the rims were folded inward to make a sort of seat that was molded to fit a body's hindquarters. Squatting on it would be as comfortable as perching on the seat of your own outhouse. Two of the division's adjutants were bunked in the forward cabin and a disgruntled staff major was hauling his traps from the rear chamber. I wouldn't be sleeping under canvas tonight.

The salon took up two-thirds of the car, was decorated like a Memphis bordello and smelled as good as Delmonico's. His cooks didn't have lobster, but they had a silver bucket of 'lobster dainties' that I reckoned were crawdaddy tails cleaned, dressed, and floated in drawn butter. We washed them down with a damn good hock and then dug into the main dish which was a short rib marinated in a queer but delicious sauce that only a dago chef could conjure up. They were the best I ever ate, but by the time Dodge shuffled the cards and we anted up the chips for a round of whisky poker my guts were running like the town drains. Highfalutin' fare don't sit well in the tripes after Army rations and pecans.

The stakes were light, we played with Confederate shinplasters, but with a half-dozen brandy-flips on top of the wine, the dainties and the ribs, I was crepitating like a beaner vaquero. I was down three hundred dollars by the time we slapped backs and bundled off to bed. I didn't care. In real Yankee greenbacks I was only down about fifteen bucks. Between giggles, I farted my way to my chamber, never giving a thought to Boone sleeping in the dew and damp on the ties beneath the car. Hell, I was a colonel. Didn't I have it coming?

And I did have it coming. Bless Dodge, he was a man after my own heart, and by the time I got my boots and britches off there was a tapping at my door and in peeked a chubby little hooker with mousey hair and cheeks rouged to match her purple dressing gown. Dodge was a great believer in horizontal refreshments and I was his guest. This would usually be a dandy after-dinner-treat but I was not at my best. The split-tail, Opelika by name, was willing, but Lord, I was drunk, the grub was inflating my gizzard like a bladder-ball and she smelled like a teamster. Opelika was an Alabama gal with no love for the Yankees. She shucked off her robe and tended to her business but she wasn't a willing worker. She wiggled her bouncers in the approved style and encouraged Little Sidney in the usual manner, trying first this and then that and then the other thing– but it was no soap. My little Bengal Lancer stayed in his thimble. I was too wallpapered to care and why a gentleman like G.M. Dodge would suffer a cheap trollop like Opelika to board his train I couldn't imagine. She was several rungs below my usual standards and didn't seem to like me. Stargazers are supposed to be frisky and fun. She was slow and sullen. I put her attitude off to Southern politics, floated a wicked air biscuit, which seemed to offend her, and fell into a sort of sleep. She didn't leave.

It was only a sort of sleep. With the good booze and rich grub after a diet of sheet iron crackers and salt horse my bowels were churning like a Dutch sausage grinder.[k] My dreams were the stuff of childhood night terrors. Brother Tom stood with Ben Rogers and Joe Harper at the front door of our schoolhouse back in St. Petersburg. We were all children but we weren't childish.

---

[k] Sheet iron crackers are hardtack. Salt horse is salted pork.

Joe Harper was in bloody Union blue and he didn't seem to have a head. I knew it was him. I heard his voice– his child's voice, "Siddy, you little sissy! You suckered me with that sucker punch outside the schoolhouse door and then at Shiloh you went and suckered me again and now I don't got no head. I'm gonna fetch you back a lickin', now won't I just?" And then Ben Rogers, dressed in grubby, bloody railroad denim piped up in his voice from our long-ago childhood, "I let you play with my train, Siddy, and you got me gut-shot and you drank all the whiskey. I ain't playin' with you no more," and then he reached into his overalls and pulled out his hand dripping with black blood. "I ain't play'in with you no more." And then Tom sang, "I'm gonna tell Aunt Polly! I'm gonna tell Aunt Polly!"

And then Auntie Polly, who for some reason looked like a cheap railroad whore cracked open the chamber door and whispered, "Slash his belly and bust his tripes– the Yankee bastard! He farts like a hog." And then squeezing through the door was Calhoun Brassard, but I knew it couldn't be because he was dead, but I also knew I was in terrible danger and this wasn't a dream any more and I was awake and knew the slut had invited a killer into my room.

By grapes they had me cold. If they'd have dared to use a gun I was a dead man but it was knives in the dark so as not to rouse the train. I couldn't scream– I was too full of terror from my dreams and now from this real nightmare to force a squeak. The killer glided past mousey Opelika like a wraith and raised his knife-hand high. My sword and pistol were hung with my duds in the tiny cabinet. The nasty boning knife I keep in my boot for just this type of emergency was still in my boot, out of reach beneath the cot. It was only three steps to cross the cabin. I was defenseless and naked under my blanket.

Opelika whispered once again to encourage her chum, "Slit his tripes, Brownie!" and he was above me like a living night terror.

I lived through those next terrible seconds for two reasons. First, the assassin reckoned me asleep and so paused to pick the best spot to bury his blade in my tripes. He should have ignored his slut's suggestion, taken a slash at my throat and been on his way. The second reason was that I never trust a whore. They *are* whores after all. As soon as she poked her head in the door, I rolled up my belt and stuffed it into the nearest hidey-hole. The hidey-hole was the commode shelved with railroad efficiency just to the left of the cot. It was meant to be found in the dark. Since I was a lad at the Academy I've never been without my belt salted with ten gold liberties sewed into the stitching– I still don't. To Opelika it was only a belt in a thunder bucket. To me it was the only salvation within reach.

My left hand fit into it up past my wrist and as the knife plunged towards my gizzard I swung it at the brute's shoulder with the strength of terror. It hit him above his elbow with a thud. The blade opened up the mattress and not my tripes. But he held onto the weapon, and with a curse, backhanded another cut at me that shattered the chamber pot with a smash of crockery.

Now I found my tongue, "Christopher Columbus!" I bellowed. Stupid you may say, but I was under stress. And then in a flash of brilliance I yelled the very best of pleas, sure to bring everyone in earshot running. "Fire! Fire!"

By now the trollop was crawling across the sheets with her dirty fingernails extended at me like talons. My commode was smashed, but in it my fist had found my belt and I slashed it at her like a whip. The heavy buckle found her teeth and she crashed into the killer, knocking him into the flimsy wall that flexed with a distinct 'crack.' Swinging the heavy belt like a demented teamster I charged from the bed, shouldered into him like a bull, and just as Boone came thundering through my chamber door with his musket held like a club, we both cannonballed through the thin panel into the next compartment. It was bedlam with the occupants of the violated chamber shouting bloody murder in their union suits squinting in the dark for the author of this sudden pandemonium. One waved a pistol and the other a sword. The gentle Opelika was lisping vulgar curses through her smashed teeth at Boone while she wrestled him for the musket. I swung my belt blindly, a mighty swing. It fetched a howl from one of the union suits, and my liberties sparkled in the dim light as they flew through the air. I caught the dull gleam of the knife coming at me again and got my hand over his on the handle and hung on for my life. Thank God I had slammed his arm a goodly smash with the chamber pot. My grip on the back of his big knuckles was clumsy but his arm must have lost half of its strength. I tripped backwards over some wreckage from the wall with the brute on top of me. I was naked with my back on the carpet, gripping the swine's knife hand like grim death while all around me were shouts, curses and thuds.

The chamber door opened with a crash, flooding the scene with light and General Grenville Dodge stood backlit in a nightgown with a pistol held high.

"Where's the fire?' he shouted and pumped a round into the ceiling. The explosion of Dodge's pistol stunned the mob to silence. My assassin was the first to recover. With a snarl he wrenched his hand from my grip and lunged toward Dodge with the big blade held like a lance. Union suit with the sword gave a scream like an offended virgin and ran the swine straight through *his* belly and busted *his* tripes.

Opelika screamed, "Brownie!" and lunged toward the killer as he toppled over with his guts leaking like hog killing time. Boone's musket butt caught her face with a vicious smack that spread her nose across her puss in a splash. She was out like a wick. The slut fell on me in a naked heap as if she was finishing the job she came in for. Opelika was a damn poor whore, but with no front teeth and a flapjack nose she'd have to lower her prices.

Dodge surveyed the carnage, lowered his big colt and his face broke out in a happy grin. “Hell on wheels, Sawyer! Ain’t it a grand life on the railroad?”

* * *

The affair was sorted out before the drums roused the rest of the camp. A captain of provost named Bluffton, who reminded me of Major Allen but without the Scottish burr or shabby brown beaver, made his report.[1] The duo of killers was clearly there to assassinate General Dodge. Only sheer stupidity sent Opelika to my door instead of the general’s. Bluffton said she was as dumb as an oyster! Opelika was known about the camp as a cheap trollop who had been escorted from the division’s lines because she had been spreading pox like a Johnny Appleseed with a grudge. ‘Poxy Opel’ had done the division more mischief than any of the rebels I’d seen hanging from the trestles. She had reentered the bivouac by granting her favors to a randy sentry who would be bucked and gagged for his lust– that and a dose of the pox. Thank God, Little Sidney wouldn’t present arms last night or I’d have some explaining to do to Amy.

Brownie was already *in* the camp. He was a sutler whose shop sold the troops a variety of patent medicines, castor oil, hair oil, snake oils, and under the counter, the oil of gladness. The sentry was found with his throat slit twenty yards down the tracks. Brownie must have offered the poor granger a swig of forty rod and when he tilted his head for the swallow he met his maker with whiskey on his last breath.

The two were in cahoots, that was as plain as porridge. Poxy Opel entered the car by virtue of her

---

[1] Major Allen was the nom de guerre of Allen Pinkerton who founded the Secret Service. Refer to the second packet of these memoirs, *The Year of Jubilee* for his adventures with Sidney Sawyer.

occupation and she simply waited until the wee hours to let Brownie in to do the bloody deed. If it wasn't for rich tucker and dreadful dreams I'd be a Frenchified corpse.[m]

Boone was under the salon car when Brownie's tiptoes ruffled the cinders. If the fool had simply stomped onto the car like an honest man, Boone wouldn't have noticed. As it was, he was almost too late to save my arse, but he made up for it by putting out the slut's lights.

Captain Bluffton had Poxy Opel escorted out at arm's length. I didn't know if the Army of the Tennessee hung women but they might have made an exception for Opelika the Hooker.

It was a gay breakfast that morning. Dodge was as merry as Puck leading the mess in crude jokes at my expense, as if he didn't look like a lunatic himself standing in his silk nightshirt, backlit with his lanky carcass silhouetted like a shadow-box, colt pointed at glory with chips of plaster and wood raining down in his beard. He made a grand joke of it and his staff snorted their scrabble out of their noses when he described me dueling his assassin with a chamber pot and winding up naked under a senseless stargazer?

My inspection was over. I'd report back to Grant that Dodge was just the fellow for the job and that everything was humming along on the Nashville line. Time to get back to the cold comforts of Chattanooga. As I boarded the cars on a southbound combination, my back was slapped and my fin was pumped by half of the loafers on Dodge's staff. While Boone hauled our traps aboard they shouted idiot jokes about Rebel hookers, snake-oil peddlers, thunder buckets and the pox. Hell on wheels, indeed! Then the locomotive's drivers ground sparks from the new rails and the train gave a lurch. I reach to slide the door shut and ice washed over me colder than the black

---

[m] Syphilis or the pox had many names. Many Americans called it the French disease. The French called it the English disease.

waters of the Tennessee when I had flipped off the pontoon. My knees quite gave out and I would have fallen headfirst onto the cinders if Boone didn't grab my belt and yank me back into the car. The locomotive gave a screech, the door slammed shut and I was left with the image of Major Melrose Middlesex standing like a bull besides a load of looted lumber. Fee-Fi-Fo-Fum!

The Adventures of Sidney Sawyer
Missouri Yankees

Chapter 24

They weren't after Dodge! They were after me! Poxy Opel didn't blunder into the wrong cabin. She and Brownie were after me, and no error. Middlesex was behind it! The fat bastard was with the Western Armies now and still up to his mischief. In Charleston he was selling medicals to the Confederates and making a fortune. His family was in New England textiles and multiplying that fortune by weaving smuggled Rebel cotton. By God, they paid for that cotton with Yankee medicine. And that blade-swinging dog Brownie was a medico sutler. He must have been in Middlesex's ring of traitors. My presence in Dodge's camp was no secret. The swine must have been licking his fat chops at this heaven sent chance to see to my slaughter. Damnation in the long grass, it was no coincidence that Middlesex was with Dodge's division of gandy dancers. What better way to run quinine, chloroform and opium south than along a railroad that *ran* south? Wherever the War would take the troops in blue and wherever there was Confederate cotton to be traded for Yankee medicals, that was where Middlesex would go. His blasted family would pull wires in Washington and he would be transferred to where the fruits of graft were juiciest. And there wasn't a blessed thing I could do about it. If I tried to peach on the brute he would see me swing for riding with Van Dorn's raiders after Holly Springs. Middlesex had his fat finger in every pie. All I could do about it was to punish the brandy that I'd had the wit to pinch from Dodge for the train ride back to Bridgeport.

At Bridgeport Boone had to prop me up by the elbows for the short hike to the steamboat. I would have tumbled into the Tennessee without him steering me up the gang. I snoozed off the booze while the boat bucked the current to Kelly's Ferry and then traveled the Cracker Line in fine officer style, snoring away on sacks of oats piled in a wagon bound for the nags in Chattanooga. In the late afternoon I was startled awake when the wagon gave a sickening swoop that almost brought up my breakfast booze. The wagon was rolling over the pontoon bridge at Brown's Ferry. The Tennessee River's current was tossing and pitching the bridge like a ship at sea. The mules brayed in terror, the teamsters swore like sailors and I was damned if I was ready to face general Ulysses Grant quite yet. I jumped ship, staggered back to the ferry and dragooned two mounts. I simply stared down the corporal minding the picket of horses and took what I wanted– I'm a colonel, by God!

I wasn't ready to report to Grant, but Hooker was a horse of a different color. I'd slept off most of my morning drunk and was ready for cards, good grub and the low company of Hooker's staff. It would be just the ticket to shake off the horror of Middlesex, and his crew of killers and poxy trollops. But it wasn't to be. Hooker's camp was all a' stir. A slim major with a paper collar and whiskey on his breath buttonholed me and brought me up on the latest gossip. The major's name was Gaylord Fritz, and I do believe he had a hint of the lavender about him, but he was free with his pint, and as long as he kept his hands to himself, who was I to judge?

First, I couldn't have finished my journey to Chattanooga that day even if I'd wanted to. It seems the Johnnys far up river had taken to rafting huge logs together. In the night they cast them into the current to drift downstream. These juggernauts would bash into the flimsy pontoons, rip them to hell-and-gone, and the

Cracker Line would be out of business until the engineers could gin up a new bridge. The bridge above the city at the east end of the line was out. Good! Rawlins couldn't fault my detour to Hooker's traveling circus.

But that wasn't the big news. That morning, Grant had ordered Thomas to line up the entire Army of the Cumberland before the Union works and parade them before the Confederate Army bunkered in along Missionary Ridge. The range was too great for Rebel artillery to reach the splendid Yankee formations, so they simply watched the grand show for what it was– a chance for the Army of the Cumberland to stretch its legs, drill in corps formation, and take advantage of the first decent weather in weeks. And then Thomas pulled a fast one. The secesh pickets and the Cumberland sentries had been enjoying an informal truce– trading Northern newspapers for Southern tobacco and in general letting the rest of the War go hang. Out on Orchard Knob and Indian Hill, two modest high-points about half-way between Union lines and Missionary Ridge, a couple of regiments of Johnnys were enjoying the show. Twenty thousand Yankees marched in parade-ground formation, bayonets shimmering in the sun like waves of rippling water, and the regiments, battalions, divisions and corps wheeled like dancers in a vast pageant. And then, at a single order, the entire mass turned on their heels, and at the double time made straight for Orchard Knob and Indian Hill. After a few ragged volleys the stupefied Confederate defenders scampered or surrendered and the Union lines were extended a full mile closer to the Rebel works on the ridge. What a dirty trick!

But that wasn't the half of it. Hooker had his orders too. Lookout Mountain towered to his front like a frozen avalanche above the mist and clouds. The Confederates had their guns and garrison there, and since the 'Charge of the Mule Brigade' they were a nagging threat to the Yankees below. They were Longstreet's boys, the same fellows who had run through Rosencrans's line at Chickamauga like corn through a goose.

Major Gaylord Fritz positively bubbled, "We have our *orders*! Tomorrow we will run those *rascals* right off Lookout Mountain. It is *our* turn. We will show Sherman's *Westerners* how disciplined *soldiers* fight."

"Ain't you supposed to show the Rebels up on the mountain how disciplined soldiers fight? They're the enemy, ain't they?"

He laughed a high tee-hee and bubbled some more, "Peas and carrots, of *course* we will! I can't *wait*! I shall go with *Ireland's* brigade. I want to be the *very first* one up. The men will have to *scurry* to get ahead of *me*!" And then Gaylord drew out his pistols for me to admire.

Damned if they weren't twin LeMats! A LeMat is usually a Confederate hand cannon. They made them in New Orleans and Philadephia before the war. They're made in Europe now and the Rebels run them through the blockade for their officers. Most of us bluebellies sported Colts and I had my Remington. What the deuce was this little prancer doing with two? And his were dandies, the metal was blackened, buffed to a luster and they were covered with fancy filigree that must have cost more than the pieces themselves.

"*Mother* brought me these from *Paris*! They're *brand new*. I can't *wait* to try them out tomorrow," and he gritted his teeth and actually said, "Grrrrrr!"[n]

Well, I reckoned him a sissy, but if he was, he was a damned bloodthirsty one. If he couldn't wait to lead an assault up that hill tomorrow, I could and I wanted no further part of him. Besides, his flask was empty and his manner was beginning to irritate.

---

[n] The LaMat was a .42 caliber, nine shot, percussion cap revolver. It had a second barrel, below the first, that fired a single 20-gauge load of buckshot. It was highly regarded by Confederate officers such as Braxton Bragg the Confederate commander opposite Chattanooga.

* * *

I wasn't with Gaylord's assault that next day, and thank Providence for that. I'm an old campaigner and should have known better, but after I handed my horse to Boone, I was foolish enough to stick my nose into Hooker's mess tent in search of some good grub. I noticed the division commanders and their staffs were absent, presumably they were preparing their commands for tomorrow's action, but Hooker was there in full martial glory. He was surrounded by his usual rabble of staff ticks. His uniform was splendid, sword and sash swinging dramatically, hogleg holstered, weak chin jutting, and his toadys striking noble poses. His cavalry boots were pulled up to his thighs, their spurs gleamed and jingled, and the brim of his wide-awake hat was pulled low to shade his eyes as he posed in his tent at nine o'clock at night. Hooker recognized me at a glance, knew I was Grant's man, and lit on me like a goose on a grub.

"Sawyer!" the pompous ass boomed, "you arrive just in time for the action. We shall sweep them off of that mountain. With General Osterhaus's division I shall have ten thousand men. While Thomas, Grant and Sherman sulk behind their trenches, I shall have my victory."

By grapes, the man *was* a braggart. He went from 'we shall' to 'I shall' in two seconds. The two-dozen staff officers packed under the canvas nodded like puppets, snickered at the hopeless-helplessness of the two western armies and drained their cups. I grabbed a mug of flip from a passing corporal who was doubling as a barmaid and joined in the bragging. I can butter up a general as well as any eastern staff loafer.

My buttering up didn't work.

"Sawyer, you are a Missouri man, are you not?

"Indeed, General Hooker, sir!"

"And you are with Grant and Sherman and their western rowdies, are you not?"

"Well, ahh, that depends– ahh…"

"And you have a soft spot for the n—rs– the Ace of Spades, eh?"

Damn, the officer corps gossiped like biddies. Did everybody know?

"General Hooker, sir, I serve where I'm sent."

"And so you shall. General Osterhaus is a Missouri man under Sherman's command. Well, for now he is under my command and I put you under his command. You can both learn a lesson in real soldiering from the Army of the Potomac!"

* * *

General Peter Joseph Osterhaus learning real soldiering from the likes of Joe Hooker was the idea of an idiot, but then Hooker *was* an idiot. If you don't believe it take a squint at the painting he commissioned to glorify his victory at Lookout Mountain. The blasted thing cost Hooker $20,000 and covers an entire wall. In the center Hooker rides in glory astride a prancing white charger while his staff flanks him right and left looking on in adoration. Fore and aft, masses of infantry swarm towards a mountain that looks to be five miles away. It was about as accurate as one of my son Ranty's finger paints and the arrogant swine left me out. When it toured through Buffalo back in '85 I paid my dime to see it. Osterhaus was there. I wasn't![o]

Osterhaus was a St. Louis Dutchman– a genuine Prussian with a cabbage-eating accent that could strip bark. I'd met him before during the Vicksburg Campaign and there was nothing Hooker's eastern crew could teach him. He had learned soldiering in Germany where they knew their business. Sherman's Corps had only lately

[o] Sawyer is referring to the 13x30 canvas by James Walker completed in 1874. It is now displayed in a National Park pavilion at the top of Lookout Mountain.

arrived from their long march from the Mississippi. They were tucked away in the tall timber north of Chattanooga all a' lather to pitch into the Confederate works on the north end of Missionary Ridge. Because of the Reb shenanigans with the pontoon bridges, Osterhaus's division was stranded on the wrong side of the river with Hooker's eastern troops. Osterhaus and his staff were disgusted with the situation but Hooker was so elated he pranced about like his Major Gaylord Fritz. Now he would have three divisions and ten thousand men for his grand assault. His two eastern divisions under Cruft and Geary would make the attack. Osterhaus would go east around the mountain, hugging the tracks along the river in support.

In the end it wasn't much of a battle. We couldn't know it then, but Braxton Bragg had watched the massive assault on Orchard Knob. It gave him the vapors. He ordered half the troops on Lookout Mountain down to reinforce Missionary Ridge.

At dawn, which in Hooker's Corps meant nine o'clock in the morning, three divisions began the assault. Hooker's two Army of the Potomac divisions crossed Lookout Creek just north of Wauhatchie. It must have been a grand review, just the kind of show Hooker loved, but alas, nobody else could see it in the fog. Then they started up the mountain. In the rat's nest of trails winding up around the rocks and through the woods, the grand review broke apart into companies and platoons laboring up through the briars. And then for two hours nothing much happened. Poor Gaylord must have been going out of his skin looking for some accommodating Confederates to try out mother's new pistols.

Lookout Mountain is around 1500 feet high. About two-thirds of the way up is a sort of ledge or bench, a couple of hundred feet wide that wraps around the point facing the river. That is where the Rebels dug their works and made their stand. It was the only place on the blasted hill *to* make a stand. Longstreet did have batteries on the point of the crest, but they could only be supported from a treacherous road that wound up from the far end of the bench. Take the bench and you took the whole hill. At about eleven in the morning the first of the Yankees reached the Rebel pickets, fire erupted from the woods, Hooker's artillery below at Lookout Creek opened up by the battery and the ball was in motion. I hoped Two-Gun Gaylord was having fun.

I wasn't. I wasn't in any particular distress but it wasn't fun. I slouched along in the saddle at the rear of Osterhaus's staff and tried not to get in the way. We crossed Lookout Creek and kept pace with the advance above from the sound of the battle. There was damned little to see. Drizzle, fog and mist covered the hill, soaked our clothes, chilled our bones and blocked our view. The musket fire above was scattered and sounded in fits and starts. Around noon the mists cleared and volley fire erupted from the bench in earnest. It became a solid roar for a quarter hour and then it stopped.

Had we won? The mist was gathering again and we squinted into it to see which flags were waving above. But the slope was too steep, the brambles too thick and the fog too dense to tell, so Osterhaus, damn him, sent me up to take a look.

"Hooker schent us to vhere ve can do no good! Hooker vas ordered by Grant to take ze point of ze bergüchen only if zis demonstration should develop it vas practical. Ze kasperlkopf[p] means to have it, practical or no."

Kasperlkopf?

"Ve are here to support. Ya? But vhat are ve to support? Go up ze bergüchen unt see."

Bergüchen?

"Go! Go now!"

---

[p] In German, Kasperlkopf means fool. Bergüchen means the point of a peak.

And I went and took Boone with me. We left our nags and went straight up the slope. It was steep, but hanging on to branches and rocks we made our way up with no danger of tumbling down. All the while we heard scattered fire from above and artillery arched high over our heads with a buzzing whiz through the damp air that I never heard before or since. In a half-hour we hit a trail that switched back and forth up the slope and the going became easier, but the sounds of battle became louder. And then we were there. Our trail merged with another where troops in blue labored up the trail past the bodies of dead pickets. Walking wounded staggered the other way holding arms, bellies and mangled faces. A file of Confederate prisoners in deplorably ragged uniforms, half of them barefoot in the late November chill, sulked down the path guarded by a company of infantry. It was a damn long file and looked to be a whole regiment. We must be winning.[q]

We were blowing like nags in the knacker's yard but managed to keep up with the troops bustling up the path. We couldn't very well rest on a log while the solders hurried towards the sound of the guns. I'd be recognized. How would it look? We weren't even carrying packs. And then, just before us was a ripping volley and cheers and what sounded like an answering volley, and we were on the bench with the ground open and level ahead.

Union troops were charging a Rebel line before a substantial house at a wide spot on the bench. They went at the run over the bodies of dead Yankees who must have fallen in the action that had Osterhaus fetch me up the mountain. And they fell too, but not many and before they were halfway to the Rebel works, the Johnnys were up and running to the rear. The union men raced forward past the house with a roar, charged around the point of Lookout

---

[q] This may have been the 34th Mississippi that was cut off and surrendered en masse.

Mountain and Hooker had his victory. The sun broke through the mist. The panorama of river and mountains spread before us and we could see all of Chattanooga and the Union works spread below us as if we were flying above it like birds of prey. We could see Hooker's artillery batteries lined up like toys at the mouth of Lookout Creek and other guns across on the crest of Moccasin Point. To the right were the Confederate works along Chattanooga Creek and in the distance Missionary Ridge stretched to the northern horizon. We could see entire armies, Yank and Reb, and they could see us. Union flags and regimental banners waved from the point of the bench in jubilation and some romantic fool watching below christened it the Battle Above the Clouds.[r]

Of course it didn't end quite there. The Rebels dug in farther down the bench and held off Hooker's boys for another few hours. Hooker didn't help. He sent conflicting orders, lost his nerve and then found it again, and for the rest of the day fighting continued in fits and starts. With the bench taken, if the Confederates didn't want to lose their guns on the summit, they had to evacuate them and during the night that's what they did. And they did it under a blood moon. The night was as bright and clear as crystal under a full moon. From below, skirmishing between the pickets looked like fireflies sparkling across the mountain. And then the earth's shadow passed over the moon. I had never seen the like before, but knew what it was– an eclipse. Under that shadow 100,000 men on both sides looked up in awe as the moon turned blood red and they wondered if it meant good or ill for the day to come.

---

[r] This romantic fool was the Quartermaster General of the Union Army, Montgomery C. Miegs. He is noted for turning Robert E. Lee's plantation, Arlington, into a National Cemetery.

The Adventures of Sidney Sawyer
Missouri Yankees

Chapter 25

I never reported back to Osterhaus. To hell with him! If anyone questioned me, and no one ever did, I simply didn't understand his orders. I don't speak Dutch. The next morning I made my way to the peak with a procession of other officers who reckoned sightseeing more important than duty. After all, this was Hooker's Corps. If I thought the view from the bench was grand, the view from the top was spectacular. Directly below, the Tennessee snaked around Moccasin Point. There was Brown's Ferry to the left and Chattanooga straight across the valley. And there in the near valley to our right was Hooker's Corps standing in formation doing nothing at all. It looked like they were ready to cross the Chattanooga River but the retreating Johnnys had burned the bridge. There was a cluster of activity along its near bank which must have been Potomac engineers laboring to rebuild the span. What the hell were those loafers doing down there? They'd had all night! When I checked their progress after a late lunch they were still at it. In Mississippi last summer I had watched Sherman's roughnecks throw up a bridge literally while the troops were marching up to it. They'd do it in hours and have time to add railings. On one bridge they even erected a navy-style flagpole. If Sherman was down there he'd have had them shot!

Away off to the east sprawled Missionary Ridge. Before it on either side of Orchard Knob was the Army of the Cumberland deployed in thick lines of blue that stretched a mile to either side. There they stood, or hopefully sat, all day. If they were waiting for Hooker to build his bridge before they'd pitch in, they would have a damned long wait. And away and far away, off to the northern-most end of Missionary Ridge there was a smoky fog that may have been mist. But it wasn't mist. It was smoke from a battle. I reckoned it must be Sherman's newly arrived men from the Army of the Tennessee, and it was. The far distant artillery, no louder than the occasional acorn bouncing off my hat, rose and fell all that morning and into the afternoon. I was too far away to hear musketry, even by the volley, but throughout the long day smoke from the guns drifted away to the east.

There was a battle going on in the distance. A fight I wanted no part of. You wouldn't get me down off of Lookout Mountain without tying me to a stretcher and strapping me into a wagon. If I had reported back to Grant I know the brutal little tramp would have stuck me into the line, chewed his blasted cigar and grunted, "Go git 'em." No, I stayed on the mountain all through that day and missed the blood, and the glory, and the miracle.

With Hooker stuck before his bridge, Thomas's Army idle before the ridge and Sherman too distant to consider, my new chums from the Potomac and I decided to see the sights. We made a picnic of it. The top of the hill was broken by huge gaps between gigantic boulders. We jumped between the gaps like mountain goats and just to show we weren't sissies, struck casual poses with the toes of our boots hanging over the edge of sickening drops. From the boulders it was twenty or fifty or one hundred feet straight down to where the tops of tall trees hid the steep slopes that ended at the bench. We rummaged through the traps and rubbish left by the Confederates in their midnight retreat. They took their guns, but left a surprising amount of gear behind, including furniture, a likely looking darkie named Cookie, a small guitar that one of the wags used to lead us in song and a carton with four quart jugs of farmer's peach brandy.

The best views were where the Johnnys had placed their batteries. The trees and brush had been cleared away to create fields of fire and there was plenty of room to pull up benches to enjoy the show. By now Hooker's men had crossed the Chattanooga River and were in position around the hamlet of Rossville at the south end of Missionary Ridge. There they waited. Three miles farther up the valley on either side of Orchard Knob waited the 25,000 men of the Army of the Cumberland, and in the misty distance the smoke from Sherman's fight was clearing away with the breeze. Had we lost? Other than Sherman's effort, it didn't look as if we had even tried.

Thank God, I had the sense to stay on the Mountain. In the wake of this fiasco my shirking would go unnoticed. Rawlins would be the only one who would give a rip, but how would he know? I had missed the blood, there was no glory and it would take a miracle to get Thomas across that mile of open land to Missionary Ridge. And then the miracle took place before our eyes. Here is what happened, if you believe it. I *still* can hardly credit it and I saw most of it with my own eyes. The next day, on the ambulance train to Nashville the wounded heroes of the fight filled me in on the bits I couldn't see.

On a fair-sized ledge of naked rock a score of yards below an abandoned battery, twelve of us lounged on the edge and watched the show. Contraband Cookie made himself useful and swept away the acorns dropped from the oaks lining the point that shaded us with the last of their autumn leaves. We dangled our feet over the void, passed around a jug of peach lightning and sang sentimental airs to the guitar strummed by a lieutenant of engineers. My companions were a mellow lot, and why not? The Potomac boys had won *their* battle. We were, after all, sitting on the very mountain *we* had captured. If Sherman was getting a bloody nose he was, after all, only leading western rowdies. If Thomas wasn't even *in* the scrap, well his men had been whipped already at Chickamauga, hadn't they?

And then we clearly heard the sharp pop of a gun. It was miles closer than the distant artillery that had rumbled since morning. And then another gun and another, and then three more sounded, clearly and distinctly. Pop! Pop! Pop! Six guns, and at the sound of the last, the floor of the valley before Missionary Ridge came alive as the thick blue lines of the Army of the Cumberland moved forward in parade ground perfection. Then the sound of 25,000 cheering men and the drummers of sixty regiments reached us on our cliff. We couldn't make it out then, but they were shouting their battle cry– "Chickamauga! Chickamauga!"

We stood up and shouted too! It was magnificent! It was suicide! By great good luck I was holding the passing jug and took a greedy swallow of the raw peach liquor that scalded my throat and set my nose and eyes to run. I was watching the suicide of an entire army and didn't know whether to cheer or cry. I'd seen slaughter at Ft. Donalson and Shiloh. At Antietam I'd seen Sumner's Corps slaughtered by the numbers before the grim Confederate killers in Bloody Lane. Before Vicksburg I had charged up Grave Yard Road with Sherman's 3rd Iowa to see my regiment butchered before my eyes, but I had never seen anything like this. Had *anyone ever* seen anything like this? Missionary Ridge was a natural fortress protected by a hundred or more guns that the Rebel red straps had months to sight in on every avenue of approach. There were prepared rifle pits along the entire base and crest, and another line dug in halfway up the slope. Before them was an entire Union Army, four divisions of infantry, marching to their deaths with bayonets shimmering in the sun and brave banners leading the way to heaven. There had been other grand assaults in other wars in other lands, but had anyone ever had a god's view of the entire pageant like the dozen of us half-drunk officers and one contraband slave named Cookie?

On marched the thick ribbons of blue– occasional groves of trees or rises and dips of uneven ground did nothing to disrupt the order of the formations– and on they came. They covered one hundred yards and two hundred and then in an explosion of smoke and thunder the entire crest of Missionary Ridge erupted. Shot ripped into the Clumberlands like the hand of an angry God. Like a single beast stung by hornets, the entire Federal line sprang into a run towards the ridge, a ridge that filled the horizon before them with a vision of flame and death. The Confederate guns roared again in a rolling volley. Then every gun fired as it was served, and the roar became a constant crash. Now the muskets from the rifle pits at the base of the hill joined in the murder but the Army of the Cumberland never hesitated– not for a single step. And then they were there, at the base of the ridge and at the end of the line nearest to us we could see the Rebels swarming from their works and crawling up the hill. They ran and stumbled and crawled with both hands. *Both hands*– they'd left their muskets to climb all the faster and all along the line as far as we could see through the smoke, the ribbons of blue reached the base of the hill and we could hear their cheers from our perch on the mountain, three miles away.

The cannon never relented– either side. Union crews served their guns strung along the valley in plain sight of the Confederate batteries on the crest. Firing upward was a disadvantage but their work was beginning to tell as their shells exploded over the Rebel works in bright flashes of light. The Southern gunners ignored the Northern batteries and rained fire on the Cumberland infantry, now crowded into the captured rifle pits at the base of the ridge.

My fellow spectators on the ledge gave out a groan at the sight of the killing before our eyes. The poor fools couldn't stay where they were. It was the same fix the Colored 94th was in when we captured the Johnny rifle pits before Battery Wagner. My God, was it actually three months ago? But then my boys had their secret weapon, two shovels for every man, and they dug themselves into solid protection before the Rebels could sight their guns.

These poor devils had only their bayonets and fingernails, but with the Rebels pouring fire straight down upon them from the heights no trench could save them. To stay where they were was death. To retreat back across the valley would invite slaughter from the back with the salt of bitter disgrace rubbed into their wounds.

And then some rude bastard gave me a sharp elbow and chirped in my ear, "Are you going to *drink* that jug or *hatch* it like an egg?"

The cheek! I dragged my eyes from the tragedy across the valley and there stood Major Gaylord Fritz.

"*Grand* show, Colonel Sidney, don't you know? I *hope* those fellows are having as much fun as *we* did yesterday."

"I thought I smelled lavender you little flit" I snarled, "and what fun is that? Those are our men down there being butchered like mutton. Fun?" The peach tangle-foot was beginning to show in my choice of words.

"*Your* men, Colonel Sidney, not *our* men. Those are all western *ragamuffins*, not *real* soldiers like Hooker's *eastern* troopers. And don't *worry* yourself. They'll be just *fine*. *See*!"

And I looked and couldn't believe what I saw. The entire line was scrambling up the steep slope of Missionary Ridge like a swarm of blue ants. They were trying the impossible. The hill was three hundred feet high and there were at least as many defenders as attackers. The entire Army would be lost! What idiot ordered this disaster?

"Now be a *good* boy and hold that jug up to my lips. With my new *mittens* I have to be *watered* like a *plant*," and he held up his paws for inspection.

His wrists were splinted and bound with crisp white bandages. There didn't seem to be any blood but the tips of his fingers were black and blue. Oh, what the hell? I held the mouth of the jug to his thin lips and he sucked at it like a baby at a nipple. When I lowered it the air sucked back into the jug like a sump. The delicate little spiv didn't even take a labored breath after swilling a pull that would have had my throat flaming around my tongue.

Our attention was drawn back to the battle by cheers from the officers on the ledge. They threw their hats and pounded backs as the blue lines made it up and over the rifle pits that the Rebels had prepared halfway up the slope. By grapes, now the Johnnys were running back and up the ridge in swarms. The Cumberlands were reforming their formations as we watched. Their officers must be taking them in hand. We could actually see the tiny flickers of a thousand musket barrels as ramrods drove fresh rounds home and they loaded their rifles by the numbers. Then off they went again, regimental flags leading the way. There and there, the Rebels in butternut would rally and make a stand, a flag would fall, but a fresh hero would raise it high, the blue would swarm and the butternut mob would scatter up the hill.

Who had ordered this madness? The guns had signaled the advance a scant half-hour before. The shadows were long, the day was spent, but by sunset the truth of it had spread through the entire Army. No one had ordered it. The entire glorious, bloody miracle had– just happened.

Hooker was useless squatting with his corps at the south end of Missionary Ridge. At the far off northern end on Tunnel Hill, where the railroad line to Knoxville was burrowed under the mountain, Sherman had attacked Rebel positions again and again. Tunnel Hill wasn't even part of Missionary Ridge proper, but if Sherman's men could take the crest they could swarm up to the ridge itself. Then they would rampage from north to south, along the entire length of the hill, and roll up the entire Confederate line. But couldn't be done– not by flesh and blood.

A mick general named Cleburne planted his division along the ridgeline and stopped Sherman cold. And I fancied that it was only *our* army that was infested with the Irish. Cleburne's graybacks fought like Mohammedan fanatics. Through the entire day we had heard the distant rumble and saw the smoke from Sherman's attacks. The men of the Army of the Tennessee charged straight up through the briars and bracken and into the teeth of the Rebel guns. They did it again and yet again and each assault was drowned in blood. If I wasn't shirking up on Lookout Mountain, nursing farm liquor down the muzzle of a crippled flit, Grant would have sent me to Sherman as sure as nits make lice. It could have been a hard day for Amy and Auntie.

Through the long day, with the Army of the Cumberland deployed as their personal bodyguards, Grant and Thomas waited on Orchard Knob for the news of Billy Sherman's victory. They sat on their nags counting the hours, waiting for the word, but the only word was stalemate. A hard Yankee defeat was in the wind– and then Grant rolled the dice. He ordered Thomas to make a demonstration before the center of the ridge to see if he could bluff Bragg into pulling troops from Cleburne to reinforce his center. Then, just maybe, Sherman could win the day. It didn't work, or it didn't work the way Grant expected.

It was to be just a demonstration. Just a *demonstration*, damn it! The Cumberlanders were damaged goods. They had stampeded at Chickamauga and starved like helpless dogs for six weeks before Grant and their betters opened up the Cracker Line. At the sound of those six guns they were to march out to only the *base* of Missionary Ridge, take the first line of works, which shouldn't have been too difficult, and then wait for orders. Sure, they'd be shot up advancing the terrible mile through the valley, but they should take their medicine like men and let the real soldiers win the war.

At the sound of the six cannon they did advance and they did take their medicine. We saw the gaps swept through their ranks by Confederate canister. And they did take the rifle pits. We saw the Johnnys fleeing in terror up the hill. But they couldn't *stay* there. They would be slaughtered. They couldn't retreat, death was less bitter than a new humiliation. So, in ones and twos and then in companies and then by the regiment, they went up the mountain. Their officers ordered them back. They ranted and raved and threatened and in the end they went up with their men, scrambling to get to the front of the mob so they could lead like officers should. They knew it was hopeless, but what could they do, and on they went, up the hill. They advanced in flocks like birds, like geese that cover the November skies in great 'Vs', but these were flocks of men in blue. They went up in fits and starts until their captains and colonels caught up with them and brought some order to the swarm. They went up! The great 'Vs' led by regimental banners carried by the bull goose, and when the bull goose was cut down the banner wouldn't touch the ground. It was picked up and waved in insane defiance by the next hero and then the next.

Back on Orchard Knob, Grant chewed through his cigar. "Thomas, who ordered that advance?"

Nothing rattled George Thomas. Calm as a trout he rumbled, "I do not know. I did not."

He was so calm that Grant spit his cigar into the weeds. He turned to Gordon Granger, the commander of the Cumberland's IV Corps, the man who had personally fired the signal guns, and snarled, "Granger, did you order them up?"

Granger was a grim regular army veteran but at the sight of his men swarming up the ridge he was bouncing in his saddle like a boy and grinning through his beard. "No, they started up without orders– but when those fellows get started all hell can not stop them." And then he waved his hat, gave a crow like the cock of the walk and grinned defiance at Grant.

What could Grant do? He couldn't stop them either. He sat in his saddle besides Thomas and Granger and fumbled with his next cigar. As Grant perched on Orchard Knob, watching a miracle but dreading disaster, I perched on Lookout Mountain watching the same miracle beside black Cookie and lavender Gaylord. I had the better view.

The Rebel batteries couldn't depress their barrels far enough to reach the scrambling Yankees. Even if they could they couldn't fire for hitting their own troops who were frantically climbing to escape the blue avalanche– an avalanche that roared *up* the mountain.

And then I realized that they just might do it. They *were* doing it! The first Federal flags had reached the crest. Confederate gunners were wheeling their cannon around to fire down the length of their own works, but the Cumberland lads were swarming up behind them, firing into the backs of the gunners who abandoned their pieces and joined the fleeing Johnny infantry that was running down the far side of Missionary Ridge back toward Georgia.

The Billy Yanks were forming into proper formations across the width of the crest. Not just one line, but formations there and there and there, advancing along the ridge line, some to the south and others marching north. The Rebel diehards were being squeezed between the Federals who were coming at them from right and left and other men in blue still coming up the hill in swarms.

And then the Confederate troops did something that Southern soldiers simply did not do. They broke. Some of them threw down their guns and threw up their hands before the menace of the Yankee bayonets. Most ran. They broke and ran. They abandoned their guns and ran. In an instant what had been a battle became a rout. Thick ribbons of blue infantry lined the eastern crest of Missionary Ridge. They and hooted and jeered and waved their banners at a sight they never reckoned to see. The sight was Confederate backs pounding and tumbling down the far side of their impregnable bastion in frantic retreat. We could hear them from across Chattanooga Valley as they cheered for the miracle they had performed.

From our ledge on Lookout Mountain we cheered too. We thumped backs, sang out three cheers and a bulldog, and broke open the last bottle of peach tanglefoot. By God, it was a sight to see, a sight that only spanned an hour from the pop of the signal guns to the roar of the Army of the Cumberland shouting themselves hoarse on the crest of the ridge.

I held up the jug for Gaylord to suck another swig and laughed at his clumsy mittens of white bandage. They practically glowed in the gathering dusk as the sun set behind the mountain.

"What the hell happened to your paws, Fritz? Get 'em slammed in a Confederate cookie jar?"

He giggled as a strong evening gust swept up the mountain, rattled the oaks and sent a shower of acorns bouncing off our hats. "It was Mother's *pistols*, Colonel Sidney, *not* the Rebels. I was in the *middle* of the fight with *both* pistols blazing. Oh, it was *thrilling*! Bang-bang-*bang*!"

He pointed his bandaged mitts like guns and grinned like a girl. "And *then* those Confederate rascals scampered away like *lambs* and it was *over* before I could give them a good what for!"

"So how did you punish your hands?"

"Oh, it isn't my *hands*, it is my wrists. To celebrate my victory I pointed *both* my pistols to the sky and fired *both* barrels of *buckshot* at once. The recoil was *simply savage* and both my wrists were sprained to *noodles*."

What an idiot! I roared with the happiest laugh I had since I bumped into Secretary Edwin Stanton on the train in Indianapolis. The army was victorious. The Rebels were gone. I was safe. Safe! There wouldn't be any more campaigning this year. The army would go into winter quarters and I was safe. I laughed at the silly little prancer who reckoned combat to be thrilling, "Bang-bang-bang!" and the other officers laughed along with me. His wrists were sprained to *noodles*!

"Haw-haw-haw!" and I tilted my head back for another pull at the sweet peach liquor, took a backward step and felt the acorns rolling beneath my boots. As if I were on skates I rolled off the cliff.

The Adventures of Sidney Sawyer
Missouri Yankees

Chapter 26

I broke both my ankles. It was my own damned fault, but you will excuse me if I felt hard used. I'd survived the battles before Chattanooga with nothing worse than a dunking with the pontoon flotilla, being set upon by Middlesex's homicidal sutlers and poxy trollops, and skinning my knees scampering up Lookout Mountain behind Hooker's paper-collar soldiers. And then, when I was out of the woods and safe as houses, I get sent over the edge by a momma's boy whose paws were in splinted mittens, a swig of raw peach lightning and a handful of acorns. Where's the justice?

I went over the edge like a puppy down a well. My yelp could be heard all the way to Missionary Ridge. It was a straight drop of twenty feet at least, through the tops of trees and into the thick brush that covered the sixty-degree slope that continued for a score of yards until the next straight drop that ended two hundred feet below at the bench. Crashing through the trees I had the sense to flex my knees, which I'm sure saved my long leg bones from ripping from their sockets and jamming their way up into my guts, but my ankles broke like cheap china. Then I went head first into the bushes and briars that tangled along the hellish slope. My face, arms and belly were cruelly scratched, but I ain't complaining. Those bushes save my life. I came to a stop with my arse tangled in the prickers and my head and shoulders hanging in space over a drop that loosened my bladder awash with peach farmer's brandy into my britches. I was sore hurt, but not embarrassed. I'd seen better men than me load their drawers with far less cause.

It took a half hour for my drunken mates to reach me and another hour to cut off my boots and strap my carcass to a stretcher. Boone and Black Cookie hauled me back up to the gun emplacement like so much dunnage. I said before that you wouldn't get me off Lookout Mountain without tying me to a stretcher and stuffing me into a wagon. In the end, that's exactly how I came down, with Boone nursing me like a bairn in arms. Thank Providence he and Cookie were there to tend me.

In the wee hours of the night we reached the dressing station for Hooker's Corps at Wauhatchee Station. The medicos had been at it hammer and tongs since the day before when the first of the shot-up boys were hauled down from the Battle Above the Clouds. Last night, a few hundred of Sherman's wounded had been barged down from the slaughterhouse around Tunnel Hill. The surgeons were drunk with fatigue. The grass beneath their feet had long since turned to a gumbo of blood and excrement that stunk like a long drop privy. The screaming of the honorably maimed, the swearing of the teamsters hauling in the wounded by relays, and the cursing of the exhausted medicos created a din from the lower pits of hell. That din matched exactly the sights and the stench and the horror.

An orderly sergeant with his sleeves soaked in gore up to his chevrons, took a quick glance at my feet. They were swollen like bladders and black and blue to the knees. With a chalk he scribbled some letters on my breast, pointed to a line of men lying in the mud and barked at Boone, "Set him yonder with them fellers."

Some of the men were screaming, one was fingering beads and muttering prayers– a Papist no doubt, and the rest were white with shock and despair. Every one of them had legs that were smashed and torn by shot or shell. As they carried me to the end of that gruesome line, another boy was tossed onto a sodden stretcher and lugged into a brightly illuminated tent where the surgeons had set up their bloody shop. His terrified keening was cut short when a chloroformed rag was draped over his face.

The sergeant saw the horror on Boone's face and said in a voice that didn't care if I also heard, "Legs gotta come off– both of 'em– above the knee. Putrify if they don't– kill 'em fer sure." And then he went about his cruel business.

I cried and screamed fit to disgrace the French. I swore and threatened and whined and blubbered. I damned Boone for a fool, a butcher and an ingrate.

"I saved your life, you bucktoothed bastard! Sent your ma off to Lincoln to fetch you a pardon. They should have shot you, you useless swine! You were napping on sentry– sleeping like a dog in the road– firing squad's too good for the likes of you. Oh, save me Boone– save me! Booney-Booney-Booney-Booney! They're gonna saw off my pins. Oh, save me you bastard! Aunt Pollyyyy!"

You know how I go on when I'm in the soup. Next I'd be praying and you know that when I appeal to the Almighty I reckon the game is about up.

In the end the bloody sergeant and his quacks didn't get my legs and I had Black Cookie to thank for it. If that filthy War had taught me anything, it was that a blackbird can be a damned handy thing to have around in a crisis.

Boone was ready to let the sawbones have at my knees with their wicked saws. "Colonel Sawyer, you will die if they don't amputate."

'Amputate'– the word sent me into a sob.

"These here medical men, they know their craft. They say they gotta do it and they are *gonna* do it. I can't let you die of the lockjaw. They gotta do it!"

"No they ain't gotta do it, Misto Boone," Cookie put in his shovel. "Looky them feets. They ain't no skin broke. Ain't no blood, ain't no putrify."

Usually when a darkie butts into a white man's conversation I shut the uppity rascal up sharp, but in this case the colored boy was singing my tune.

I wiped my nose with a long swipe of my sleeve and told him to explain himself.

"My marmee, she was a healin' woman. Folks brung n—rs from all around to her when dey git busted up. Happen all de time. I's seen dis lots a' times. Yo foots be broke is all. Maybe just twisted bad. Don't gotta cut 'em off. If'n I reckoned dat be what dey was gonna do, I wouldn't a brung you here."

My ankles hurt like blazes and my face, arms and belly were scratched to ribbons, but for the first time since the acorns rolled under my boots, things were looking up.

"If not here, then where would you have taken me?"

"Take you to de crick. Soak you in de cold water 'till de swellin' go down. If'n it's winter, I'd pack it with de ice. Marmee say de cold be de best thing for de swellin'. But I tain't gwain to cut off yo feet. Dat fo' sure!"

In the end, Boone and Cookie bundled me onto the same stretcher I was carted in on and they didn't have to soak me in any creek. Hooker's mess was only a hundred and fifty yards down Lookout Creek from where his men had frozen their brogans the day before yesterday on their way to battle up Lookout Mountain. Cookie reckoned the creek water would be cold enough to work its magic, but I reckoned the ice Hooker shipped in to chill his flip, and render his sherbet would be colder still. Any other commander would figure that the last thing an army facing desperate battle would need in its commissary would be ice to cool his dainty treats, but Hooker was Hooker and there it was. Boone barged into the kitchen as bold as a razorback boar hog, dug out a block of ice from its nest of sawdust and claimed it for General Hooker's good friend, Colonel Sawyer. In a half-hour my legs were bundled in a measure of canvas and packed in chunks of Vermont's coldest. In another half-hour the three of us were on an empty ambulance bound back to Chattanooga to fetch another load of wounded.

It took a full week of bad food, whining, and fighting off the quacks who still wanted to ply their saws on my legs, to finally win my way onto a riverboat jammed with convalescents bound for home and mother. I believe that if I wasn't a colonel and didn't have Boone at my elbow for that week, some medico would have draped a chloroform snot-rag over my nose and I would have woken up three feet shorter.

As it turned out it was my old chum General Rawlins who personally saw to my furlough. He couldn't believe that I was actually wounded– malingering was more my style. He had to see for himself and he did. The fussy housewife would never know that I was watching the battle as if it were a baseball pitch and fell off a cliff. I certainly wasn't going to snitch on myself.

Cookie was right. The ice *had* brought the swelling down a bit, but my ankles were a deep purple, shot through with sickening yellow patches, and when you poked at the skin it stayed poked in like a thumbprint in sourdough batter. Rawlings took one look and snapped to a staff flunky to draw up the papers and pack me away to Nashville by soonest transportation. To Rawlins I wasn't an asset. I was only one more threat to his boss's sobriety. He wanted me gone and pronto, bless him.

I was hauled in an ambulance packed with its reeking cargo of invalids across the newly repaired pontoon bridges to Kelly's Ford. From there we were packed like cordwood onto a grubby steamer bound for the railhead at Stevenson.[s] There was some fuss about taking Cookie along. In the end I played the slave card. I was

---

[s] The steamboat was almost certainly the *Chattanooga*, built by General Baldy Smith with the same rough planks as his pontoon flotilla. It was powered by an engine scavenged from a steam-powered cotton gin.

from Missouri and that was still a slave state. Lincoln's proclamation only freed the n—rs in the *Confederate* states. An officer should be able to take his property along with him now, shouldn't he? Cookie had been a *real* slave up to a week ago. When his Rebel masters retreated down Lookout Mountain they neglected to haul him away with their other traps. He was as free as air when the first blue soldiers found him sulking in the shrubbery and he wanted to *stay* free. If the surest way to do that was to tend to my poor feet and call me Mares Sidney, then that was dandy with him.

It was on that riverboat that my colored quack judged my ankles fit to be properly splinted. He did a neat job, as good as any army medico could have done, and even though it hurt like Lucifer I didn't bawl over much. I was surrounded by men who were wounded in real battle–most missing a pin or fin, and it wouldn't do to have a man wounded by acorns and sweet liquor raise a fuss.

At Stevenson we took the cars to Nashville and from there to Louisville where I used the gold liberties in my belt to set up housekeeping in the Galt House.[t] By God, I deserved it. The Galt was the fanciest hotel between Cincinnati and New Orleans. My feet hurt like blazes and my arse was rubbed raw from bouncing on horsehair seats for three days over war-ravaged rails. I stunk like South Buffalo shovel labor and I hadn't had decent grub since Hooker's traveling clambake.

I had plenty of coin and I spent it. While I breathed in the steam from a tub hot enough to soak the crud off of me in layers, a colored barber scraped away at my jaws and trimmed the rat's nest under my hat. A boy ran my poor punished uniform to the tailors and it came back stitched, brushed and pressed neat enough to pass

---

[t] The Galt House is an institution in Louisville. Lincoln, Jefferson Davis, Grant and Sherman stayed there. In 1972 a totally new Galt house was built with 1300 guest rooms.

muster in the lounge. I kitted Boone out in uniform fit for a Colonel's valet and duded Cookie up in duds suitable for a gentleman's darkie domestic. I had the bell-boy whistle me up a wheeled chair, all decent hotels have them, and when Cookie rolled me into the dining room with my hair brilliantined into its pompadour, my whiskers fluffed, my shoulder bars gleaming and my feet dramatically splinted in snowy bandages, I turned the heads of every lady in the room away from their suppers and spouses. The world loves wounded heroes as long as the wounds ain't vivid and the linen's clean.

And a certain class of ladies *also* loves a wounded hero. I had planned on spending one night in Louisville but I made it two when a Mrs. Lucy Newcastle from Bowling Green took a solicitous interest in nursing my wounds. She was one of those women of a certain age that brings delight to younger men who find themselves at loose ends in strange cities. Mrs. Lucy had a full figure with half an acre of powdered bosom rambling from the top hamper of her gown and thick chestnut hair pinned up high enough to brush the chandelier. Her husband was in the Kentucky legislature back in Frankfort, her son was squirreled away in New Jersey, safely out of the War at Princeton University, and her daughters were comfortably married off. What's a lady to do?

Well she did it three times, twice in the night and once for breakfast. I was as randy as a ram-cat and my scratches and ankles didn't consider. I hadn't come to grips with a willing goer since bouncing Libby on the boardwalk. That was back in October and it was already the first week in December. Young men, here's that lesson again from old Professor Sidney and this time take it to heart. If you ever get the eye from an older woman, don't be an ass and let the opportunity pass without investigation. Remember my instruction from when Missy Ruth wrestled me around her counterpane back in Washington City. Mature ladies know more about the capital act than you have dreamed of in your less extensive experience. They may have a bit more flesh than the fillies, but that simply means bigger bouncers and if you don't cotton to a stretch or sag, turn down the light. You may have to watch out for a betrayed husband, but not a daddy with a shotgun and most of them are widows anyway.

Miss Lucy gave me a once over in the Galt House dining room that was as obvious as a railroad flare. Ten minutes after Boone and Cookie hauled me up the stairs Miss Lucy had my britches peeled down past my splints and had fully taken charge of the situation. Usually, I like to drive the trolley but I was off my pins. Feet are damn important when a buck wants to bull a belle. You need them for traction. What could I do? What I did was lie back, let her do the work and enjoy the show. And what a show!

Lucy stripped down to her corset, loosened the strings and climbed aboard. When she pulled the pins from her hair a wild mop spilled out in all directions fit to scatter the birds. To keep it from covering her face she threw back her head and arched her back, which was splendid because it thrust out her dairy tackle fit to pop my eyes. They had me reaching for them with both hands and thank heaven I didn't have splints on my wrists. Her nipples were huge and well worn and were too big to nibble all at once. Below her corset her hips rolled over me like waves at sea and I was actually hooting with lust when– she stopped. She just stopped– froze! I almost exploded, but what could I do? I was on my back sunk deep into a feather mattress and pinned there by twelve stone of matronly flesh.[u] What the hell?

I told you older women know what they're doing. Cool as you like she fumbled in her purse and pulled out a tiny cigar wrapped in white paper. It was the first time I

---

[u] A stone is a British unit of weight equaling fourteen pounds. Mrs. Newcastle must have weighed around 170 pounds.

ever saw a woman smoke a cigarette. I was as shocked as if– well, as if she was naked! She struck a Lucifer on the headboard as brazen as one of Hooker's girls, sucked the smoke deep in her lungs, gave me a slow smile, gave her big hips a little wiggle and was off to the races again like a derby winner.[v]

Aye, older women can be grand tumbles and Mrs. Lucy Newcastle of Bowling Green, Kentucky, was all of that. That afternoon I had Cookie wheel me to the telegraph shop where I sent a wire to Amy that her Sidney would be home from the War on the thirteenth. I didn't say I was laid up. I didn't want her to worry.

* * *

We took a riverboat to Evansville on the Ohio and from there the E&C to Vincennes. Again, the blasted seats blistered my arse, and every rail-butt jolted my feet to distraction, but my route committed me to the cars, at least until the St. Louis ferry. I whined like a brat across the entire state of Illinois and by the time Boone and Cookie hauled me off the O&M across the Mississippi from St. Louis I was ready to swear off railroading for life.[w] We took the *Mt. Carmel,* a stern wheel river queen north from St. Louis. I stowed Cookie in the bow with the rest of the deck cargo. Boone stood at the rail taking in the sights like the hick that he was. I perched on the Texas deck with pillows fluffed under arse and ankles, sipping a damn decent bourbon and smoking Dominican cheroots,.

---

[v] By the Civil War hand-rolled cigarettes were common among soldiers. In 1881, James Bonsack's mechanical cigarette rolling machine revolutionized tobacco consumption.

[w] The E&C was the Evansville and Crawfordsville Railroad, the O&M was the Ohio and Mississippi R.R.

It was well after dark when the boat tied up at the Temple & Son wharf in St. Petersburg, but I had telegraphed ahead and there was a mob waiting for the *Mt. Carmel* and their hero. There was kin from the Sawyer and Lawrence sides, including Amy's pa, July and her ma, Mildred. The Rogers and Harper clans were out in force waving hankies and tiny flags. Schoolmaster Dobbins and the Reverend Mr. Sprague were at the front of the mob looking like cadavers out for an airing. My first boss Mr. Temple and his wife, Miss Margie were there with my old chum, Alfred. Of course they were there to greet me. The Temple clan had gotten rich off of the Army payola I shoveled their way. If I have the coin to run with the Buffalo Brahmans today, it's because of Temple & Son kickbacks I earned back in the War. All wars are greased by graft and if a body can't get rich victualling one side or the other, or better still both sides, than shame on you.

Off by the livery shop were my darkie pals beaming with hats in hand and sporting Sunday best. Jim Watson and little Lizabeth stood with the Widow Moses and half the population of Dark Town. Beside them was Roseasharen with her bosoms catching up with her arse in poundage and a pickaninny brat on her hip. The boy had a red mop of wild hair so I knew he couldn't be mine, praise the Lord. The 94th not withstanding, I'd always gotten along well with darkies. I never hated them on principle like most Missouri men, and back when I was a lonely boy they made damn good friends. The rest of the crowd was the usual flock of loafers you'd expect to be drawn to a circus by jugs of forty-rod liquor provided by Alfred and Mr. Temple. The tangle-foot was a gesture of goodwill to the customers he cheated the rest of the time.

And there, before the crush, was my Amy, arm-in-arm with Auntie Polly. Beside them was our colored maid Scotland, holding up my boy Grant like a trophy. Auntie looked grand, a few extra pounds filling her out to true matronly respectability, and her pearl-gray silk frock and pleated bonnet set her up as river gentry. Amy was a wonder in yellow muslin, with a wide green belt high under her breasts, lace at throat and wrists, and hair thick in a French braid. Grant was as fat as a suckling porker and Scotland couldn't pry his thumb out of his mouth.

The crowd 'ooohed' when Boone and Cookie carried me down the gang with locked hands under my arse. They 'aaahed' when I propped myself up bravely on crutches. They cheered me three-times-three when I wrapped my arms around Amy, Auntie and little Ranty. I was home from the Wars again, and this time it would take more than a dirty trick by that swine Tom Sawyer to fetch me back into the soup.

The Adventures of Sidney Sawyer
Missouri Yankees

Chapter 27

We celebrated Thanksgiving that Sunday. It was December thirteenth if I recall. The family had already had its banquet a couple of weeks before, but my homecoming rated another feast. Hell, two weeks ago the entire nation celebrated Thanksgiving on that *same* day. Of course, us Americans had been slaughtering poultry and tipping our hats to the Almighty since the Pilgrim Fathers and the Indians had their sit-down. But for the first time back in '63, Old Abe made the day official. Us Sawyers had always had our Thanksgiving in October after Auntie, Amy and Mrs. Lawrence had laid up the last of the preserves. This year, and for every year ever after, us Yankees would give our thanks, carve our birds and ladle out the gravy on the last Thursday in November. I hadn't heard the news.

It seems that our Civil War was a political war and after Chickamauga the politics didn't look good. The trolley was again off the tracks. By the end of the summer the victories at Vicksburg and Gettysburg had lost their luster. Rosecrans's pickle in Chattanooga had the North wondering if the War was, after all, winnable. Just what the dickens would we have to do to actually end the thing?

Lincoln knew– pray. Two weeks after Chickamauga the Ancient issued another proclamation. Since Plymouth Rock every state, hell, every congregation could have their Thanksgiving banquet whenever it took their fancy. Lincoln decided it would be politic to get the whole nation to give the Lord his marching orders at the same time, the last Thursday in November.

"Thanksgiving and praise to our beneficent Father who dwelleth in the heavens," and now gentle Lord, how about rolling up your big sleeves and helping us slaughter those impudent Southern rascals who use your Good Book to justify lashing their darkies, wrecking their country and shooting at the Old Flag– Amen! Oh, and one more thing Jesus, please reserve a special place in hell for Nathan Bedford Forrest and George B. McClellan and, if possible Lord, let them be roommates in the deepest pit– Amen."

Aye, Lincoln knew his politics. By the end of November the crisis in Tennessee was over, the Union had a new messiah named Grant, the campaign season was over and the entire nation could sit down to a good meal.[26]

And, by George, the Sawyer clan's second Thanksgiving of 1863 was a *grand* meal– ham and lamb and smoked fish, spuds both sweet and Irish, turnips, squash, beets and beans, gravy, cider and a cranberry pudding that puckered my mouth. Dessert was Amy's gingerbread, Auntie's pumpkin pie with sugared whipped cream, two of Little Lizabeth's apple pies, and coffee with the new Bordon's canned milk.[x] The Sawyer clan including Cousin Mary, her husband Elkton, and their three brats were present. The Lawrences and the Temples squeezed around the table, including Alfred's fat new wife, Birdie– a more useless woman I never met. While the other ladies happily bustled about setting the feast and clearing the dishes, Birdie squatted on the sofa stuffing her face with nuts and figs like a whistle pig.[y]

And a new couple attended our celebration– Captain Terrebonne Blanche, late of the Confederate

---

[x] Sawyer attributed his postwar prosperity to investing his wartime graft and plunder in Gale Bordon's new condensed milk industry.

[y] A whistle pig is a ground hog or a woodchuck.

cavalry and Pietronella Turner, widow of fallen hero, Harper 'Ducky' Turner of the 8th Wisconsin. If you're wondering what a Rebel officer was doing breaking bread in a Missouri Yankee household and playing footsies under the table with a Union widow woman, than you don't understand the nature of the War along our stretch of the river. The late War was lousy with stories just as improbable as ours. Terrebonne, Ducky and I were pals in our cadet days back at West Point on the Hudson. Ducky got himself killed at Belmont, but his bride was chums with Amy, so here she was. Terrebonne saved my life at Vicksburg, which cost him an arm. I saved his life back and fetched him home, so here he was. With one arm he was out of the Johnny horse troopers, but he still had his Academy training and knew the ways of the river. I landed him a job with Temple & Son and now the three of them were looting the Yankee treasury like river pirates. By working with the Temples he was doing greater service to the Southern cause than if he still commanded a troop in Joe Wheeler's division. With the prices Old Man Temple was gouging the Union Commissary, selling them everything from shoddy brogans to lame mules, it's no wonder that Chase had to keep his presses fired up printing greenbacks night and day.[z]

Aye, it was a grand meal and a grand day for all concerned except for that one little thing that set my teeth on edge and my gizzard to churn. Terrebonne and Pietronella couldn't keep their eyes or their hands off of each other. She had always fancied me and I always reckoned it was just a matter of time before I'd have at the woman in the pantry or on the porch or below stairs when Amy and Auntie weren't looking. We had almost come to the capital act before, several times, but there was always

---

[z] Salmon P. Chase was Lincoln's Secretary of the Treasury. Greenbacks were demand notes, not backed up by gold. Chase put his face on the $1 bill so he would be recognized when he ran for president.

some blasted busybody to barge in when just when my hands found her nipples under her linen or when she was pawing away at my front-fly buttons. It's damn hard to find privacy in a small town where everybody knows your name. Oh, I loved my Amy and she was the best bounce any lonely soldier could imagine marching home to, but you know me. Pietronella was beautiful to distraction, with corn-gold hair, the blue eyes of the truly simple, the face of an angel, a figure to set altar boys to slurping the sacramental wine, and the morals of a dedicated mattress galloper. The last time we sat a table it was *my* socks she was pulling down with her toes under the table. Now it was Terrebonne Blanche's little stockings. Terrebonne was my friend, but along the river he was what we called a killing gentleman. He was a small man and whipcord thin, but one arm or not, he cut a damn fine figure in his tight cut suit, silk vest and cravat, gleaming boots and .31 caliber Bacon five shot holstered under his missing wing. I'd be back on my pins in a few weeks and had figured to have a run at the Widow Turner, but now I wouldn't dare.[a]

* * *

Two weeks later we celebrated Christmas on the proper date. I had been married to Amy since before I went off to West Point back in '56. I was only seventeen and the marriage was the shotgun variety but I learned to love my girl, and still do. In all that time, I had been able to spend only one other Christmas at home. That was the December before Sumter, when I was assigned to Jefferson Barracks outside of St. Louis and was able to wrangle holiday leave. My last Christmas, the Christmas of '62, found me crawling under the wire of a Union

---

[a] For Sawyer's adventures with Ducky and Pietronella Turner, and Terrebonne Blanche refer to the first four editions of the Adventures of Sidney Sawyer.

prisoner stockade and running for my life. How the wheel does turn.

The womenfolk had decorated the old house with wreaths, and boughs of fresh pine and holly. The picket fence was festooned with garlands, and candles illuminated every window. Amy braided her hair with red and green ribbons and Auntie's cheeks were at their rosiest. I was fluffed on our big davenport with my feet to the fire, a spiced cider in my mitt, our cat, Mary Todd warming my lap, and the Sawyer females waiting on me in relays. Carolers stopped by to serenade their wounded hero singing "Green Sleeves," "Do You Hear What I Hear" and "The First Nowell" in three part harmony. If there had been more rum in my cider it might have set me to weeping. I'm a sentimental sort. Auntie rewarded the carolers with gingersnaps and coffee, but when the fools broke into "Oh Christmas Tree" I would have paid them off with the toe of my boot. There is always some damned thing to blight even the finest moments. "Oh Christmas Tree" is set to the music of "Maryland, My Maryland." Bobby Lee's Army of Northern Virginia sang the blasted tune when they splashed across the Potomac fords on their way to Antietam and the worst day of my life. It was certainly the worst day in the lives of the 23,000 boys in butternut and blue who were shot there.

I know I'm sounding like Scrooge, whining my "bah-humbugs" over holiday trifles, but the novelty of home and family was beginning to wear off, my feet itched like thunder beneath their splints, and I never was one for wholesome, hearth-centered festivities to begin with. And one *other* trifle was taking the bloom off of my Christmas rose. Tom Sawyer was infesting the premises for the holiday. He'd stopped by without a word of warning two days before Christmas dressed like a banker in a tall black beaver with an armful of packages and a colored boy toting his pigskin luggage. It looked like he'd come up in the world.

Brother Tom was passing through St. Louis on his way to Washington. On a lark he had decided to bless our Christmas with his presence. Since his last visit he had been back to Nevada to stand for reelection to the Legislature. He won, spread his mischief throughout the territory and earned his boodle of honest graft from the silver barons in San Francisco who controlled the Nevada mines. He'd stopped off home to crow.

Amy was cool, Auntie Polly watered her hankies and Pietronella flirted. I didn't blame her. Tom Sawyer was a pretty man. He was too small to be properly handsome but the lasses flocked to him like bees to sweet-buns. I may not have blamed Pietronella but Terrebonne blamed Tom. He sized up my big brother with a glance and greeted him with a handshake that ground Tom's soft knuckles. When Tom grew too bold peeking down Pet's frontage, Blanche stood left hip forward so that his coattails cleared his five shot. My brother got the message, and within the bounds of his natural insolence, behaved himself. Besides, Terrebonne knew it would spoil Auntie's holiday to gun Tom Sawyer down over the Yule-tide goose. Through it all, I watched the booze. The last time I got wallpapered in front of Tom Sawyer I wound up leading eight hundred darkies against the Rebel works under the glare of calcium lights.

After our Christmas feast of goose, stuffing, giblet gravy, wintergreens and mashed spuds, the men folk retired to the parlor for brandy, cigars, man-talk and to rub our swollen guts. It was there that I first heard about Red River cotton.

"Two hundred thousand bales and five hundred pounds to a bale and a pound of delta white going for a buck fifty in Lowell." Mr. Temple was off on his favorite topic, which was making money on other people's efforts.

"But the Red River's still in Reb control, and what can *we* do about it?" piped in Alfred. "They ship it through Texas and we don't even have a toe-hold along that stretch of the Gulf."

"But just think on it, Alfred. Two hundred thousand bales! At a buck fifty that's a hundred and fifty *million* dollars, hard money! Why, just one riverboat loaded with Red River fiber would be worth over three hundred thousand bucks! Damnation in July, that would set us up proper now, wouldn't it just?"

This had me scratching my head. "Ain't the navy blockading Galveston and the rest of the Lone Star coast? I've seen for myself that the blockade has sewed up the Atlantic from Cape Henry to the St. Johns River. Down in the Gulf a blockade runner may pop in and out of Mobile but that don't consider for Red River country."

"Blanche, you're a Louisiana man an' a cotton man." Old man Temple was rubbing his hands together like a gypsy tinker. "You know the Teche an' Atchafalaya, the bayou country and the Red. Is there any chance of *us* gettin' a load of contraband cotton upriver to St. Petersburg?"

Terrebonne swilled his brandy in his glass and gave the question a good consider. "The Yankees don't hold no sway up the Red River, but they have it bottled up with their gunboats on the Mississippi. From Alexandria to Shreveport is all prime cotton country but the planters can't ship it out of New Orleans. The cotton's been pilin' up. And more cotton gets smuggled along the Red from across the Mississippi and up to Shreveport from Arkansas. Yes indeed, it's pilin' up! Mr. Temple, I don't doubt that there's a powerful lot of cotton along the Red River, but the citizens of Louisiana ain't gonna sell it to you– to us. They'd rather ship it to Texas and try to run it through the blockade. That or burn it."

Alfred scoffed, " But there ain't no railroad that runs all the way from the Red River to Houston. An' shipping it out of Galveston Bay won't answer. They sure can't ship a quarter million bales out that way."

Terrebonne sighed, "You're right there, Alfred. Shipping that much cotton through Texas won't work and the occasional blockade-runner ain't enough. And remember, Texas grows its own cotton that they can't sell either. It's worth millions but it may as well be on the moon. The only way to get at that cotton is to take it, and that means a full-scale military campaign, and that ain't in the cards."

The room fell silent at the thought of all that wonderful money going a' glimmer. We gazed into our drinks with regret. That's when Brother Tom put in his shovel.

"There *is* gonna be a campaign, and soon– this winter. The news is all over St. Louis, if you know where to listen, and I do."

The little dandy man had our interest now, and Tom Sawyer loved to be the center of attention.

"Remember General Bank's expedition up Bayou Teche last spring?"

The Temples had heard. I hadn't.

"Banks ain't much of a general but he's always up for the main chance. He went up the bayou with a fleet and an army. He came back down without much military result but he didn't go up the Teche looking to lick the Rebs. He went up for what everybody's lookin' for–cotton. He came out with 5,000 bales. What with his other loot it was over five million dollars. Tain't bad for a bayou boat ride. Tee-hee!"

"Five million dollars! By thunder, now you're talkin'." Temple's fat face was red with lust.

"And the Red is a proper river and not a damn backwater bayou!" Tom crowed. "Instead of fifty miles of cotton there's a hundred an' eighty crow-fly miles of prime plantation country between the Mississippi and Shreveport and the Rebels have damned all to protect it."

Tom seemed to forget that he was a Rebel himself. After Sumter he'd raced to join the Alabama line. He deserted when Shiloh taught him that real soldiering wasn't as much fun as when he played at it as a kid.

"Who's gonna ram-rod the campaign?" I wanted to know. I was hoping to have a personal interest in the result. "Sherman? Thomas? Oh, Lord, not Hooker?"

Tom gave me the same grin he used as a boy when he was caught with his fingers in the jam."

"Grant?" I squeaked, "Hit the binders, they can't send Grant! He hates cotton jobbers and all their works."

"Tee-hee-hee," Tom giggled. "It ain't old Grant neither," and he giggled again.

"Who?" the four of us demanded at once.

"It's Banks! Nathanial P. Banks!"

Banks! That was Tom's rumor and in the end it proved to be true. And that's why he thought it was so funny. Damnation in a breadbox, the expedition was scuttled before it began. I've written about General Nathanial P. Banks before in these memoirs. They're locked in the gun cabinet with my other rubbish and I'm not going to paw through them now to remind me of what I wrote. Just note that that Banks had already pitched me into the gumbo during other Union disasters he had authored. He was *the* bright light in Massachusetts politics and Lincoln knew that to win the War he needed Massachusetts to shoulder the wheel with a will. Banks wanted to be president and to get the '68 Republican nomination he needed military glory. To win his laurel crown he needed to be a general, and so Lincoln created him a general. He was a damn fine clerk, and ran his department in Louisiana like a China tea clipper, but when he was leading troops in the field the wheels came off his buggy. In the Shenendoah Valley in '62, Stonewall Jackson ran rings around him and the Johnnies pinched millions of dollars of loot from his supply trains. The Confederates called him Commissary Banks and they loved him like no other Yankee general. Jackson's troops never had better rations than when they opposed Banks and dined on his grub.[27]

* * *

Tom stayed until after the New Year. We stood in a sleet storm to wave our goodbyes as a Temple packet took him across the River to the train depot in Quincy– and good riddance. It was high time for him to go. Amy could barely control her disgust and I do believe Terrebonne was ready to call him out for the way he had leered at Pietronella's frontage and nuzzled her knuckles at every opportunity. His parting was hard on Aunt Polly, though. I always wondered why she loved him best.

By February I was up and off my crutches. My feet were growing more sound each day and there seemed to be no lasting damage– bless Cookie for being a competent black quack. Cookie was established across O'fare Creek in Dark Town, living the life of a free colored boy. Big Jim Watson found him useful employment on the Temple docks. Jim was the top n—r on the riverfront and could hire or fire colored help for the Temples as he saw fit. And Cookie was a family man now. He and Roseasharen had set up housekeeping, the lucky rascal. If she favored him to the same tricks she taught me when I was a randy brat, Cookie would be living in darkie heaven. And Roseasharen was the Temple's cook. He'd eat like the King of Siam.

And Boone was back from Kansas. I didn't want the bucktoothed rustic hanging about for our holidays so I ginned up furlough papers for him to visit his kin back in Kansas. I didn't have any legal authority to send him home, but I was a colonel, so what the hell. The papers seemed to work. The provost didn't arrest him off the trains and he was back with blessings from his ma in time to prop me up when the splints came off.

I had no intention of reporting back for duty. Rawlins had sent me off in a huff and if the gods of war were kind he'd forget about me. I was only a staff colonel and that breed was a dime a dozen. They could reckon me dead or crippled or lose my paperwork or just not bother. All was well through February. By the 29th (64 was a leap year), I was riding the Temples spitfire mare, Juno through the back lanes of Lewis County. I still sported a gutta percha cane, but that was more to keep up the appearances of a wounded hero than for need, and it was damn handy to thrash Juno when she tried to bite my face.

And I was happily riding topside again during my riverboat games with Amy. By damn, it was dandy to have two working pins again to plough into the act with proper leverage. As Mrs. Lucy Newcastle taught me back at the Galt House, a man needs knees and toes to properly engage in Adam's antics. With a strong, willing woman like my Amy it's all hands on deck when the wick is turned down and the knickers come off. Toot toot!

At the end of January Pietronella took Terrebonne north to Green Bay to meet her folks. It seemed that Cookie and Roseasharen weren't going to be my only chums to jump the broom. Without the distraction of Tom or Blanche or the Widow Turner, and without the hindrance of my busted ankles, Amy and I were practically jumping at each other when the supper dishes were cleared. 1864 wasn't a leap year for nothing.

Alas, nothing good lasts forever. In the end, Grant didn't send for me. Neither did Rawlins. Sherman did!

The Adventures of Sidney Sawyer
Missouri Yankees

Part IV: Red River

Chapter 28

My orders were to report to the Galt House in Louisville no later than March 17 to await orders. The Galt House? Sherman? I wonder if he knows Mrs. Lucy Newcastle. I couldn't imagine why that redheaded lunatic wanted to see me or why in the blazes he even remembered me. I knew him well enough from the Vicksburg Campaign when he was Grant's chief honcho from the Yazoo to Jackson, but he didn't know me, at least not enough to consider. The last time we had crossed paths was right after his XV Corps's bloody repulse before the Vicksburg works when I was fool enough to congratulate him for occupying Chickasaw Bluffs.

"Hayne's Bluff is ours and fairly won!" I had crowed to him while his whipped infantry was limping back from the slaughter before the Confederate trenches. God in heaven, what a damn fool thing to say to a Major General who had just stepped into a mutt's mess. That must be why he remembered me, but why would he send for me? Three days later I was captured by the Rebels and spent the rest of the campaign in a Confederate hoosegow.

At any rate I had five days to report to Louisville and it was only a two day ride on the cars so I set out to make the most of those extra days with Amy. A trooper never knows when he will have another opportunity to rattle his wife around the crazy quilt and I didn't want any regrets over lost opportunity. I've made my fare-thee-wells to kith and kin a hundred times during my misspent life in the service of the republic and this goodbye was about what I had come to expect. As I boarded the Temple packet to Quincy I spun Aunt Polly around in a great circle to make her laugh through her tears. I gave little Ranty a bounce on my knee and a chuck under his fat chin. Amy gave me a hug that had me recalling the scent of her hair and the feel of her waist across the width of Illinois. I hopped up the gangplank with Boone a step behind hauling our traps and waved until the March Mississippi mist swallowed the boat. The train ride was a sight more comfortable than my ride home three months before. Now that I could use my feet the benches didn't chafe my arse. I had a basket full of home cookin' instead of the greasy cheese on stale rolls they serve up at the whistle stops, and Boone watched my grips while I snoozed. On St. Patrick's Day morning I limped into Galt House like I owned the place.

I didn't need to limp but I leaned on the gutta percha as though I did. The last thing I wanted was for Sherman to know that I was fit for duty. I wanted to be on Grant's staff, not his bloodthirsty lieutenant's. It was the talk of the nation, North *and* South, that Lincoln had put all his eggs in Grant's scruffy basket. Congress had reestablished the noble rank of Lieutenant General and laid the Olympian mantle on Grant's humble shoulders. Only George Washington and Winfield Scott had held that exalted rank before. Grant was now the commander of all the nation's armies, east and west. He outranked Old Brains Halleck. He outranked all the generals who had graduated ahead of him at West Point. He ranked all the officers who snickered and gossiped when he sulked out of the Army after his bout with booze. Now he only took orders from Lincoln, and Lincoln wasn't giving him any orders. I had hitched myself to Grant's wagon way back in the summer of '62 when the War was young. I had picked the right horse. I knew where my bread was buttered and I was Grant's man, especially now when his staff would billet in comfort and safety in Washington. What the hell did Sherman want with me?

Well, I hobbled into Galt House and five minutes later hobbled right out again. Sherman's adjutant had set up shop in the dining room where I'd met Miss Lucy back in December. He gave me a nod, my hand a quick shake, grinned a "Welcome aboard," and scooped his papers into a canvas valise. I followed him and a half-dozen other staff minions back to the lobby and there was Grant, arm in arm with Sherman marching out the door. In ten more minutes I was back on the same blasted Jeffersonville Railroad train that took me to Louisville. With a whistle and a jolt we were on our way to Cincinnati.

The meeting is famous now. Grant and Sherman, America's twin warlords, heads together in Parlor A of the fabulous Burnet House, the grandest hotel in the world, plotting the destruction of the Confederacy over cigars and coffee. And damned if the Burnet House wasn't grand. I'd been to Chicago's Palmer House with Amy and Washington's Willard Hotel with John Hay, and the Galt House with Mrs. Newcastle, but the Burnet took the biscuit. It was five floors, covered an entire block, had six grand pillars on the portico, and was graced with a dome that was crowned with a majestic cupola. The cupola's flagstaff offered Old Glory to the winds where it could be seen in Kentucky. The Burnet House was only ten years old and had all the accoutrements of the modern age. There was steam heat in every room. Flush water closets were available for every guest (just down the hall) and hot and cold water flowed from the taps. If you had the tin to book a suite, you had a "bath room" with a sink tub and flush-bucket all your own. The wonders of the age of industry in a rich republic!

I wasn't invited to sit in on the powwow in Parlor A, but I was in and out with the rest of the staff often enough to get the gist. Both generals were sick and tired of the sideshows. Why the hell was Secretary of the Navy Gideon Welles allowed to waste an entire year, shed a river of blood and squander millions in treasure, sending half of the navy, twenty thousand troops, General Quincy Gillmore and me to Charleston to take a city that didn't have to be took? If Charleston fell, the war would go on as before. It was a damned sideshow. And why the hell was Banks going up the Red River with thirty thousand men in five divisions to seize Shreveport, Louisiana? Shreveport was a dandy city. It had factories churning out booties and britches and biscuits for the Confederate armies– so what? Those armies were on the wrong side of the Mississippi and couldn't have the slightest impact on the outcome of the greater War. It was a damn sideshow, the same nonsense that had been queering the Federal cause since before Shiloh. The likes of Halleck and Frémont and McClellan and Banks had been scattering our armies all over creation to take *this* junction and guard *that* crossroads and secure *those* chicken coops. If Shreveport fell, the rebellion would still live. Grant knew it and Sherman knew it and I knew it because Sergeant Major Huckleberry Finn of the 3rd Iowa had told me, but it didn't seem that anybody else on the Union side knew it. But now all that wasted motion didn't matter. Grant's was the only voice that counted and the sideshows were over.

Here was the grand strategy and if it seems obvious now to the village idiot– well, it didn't seem obvious then. The Confederacy lived while its armies lived. We had taken and held Rebel state capitals like Nashville, Baton Rouge and Little Rock. We had raided and ruined others like Jackson. We commanded the Mississippi including the South's greatest city, New Orleans. Our navy bottled up the insurgent coast with only an occasional blockade-runner to succor the Southland. None of that mattered. While Joe Johnson commanded the Confederate Army of the Tennessee before Atlanta and Bobby Lee's Army of Northern Virginia stood foursquare before Richmond, the Southern Confederacy lived. We could take Atlanta and take Richmond, and in the end we did, but until we could smash those two armies and take the swords of those two commanders, Southern independence survived.[b]

In Parlor A Grant smoked a hatful of cigars, Sherman squinted mightily through the smoke, maps were summoned, tables of supply and transport were referred to, staff flunkies like me were kept hopping, sentries turned away mobs of the curious and in the end here was the essence of victory distilled. Grant would go for Lee and Sherman would go for Johnson. If Grant went for Richmond, Lee would fight him. If Sherman went for Atlanta, Johnson would fight him. Richmond was incidental. Atlanta was incidental. It was the armies that had to be killed. They would kill us back, but we had more men so in the end we would win. No more sideshows.

You can see why I was concerned. If I was with Grant I'd be safely in Washington, shuffling papers, tut-tuting over casualty figures and rogering my new chum, Missy Ruth. With Sherman I'd be in a headquarters battalion, sleeping in a reeking Shelby tent with a dozen other staff loafers and chewing on salt-horse and sheet-iron crackers. Again, what the hell did Sherman want with me?

In the end Grant decided that the old snapping turtle, General G. Gordon Meade needed his personal supervision when the Army of the Potomac tackled Marse Robert, but I didn't know that then. I was in a stew that I'd be riding south with Uncle Billy and of course that's exactly what happened– but not quite yet.

Grant ordered no more sideshows, but before he got the top slot at the beginning of March, Halleck had set one more in motion. It was already rolling and there was nothing for Grant to do but try and mitigate the damage. Commissary Banks was on his way up the Red River with the biggest expedition the Union had launched into the

---

[b] After the Confederate rout at Missionary Ridge, Jefferson Davis replaced Braxton Bragg with General Joseph Johnson.

trans-Mississippi during the entire War. He would take twenty thousand men from his department and a train of ninety pieces of artillery of all types. Rear Admiral David Porter would escort him up the Red with a brigade of marines, twenty-two gunboats, including thirteen ironclads mounting two hundred and ten big guns, and forty quartermaster boats and transports. All this was effort enough away from the main objectives, but to add insult to injury, ten thousand of Sherman's veterans in three divisions under General Andrew Jackson Smith had been ordered west to join Bank's chowder and marching society. And *that* is why I was ordered to Sherman's command.

* * *

Sherman wanted A. J. Smith and his ten thousand men back and no mistake. He wanted them back where they would do real service to the master plan, and floundering up a bayou in Louisiana with Commissary Banks wasn't it. Grant had already seen to the matter but Sherman wasn't satisfied by a long reach. Three days before in Nashville, when Grant and Sherman met to begin their grand meeting (that was before they traveled to Louisville and before their big powwow in Cincinnati), Grant sent a staff major to Banks with a letter. If Banks wasn't cast-iron sure of taking Shreveport by the end of April he *must* send Sherman's divisions back to him east of the Mississippi. It was an order, by God!

By that St. Patrick's Day Sherman's men had already joined the Red River Expedition. Now the combined army was marching to Alexandria. Alexandria was a substantial river port on the Red that was over a third of the way to Shreveport. There was nothing much the Confederates had to stop them. If Banks marched his legions a measly ten miles a day they'd take Shreveport in a week and a half. What could go wrong?

It was *Banks* that could go wrong and neither Grant nor Sherman gave the Red River Expedition a rat's chance in a terrier pit. That is why only two weeks after Grant was promoted to Commanding General of the Armies he sent the staff major to Banks with his order. It was an order from U. S. Grant, Lieutenant General of the Armies of the United States of America. Banks would have to hear and obey– wouldn't he?

Sherman wasn't so sure, and *that* is what the hell Sherman wanted with me. The redheaded swine knew all about Grant's April deadline for Banks. He also knew that Banks often took his orders as mere suggestions– hadn't Banks almost scuppered the entire Vicksburg Campaign by kiting off with his army up the Atchafalaya just when Grant needed him most? No, Sherman wanted to make damn sure that he got A. J. Smith's three divisions back before he set out on his spring campaign against Joe Johnson. He decided to send a letter of his own. Grant sent a staff major. Sherman would trump him with a colonel! Now where would he find a staff colonel that he could spare for a wild goose chase down the Mississippi and up the Red? How he knew I was laid up in St. Petersburg as useless as buttons on a dishrag I couldn't cotton, but two days after Whiskey Smith led his three divisions aboard the transports to the Red River, Sherman wired me my orders to report to him on the 17th. On the 18th I had his letter to Banks in my pocket and I was on a riverboat down the Ohio, bound for the Red.

"Sawyer, you've always done your best fighting with your mouth. I want you to fight for me."

Sherman knew me better than I reckoned.

"That blasted politician has three of my divisions under Whiskey Smith and I need 'em back by the middle of May. Grant sent him his orders that I get 'em back but Banks ain't a soldier and orders to officers of his stripe aren't taken as they ought. Here's a letter from me that backs up Grant's. Don't give him any room to wiggle. Use your rank like a bludgeon. If Banks takes Shreveport, that's dandy. But if he don't, and he won't, don't come back without my men!"

Crackerjack, hot damn and hallelujah! I was off to the Red River, but not right away. Sherman assumed I'd fly like a Yankee Mercury to Banks with his message, why wouldn't he? He was a general with a bee in his bonnet. I was staff. I was an officer, a gentleman and my duty was clear. But the message was to fetch his men back by the end of April. That was over a month away and besides Grant had already sent his orders. I was only lard on the biscuit. I'd get there, but first things first. I hopped off the boat at Louisville and was back where I started. I'd take the cars back to St. Petersburg in the morning, but first things are indeed first and I strapped my gutta percha to my carpetbag and strutted into the Galt House dining room.

Now that Grant's staff rabble was gone it was a dining room again and there sat Mrs. Lucy Newcastle like the Empress of China at her table across from a stout fellow with gray whiskers and a hopeful look on his red face. I gave her a leer. She gave me a look. I gave a quick two-step to show my feet were in marching order. She turned as red as her companion and gave him a quick excuse. He gave me a glare. I fluffed my whiskers at him, tipped my magnificent Jeff Davis and was up the stairs with Lucy without saying a word. I love a short courtship.

I had reckoned that her udders bounced when my pins were splinted and she was topside, but now that I was a going concern and we frolicked with Sidney properly aboard, her Sundays rolled and swayed and bucked fit to frighten the French. I usually like to try this and that and take my time and tickle and slap but Mrs. Newcastle held on to me with arms and legs and there was nothing for it but to soldier on and give the lady what she wanted. I always defer to my elders. Back in December she had entertained me for the pure naughty fun of it. Now she was putting her heart and soul into the game– twice! We finished with scratches on my arse and a screech that could be heard across the Ohio River in Indiana. How would I explain those scratches to Amy?

I made all my connections and by Sunday afternoon stepped off the packet onto the Temple's dock. This was a business trip, first things first, so I quick-marched straight to the Temple's. There are those that consider business on the Sabbath a sin and a disgrace, but Old Man Temple and Alfred ain't among them. We put our greedy heads together like the brown water buccaneers we were. A quarter of a million bales of Red River cotton at a dollar fifty a pound and five hundred pounds to a bale!

After a quick stop home to change my linen, buss Auntie's chin, give Ranty a bounce on my knee and freshen my wife, I was off to the Red River. Amy never noticed the scratches on my arse.

* * *

I love to ride in the pilothouse of a tall river queen. The view is grand, the company is first rate and the jargon of the river is music to any river-bred boy. The pilot of the *Hannibal* was an old Temple boat captain named Gerald Patrick Dennis Regan. He was one of those professional Irishmen, complete with clay pipe and Miraculous Medal, but he knew every bend and bar in the Missouri from St. Joe to St. Louis and every twist and snag in the Mississippi from St. Paul to New Orleans. We were southbound with a light cargo of fodder, timber, and two score mules for the Union garrisons at Vicksburg and Natchez. Then it was up the Red River to Alexandria and Commissary Banks. The plan was to fill our empty boat to the railings with all the cotton we could plunder. Under my belt, stitched with its usual string of gold eagles, was a canvas money belt stuffed with Temple & Son greenbacks. We knew that I'd need plenty of ready boodle for bribes. In my carpetbag I had notarized letters of credit for buying "legal" contraband cotton from the Army. Once I delivered my message to Banks I was in the cotton business.

It was forever getting down the Mississippi to the mouth of the Red, but then I wasn't in all that ripping 'a hurry. Vicksburg was a trial, though. We tied up below the bluffs and I spent a day and a night squinting up at the cupola of the blasted courthouse where I had spent the siege as a prisoner of war, picking nits and fighting rodents for my swill. The holdup was waiting for cordwood for *Hannibal's* bunkers. Then we were off to Natchez to drop off our mules and fodder to the garrison. The Union soldiers occupying Natchez were mostly colored. Their bivouac would have disgraced the greasers, filthy tents pitched every which-way, uniforms shabby and discipline shot. These Corps D' Afrique troops were mostly former slaves fresh out of the patch. They didn't have the luster or snap of the old 94th. If the Corps D' Afrique was what the rest of the n—r Army was like, I was well out of it.

On the twenty-third, the *Hannibal* steamed opposite the mouth of the Red but was met by a Navy packet before we could enter the stream. A lieutenant in trim navy blue fig and a tight brimmed cap presented his compliments to Captain Mash Regan gave us new sailing instructions. We were under the jurisdiction of General Banks's Department of the Gulf and we had no choice, but were glad for the detour none-the-less. It seems that smallpox had broken out in Admiral David D. Porter's marine brigade. They were to be replaced with the only troops handy, which was a Corps D' Afrique battalion from the garrison at Baton Rouge. Would we please run down to Baton Rouge to pick them up– no, we didn't have a choice, and yes, we would be paid four-fifty a head to transport a four company battalion of the 3rd Louisiana Colored Engineers.[c] That would be around three hundred and fifty officers and men. (I took a fifteen percent finder's

---

[c] Only a week and a half after Colonel Sawyer reached Baton Rouge the Corps D' Afrique's 3rd Engineer Regiment was reorganized as the 97th USCT Engineers.

fee. Old Man Temple would understand.) Thank heaven these darkies weren't the rabble we saw the day before in Natchez, although they were probably of the same vintage as the rest of Louisiana's black troops. Natchez was only one day down the Mississippi and a day back. We had the extra time and the Army paid us damn well for it. After all, the *Hannibal was* a Temple & Son boat and money *was* money and Baton Rouge *was* the capital of Louisiana. If I couldn't bribe a likely general to sign some blank cotton licenses while the darkies jigged aboard, you could call me Uncle Remus.

Hannibal reached the levy at Baton Rouge in the late afternoon and our arrival touched off a series of surprises that could only happen in wartime and could only happen to the likes of me. I was the only officer aboard, so it was my task to meet the battalion commander to see to boarding and victualling.

To my vast surprise while the deck apes were still heaving the mooring lines to the wharf, the four companies marched onto the levy in a column of fours as neat as a Quaker bonnet. Their kits were neat, uniforms brushed, boots buffed and musket barrels sparkled in the bright springtime sun. To the bark of officers who knew their business, the battalion mustered along the dock and stood to attention by the platoon. It took less than five minutes. That's a damn good show in *any* army and these troops were, if anything, even blacker than my old 94th. Before each company was its captain with his lieutenant by his side. Before the battalion was the lieutenant colonel with his staff, and beside the colonel, in a green sash fit for a field marshal, was my second surprise.

He was only a sergeant major and I was a colonel, but damnation in July, there stood Sergeant Girardeau Smith in all his black glory. No wonder the 3rd Louisiana Engineers was such a dandy outfit!

I strutted up to the big rascal with a grin that I felt to my boots, "Smitty! Glory in the long grass, man, but its damn good to see you again!"

He greeted me with a wooden face and a salute that could have been snapped by a railway signal. What the deuce?

The colonel looked at me like I was unhinged but I blundered on.

“Smitty, its me– Colonel Sawyer. Must be quite a surprise. But… But…”

Smith stood ridged as a statue with no recognition on his broad face, but his eyes did slide for a second to his left and like a fool mine followed his to my third surprise of the day.

There was Liberty, or should I say Miss Libby standing by herself beside one of the wagons that toted the regiment’s dunnage. She was dressed as a woman, no hint of the drummer boy, and she was looking at me with curiosity and a hint of sadness. Six months ago Libby was a thin, pretty girl. Now she was neither. Now she had the mature beauty of a full-grown woman. She was lovely, but no longer cute or pretty like a girl. And she wasn’t thin. Her face had filled out along with her breasts that a loose frock couldn’t conceal. In that instant I understood why Smitty was with the Corps D’ Afrique here in Louisiana. And I understood why the man wasn’t at all pleased to see the Ace of Spades! Miss Liberty Smith was huge with child.

The Adventures of Sidney Sawyer
Missouri Yankees

Chapter 29

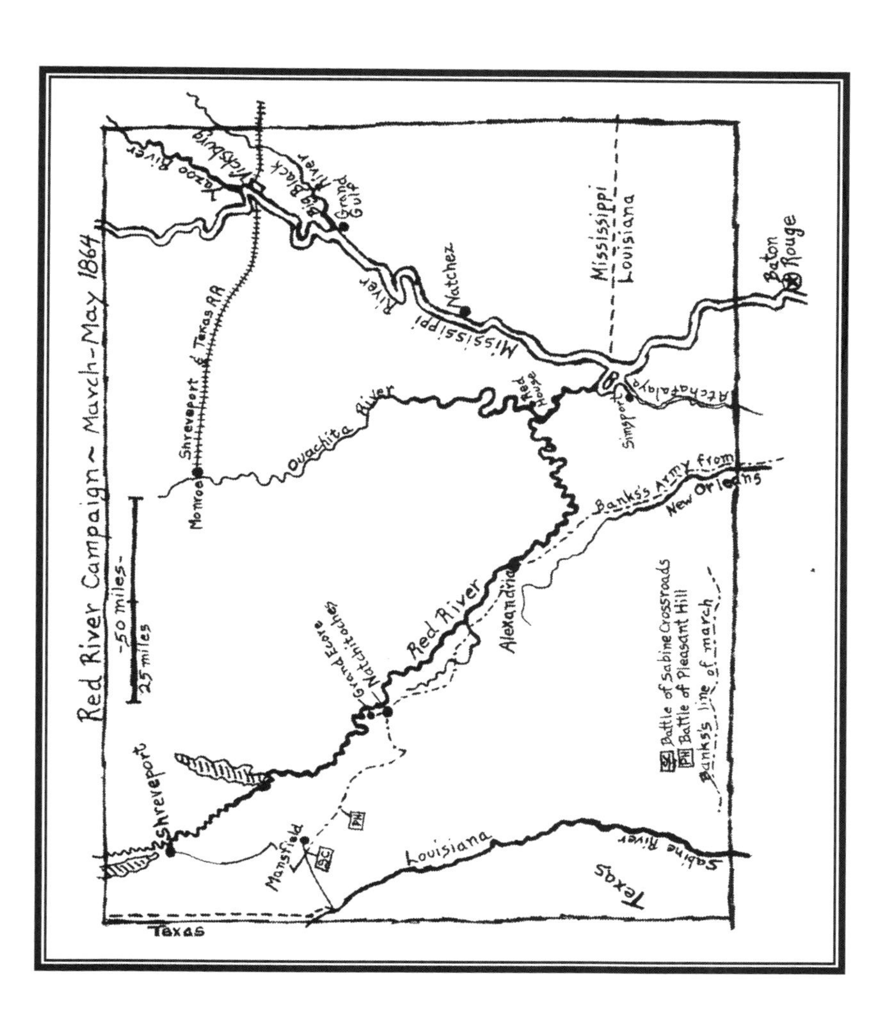

I don't get rattled much except when the security of my arse is on the line, but seeing Liberty in a family way rocked me to my boots. A family way– that was a damn poor way to put it. Her family was her ugly black pappy and a regiment of delta field hands masquerading in Union blue– and *me*. I knew the bairn was mine and that was gospel. I didn't even have to tally up the months. I knew! Liberty wasn't the type of girl to invite advances from any Tom, Dick or Sidney. No, it was just the noble Colonel Sidney, champion of emancipation and the hero of Sea Island combat. In other words, she gave her flower to a man who didn't exist– *me*.

But shock wasn't my only reaction. I wanted to run over to her and swing her in the air before the entire battalion. I wanted to plant my cheek on her belly and feel the baby kick. The white officers of the 3rd Engineers, Corps D' Afrique could stand and scratch themselves for all I'd care. I wanted to slap black Smitty on the back and offer him a cigar and grin and smoke one with him and let the three hundred darkies in blue shuck and grin and elbow each other at the notion of it. You see, I was happy. You know me– and I know me too, and the idea that my first reaction after my jaw dropped would be joy, actually gave me the giggles. I was going to be a pappy again and that the brat would be a half-caste high-yeller pickaninny didn't consider. Splendor in the tall corn, I had freshened little Sergeant Liberty Smith and the baby was mine! And in that instant Smitty saw the joy bubble up in me. I do believe that instant is when he stopped hating me for what I had done to his girl. I can understand any black man hating any white man for bulling his baby gal into maternity and I believe that Smitty hated me for it. But then, in my surprise, my face was as easy to read as the daily news. There was no embarrassment on my face, or anger or shame or bother– just slaphappy joy. I believe that that brief but honest expression on my silly puss is what saved my life seven weeks later when an army of bums and looters swarmed with torch and knife, two monsters lusted for my blood, and a city exploded into flame around my ears.

* * *

I didn't spin Libby about and I didn't suck a cheroot with Smitty. It simply wouldn't do. Instead I did what I was expected to do which was greet the top rail of the 3rd Engineers. The colonel was a New York man named Brant who was as dark as an Indian with a nose as big as mine, and a fat round face. After my interlude with his sergeant major he was looking at me like I had a slate loose, but I returned his salute like all was right with the world and invited him to carry on. Before you could say 'Uncle Cracker Jasper' he had the men filing aboard the *Hannibal* by the platoon. It took a while longer to load the wagons. There were six of them stowed on the bow deck and they carried canvas pontoons. I guess the 3rd was a *real* engineer outfit after all. The rest of the regiment with their nags, mules and the bulk of the pontoon train would follow along in other boats. Libby boarded with the wagons and pushed through the mob to the afterdeck. None of the stevedores, roustabouts, deckhands or troops thought to question her presence on a troop boat. If they reckoned it a bit queer this was, after all, the African Army.

I wanted to scoot to the stern deck to powwow with Smitty and see to Libby but I had to powwow with Colonel Brant first and there was nothing for it. Brant was a Department of the Gulf soldier who knew the lay of the land and the ways of the bayou war. If I was going to load the *Hannibal* with Red River cotton I had better gather as much local information as I could. And powwow was the word to use for a meeting with Brant. It turned out that the red rascal was a full blood Seneca Indian from the Iroquois nation.[28]

Brant didn't talk like an Indian. He spoke better English than I did, like a preacher, with no 'ain'ts,' 'tain'ts' or 'gits'– and no curses either, but he had damn little to say. He was all business and only business as we climbed to the railing of the Texas deck to observe the loading. I tried to pump him for gossip but he was as quiet as the cigar store variety of Indian. I'm a neighborly fellow and more open-minded than most, so I sent Boone running to my stateroom for my pint. I figured to loosen Injin' Joe up with a swig. When I offered him the bottle he gave me a look that could have frozen the whiskey in my flask.

"I joined the Union Army to inspire my people and I cannot inspire them with intemperance! Drink is the curse of my race."

Well, la-de-da! I tucked the tangle-foot back in my blouse and offered him a cigar. At least Indians smoke, but when he fired up my cheroot he turned to me with a formal salute and made his leave.

"Colonel Sawyer, I must remain here to see to the transport of the rest of the regiment and its baggage. This battalion is under the command of my second in command, Lieutenant Colonel McCracken," and he gestured behind me.

I turned and there was a big lout with shoulders a yard wide and a gut like a bow fender. But his size wasn't what drew attention. It was his hair and whiskers. Under his Jeff Davis, a rough mop of reddish-brown wool bristled as if it was fighting to escape confinement. His mustache had me wondering how he could eat through it. It was as big as a cowcatcher and completely covered his mouth. A beard of the same brown thatch as his hair cascaded in a tangle to his belly. His eyes were as merry as a younger Pickwick, and under his soup-strainer he was smiling like a fool.

What the dickens? I knew the n—r army was officered by some damn odd types, consider my new Indian acquaintance, hell, consider *me*– but this fellow was clearly addled. And then the last eight years seemed to roll away and I was climbing the bluff at Gees Point to the parade ground at West Point for my first memorable day at the Academy. I was a greenhorn and with me was another greenhorn, a boy from Sandusky, Ohio with the wispy beard of a youth, and a mop of ridiculous hair stuffed beneath a farmer's straw hat, but the merry eyes were the same. In an instant we were pounding each other's backs and pumping each other's fins.

Amos Marriwheather McCracken, my plebe roommate and my chum. He was the very first fellow I had met in the Army. Together we suffered through the cruel hazing dished out to plebes by the upperclassmen in their efforts to create officers and gentlemen. And in my fateful duel above the Hudson, when I met Cadet Calhoun Brassard over the sights of pistols, he stood as my second. We had drifted apart after that first year. Amos didn't have quite enough style for the likes of me. He was temperance and went to church as if he meant it, but we were always friends. Now, here he was, ramrodding four companies of blackbird infantry– engineers no less. And Amos was a born gossip, which was *exactly* what I needed.

Brant gave a sniff at the joy of our reunion– white men are so emotional– and after a formal bow, trooped down the stairs. The second he stepped onto the levy the *Hannibal* blasted its whistle, the big wheel churned up the Mississippi and we were bulling back against the current to the Red River.

It was grand seeing Amos again, but those I really wanted to see were Smith and Liberty. Smitty was busy with the men and the dunnage so that wouldn't do. Libby was surrounded by colored soldiers on the aft deck, so how would that look? I *had* to see them. I *had* to talk to them. I wanted to– really! After all, we were family now, but this wasn't the time or the place. It was time to talk to Amos and find out what was trump with General Nathanial P. Banks and his Shreveport Expedition.

We stood at the forward railing above the Texas deck to catch the breeze and started where we had to start, with our Academy friends.

Billy Ives had gone South.

Ducky Turner was dead.

Terrebonne Blanche lost a wing at Vicksburg saving my hash. Now he was in Wisconsin with Ducky's widow to meet her family. Yes, that does seem odd, don't it!

Yes, Calhoun Brassard was dead. Was I sure? Pretty sure. And on we went, down the roll of old chums.

After I bragged about Amy and little Ranty, Amos dug into his blouse and fished out a picture of his sweetheart. They had been married since last winter and he was as proud as a Spanish Duke that she was in a family way. Her name was Marian. She had no chin, thin lips, and her nostrils were so wide I could see up her nose into her forehead. But she was comfortably chubby, her eyes were wide and happy, and she looked so overall silly that I liked her from the first squint.

"You're a family man now, you old buffalo! Marian's a doll an' you're a lucky man. Atta boy, hoss!" I pounded his back, pulled out my pint, spit the cork over the rail and tipped the flask in a toast. Amos was still temperance, bless him, so I had the liquor to myself.

Now it was time to get down to business.

"How came you to be with the African Army, Amos?"

"Don't ye go holdin' it against me now, Sidney. I was a lieutenant an' likely to stay one. I'm a colonel now, thanks to requesting duty in a colored regiment. I ain't ashamed. But you're a full colonel, goll darn! Aint' ye too young?"

"Not for Lincoln. He gave me my straps himself for political service."

Amos was suitably impressed, but if I was going to brag why not up the ante?

"That was before I joined the African Army myself."

McCracken's hairy jaw dropped. "You?"

"Yep, me! Halleck and Stanton heard about my work with the Underground Railroad and personally offered me command of the 3rd Missouri USCT. We had the honor to take the Confederate battery at Fort Wagner."

"You?"

"Yep, me! An' I ain't the Ace of Hearts no more– I'm the Ace of Spades, an' it was the daughter of your sergeant major that gave me my new tag. No wonder your 3rd Louisiana is such a crack outfit, Smitty's a hell of a top kick."

And this really got Amos to talking. Lincoln, Halleck, Stanton, Battery Wagner, the Underground Railroad and more to the point, Sergeant Major Smith. Lieutenant Colonel McCracken was quite star struck. He couldn't tell me enough, quick enough.

"Sidney, my Colonel Brant ain't usually so stand-offish. He's just disgusted. He's an Indian you know."

"I know."

"Back at the Cattaraugus Reservation School he was a native preacher an' teacher and he joined up to save the Union and to free the darkies and to inspire his people."

Damnation in a feather bonnet! That redskin didn't just talk like a preacher. He *was* a preacher!

"He says this entire expedition is only a raid– a gigantic cotton raid up the Red River to line speculator's pockets and to puff up Banks back in Massachusetts. He covets Rebel cotton as a drunkard covets liquor."

I took a swig to punctuate his point.

"Banks wants to be president. There's tons of cotton up the Red. He wants to grab it and send it to the mills back in New England. The looms will thunder. He'll blow his trumpet, 'Vote for me– I'm the savior of the Republic!' Colonel Brant didn't sign up to be a part of that… that…"

Amos didn't swear so I helped him out, "Bullshit!"

"Folly!" he snapped back. "Ye have heard of the reasons for this campaign, ain't ye Sid?"

"Actually, no I ain't."

He ticked them off on his fingers, "Banks says we gotta pacify western Louisiana. Then we can fetch more Rebels back to the Old Flag and have 'em swear the Union oath. That way Louisiana can be a state again. He wants the credit. He brags we're gonna seize Shreveport like a low hangin' plum. From there we're gonna advance into Texas and over-awe that Maximilian feller in Mexico."

I'd heard of Maximilian. Who hadn't? He was a square-head duke with a French army behind him who had filibustered into Old Mexico to carve out an empire. I didn't care a wet cracker about him or his beaner dreams. I reckoned the Mexicans would settle his hash in short order or I didn't know my greasers.[29] And I didn't care about Banks's political daydreams either. Lincoln would be reelected, wouldn't he? And after him, if the War was won, Grant or maybe Sherman would be president. I reckoned there were already platoons of politicos elbowing each other for the top job, but after a war we Americans always elect a general, don't we? And if the war *wasn't* won nobody would give a lick *who* was president. The only thing *I* cared about right now was cotton.

I screwed on my most innocent face and steered the conversation back on course. "Cotton raid? Amos, this War's about saving the Union and freeing the n—rs, ain't it? All we gotta do is lick the Rebs in the field and take their cities, don't we? What's all this fuss about cotton?"

Good Christian that he was, Amos couldn't resist the scandal. "Do you know how much cotton is worth, Sid?"

My face stayed an innocent blank.

"Why, it is worth millions to those who can seize it and run it north to the mills. Banks an' his Army are in a race with Admiral Porter an' his Navy to get up the Red River. It's winner take all."

"A *race*? I thought they were in cahoots."

"They're rivals. Colonel Brant says that all white men are rivals to all other white men. Porter's already up the river to Alexandria with his flotilla. They're grabbin' cotton far and wide. General Banks is still marching his Army up through the bayou country from the railhead at Brashear while the Navy's gettin' rich."

"Rich? How can the bluejackets get rich? Ain't all the plunder they grab the property of the government?"

"Not if ye are in the Navy. Alexandria is swarmin' with speculators, all of 'em with licenses to buy contraband cotton at whatever price Banks approves. Them licenses are all signed by your friends Stanton and Halleck and even President Lincoln. But they won't do 'em no good. Navy's gonna grab up all the cotton in Red River country."

"What the blazes is the Navy going to do with the stuff? Their jumpers are made of wool. They can't drink it!"

"That's why Colonel Brant reckons it all a big raid and nothin' else. When the Navy takes a ship on the seas they can sell it as a prize-o'-war and then they divvy up the plunder."

"But this ain't the high seas. It's a damn river. Porter's a hundred miles from blue water. You're talkin' nonsense, Amos!"

"Tain't me, Sidney. Porter's claimin' that any Confederate cotton is a prize."

"But the Reb government don't own no cotton. What the hell would Jeff Davis do with a bale of cotton?"

"Tis a Rebel bale once the Navy quartermasters stencil 'CSA' on it. Then they cross it out and stencil 'USN' above it."

"But that ain't legal!"

I was outraged! Porter's theft was interfering with my larceny. I had a fistful of signed licenses in my pocket from Baton Rouge. Now my hairy friend was telling me they weren't worth the ink on the paper or the bribes I spread around this morning before my powwow with Chief Brant.

"Damnation in July– those sea-biscuit bastards!"

First it was the shock of seeing Smitty at the head of his new regiment of Louisiana field hands. Then it was the jolt of Libby six months along with my mongrel. Now this! As the *Hannibal* made its stately turn to port out of the current of the Mississippi and into the sluggish Red River, I finished my pint and tossed the bottle over the rail. I didn't give a snap for the look of disapproval I got from my Sandusky paragon of temperance. My only thought was how to get into the Navy.

* * *

We entered the Red River on the twenty-fourth of March. After the broad, grand Mississippi, stained brown with honest mud, the Red River was a slough. The Red earned its name from the thick maroon silt that swirled in slimy eddies thick enough to plow. It was never more than three hundred yards across and twisted like an eel with meanders that had Captain G.P.D. Regan wrestling the wheel from the helmsman. I heard him booming orders into the speaking tube to the grease apes tending the engine and snarling at the bluejacket in the bow with the sounding line. The Red River was ugly, but it didn't seem dangerous, and the *Hannibal* only drew forty inches of water. I strolled into the pilothouse to chat up Captain Regan.

"What's the fuss, Captain? This creek giving you the sizzles?"

He didn't take his eyes from the water. "It's low, damn low. Been up the Red a dozen times. Never seen it this low. The river failed back in '55. Time before that was in '46. That's every nine years. '55 was nine years ago. Don't know why she does it– don't nobody know. But on me life, Banks and Porter are damn fools to send an army up this river now. They git up– water might just git too low to git back down."

We were rounding another meander and Mash had the boat hugging the outside bank where the current gouged out the deepest channel. The top of the bank was high, on a level with the pilothouse, and I could see the marks along the soil from the spring high water level. It *was* low– damn low. When we passed where the Ouachita River joined the Red it got lower still.

I never *did* get to meet with Liberty or her pappy on our run up the Red River into the deep Louisiana Bayou country. There were three hundred and fifty troops aboard, crammed into the lower decks like tadpoles in a bucket. A tender reunion with Libby wasn't in the works. I had no credible reason to be down among the darkie troops and n––rs weren't allowed on the upper decks. The next morning we tied up to the Alexandria levee.

The river was bedlam and the city was worse. The levee was lined with Porter's fleet tied up rail to rail. We were squeezed between a Navy quartermaster boat loaded with cotton and the *Cricket*, an ugly tinclad gunboat. Other than the Pook turtles no two boats were remotely alike. Proud stern wheel river queens, elegant side wheelers with rails and upper decks painted like fairy castles, grim tinclads and rams swarming with bluejackets, ugly quartermaster boats shoddy built for quick wartime profit, jollyboats, packets, and barges filled the riverfront. I recognized the *Corondelet* and *Pittsburg* from their stack rings and there were at least two other city class boats farther up the levee.[d] Anchored out in the river was a hideous black tub of a warship that looked too big to dock.[e] It was surrounded by a swarm of bum-boats, cutters and bateau. Hell, the entire river was a' swarm with boats of all sizes and descriptions literally butting each other for passage. Barges looking like snow hills, piled high with

---

[d] Sawyer's spelling of *Pittsburg* is correct. The other two Pook turtles present were the *Mound City* and the *Louisville*. Three of the original seven city class gunboats had already been sunk by torpedoes.

[e] This was the *Eastport*, an ironclad ram cut for six guns.

cotton bales, bulled their blunt bows through the red water bringing more plunder to the mountains of cotton already piled along the levee. The din from the riverfront was deafening. Pilots roared for right o' way, roustabouts in Union blue and civilian drab bellowed curses and threats, and swarms of black stevedores moaned their songs in low baritone to lighten their loads. Above all this clamor and adding to it with shrill punctuation were the toots and whistles and bells of a mighty fleet bent on war and plunder.

The Alexandria riverfront was many blocks long and serviced with a wide avenue beside the levee. The promenade was lined with warehouses, shops, saloons and markets. They were solid structures of brick, two and three stories tall with awnings and shutters, and each door was serviced by a liveried darkie in top hat and spats. Behind the riverfront was a fine city that had grown rich on red soil, white cotton and black slaves. And as I watched from the Texas deck the street opposite the *Hannibal* suddenly filled with marching men in blue. At their front were flags of peppermint stripe and a military band that struck up "Columbia the Gem of the Ocean." In a moment the marching men reached the avenue. In ranks as neat as the Corps of Cadets they swung to the left in a column of fours onto the levee. Before Porter's flotilla they paraded in review with bayonets gleaming.

After its long march up the bayou back roads, the Army of General Nathanial P. Banks had finally arrived. I had a letter to deliver.

The Adventures of Sidney Sawyer
Missouri Yankees

Chapter 30

It was my blasted hat. Damn all vanity– I was staff, but the insignia for a staff loafer looks more like Aunt Polly's scrambled eggs than a laurel wreath so I still sported the cavalry's crossed swords on my bonnet. It has more flair by a long reach and the lassies love the glamour, but Banks jumped on it like a duck on a wooly bear. That is how I wound up at the very head of an army of invasion beside a towheaded major who could barely sit his horse. That army straggled behind us for twenty miles on a road churned to gumbo by relentless rain, the booties of twenty thousand infantry, ninety guns and a thousand wagons. The major's troop had just ridden through a scruffy hamlet named Pleasant Hill and there was nothing between us and Shreveport but a scratch Confederate force that we reckoned would flee at the sight of us.

Our highway cut through winter cotton fields, up and over a rise and there they were. There must have been five regiments, a full brigade, and these Confederates were deployed across the fields with their flanks protected by woodlots of pine. By God, they didn't look like they were going to run! They meant to deny us the road and if these Johnnys were anything like their cousins across the Mississippi we were in trouble, neck deep and the water rising. And then an officer raced across the front of the Rebel line, guidon snapping in the wind, and an order was shouted that reached our ears as clear as a chime. Commands barked, and from across the muddy field wild Texas and Louisiana Confederates drew their sabers with the sound of a great serpent hissing hate. Trumpets sounded high and thin, a thousand hysterical men screamed their Rebel yell and on they came like a wave of demons.

This wasn't supposed to happen. From Alexandria to Grand Ecore and now on the road to Mansfield, the Rebels were falling back before the irresistible force of the Army of the Gulf. We'd be in Shreveport in three days, four if the blasted rain didn't relent. It was turning the road to porridge. But it *was* happening! Beside me the towheaded major drew his sword to receive the Confederate attack, brave lad, but he was the only hero in the Yankee line. Our column was strung out in marching order along the road. Good troops could have deployed into skirmish lines as quick as you like and met the Johnnys halfway, but these weren't good troops. They were mounted infantry that had no more business on horses than your grandma's cat. The screaming Rebel charge wasn't halfway across the winter cotton field when the gallant men of General Banks's vanguard broke and ran, and I broke with them with Boone behind hanging onto his fat gelding with both hands around its neck. The Texas boys emptied their carbines at our backs and it was a race to the safety of the main Union column with the devil taking the hindmost. The Union cavalry was disgraced. I *should* have been humiliated, but I don't consider humiliation when it's my arse in the balance and there would be more than enough disgrace for all hands before this campaign was finished.

General Albert L. Lee, Banks's cavalry commander had at least four thousand troopers and a battery of light artillery passing through Pleasant Hill. We could see the redstraps servicing their guns as we swarmed towards the village and stampeded through the line with no more order than a flock of birds. The Rebels weren't fools and wouldn't follow us into Lee's guns, but notice was served that the Confederate Army was present and ready to deal us mischief.

This was all Sherman's fault– him and his damn letter. Porter's fleet had been in Alexandria for over a week before Banks's army marched into town. Banks wasn't with them. He arrived the next day on a boat filled with speculators greedy for cotton. God in heaven, it was a fiasco that would have shamed the Dagos. First, Banks's boat was named *Black Hawk*. Dandy name for a boat, ain't it? It was so dandy that it was also the name of Porter's flagship. The Navy's *Black Hawk* was a side-wheel tinclad that was big enough to accommodate Admiral Porter's entire entourage in martial comfort. Porter was damned proud of his *Black Hawk* and fell into a snit over Banks's *Black Hawk*. The two commanders were barely speaking. *The nerve!*

And then Banks found out that the Navy had already swiped every bale of cotton from Simmesport to Grand Ecore. The jobbers on Banks's *Black Hawk* would have at least *paid* the Louisiana planters for it at the official rate. Porter's quartermasters simply stole it. Now, at the first sign of Yankee blue, the planters were burning their own cotton in a fit of patriotic pique. A week later Banks ordered the outraged speculators back to Baton Rouge where they spread bitter rumors of incompetence, corruption and defeat. *The insolence!*

Finally there was Grant's letter. Banks knew that Whiskey Smith and his three divisions were only along to guard the fleet. If Banks was licked Grant reckoned that he would toss Porter's boats to the wolves. Grant's letter rubbed more dirt into this implied insult. If Shreveport wasn't occupied by the end of April, which would mean that Banks was indeed licked, then Smith's ten thousand troops would be sent back to Sherman where they could do some good. *The cheek!*

And not an hour after Grant's letter was delivered, I marched up the *Black Hawk's* gangplank sporting the crossed swords cavalry button on my Jeff Davis with Sherman's letter to rub even *more* salt into the wounds.

General Nathanial P. Banks was a handsome fellow with a great sweep of hair parted from the left over his noble head. He was clean-shaven but his nose, which was as big as Chief Brant's of the Colored 3rd Engineers, rested on a mustache as big as Amos McCracken's. I reported to him in the ladies' salon of his *Black Hawk* where he had set up an office fit for a field martial. He wore thigh-high cavalry boots complete with spurs as if he was riding at the head of a troop instead of sipping port in a parlor. A double row of brass buttons gleamed on his chest and the gold epaulets on his shoulders damn near made me squint. He was surrounded by a half-dozen staff and a civilian clerk who was shuffling papers by the handful.

"General Banks, sir, I am Colonel Sidney Sawyer." I presented myself foursquare before his desk and threw a crisp salute. "I bring compliments from General Sherman."

General Banks was not pleased to see me. He flashed me a look of thunder from under his hairy eyebrows.

"Sir, you do not bring compliments. You bring interference! Unwelcome interference from distant quarters to confound this command. Do not forget that I outrank your Sherman. He may not order me about. Do you hear, sir?"

"Sir, I am simply a messenger." I handed him the letter with a flourish and almost added, 'Don't shoot the messenger!'

Banks read Sherman's blunt note and turned scarlet. "The nerve! The insolence! The cheek!" He glared at me and demanded, "Do you know the contents of this epistle?"

Like a fool I said that I did.

"Than you are more than simply a messenger, sir. You are a colonel, sir! A colonel to do the work of a corporal! May I presume your orders, sir? You are to stay with this army, are you not, sir? You are to stay until the end of April, are you not? You are to see to it that Grant's order is carried out, are you not, sir?"

Well this was unpleasant. All I wanted was to use Sherman's letter as an excuse to job some Red River cotton, and here I was with an aroused major general snarling in my face.

"Yes, sir." I replied. If I had a tail it would have been tucked between my legs.

"Grant may give me orders, sir. Not Sherman! I do not need his men. His General Smith is not my nanny, sir. His men can ride along with Porter's fleet and be damned! Those that will not fit on the boats may follow along at the end of the column. They may eat the dust of the Army of the Gulf all the way to Shreveport and the devil take them!"

By grapes, this was a hissy fit for the ages. Banks was going to pack off his best ten thousand veteran troops where they could be of no possible service to him on the eve of a march that would take him one hundred and twenty miles into hostile country.

He glanced at my hat. "And you are cavalry, sir!"

I was staff, but I didn't think he wanted me to join his. "Yes sir."

"I have heard of you, sir– Colonel Sidney Sawyer, late of General Gillmore's n—r army at Charleston. I have heard of you, Sawyer, and have heard nothing good. You are a duelist and a brawler and find your company with whores and drunkards, sir! And here you are on my *Black Hawk* with an order your General Sherman has no business giving."

Had somebody been telling tales about me? What the deuce? I had to defend myself, "General Banks, sir, I never brawl. I am…"

"You are cavalry. If you must stay here, you may not stay *here*! Captain Camden!"

A skinny staff plunger, also in boots and spurs, sprang forward with a supercilious look of righteousness on his pale puss. I wanted to punch him in his pasty face. Maybe I *was* a brawler.

"Draw up orders for Colonel Sawyer. If he is cavalry, let him ride with the cavalry. He will ride with the foremost troop. He is General Lee's problem. I do not require aid from General Sherman nor Admiral Porter nor you, Sawyer. On your way!"

Captain Camden actually took my arm to hustle me out. I really *did* want to punch his pasty face.[f]

* * *

I spent the next day loafing about Lee's cavalry bivouac across Bayou Rapides, west of the levee. It was easy to loaf. I was a colonel, I didn't really belong there and who was going to put me to work? The brigade reminded me of the Yankee horse troopers from the early innings of the War. Most of the men were farm boys who could sit a horse but you couldn't really say they could ride one– at least not like any Texas Confederates they were likely to meet. And they were loaded down with so much dunnage that swift movement would be impossible. Besides all the frying pans, spades, shelter halves, blankets and Bibles strapped onto every nag, the brigade was fixing to drag three hundred wagons along with them on the march. I saw one trooper with a cane fishing pole and a rattan creel bag buckled to his screw's withers. Nathan Forrest and Joe Wheeler would have laughed themselves silly.

I used Amos McCracken as an excuse to seek out the Corps D'Afrique, 3rd Engineers– I couldn't very well say I was looking to see to Liberty and her daddy, but the

---

[f] This is a good spot to straighten out the Smiths. General Andrew Jackson Smith (Whiskey or AJ) commanded Sherman's three divisions of infantry sent to Banks. General *Kilby* Smith commanded one of these divisions, which rode with Porter's flotilla. General *Kirby* Smith was the Confederate commander of the entire trans-Mississippi region.

regiment had already moved up the river road with their pontoon train. If they were gone, the rest of the Army wouldn't be far behind. Sure enough, the next day Lee's brigade set out at the lumbering speed of their three hundred wagons to begin General Nathanial P. Banks's glorious Red River Campaign.

We did see Rebel cavalry, but only as they trotted away before us. There was no opposition and nobody expected any. We followed the river in easy stages, occasionally catching a glimpse of the fleet when a meander brought the river and road together. It was at the Cane River that I finally had my reunion with Liberty and Smitty.

The Cane is a considerable bayou that joins the Red about halfway to Grand Ecore. Grand Ecore was just north of Natchitoches. It was important because it was halfway to Shreveport, had enough high ground for the entire army to camp out of the mud, and was a handy place for the army and navy to rendezvous. The 3rd Corps D'Afrique's pontoons bridged the Cane and they couldn't move forward until the entire army had passed over. At the rate Banks was driving his army, we had all the time in the world.

It was easy to get away from Lee's brigade, and it wasn't as if they were moving too fast to catch up. And it was easy to find the 3rd– they had to stay with the bridge. And it was easy to find Smitty and Libby– regiments revolve around their sergeant majors. After dusk around a small campfire along the Cane we had our chat. It was damn awkward at first, what with the situation, but at bottom we like each other and I did have a pint. I passed it to Smitty and he took a swig. He passed it to Libby and she took a sip. She passed it back to me and I took a slug without thinking to wipe the n—r off of the mouth of the bottle. That seemed to break the ice. I was still the noble Ace of Spades.

"Had a' leave the 94th, sir. Weren't no point stayin'. Dey was gonna break up de regiment, mix it with a

South Carolina Colored outfit. Give it a new number an' mix us all up. An' we wouldn't a' been a fightin' regiment no more. De Carolina War is over. Ain't even tryin' ta take Charleston no more. We'd jist dig all around it. Lay down de musket an' pick up de spade."

He took another slurp and said, "And den dey's Liberty."

And there she was, looking ripe and beautiful in fresh calico with her hair longer now, surrounding her face in a perfect sphere of black softness. Not a drummer boy at all.

"Mr. Colonel Sir, I couldn't be no drummer boy no more. It ain't just this," she circled her belly with her hands. "I'm a woman an' didn't *wanna* be a boy no more. An' I was gittin' to look too much like a woman to pass."

Libby looked far off into the fire, "I was a soldier, a sergeant. I fought in battle for my race. I was a spy in the camp of the enemy." She looked from the fire into my eyes, "An' I fell in love with the Ace of Spades. An' I'm gonna be a mama. Time to move on."

She still loved me and made no bones about it, but she didn't burn for me as she once did. And she wasn't simple. She knew there was no happy ending for the likes of us. And I didn't burn for her anymore either. Hell, she was six months along and there was no hiding it. But in a way *I'm* the simple one. I often get a soft spot in my heart for my girls and the memory of them will pop into my head at the damnedest of times. Oh, not casual gallops like Mrs. Lucy Newcastle of Bowling Green, but lasses like my first tutor in love, Professor Roseasharen. The jolly ones have a warm home in my heart, like Martha Jane or chubby Nurse Marybeth from Terre Haute. I was more than a little in love with a few truly noble ladies like little Lizzy Watson, who I never did get to bounce, or Sojourner Ursa Major who I did. And Dust Mop and fat old Missy Ruth and Sweet Pea will roll through my memory now and then, and thank heavens the decanter is at my elbow and I can slop some more into my tumbler, and here I am sniffing into my sleeve and damned if I ain't just a simple old fool.

Around that fire along the Cane was my family– Smitty, blacksmith, soldier, father and one of those capable men who are so rare upon the face of earth, and Liberty– her pure African face shining across the fire, carrying my child who wouldn't be pure anything. A family is a fine thing to have and some men are lucky enough to have two. And if you're really lucky you can keep them both. I'm damn glad I did, because if I didn't, a monster and a bitch would have burned me to ashes on a pyre of Louisiana cotton.

* * *

The Army met the Navy at Grand Ecore and then wasted days as if days don't matter in war. In the Valley back in '62 Stonewall Jackson taught Banks hard lessons in the value of a quick march but Banks was a poor pupil. A full week after Lee's cavalry rode out of Alexandria, the Army was only sixty miles up the river. In Natchitoches the Army of the Gulf staged a grand review for no particular reason, impressing nobody in particular, that had Whiskey Smith's veterans laughing up their sleeves. Smith's men had begun to call themselves Sherman's Gorillas and took to calling their general Napoleon P. Banks. They'd chant it loud and often, and Porter's sailors would have thought it was funnier if the level of the river didn't keep falling.

Not all of Lee's cavalry was of the clodhopper variety. Only half of his troopers were what he called 'amateur equestrians.' The rest of the brigade could have done the real job of cavalry, which was to ride ahead, scout out the roads and ground, and see what the hell the enemy was up to. They could have done it, but of course they didn't. I was cavalry, bred and trained and I could have called Lee on it, but of course I didn't. If I was to nag him into doing his job he might just do it. He could thank me for my troubles by putting me at the head of a battalion of green dragoons way out beyond any possible support. And if we met the Johnnys we would need help. No, I kept my trap shut and let nature take its course. We didn't send out scouts and of course Banks sent us up the wrong road.

There was a dandy road right along the river that we could have strolled along all the way to Shreveport. The entire way we could have been in the shelter of the guns of the fleet and even Napoleon P. Banks's blunders couldn't deny us our prize. But we didn't bother to scout it and we certainly didn't take it. Instead, Banks looked for an excuse to march away from that vulgar cotton thief, Admiral David Dixon Porter and his crews of rascals. He found a scoundrel named Wellington W. Witherbury who claimed local knowledge. He was the pilot of one of Porter's commissary boats. Nobody knew it then, but Witherbury also leased a few hundred acres of cotton growing along the river road that he didn't want confiscated or burned. He chirped to Banks that the inland road through Mansfield was a *fine* road, a *better* road, and if *he* was the general, that's the way *he'd* go. After a pleasant hike the army could sashay into Shreveport as crisp as hard cheese.

On the fifth of April, the day after the Grand Natchitoches Review, Porter steamed his fleet into the maroon current of the Red River. Along with him was General Kilby Smith and 2,300 Gorillas of XVI Corps. They were supposed to meet with Banks farther up stream but not a man in the ranks or a bluejacket on deck ever reckoned to see him again.

The next day in a driving rain I rode out at the head of the first troop of Lee's amateur equestrians towards Shreveport and glory. The day after that, just past Pleasant Hill, Johnny cavalry chased a towheaded major, a troop of pie-eaters, Boone, and me back to the shelter of Lee's line of guns. The next day the wheels fell off of Napoleon P. Banks's wagon.

The Adventures of Sidney Sawyer
Missouri Yankees

Chapter 31

I rode with Lee's staff from our bivouac that morning and I wasn't the only one in Lee's party with butterflies churning in my guts. This Lee wasn't Robert E. by a long branch. He was only a Kansas lawyer of the Jayhawker persuasion, but he was soldier enough to know that with three hundred wagons between his troops and any possible infantry reinforcement he was out at the end of a very long branch indeed. Our embarrassment of the day before occurred four miles beyond Pleasant Hill and that night we camped at least four miles farther out from there. But now we did have at least some infantry with us–Banks had a rare flash of common sense and sent up a division from XIII Corps last night, but it was a thin division and there were still all those wagons hogging the road between us and any further aid.[g] What the dickens *did* cavalry need with three hundred wagons?

We lumbered through the muddy lane up a rise flanked by piney woods and then down past fields and more gloomy pine. We kept on for several miles until before us, bold as stud ducks silhouetted along a ridgeline, we found the Rebel cavalry. They were probably the same rascals who bullied us yesterday. This time Lee had his fellows deploy into line of battle and today, with the

---

[g] This was the 4th division of XIII Corps commanded by Colonel William Landram with 2,500 men.

infantry among them, they did it smartly. Lee advanced toward the ridge like he meant business and the Confederates melted away down the far side of the hill. When we reached the top, the blood chilled in my veins. *There* was the Rebel Army, an army that Banks didn't think could exist west of the Mississippi. There were at least three divisions arrayed in line of battle astride the crossroads three quarters of a mile out. The roads led either North to Shreveport and victory, or west to the Sabine River and Texas, or east to the Red River and the shelter of the Navy's guns, or south to defeat, back through the mud that we churned axle-deep with our march. The Rebels were deployed in an 'L' to the left and right of the crossroads and their center was anchored with a battery of guns.[h]

Guns! That is where Colonel Sidney belonged in a fix like this– behind our own guns where there was power to our front and dozens of obliging artillery nags to hide behind when the shooting began. I had been riding in the company of a half-dozen officers on the right side of the line as we advanced to the crest of the ridge. I gave them a tip of my hat, a calm smile and with Boone bouncing along behind on his fat horse, trotted my mare to the center of the line. I wanted to gallop, but appearances matter. Wouldn't want the troops to see a colonel with wind up his backside now, would we?

We were outnumbered– that was as plain as boiled potatoes. Lee was with the guns and as I trotted up he shoved a scribbled note to a mounted messenger. The boy stuffed it into his gauntlet, spurred his horse and raced back down the road, splashing gumbo in all directions. Damn, if I'd galloped my mare instead of trotting it could

---

[h] The Rebel Army at Sabine Crossroads (also known as the Battle of Mansfield) consisted of Alfred Mouton's Infantry, John Walker's Texas Infantry, Thomas Green's Texas Cavalry Division and William Vincent's Louisiana Cavalry Brigade. During the battle they were reinforced with two additional divisions.

have been me delivering the message to Banks and I'd have missed the worst fiasco I cringed through in the entire War. I had been in more battles than I care to remember, through no noble impulse of my own and always sulking for the egress, but I'd never had the sour taste of defeat rubbed in my face. I was at Forts Henry and Donalson, and Shiloh, and Antietam and Champion Hill and Vicksburg and Battery Wagner and lately Chattanooga and Lookout Mountain, but all of those had been victories. By God, when you look at the list it's a wonder any man could have survived them all but I fought them with self preservation as my sole objective and let the other heroes pitch in with a willing heart. I'd missed the muck-ups like Second Bull Run, Fredericksburg and Chancellorsville, thank providence, but sitting besides Lee looking down at the trans-Mississippi Confederate Army licking its chops like a great gray wolf, the gorge flooded the back of my throat. And then their guns opened up and ours responded in kind and both armies watched the long range duel as the afternoon wore away.

I knew who the Rebel commander was–everybody in the Army knew. He was a sassy devil named Dick Taylor. He could afford to be sassy. His pappy was Zachary Taylor, 'Old Rough and Ready,' hero of the Mexican War and President of the United States. His sister was Jeff Davis's first wife. The bastard was damn near Confederate royalty. He had earned his military spurs with Stonewall Jackson in the Valley by spanking our own N. P. Banks like a delinquent brat. History was about to repeat itself.

The crafty rascal didn't attack. Taylor had cavalry that *behaved* like cavalry and he knew that Banks had double his numbers. They had been ghosting along our flanks since we'd left Grand Ecore and knew our order of march as well as we did. They also knew we were strung out for twenty miles along a single road that drumming rains had turned to quagmire, and they knew we had a train of wagons hogging the route that would make timely reinforcement from point to point impossible. Taylor couldn't have known that Sherman's veterans, the best troops in the Army, were bringing up the rear a full day's march away–could he? No, Dick Taylor was waiting for Banks to attack *him* with only part of his Army in the field. It would have been folly, but Taylor knew his man.

And speak of the devil and up he pops. After two full hours of the guns banging away at each other from ranges too long to be effective, Banks arrived with his full compliment of staff, including the skinny swine that wrote the orders putting me here. I still wanted to box his jaws. I should have stayed away. Nothing draws artillery like a swarm of officers, but it was my neck and I had to know what was trump. I trotted my mare into the growing gaggle around Banks.

Banks was immaculate from the knees up, but nothing could keep the mud from caking on his high boots. His horse was running with muddy sludge from the belly down.

"General Lee, sir, you have them, sir. You have them!" Banks was exultant.

Lee looked at his general as if he had a slate loose. "General Banks, sir, we need reinforcements– infantry and more artillery. When they attack, we may not hold. They have us outnumbered on this field."

"Nonsense, sir! They would not dare such a movement. This is only a display. Do not concern yourself, sir. This is just what I had hoped for. They are ours!"

Lee tried again, "Sir, we need reinforcements from General Franklin, now! His entire corps if they…"

"Franklin is coming up now. Do you think I do not know my duty? But if he does not hurry he will miss the glory. I will ride now to see to his progress. Await orders!" and with that he wheeled his mount, gave his hat a dramatic wave and almost lost his seat when his horse slipped in the muck.

I was Johnny-on-the-spot. While he was hanging onto the mane with both fists I reached down from my saddle, grabbed the dropped reins and handed them back to the general with a flourish. You would think the bastard would have been more grateful to a fellow that saved him from tumbling into the mire in front of half the Army.

"Sawyer," he snarled, and at the same second trumpeted a petard that almost boosted him out of the saddle again. His fart could be heard above the guns.

"Sir!" I threw him a crisp salute.

"I thought I was rid of you, sir. What are you doing here with the guns, sir?"

By grapes the puffed up martinet was mad at me! I hadn't floundered his nag in the mud and I hadn't given him a dose of the Red River two-step. Hell, most of the Army was down with the trots. I hadn't led them into sixty miles of mud with rain to foul the rations. He had a bee in his bonnet about me, and no error. I wonder who the blazes put it there?[i]

"I sent you to the cavalry, sir! Report to your troop at once!"

With another crepetation that triggered giggles in the crew serving the nearest gun, Banks wheeled his mount again, this time didn't almost fall off, and rode back to see to Franklin's Corps.

If that wasn't enough to alert Lee that the commanding general was a military imbecile, the orders he received from Banks fifteen minutes later did. Lee was to advance and take the town of Mansfield that was three miles *past* Sabine Crossroads where Taylor sat with the whole Confederate Army. Lee scurried back to Banks to politely inform him that he was indeed an imbecile and it couldn't be done before Franklin's men arrived on the

---

[i] Virtually all soldiers in the Civil War suffered with dysentery or diarrhea, most of them repeatedly. There were dozens of droll names for the malady, but more men died from it than from combat.

scene. He returned to his command just in time for Taylor to make any notion of a Union advance a moot point.

*   *   *

They came in on our right in a stately march in echelon with tight formations and mounted officers to the front like a parade ground review. I remember thinking it damn queer for the officers to lead from horseback. One thing three years of war should have taught these Louisiana and Texas Confederates was that mounted officers are little better than targets in a turkey shoot, but on they came, pacing their infantry and gesturing bravely with swords. One gallant buck held the reins in his teeth, pistol in one hand and sword in the other, looking like a doll in his tight gray tunic. His gold braided frogging glittered in the dim sunlight as he rode.

And from my right an order barked, a troop of dismounted cavalry fired their carbines in a crashing volley, and the gallant cavalier and his mount went down under a hale of minié balls. The Rebel line gave a vast groan and broke into a wild charge fueled by hate. Our green cavalry was shooting at the officers! By God, the officers won't kill you, you fools– the infantry will! Then our entire right flank fired by the volley and the Battle of Sabine Crossroads was on.

I hate battle, but we were in one now with both boots and we had to slaughter these Confederates before they got much farther up the hill within killing distance of *us*. We had squatted on this rise all day! It was four o'clock at least, and nobody had thought to entrench the line. We were going to attack– Banks had said so! Who needs entrenchments? And now, here we stood, in the open as if it was 1861 all over again, and entrenchments were for cowards who didn't understand the romance and pageantry of war. I spurred my mare and galloped to the right of our line with Boone following along as best he could.

"The hell with the officers!" I screamed above the oncoming Rebel yell that was getting closer by the second. "Shoot at the men! Aim low! Shoot low in their guts. Shoot the infantry! The men!"

I was almost as hysterical as the Confederates, screaming their hideous yell and storming up the hill like demented demons. Their officers, their beloved officers, were being swept from their saddles like God's own angry hand was smashing them aside, but the line of Rebels swept up the hill unchecked. They were closer now and now the men could see their faces, twisted with hate and vengeance for their officers. The first cowards in the Union line began to waver.

"Stop them, you swine! Hold your place, you dog! Reload by the numbers, you bastards! Remember your drill,"

It wasn't the most inspiring brand of leadership in the register but most of the soldiers in the line did steady and finally let loose volleys that tore into the onrushing Confederates, blowing every tenth man back down the slope. The slaughter shocked them to a stumbling halt a scant hundred yards before our thin line of dismounted Yankee cavalry.

"Remember your mothers and sisters! Remember your dead and buried! Remember..." Remember what? I didn't know what state these fellows were from. I couldn't rally them with memories of the wrong place, but then there was a great crash of fire from the left side of our position and there the rest of the Confederate line was charging up the hill to engage our other flank. The sound of it encouraged the hesitant Rebels to our front and with a great screaming yell they surged up and at us with regimental banners waving and bayonets flashing into our faces. In an instant the entire Union right became unhinged. Men sobbed in terror and ran. Most threw their carbines at the oncoming Rebels who roared and charged on like insane terriers. I was surrounded in a mass of men, faces twisted in fear, their only thought to flee the monsters who were cresting our hill and cutting down the brave and the slow with their terrible bayonets.

I forced my mount through the swarming cowards and pulled up behind Lee's guns in the center of our line. The left was still holding and the guns were firing into the Rebel formations with vicious effect. For one hopeful second I felt that, despite the shambles on the right side of the line, we might hold until Franklin's Corps arrived. That is *if* he hurried to the sound of the guns. But then, to the left and the right, distant bugles shrilled disaster. I positively sobbed in fear. The Confederate cavalry raced from the shelter of thick piney woods on our far left and right and Lee's entire line disintegrated as if on command.

What had been stout lines of troopers to the left of the guns, holding ground before the assaulting Johnnys, became a swarm of sheep pelting for the rear as fast as boots could propel them through the mud. This was no place for Auntie Polly's little boy and I spurred my mare with a savage kick that sent her into the mob like she was pushing through a thicket of briers. Men snarled and beat her with fists. If most hadn't thrown away their guns they would have shot her, and me. I couldn't get through. The Rebels were around our own guns, no more than fifty yards behind me. They were shooting into our backs with musket and pistol and now turned our own cannon onto us with cruel effect. Men were throwing up their hands, crying for quarter and my mare went down in the sobbing mass and I was thrown into the mud. I struggled like fury but couldn't win to my feet with the crowd crushing me down. I was doomed. There was no escape. It was a bullet in the back or a Rebel prison camp for me, and no way to run. Men were crying for Mother or Molly or Sweet Jesus and the tears came to my eyes and the snot to my nose and I cried with them.

"Aunt Polllly!"

A strong hand grabbed me by the collar and roughly dragged me from my knees. I looked up and there sat my salvation on a fat horse. Boone!

"Jump up behind me, Colonel Sawyer! I'll save you! I'll save you or die!"

He reached down his hand to haul me up onto the back of his mount and I took it. My decision was instant and if you think me a craven, well you are right, I was, but here I sit five decades later sipping a decent bourbon with my feet to the fire and my family on the way over for supper. They'll never know what I did that terrible April day back in '64 with hysterical men sobbing for quarter, vengeful Texans firing point-blank into our backs and mud balling thick around our boots, slowing our flight through a wallowing nightmare.

Boone could never save me. He could barely sit a horse and his mount was foaming with terror and exhaustion. It could never carry us both through the mass of struggling men. And I was an officer!

I gripped his wrist with both hands and instead of swinging astride the rump of his horse I yanked as hard as I could, sending him headfirst into the swarm. I was up and aboard in a second and lashing the flat of my sword left and right to clear a path. I'd kill any man that tried to stop me.

"Way, make way you men! I have a dispatch for Banks. I'll be back with Banks and the Army!"

I slashed my blade at a hand grabbing for the bridle. Fingers flew and blood splashed. Hands clawed at my belt and boots. I kicked at a screaming face, hands fell away and I spurred Boone's horse through the last of the mob.

"Make way for a dispatch to Banks! I'll fetch Franklin. We'll be saved!" and I bowled through men with arms up begging me to stop and save them.

And there was Banks himself. Napoleon P. Banks was swinging his sword like me, but not to cut off grasping fingers. He was a fool, but not a coward.

"Rally to the colors my men. Oh, my dear men, rally to me! Franklin is here! Oh, my dear soldiers, rally to me!"

Franklin *was* here. Too late! I had only ridden a hundred yards and there were Franklin's men trotting at the double time, struggling through the ditches and mud on both sides of the lane. The road was of course clogged with Lee's wagons. As far as I could see, wagons were blocking the way with wheels sinking into the muck and muddy mules sagging in their harnesses. God, what a shambles!

"Hoo-hoo-hoo!" the men shouted at Banks as they stampeded past his horse and around his bewildered staff. "Where's yer mule? Where's yer mule? HOO-HOO-HOO!"

The sound of Confederate fire was coming closer. The Rebel yell was rising above the shouts of the routed Yankees. Frightened teamsters began abandoning their wagons. Some cut the traces and climbed on their mules bare backs, slapping and kicking the beasts into a trot past their cursing officers.

The first of Lee's panicked men were swarming around the vanguard of Franklin's Corps.

"Run! Run! They're killin' us all! Run! Save yerselves– HOO-HOO-HOO!"[j]

Franklin's were mostly green troops, exhausted from their forced march in the mud. All around them was chaos and terror. Their division was stretched out behind them for miles and could not possibly help in any fight. They saw a colonel, covered in mud, bloody saber in hand, hatless and wild-eyed, spurring his fat horse in the other direction. They broke and ran, joining the rout, abandoning the wagons, the guns and their thousand Union brothers surrendering to the Rebels with hands high and cries for mercy.

We shouldn't have stopped to steal cotton. We shouldn't have wasted days with parades in Alexandria

---

[j] Hoo-hoo-hoo' may seem an odd cry from the throats of panicked soldiers but independent accounts confirm Sawyer's description of the battle and the rout.

and Natchitoches. We should have taken the river road. We should have let Whiskey Smith's veteran Gorillas take the lead. We shouldn't have taken three hundred wagons. We should have entrenched. We shouldn't have aimed at the Rebel officers. Napoleon P. Banks should have stayed in New Orleans.[30]

Chapter 32

I never saw Boone again. Killed or captured, it really made no difference. I had saved his life and he'd saved mine back and I'd call that even-Steven in any book. It was dandy to have a personal flunky all my own, and a white one no less, but he was always under foot and had no style. And for what I was about to do now, I didn't need any witnesses. I was deserting in the face of the enemy.

I knew the graybacks would be on us like fury the next day. I was in the Army, but I didn't belong with *this* army. Who the dickens would miss me? I was mounted and moving faster than the rest of the panicked rabble stampeding in retreat. I reached what looked to be a stalwart line of troops from Franklin's Corps about four miles back from the crossroads. They hadn't been touched by the rout, looked to be good boys and there were certainly enough of them. I rode through the line as if I had a mission, but my first mission was to snatch a decent mount. Boone's nag was shaking at the withers and blowing with the croup. There were always spare mounts to be had about any army's headquarters and Franklin's didn't disappoint. A rolling kitchen was parked close to the center of the line where a dozen staff loafers were sipping rio and stuffing their faces with biscuits. I hung back, biding my time for a chance to pinch a fresh screw and sure enough Providence provided.

Major General Billy Franklin himself provided it. He and another gaggle of staff came trotting through the line looking like a spaniel's breakfast. His boot was gone, there was a filthy bandage wound around his shin and he was riding *my* horse![k] An officer with a half-acre of magnificent auburn whiskers helped him off his mount, *my mount*, and two stalwart troopers carried him twenty yards down the line and propped him up on a caisson.

Franklin was the center of attention. In a twinkling I was up and away and nobody gave me a second look. My mare still had my carbine strapped across her withers and my bag and blanket secured behind the saddle. I took to the winter cotton fields beside the road. An endless line of wagons blocked the lane itself. Damnation and dead mules, there were even more of them behind the infantry than there were behind Lee's cavalry. What a cock-up!

That night I made it as far as Whiskey Smith's Gorillas. They were bivouacked in a dull village of scattered houses and barns that was misnamed Pleasant Hill. If Banks had put these Gorillas at the other end of his line it would be Dick Taylor's graybacks reeling back in defeat instead of him. I could have done my duty and reported the fiasco at Sabine Crossroads to Smith, but I knew there would presently be some bona fide galloper along with the grim news. Instead I walked my mount through the camp, found a likely place to spread my blanket just inside the far picket line and slept rough.

I didn't sleep well and I didn't sleep for long. The infantry wagon train that had been strung along miles of road between Franklin's Corps and Smith's was rumbling through the bivouac heading back towards Grand Ecore. The Army was retreating. No one can curse with the eloquence of teamsters and these teamsters were driving their wagons through midnight mud behind exhausted

---

[k] Major General William Franklin led Banks's army on the march to Alexandria. He was wounded in the shin at Sabine Crossroads and rode a borrowed horse back to prepare his remaining corps to meet the onrushing Confederates. Evidently this was Sawyer's mount.

mules. In the wee hours bugle and drum officially roused the camp and I set about organizing my own retreat. I pinched a sack of fodder from a stalled wagon. The teamster was too busy swearing at its broken spokes to mind a colonel rummaging through the cargo. I'm cavalry and know my priorities. Feed the horse first! Then I bullied some scrapple and coffee from a company of Pennsylvania Gorillas who were enterprising enough to have stolen a hog the day before.[1] I scribbled a dispatch outlining the scope of the disaster, addressed it to the garrison that Banks had left to baby-sit Alexandria and stuffed it down my blouse. If any busybodies along the way demanded my reason for being on the highway, why, I'm delivering the mail, ain't I? I started on the road back to Grand Ecore before anyone knew I was even there. And I missed the Battle of Pleasant Hill and thank God for that blessing.

I heard all about Pleasant Hill from the layabouts on Whiskey Smith's staff during the idle weeks we sat in Alexandria waiting for the fleet to evacuate. They reckoned me one of their own. I had charged with Sherman's Corps up Grave Yard Road at Vicksburg and ridden with Grant into Chattanooga through sixty miles of dead mules. The officers of Smith's staff treated me like one of the boys. Over jars of Oh-Be-Joyful they were happy to brag. After all, the only credit squeezed from the entire campaign was the glory won by the Gorillas at Pleasant Hill.

By morning, Smith and his Gorillas knew all about the rout back at Mansfield. They formed their line on a slight plateau with houses and outbuildings scattered here and there and waited to receive the graybacks. At dawn the

---

[1] Scrapple is a fried loaf of hog scrapings (head, glands, ears and other unappetizing parts) mixed with flour or corn meal. The Pennsylvania Dutch called it 'panhaas' or 'pan rabbit.' Soldiers in the Civil War would have used crushed hardtack instead of flour.

whipped troops from the crossroads began limping through their lines. This parade of refugees continued until Taylor's Army showed up in the early afternoon. And then nothing happened. Most of the Confederates had made an exhausting forced march just to get to Mansfield. Then they fought the battle at the crossroads and chased the routed Yankees another four miles to the line held by Franklin's only remaining corps. That was where I reclaimed my horse. It was almost dark by then but Dickey Taylor had studied war at the knee of Stonewall Jackson who taught him that there is never a minute to be wasted. He piled his troops into a wild attack on Franklin's line, but the Rebels were almost as disorganized from their victory as the Yankees were from their defeat. Franklin's line held just long enough for darkness to close the day's festivities.

As soon as the firing died down Banks ordered a retreat, leaving the wagons and wounded for the Confederates. At dawn Taylor found the Federals gone and took up another forced march to catch them. The Yankees weren't about to be caught and high-stepped through mud and mire the dozen miles back to Pleasant Hill. Those that still had their muskets fell in with Franklin's men on the left of the line. A. J. Smith's Gorillas sneered with self-righteous contempt and held the center.

Presently Dick Taylor showed up with his men too fagged to stand, much less fight. The idea of a counter attack never entered Napoleon P. Banks's wooly head. His army simply squatted in place and gave the Johnnys time to catch their breath and pull up their socks.

At around five o'clock Taylor opened the ball by thundering his men into the far end of the Union left flank. That was exactly where Franklin's shaky troops were slouching after their all night skedaddle. These Confederates were Arkansas and Missouri boys who had missed out on the glory of the Southern victory at the crossroads. They had arrived late to the field after a tardy march from beyond Mansfield. Now they lusted to be in at the kill and they hit Franklin's flank like the crack of doom. They came in like furies with their terrible yodel screeching above the glint of bayonet and steel. Franklin's soldiers did what troops in any army commanded by General N. P. Banks did so well. They broke and ran. It should have been another Union disaster, but Whiskey Smith was holding the center with his Gorillas and they didn't consider themselves to be any part of Banks's crew. Cool as you like, Smith sent his reserves far out and around to the left. Old Stonewall couldn't have done it neater. The Gorillas hit the charging Rebels in *their* flank and smashed through regiment after regiment like a runaway locomotive. Smith never even consulted Banks. Banks would have dithered. He simply did what he had to do and kept feeding more and more of his troops into his attack on the left until it was hand-to-hand, clubbed muskets and cold steel. The Rebel yell turned into cries for quarter and the graybacks fell back in a rout of their own. Dickey Taylor ordered retreat and glory hallelujah, the day was won. And then Napoleon P. Banks turned his Army around and marched them back to Grand Ecore.

I don't believe in heaven, and won't until I'm on my deathbed whining for a padre, but I do believe in hell. There has got to be a special place set aside in the hottest, deepest pit to accommodate conceited generals. I'm a general, but if I wind up in the fires it won't be because my conceit filled graves with men unlucky enough to have been placed under my command. In the Navy, an admiral is literally in the same boat as his shellbacks. If they sink, he sinks. That's the line I took in the few times I ever commanded a brigade in the field. If they went down, I'd likely go with them, so I was as stingy with their lives as any miser with his bullion. And I wasn't a general because of any conceit. Oh, I think I'm as dandy as any Yankee Doodle and my privy don't stink, but I've never entertained any notions of martial mavenhood. The Army's a bureaucracy, and in any bureaucracy, if you hang around long enough, you'll wind up in charge of *something*. I'm a general because I hung around for forty years. With Banks it was conceit. The Civil War was full of generals who couldn't have run the local post office but who were put at the head of brigades and divisions and corps. Any civil war is a political war and these birds were politicians. McClernand was one and Beast Butler was another, but Napoleon P. Banks won the quilt. He had the conceit to be president of the United States. He had the clout to demand a command, and so wherever the winds of Civil War blew him disaster followed. By 1864 the Transmississippi didn't matter to the outcome of the larger War anymore than Gillmore's folly before Charleston did. But Banks craved glory and so soldiers marched where they didn't have to march, fleets sailed up rivers that couldn't float them, battles raged to no purpose, and graves were filled by men who didn't have to die.

The half-acre in hell reserved for conceited generals must be damned crowded. If I'm doomed and damned for my sin and folly I can only hope that Satan parks me in another corner of perdition where I won't have to see the likes of Frémont or McClellan or Gillmore or Hooker or Custer or Banks ever again.

There are many good reasons to be a general. Humble Ulysses Grant simply did what he was best at doing, Rawlins was a busybody, Thomas was true blue, Forrest was a born killer, Wheeler was gallant, Dodge was a driver, A. J. Smith was a warhorse, Dick Taylor was born to it and I had hung around long enough. Sherman may have had the best reason of all– he was crazy. Conceit ain't any kind of reason. Conceit is fine for a bride at her wedding or a corpse at his funeral, but it has no place at the head of an army.

* * *

I didn't push my mount and kept to the fields and brush until I was past the first of the wagons heading back to the Red River. I was worried about Johnny cavalry lurking in the pines to intercept the odd wagon, the unlucky messenger or deserting colonels, but they must have all been rallying to Pleasant Hill to support Taylor. In the mid afternoon when I trotted into Grand Ecore I heard the distant muffled booming of artillery that was the beginning of the battle back at Pleasant Hill. Good luck to 'em. I had other fish to fry. I had to buy a boatload of cotton. After all, that was what I was here for.

I had reckoned that I would have to ride my mare the sixty miles back to Alexandria by the river road, but luck was with me and about damn time! Luck had a name, *Lady Leavenworth*, a commissary boat, and she was headed back downriver to Alexandria from Porter's flotilla. *Lady Leavenworth* was escorted by *Cricket*, the same tinclad that had hemmed us in on the Alexandria levee when the *Hannibal* docked to unload the 3rd Colored Engineers. And *The Lady L* did indeed need an escort. She was loaded with white gold– cotton! It wasn't a big boat, and she didn't have a full deck load, but at a buck fifty a pound she didn't have to be.

I did some quick ciphers and came up with a cargo of at least three hundred bales. Five hundred pounds to a bale times three hundred bales times a dollar and fifty cents and that comes to– let's see, carry the two... Damnation in a biscuit box– a quarter of a million dollars! And my deal with Old Man Temple was a cool ten percent of gross value. Twenty-five thousand dollars under the Sawyer mattress– what a daydream, but I had a better chance of billiards with Bobby Lee than I had of pinching that load. Or did I? I had a fistful of signed licenses to purchase all the cotton the Temple's line of credit could handle and a stash of gold eagles for ready bribes. *The Lady L* was a *Navy* commissary boat. That meant that its cargo was under the authority of a *Navy* quartermaster. I never heard of a bo'sun who wouldn't pry the gold teeth from a drunken shipmate's gums. Bo'suns are a larcenous crew, pinching the best rum, selling off the ship's rations and shaking down the shellbacks for services, shillings and sodomy. I had an even chance! But was the quartermaster of the *Lady Leavenworth* a fair representative of his breed?

It turned out that he was. He was a red-faced, big-bellied saltwater sailorman named Jekyll Winchel who was disgusted beyond endurance with the entire brown-water Navy. He longed for the wide sky and blue water of the open sea. He hated all rivers on principle and the Red River in particular. When I offered him fifty bucks in greenbacks to stow me and my mare aboard the *Lady L*, for a ride to Alexandria, where we had no legitimate business being, he snapped at it like an eel. On the way downriver we shared a pint of Red River rooster-juice and had quite a talk.

Winchel leaned his big mitts on the rail and gave the river a spit, "River's fallin'. We'll be lucky to get this washtub past Bayou Rapides and down to the Mississippi. The gunboats 'ill never make it."

I could see he was right. Mudflats along the inside of the bends were showing above the sluggish water. I knew rivers and this didn't make sense.

"But since we started the campaign its been raining like Father Noah's flood. The Red should be rising, shouldn't it?"

"Nope, it takes more rain than we got this past week and its been a dry year, but the big problem is that the Rebs blew their damn dam."

"Dam?"

"Damn right! Below Shreveport there was a dam to keep this damn river from flowing into an old channel. Damn Rebs blew the dam and the whole damn river flowed the wrong way leaving Porter high and dry. The fleet won't be able to get past the damn shoals at Bayou Rigolette, an' if that don't stop Porter, the damn rocks at Bayou Rapides will. They don't call it Rapides for nothin'"

"Damn!" I sighed. (Or did I sigh, "Dam?")

"But see here, this boat can't draw more than a foot of water. She can run on dew. She can make it downriver, can't she?"

"Damn right she can, the *Lady L's* just a little barge– might have to unload the cotton and carry it around the riffles, but she'll make it. It's the ironclads that won't have a chance in hell. Have to scuttle 'em or leave 'em for the Confederate Navy."

"Damn!"

After a few more sips of rooster-juice I turned the conversation to the matter at hand– cotton. I already knew Jekyll Winchel was crooked, he'd pocketed my bribe without a wink, but I had to find out the scale of his larceny.

"I see USN stenciled on all of these bales of white gold on deck. You're a lucky man, Bo'sun. Damn white of the Navy to spread the prize money around to the ranks. Wish the Army did. You're gonna be as rich as Croesus. Good for you!"

The selfish swine finished my pint, tossed it over the rail and rounded on me with a snarl, "Rich man? The only men who are going to get rich are Porter and his blasted officers on the gunboats. The lads get two shares and that's divvied with the crews of twenty-two ships-o'-war, and I ain't countin' the quartermaster boats. My share of the plunder will buy me a warm belly for a night and a bottle of rum. Prize money– bah!"

I had found my man![31]

* * *

By the time the *Lady Leavenworth* shot through the shoal water and tied to the Alexandria levee we had made our deal. Winchel was right about our small boat floating the riffles. Going full steam to keep steerage through the fast water we slid past the exposed rocks to our starboard, continued under the looming cliffs to port and shot rapids that flooded half of the bow deck passing Bayou Rapides, but my cotton was safe. *My* cotton!

Bo'sun Winchel was a bitter man. He reckoned that he'd never see dime-one from Navy prize money so he took his prize from *me*. And better still I gave him an opportunity to win his own fortune by the main chance. I gave him two hundred dollars in gold coin just to let him know I was serious. He took another thousand in greenback dollars, which didn't have the luster of my gold, but you could spend them just as well, and I signed a check to Temple & Son's account for another four thousand. He had heard of Temple & Son and knew they were a square deal. To *really* sweeten the pot I gave him a cotton license signed by the military governor of Baton Rouge. If Winchel was half as clever as he was felonious he could make a bundle and I wished the bastard well.

The dead of the night is a grand time for the likes of rogues, reivers, swindlers, and scoundrels, and that first midnight back in Alexandria was a grand time for the likes of me. I had genuine Navy vouchers signed by Lieutenant Samuel Clemens, the quartermaster of the man-o'-war, *Eastport*. Lieutenant Clemens's handwriting looked suspiciously like my own, but who'd ever check? Besides, I'd be burning them once they served their purpose. The vouchers stated that three hundred and seventeen bales of cotton, seized by the Navy as legitimate prizes of war, were to be transferred for storage to any suitable location. This wasn't the only time that I had used Cousin Sam's name on a dodge. I like to think that there are still unserved warrants on that pencil-pushing fraud out in a half-dozen states.

The suitable location I found was the Antioch Faith Baptist Church on 4th Street, kitty-corner from the Catholic Church and only two blocks up from the levee. I would have preferred using the Catholic Church, it was bigger and a damn sight more solid, but half of the crew rounded up by Winchel were mackerel-snappers and I don't like to mess with the local gods. The Baptist Church would do. It was timber and clapboard and when the men piled the benches to the side there was plenty of room for the cotton. The preacher tried to raise a fuss but he was no more effective than the Reverend Mister Sprague, Auntie Polly's parson back home. I waved my forged papers and Winchel waved his big fists, and the argument was over.

Winchel whistled up a labor-gang from the swarm of contrabands loafing about the riverfront, and while the city slept my fortune piled up before the Old Rugged Cross. By morning, the darkies were on their way with two-bits each for their trouble and the church was secured. I nailed the doors shut for good measure.

I stabled my mare at a private livery and I checked into a boarding house around the corner on 2nd Street. The Army wouldn't even know I was in town, and the Navy would never miss their cotton, not that it mattered. Banks was still far upriver ushering his whipped Army back to Grand Ecore. Porter was nursing his fleet, including the *Eastport,* which was too fat to ever shoot the riffles of a river that was falling before his eyes. I was in a featherbed by dawn and slept the sleep of the satisfied.

The Adventures of Sidney Sawyer
Missouri Yankees

Chapter 33

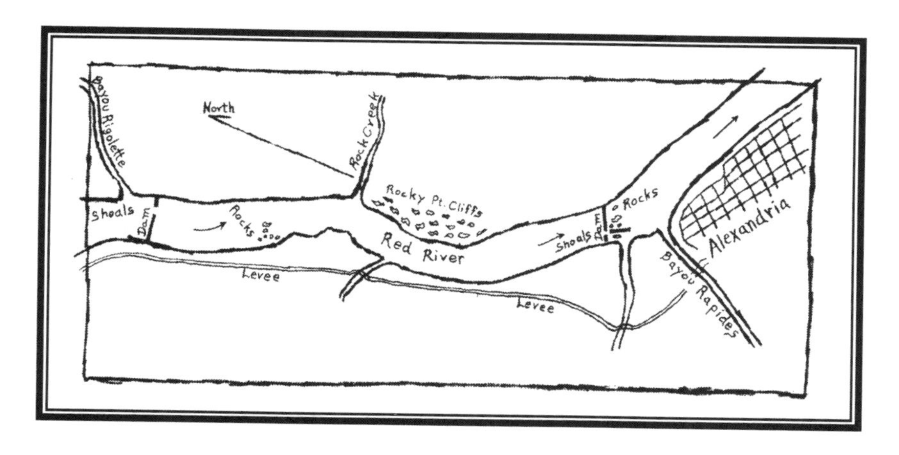

If I knew I was going to be stuck in Alexandria for another month I would have abandoned the cotton and deserted all the way back to Amy's arms and Auntie's cookin'. How was I to know, and why in the blazes would anyone even *consider* that Banks would dither in Grand Ecore for another two weeks?

At first he waited for Porter who had steamed his fleet fifty miles farther upriver in the forlorn hope that Banks would rendezvous with him for the final drive to Shreveport. When that hope went a' glimmering, Porter turned his boats around to find the riverbank lined with

Johnny irregulars who used his flotilla as target practice. The transports ferrying Kilby Smith's gorillas were shot through like sieves. And the Red twisted like a serpent. Navigating the treacherous bends sent the boats bashing into snags, mud banks and each other. Rudders were unshipped, woodwork was splintered, railings swept away and stacks toppled. Every bluejacket that exposed himself on deck to effect repairs attracted the attention of every bush-popper and window-shooter in Louisiana.

When the flotilla finally limped under the shelter of the Grand Ecore bluffs, it took another four days for Porter and saner heads to convince Banks that it was time to go. By then Banks was also convinced that he was hopelessly outnumbered, so when he finally *did* skedaddle, he went like a scalded cat. His men marched until their tongues hung out. The column leaked gear and stragglers with every mile. If the silly swine had gone after Shreveport with the speed that he ran away from it, he'd have been in Texas by now. Along the way his stragglers burned Grand Ecore, Natchitoches and every house, barn and chicken coop along the road. On April twenty-fifth, Napoleon P. Banks rode his lathered horse back into Alexandria leading a whipped Army that was shy a thousand mules, ten score wagons, two dozen pieces of artillery and four thousand men. He'd been gone less than a month.

Three days later, the fleet steamed back to the Alexandria levee looking like the Celestial Chinese Navy after a typhoon. There wasn't a boat that hadn't been shot through a score of times and their decks were littered with rubbish and smashed tackle. The stacks of the Pook turtles were so peppered that I could see sunlight twinkling through the shot holes as they passed. No wonder their sailors called their ironclads teakettles.

Just out of Grand Ecore, the *Eastport* had blundered into a torpedo. Pump-boats re-floated the ugly ironclad but she hit a snag a bit farther along. The sailors re-floated her again, but by then Rebel artillery had taken that stretch of the river under fire. The Johnny twelve pounders couldn't dent the mighty *Eastport,* but a pump-boat was lost in the effort. Then the *Eastport* grounded on another sandbar while the level of the river dropped another foot. The gallant little *Cricket* steamed to the rescue with Porter aboard to direct the salvage. The *Eastport's* giant guns were piled onto the *Cricket's* deck to lighten the load but the great ironclad was stuck fast. Rebel batteries on shore slaughtered the *Cricket.* Half the crew was killed, its thin armor blown into the river. Porter himself took the wheel when the helmsman was mutilated by shot. Charges were finally laid in the *Eastport's* vitals and she was blown up to keep her from enemy hands.

If that wasn't humiliation enough, the fleet now filled the riverfront above Bayou Rigolette and unless the Red River rose there wasn't a chance in hell it could get past the rocks, riffles and shoals. The water kept falling.

It was a disaster, but it's an ill wind that doesn't blow sunshine into somebody's backyard and the sun shown brightly on Sidney Sawyer. With the fleet in a shambles there wouldn't be any busybodies from the *Cricket*, and for damn sure not from the *Eastport*, to stick their noses into the matter of forged invoices and three hundred and seventeen bales of missing cotton. And with the Army at sixes and sevens it was easy for an unassigned colonel to lay low. All I had to do was avoid headquarters on the *Black Hawk* and behave myself. Every few days I'd visit Smith's Gorilla's mess to pick up the gossip. When I had to be on the streets I pasted a determined look on my noble brow, strode down the boardwalks with a purposeful gait and always carried a dispatch portfolio that must have been stuffed with urgent orders and vital documents. It carried my pint, forged cotton licenses, Old Man Temple's greenbacks and a deck of cards. I was never questioned.

I had beaten the Army and Navy back to Alexandria by a good two weeks. In that time I had work to do. After I woke from my well-earned slumber at the boarding house and stuffed myself on the landlady's pork and potatoes, I returned to the Baptist Church with a claw hammer, pried out the nails and let my self in. A claw hammer is a dandy key. I spent the rest of the day covered with lint. Each bale had 'CSA' stenciled in black with an 'X' painted through. Beneath was a scarlet 'USN.' This cotton wouldn't belong to Temple & Son until I ripped out the incriminating cotton and repacked it with virgin fiber. The first bale took me half an hour and it was a lame effort. The patch showed like a whore at a camp meeting and stuck out every which-way. This would take forever. I'd need help.

Back home in St. Petersburg the darkies lived across O'fare Creek in 'Darktown.' Alexandria was less genteel. They called it 'N—r Town.' It was up Bayou Rapides past the levee, and beyond the tanner's yards, and the dump. That's where I found Liberty.

Smitty wasn't the only soldier from the Colored 3rd that had brought his women folk to war. There are always women who tag along with any regiment. Darkie outfits had more than most. The year before most of the men had been slaves, and what else were their women to do? But they couldn't go on the campaign so the women stayed behind in N—r Town. Libby seemed glad to see me. I was damn glad to see her.

*   *   *

I don't know how they do it, but they do. Women can take a domestic problem that has the men shaking their heads and scratching at their arses, and with a tut-tut and a sidelong glance that sums up their opinion of men folk, they simply go about doing it. Liberty set my hash-job on the first bale to rights in fifteen minutes. I couldn't tell where the patch ended and the bale began. In another fifteen minutes she worked the same magic on a second bale. I was in business.

Liberty Smith was as ripe as a plum. I hadn't seen her in two weeks but she was six months along now, and it showed. But she was just as pretty and just as full of ginger as ever. When I told her my plan she jumped at it with all the eagerness that had sent her into the Army with her pa, dispatched her into Charleston as a spy and fetched her to the Swamp Battery boardwalk to make love to the Ace of Spades. The girl had sand!

The only thing I held back was my desertion. I'd had a chance to buy cotton from the Navy. "Yes, little lady, the Navy stole it to begin with but now it's mine– but it ain't mine quite yet. First I have to re-label it. It's deuced hard. A man's fingers just ain't fit for the work. *Yes*, I have papers to prove ownership. It's all legal, it just don't bear close scrutiny. The sooner it's shipped it the better. Will you help? You will– dandy! You get one percent of gross."

She would have helped for free, but what the deuce, she was family. If Old Man Temple bristled at forking over two thousand five hundred bucks to a darkie wench, well, I couldn't have done it without her and slavery's dead now, ain't it old man?

Liberty slept in the enclosed porch of the rooming house and took her meals in the kitchen. The landlady tried to make a fuss, but I was a Yankee colonel with plenty of tin and well, slavery's dead now, ain't it old woman?

Libby could only doctor about thirty patches a day. Each morning I had to pile the finished bales by the door and manhandle fresh ones forward so she could ply her handiwork around her growing belly. I cut a four-foot measure of hickory from a hoe handle to use as a lever, but it was still no work for a white man. I had to strip to the waist to keep lint from fouling my uniform. I coughed like tabby with a hairball from the dust and sweated like– well, like a darkie stevedore. Five hundred pounds to a bale– it was like levering sleeping bears. I swore! Libby giggled!

And rum and rosewater, when it was only her and me in the church surrounded by handy bales of soft cotton laid side to side like King Henry's bed, I hankered to have another crack at little Liberty Smith. She was just so damned fetching with her cloud of African hair softer than any cotton surrounding her merry black face, laughing at me as I wrestled the bales about. The bales were piled four deep, ten feet high, and she clapped her hands like a child at a circus when I forced the hoe handle between them, pried the top bale down and sprang aside to avoid being squashed like a bug under a boot.

"Oh, Mr. Colonel Sawyer, sir! Y'all jump like a big toad," and she laughed fit to redden her cheeks beneath the black.

"A toad?" I thundered, spitting cotton from my mouth and sneezing in the dust, "That's Colonel Toad to the likes of you, drummer boy!"

"Mr. Colonel Toad, sir, I ain't in de Army no more. I'm in de cotton business," but she came to attention and threw me the sweetest salute I ever saw. "Y'all kain't give me no more orders. We's partners!"

"*Business* partners, Sergeant Smith," I sang out as I grabbed her by the waist and pulled her close, "what about some monkey business!"

My shirt was stripped off so I was already halfway ready for monkey business. Little Sidney was *definitely* ready. I gave her my best leer and shouted, "Ha-ha!"

I was about to add a randy jest about being ready for the monkey kind of business, when I felt her belly hard against mine. Her belly! In that belly was my child! Damnation in a jelly jar, why am I always such a gentleman? And to a colored wench, no less! I pulled my hands off her arse, gently pushed her away and tried to wipe the lust out of my smile. I'm so noble!

I patted her head like a Dutch uncle, gave her bottom a friendly swat and we went back to work. At lunch we propped up on the bales, dined on buns, butter, cheese, and cider, and chatted like old chums. We were family.

While she labored in the church I set about arranging cargo space for my treasure. Riffles and shallow water blocked the Red above the city, but it was open below down to the Mississippi. Everyday boats steamed up to Alexandria with tucker for the garrison. The boats arrived loaded but went away empty. The only real cargo they could ship out was cotton and contraband slaves. The darkies were happy to go but the cotton was already gone. It had been looted or burned weeks ago– except mine!

I had learned the business of the rivers when I was a brat fresh from school. Temple & Son's shop was my first employment before West Point and I knew the price of cabbage and cargo. I also had a dispatch portfolio stuffed with signed licenses, forged invoices and cash money. The riverboat captains were glad to make my acquaintance. Every few days I'd rent a wagon, hire a pair of colored boys from N—r Town and haul another treasure to the levee.

That Red River cotton I shipped up the Mississippi to Temple & Son made me my fortune. Oh, I'd already made a tidy bundle grafting Army contracts to Alfred and his daddy. Whenever I booked Temple boats to haul military cargos I counted my boodle and banked my kickbacks. This plunder had let the Sawyers live mighty high, but we weren't wealthy. We were rich, but we weren't *wealthy*. I was a staff officer, a damn good one, and being on staff in the Army is a lot like being a bo'sun in the Navy. Any war is fought as much with coin as with cannon, and if you can't turn that to advantage you should stay home. But I didn't stay home, and don't forget that. Yes, I got rich and then I got wealthy, but I *went* to war and have the scabs, scars and night terrors to prove it. If Amy and my daughters glory in taking tea with their Twentieth Century Club chums down Delaware Avenue it is that plundered cotton from the Red River that pays their freight.[m] When you're rich you live high on the money you

---

[m] The Twentieth Century Club of Buffalo, founded in 1894 is one of the most prestigious women's clubs in the United States. It is dedicated to self-improvement and public service.

earn. When you're wealthy you live high on the money your money earns. Before the War was over I'd invested the lot in condensed milk. I'd seen troopers pour the stuff into their coffee by the gallon. I knew that when the War was over the veterans would fetch it home to their wives. They'd see the light and keep their bouncers buttoned up in their bodices and feed their brats Bordon's best. If you don't reckon there's a fortune in condensed milk, take a squint into Amy's jewelry box.[n]

* * *

Twenty blasted bales of cotton! By the time Banks led his defeated army back into Alexandria there were only twenty bales left to lever, label and ship. They were piled in a line four bales high, a yard in from the moldy wall of the church. That three-foot space kept them from the winter damp that had turned the baseboards green with mildew. That cotton was worth over ten thousand dollars but with the Army back in town it would be damn dicey to ship it downriver. My first idea was to simply wait until the wee hours and truck my haul to the levee. After all, larceny is best done under a dark moon, but the provost crushers were following their nocturnal rounds with a vengeance. It would seem that there was a host of rough customers who wanted to burn the city and Banks wouldn't have it.

Alexandria's riverfront saloons swarmed with pro-Union Missouri men and former Kansas jayhawkers. They had seen kin murdered and had been run from their homes by Rebel bushwhackers and Confederate irregulars. These bitter men had lost everything to the likes of Quantrill and Bloody Bill Anderson.32 Now they were in a Southern city with revenge in their hearts and lucifers in their pockets.

[n] Sawyer is referring to Gail Bordon's invention of canned, condensed milk, patented in 1856.

And Sherman's gorillas were back in town– Kilby Smith's men from the fleet and Whiskey Smith's from the march. They had been tutored in arson by the master himself, Uncle Billy Sherman. In '63 they had burned Jackson– twice! Just last February they had burned Meridian and everything on the road there and back. They reckoned to burn Alexandria on general principles.

And the mood among the sailors was ugly. The big gunboats drew six or seven feet of water. For a mile north of the city the riffled waters of the Red flowed only three feet above rocks and shoals. Porter would have to scuttle the entire fleet. The bluejackets were going to have to ride shanks mare back to the Mississippi with the infantry.

But business was business and I still had ten thousand dollars in white gold to ship to Temple & Son. The smaller commissary boats that only drew one or two feet of water were shooting the riffles in fine style. As soon as they tied up at the levee workers swarmed aboard to set to rights the damage inflicted by Rebels with a grudge. The Army poured back into town on Monday. The Flotilla arrived on Wednesday. By Thursday the riverfront was a madhouse of motion and noise with provision boats arriving from downriver by the hour. You would think that amongst all this tumult I could find at least one riverboat pilot who would take an honest bribe to stash a score of bales on the bow deck, but you would think wrong. The lid was on. The Army had their provost and the Navy had its own patrols of shoulder hitters. Captains, who a week before would have taken my money and cotton with a wink and a drink, now gave me the bum's rush down the gangplank.

I reckoned it would only be a day or so before Porter would spike his guns, blow the bottoms from his boats and Napoleon P. Banks's entire chowder and marching society would take to the long road back to New Orleans. I had no stomach for another retreat. I had seen what happened to Rosecrans and his Army of the

Cumberland after their rout from Chickamauga. They'd spent the next six weeks dining on putrid mule and their own boiled belts. And I had fought through the mob of terrified rabble in Banks's retreat from Sabine Crossroads. It was Satan take the hindmost. An Army marches on faith and pride as much as on beans and bacon. Banks's blunders had destroyed this Army's faith and without the magic of that emotion a retreat would crush their pride. With Sherman's mocking bummers and thousands of marooned sailormen, any retreat would degenerate into a panicked stampede after the first ten miles. It would take a miracle to save this Army and Navy. (And more importantly, me, my cotton and my colored drummer boy.)

And then a miracle happened in the person of General Franklin's chief engineer, Lieutenant Colonel Joseph Bailey. I'd seen the rascal before. He was the officer with the magnificent auburn beard who had helped Franklin from his horse, *my horse*, after the rout at Sabine Crossroads. I must have remembered him because his whiskers were the same color as my Amy's hair. He was a pretty man, if you like that type. He should have been in the Navy.[33]

Here was his scheme and if it seems like the blithering of a ninny, well, in the end it worked and it saved a fleet and an army. It almost worked soon enough to save me.

A dam, that was the plan, built just above Bayou Rapides. If the Johnnys could blow up a dam far upstream to divert most of the water from the Red, than we could build one of our own to catch what water was left–couldn't we? I wasn't at the meeting where Bailey presented his dunderhead scheme but I heard all about it. Soldiers love their gossip.

At first Porter rejected the notion out of hand.

"Damnation in a bum-boat, if damning could save the damn fleet it would have been damn well saved by now!"[o]

Banks was desperate to try any notion to save what little was left of his reputation and made his only intelligent decision of the entire campaign. He told Porter that the dam would be the Army's bailiwick. The Navy could simply sit and watch and what else did they have to do? By May Day three thousand soldiers were hard at work building Bailey's dam, including the Corps D' Afrique's 3rd Engineers.

The troops worked with a will, especially Sergeant Major Smith's blackbirds. The 3rd Engineers were one of the few outfits in the Army that were stepping high. After a nasty skirmish along the Cane River where Taylor tried to block the Federal's retreat, the 3rd threw its pontoon bridge across the bayou and the entire force made good their skedaddle. The men were cocky and had a right to be. Building dams would be just another day in the barnyard for those dusky engineers.[p]

The deck apes on the armored teakettles openly hooted the idea. They were already resigned to scuttling their boats, but they shut up when after only a week the river began to rise before their eyes. Every day of that week while the Army labored to build Bailey's dam, Libby and I picnicked on the levee to watch the pageant. If I ever wondered how the Egyptians could have built their pyramids I stopped wondering. If you muster enough strong backs to any labor and lay enough strong hands to any rope any task will be accomplished. It *almost* inspired me to report back for duty.

---

[o] According to *The Civil War A Narrative*, Vol III, by Shelby Foote, the quote was, "If damning would get the fleet off, we would have been afloat long ago."

[p] This action was the Battle of Monett's Ferry, April 23, 1864.

They worked from both sides of the river. By day they sweated, half-naked under the spring sun, and at night the work went on illuminated by bonfires. Huge trees were sunk, branches toward the current, with timbers interlocking their boughs. Buildings were ripped apart, their brick and stone filling huge baskets to be sunk in the stream. Lunch along the levee became crowded as half the town came out to watch the miracle. And there were other miracles coming my way– one from home, the other from hell.

On the eighth of May the dams were all but complete. As a final touch, barges full of rubble and rock were sunk to extend the wings of the dams to leave only a narrow channel for the boats to shoot through to the sheltered waters before the town. Water was rising nicely behind Bailey's wonder and the flotilla was swarming with bluejackets working like blazes to ready the boats for their run to glory. They stripped armor and unshipped guns to lessen their drafts, and they battened down anything that could rock, roll or rattle.

I still had the matter of twenty bales of cotton to attend to, not to mention my own personal retreat back to St. Petersburg. Liberty would have to take her chances with the regiment. I would have to abandon the cotton and ride with the Army on the long river road back to the Mississippi. Andrew Jackson on a sled, what a bitter prospect, but then salvation steamed up the Red River with its black stacks belching smoke above gleaming gingerbread. I was moping on the riverfront when I heard it– TOOOOOOOOOT! TOOT TOOT TOOT! Temple & Son's whistle! A long and three shorts, Morse code for 'T' and 'S,'– Temple & Son! And there she was, tall and handsome, with *Hannibal* lettered proudly on the wheel-barn in scarlet and gold.

I didn't wait for the plank, but jumped aboard the second the bow butted the levee. Captain G. D. Regan had been loading up my cotton cargos at Natchez. I would have been shipping it to Simmesport but A.J. Smith's gorillas burned the place flat back in March. Sherman's boys did love their friction matches. Back at Natchez for two weeks there had been no word and no cotton so Regan brought the *Hannibal* up the Red to see what was what. He almost tossed his cap when I told him there were only twenty bales left but he was an operator and would fill the boat with *something* to turn a profit. After all, the whole city was clamoring to get out.

I was well satisfied with my little expedition up the Red. It was only seven weeks ago that I had met Smitty and Libby in Baton Rouge. In that time I'd seen battles lost and an Army disintegrate. I'd deserted, embezzled, forged and stolen. But I had found a family, such as it was, banked a fortune and would ride home in style on the queen of the river. I wasn't worried a snap about consequences. As soon as the *Hannibal* tied up to the Temple pier I'd burn all evidence. Sherman had sent me up the Red but he didn't give me any orders about when to return. As far as he was concerned I was with Banks. As far as Banks was concerned I was back with Sherman, that or dead. In any event Banks wouldn't matter a weeviled biscuit once Grant and Lincoln learned the full dimensions of his disaster. No, when I was home, I was home free. I flicked the ash from my cheroot on the pilothouse floor, gazed out the wide windows with their grand view of the Alexandria riverfront and took a deep pull of Captain Regan's Irish whiskey.

And then the whiskey came out of my nose in a rush and I fetched a coughing fit that sent me to my knees with Regan pounding my back like a housefrau lashing a carpet. Along the levee promenade a couple strolled arm in arm. Crowds swarmed along the way but the couple was singular and stood out from the mob. He was a huge officer made all the taller by the tiny lady on his arm. She looked like a pretty china-doll and he was the size of Jack's giant. What a droll pair! And then the whiskey shot from my snout, my knees gave out and Regan's thumping almost unhinged my ribcage. Major Melrose Middlesex and Mrs. Hazel Brassard Ballentine were taking the air.

The Adventures of Sidney Sawyer
Missouri Yankees

Chapter 34

Bad dreams and dead dogs but I've had some shocks. I knew the two swine were in cahoots back in Charleston but what the blazes where they doing here on the Red in a frantic city on the verge of a desperate evacuation? When the last of Captain Regan's booze trickled out of my snot-locker and the fool stopped pounding my spine with his tender brand of nursing, I excused myself to the Texas Deck and nursed myself with my own brand of mercy. I snapped at the colored porter for a bottle of Tennessee Bourbon and none of Regan's Irish rot-gut– and don't bother with a glass. I was wallpapered in a half-hour. Wallpapered, but not too drunk to reckon why Middlesex and Miss Hazel were in Alexandria. For him it was cotton, for her, medicines. If those monsters had a notion I was in the city they'd have another reason– revenge.

But there wasn't any more cotton in Alexandria, was there? Of course there was. If there wasn't, why was that tub of suet Middlesex in town? But where could I find out without announcing my presence to the Army? And then, just before my booze-soaked brain tumbled off into a well-lubricated sleep, I remembered that I knew just the fellow. I woke up in the wee hours with my head pounding like the village forge and my mouth as furry as a squirrel's hindquarters, but with the fellow's name still in mind. The fellow was Bo'sun Jekyll Winchel and remembering his blasted name almost got me scuppered in a Niagara of red water aboard the ugliest ship afloat.

The *Lady Leavenworth* was still tied up on the levee. It had nowhere to go. The Rebels had finally blockaded the Red River to the Mississippi and if the fighting fleet stayed marooned above the fast water it would stay that way. A few days before, Confederate gunners took a transport and slaughtered two escorting gunboats on their way to Simmesport. Temple & Son's *Hannibal* was one of the last boats into Alexandria. The night watch on the *Lady L* informed me that Winchel wasn't aboard. He had shipped onto a boat more to his liking– a fighting boat, the *Neosho*. Its own bo'sun had lost an eye to a Rebel shell that had hit too close to a view-slit. I was in luck, if you can call it that. The *Neosho* wasn't upstream with the rest of the flotilla stuck on the wrong side of the rocks and shoals. When the river began to rise behind the dam, three of the shallower draft boats risked the upper rapids, a tinclad and two broad-beamed river monitors. One of them, the *Neosho*, was riding at its stern anchor not two hundred yards above the dam. I paid a nickel to a likely colored boy with a bateau to row me out to the monitor. A snotty escorted me around the deck gear and tackle to forward of the turret where Winchel was squinting at the river.

"Sawyer!" If he was surprised to see me again it was only because of the early hour. Dawn was brightening the sky to our left. The boat's single stack and its pilothouse, perched atop the armored barn protecting the stern wheel, stood out in silhouette. "You picked a helluva time to come a' callin', and I don't mean the filthy hour. Is it more of the cotton business that you're after?"

I said it was and we got down to business, this time without the pint. He never took his eyes from the water. I told him about the new jobber in town, a fat major named Middlesex who wouldn't be here if there wasn't a white mountain of fiber to be had. It *had* to be here! Where the hell was it?

"The country here 'bouts is cleaned out. Your Navy grabbed it all and what little they missed the Army gleaned. Middlesex ain't a fool. Where the dickens is it?"

Winchel gave a low laugh but still didn't take his eyes from the river. "Why, the country ain't cleaned out–only the parts along the Red where Porter could plunder it, or where the Army marched if they had wagons to haul it. This neck of Louisiana is laced with bayou and backwater. Go ten miles up any of 'em and every barn is piled with cotton to the rafters. The planters ain't been able to sell it for two years. It's just pilin' up. It's there, we just can't get to it."

He took a quick squint at me and gave the water a mighty spit. Then he looked up and down the boat. The railings were lined with jacks. They stood on the turret and the wheel barn, and some had slid down the sloped armor to stand on the narrow deck with their feet only inches above the water. I hadn't noticed them before. They were silent with the glow of their smokes fading in the growing light.

In the still of the morning I could hear a low roaring like steady distant thunder from downriver.

He saw me listening and said, "That's the Red, running through the gap betwixt the wings of the dam. Gittin' louder. Water's gittin' deeper. Fleet's gonna run the upper riffles today if the dam holds. Don't think it's gonna." He gestured fore and aft to the bluejackets lining the decks. It must take a hundred sailors to man a monitor and it looked like every one of them was up early and listening.

Winchel returned to the matter at hand. "To git more cotton you need three things. You need passage through the Reb lines to territory that ain't been picked over. Then you need something to buy it with. Money ain't no good. The Confederates got no place to spend it. You need something to trade, gold or silver or something they need, like guns or boots. And then you need a way to get it down the Red to the Mississippi. You git them three things, Colonel, and then you let me know. I'll help all I can. I like the color of your money."

"First call!" It was a sharp cry from the deck before the pilothouse. "First call to colors!" The ship's bell clanged, the whistle gave a blast, and feet pounded the deck as the sailors scurried to position for the morning ceremony. Bo'sun Winchel quick marched to the main deck to muster his men, and landsman that I was, I knew my place as an officer was the flagstaff. I made it just as a seaman's bugle blew the sharp notes of "Call To Attention." The flag was yanked up the short pole aft of the pilothouse and the officers assembled and the crew, stiff at their stations, threw the banner their salute.

When the last shrill note ended and the chief of the boat roared his "Dismissed!" every eye turned downriver. The distant roar of the river shooting through the gap had become a thunder that filled the day. The ugly red waters of the river had broken through the dam.

* * *

In the pilothouse there was paralysis. The pilot, a rail-thin fellow named Ferrell, with Napoleon chin whiskers and the arrogant look shared by all river pilots, demanded that the captain run the breach before the river drained and all chance for escape was lost. The captain wouldn't hear of such suicidal foolishness. His name was Howard and he was a real river man and not a transplanted saltwater sailor stuck on the brown water for the War. They argued like fishwives until Captain Howard won the debate by throwing rank.

"We'll not go! It's not a risk– it's a dead certainty. The *Neosho* will smash to rubbish running that maelstrom. I'm in command and by God we will not do it!"

And then he noticed me. "And why does the Army grace us with its presence?" He didn't seem happy to see me. "Another busybody from Banks's staff of loafers? Show me your orders, sir!"

I didn't have orders, but as events went, I didn't need them– and events happened quickly. Ferrell gave a shout and pointed upstream. There, showing around a shallow bend was a gunboat under full steam booming along with the swift current and steering to cut close along the *Neosho's* starboard side. It was a timberclad gunboat with "*Lexington*" painted tiny on its mammoth side wheels. She was cut for eight guns, her twin stacks far forward, and was almost as ugly as the *Neosho*. Lexington flew by with bell ringing, whistle shrieking and every manjack lining its decks, cheering like bedlam.

"She's run the upper falls!" Ferrell roared, and reached for the lanyard to add the *Neosho's* whistle to the din.

Howard shouted to be heard, "The fools going to run the gap, God help him, it can't be done!"

But the timberclad never hesitated. If anything she went faster as the current sliding into the falls locked it in its grip. And then it was there between the sunken barges that had shifted to let the Red River run wild. The *Lexington's* bow was tossed high and water cascaded over the bow. It rolled hard to its starboard and we saw the paddles of its great wheel spinning in the air for a count of one – two – and three before it crashed down into the river, and the boat lurched forward to show its bottom from stern to midships. And then the boat was gone. It was simply gone into the towering splash of falling water and smashing ship.

Ferrell roared again, "There– there she is!

And there she was– a hundred yards farther downstream from the gap. She only showed from her gunports up, so steep was its drop, but there she was, still afloat with smoke pouring from her stacks and the howl from the mob of spectators lining the shore reaching our ears.

"Hurrah! Hurrah!" The whole town along with the entire Army had turned out to see the catastrophe of the collapsing dam, and instead they were treated to the salvation of the brave *Lexington.* And then Captain Howard was shouting down the speaking tube to the engine spaces bellowing for full steam. Winchel and a pair of deck apes flew past the pilot house at a run to slip the stern anchor, Ferrell tossed his pipe over the side, squared his cap and gripped the wheel– by God if the *Lexington* could do it so could the *Neosho.* The maniacs! The *Lexington* was a timber clad. It couldn't have drawn two feet of water. Ferrell was driving an ironclad monitor with a great armored turret at the bow that must have weighed fifty tons. It sported two eleven inch Dahlgren smoothbores that weighed sixteen tons between them. This ugly tub must have drawn six feet of water.[q]

And we weren't the only mad ones. Behind us the two other boats that had run the upper falls were billowing cinders from their stacks, their whistles were blowing and bluejackets were swarming the decks to secure every loose end for the plunge. Captain Howard was a game bird. Once the *Lexington* showed the way he never hesitated. His orders were given, it was neck or nothing and his work was done. Ferrell was the pilot. Howard left him to do his job and steer the boat! He strode to the signal staff before the pilothouse and stood foursquare with hands on hips and face to the wind. I headed for the signal staff too. I wrapped arms and legs around it like a squid and hung on in terror.

A monitor can do ten knots without blowing its boilers. The deck was quivering beneath my boots like a living thing. The river was booming along at another eight knots and when the current caught the boat and sucked it into the maelstrom between the torn wings of the dam we were clipping along at the speed of a galloping horse.

---

[q] Four boats, *Neosho*, her sister ship *Osage*, the tinclad *Ft. Hindman* and the *Lexington* ran the ruptured dam on the morning of May 9, 1864. The *Neosho* and *Osage* were single turret monitors, 180' long, 45' abeam with a 4'6" draft and displacing 525 tons.

And then the deck gave a lunge and Howard stumbled into me and grabbed my jacket to keep his feet. The great stern wheel had stopped! I looked up to the pilothouse and Ferrell's face was frozen in terror. He had lost his nerve and was trying to stop the *Neosho* from its plunge to destruction. Too late! Too late! Any fool could see that we were committed. The pull of the roaring, rushing red water had us and wouldn't let us go. Our only hope to avoid the rocks and sunken barges was a cool hand on the wheel and enough speed for the rudder to bite and Ferrell was paralyzed with fear. He had ordered full stop. We had lost all way in relation to the current and the rudder was useless. He opened his mouth in a scream that was lost above the rush of foam and water. I turned to forward and joined him with my own scream.

Thirty yards ahead the river disappeared. It was there racing before us in waves as thick and slick as oil, and then it wasn't. We were racing over a cliff and then the current gripped us like a dog with a rat and the monitor lunged sideways, out of all control and slammed into a half-sunken barge like a drunken dancer. The collision slewed us back around and the *Neosho* went over the falls bow first in a swoop that brought last night's bourbon up and out. The bow went under up to the great turret and then the river boiled around it and up past to the stack. She hit bottom with a jar that set the signal staff whipping like a cane pole. My hands tore from the mast and I tumbled half the length of the deck before I came up hard against a davit, gulping like a catfish and howling like a wet dog. It seems that I broke my right thumb.

The *Neosho* spun around like a kiddy's top in a complete pirouette before that fool Ferrell gathered his guts and began to pilot his boat. The craven had almost scuppered us all, losing his nerve in the breach, stopping the engines and letting the boat find its own way over the falls. If we hadn't fetched into the barge we'd have gone over the drop sideways. The boat would have turned turtle and I would have been smashed on the bottom of the Red

River with the weight of an ironclad river monitor driving me into the mud.

Damnation in a berry basket, but I was hard used. I was sopping wet, blowing snot from my snoot in slimy ropes and the knees were out of my britches. My poor thumb, twisted behind my knuckles was turning purple, hurting like blazes and swelling like a blood-gorged leach. The bluejackets ignored my distress, rot their rations, and began a cheer of salvation and pride. It was returned three times three from the mob along the levee. I looked upstream to the dam and it was a sight to see. Red water boiled in a Niagara over the gap that tumbled down a ten-foot drop into the placid Alexandria riverfront. How the blazes could we have done it without smashing to bits? And then I saw *exactly* how we did it. The bow of the other monitor appeared like a specter through the mist thrown up by the cascade. It flew out over the drop for half its length before it tipped in a sickening plunge that took it underwater to its turret, but there was no smash from hitting the bottom. This boat had gone over under full steam and control and she shook the water from her bow like a spaniel. With flags flying and whistle blowing it bobbed even with the *Neosho*. A few minutes later the tinclad made her run with spectacular splashing, frenzied cheering and the spectacle was over.

By evening the river had drained, leaving Porter and six of the Navy's biggest ironclads stuck above the upper falls. My right arm was slung in a sling, covered with plaster from fingertips to elbow and throbbing with every beat of my yellow heart.

* * *

Banks and Porter were persistent; I give the devils their due. By afternoon they had thousands of soldiers at work on *two* dams. Colonel Bailey knew the drill now and work flew. A new dam, an upper dam, was begun below Bayou Rigolette. Working in shifts day and night from both sides of the river, this upper dam was ready in only two days. The water behind it rose before our eyes. The burst dam above Bayou Rapides was repaired and reinforced and with the upper dam working in tandem, it only had to hold enough water to cover the lower shoals and rocks. By God, if the campaign was a fiasco for the ages, the Army at least covered itself with credit by taming the mighty Red River.

On the eleventh of May three boats made their run. They were all original Pook Turtles, the same boats that Grant and Foote had used as far back as Forts Henry and Donalson including the ugly, gallant *Corondolet*. The town and garrison turned out to cheer the Navy, and the next day they turned out again to cheer as the last three of Porter's gunboats shot the dams.

Of course I turned out with the rest of the town to watch the show and why not? I'll tell you why not. The last ship in the flotilla was lining up to make its attempt over the millrace between the wings of the dam. It was the mighty monitor *Ozark,* with its turret amidships and her tiny pilothouse perched on the turret like a cupcake on a washtub. She was a screw-driven boat and had a low, predatory look without a great wheelbarn at the stern. She blasted her whistle, sparks billowed from her stacks, a band on shore struck up "Columbia the Gem of the Ocean," and like a dunce I bellowed along in my glorious baritone. I love to sing.

Oh Columbia the gem of the ocean,
the home of the bra-ave and the free-ee
The shrine of each patriot's devotion,
the world offers ho-o-mage to thee!

Auntie Polly loves my voice and singing next to her in church is the only thing that makes the Reverend Mr. Sprague's services tolerable. I belted out the verse and around me Alexandria ladies were nudging their husbands with their fans and pointing out the wounded Yankee officer with the magnificent whiskers and grand voice. I'll say it again– the world loves a wounded soldier as long as the wound ain't vivid and vulgar. With the chorus I'd give them something to remember the Union Army by. The *Ozark* was in the fast water now, and would be over the falls in a flash. I lifted my voice for a grand finale.

When borne by the Red White and Blue!
When borne by the Red White and Blue!
Thy banners make tyr-r-anny tremble,
when borne by the Red White and ...
SON OF A BITCH!

My curse was drowned out by the cheers of thirty thousand people as the monitor's bow sent up a wave that glittered into rainbows when she joined her sisters in the still waters of the lower Red River. Glorious baritone indeed! My dimwitted singing hadn't just drawn the attention of the local ladies. Across the bandstand was another lady, a tiny one with her hair tugged back in the severest of buns. She was using her parasol as a headhunter would a spear to point me out to her companion, a giant in Union blue. They looked at me from across the mob, eyes burning with pure malice. Mrs. Hazel Brassard Ballentine and Major Melrose Middlesex now knew that Colonel Sidney Thomas Sawyer was in town.

The Adventures of Sidney Sawyer
Missouri Yankees

Chapter 35

It was a secret. Maybe if I'd reported back for duty with Banks I'd have known, staff officers usually know all the juicy bits, but the only officers I'd confabbed with for the last two weeks were the wild boys with Andrew Jackson Smith's crew. They'd have nothing to do with the wilted-collar duds in the Army of the Gulf, they were a damn sight more fun, and they reckoned me one of Sherman's boys. Banks had his antlers out for me and he would have probably sent me back to what was left of his cavalry. I didn't know who had put the bugbear in his britches about me but it was clear he loathed me from first acquaintance. The city was to be evacuated and nobody knew until that morning when the fleet got up steam, wagons began to roll and the troops fell into column of march.

Of course it was the logical move– the campaign was lost, the fleet was saved, and there was no reason to stay, but when the hell had Napoleon P. Banks ever made a prompt and logical move? The last of the ironclads had run the rapids just yesterday afternoon. I was counting on official dithering and procrastination to give me time to see to my cotton. Hell in a wicker basket, there was no time to even see to Liberty! If she was with her daddy she was far along at the head of the column. Smitty's colored soldiers were pontoon engineers and any advance would need the pontoon troops with the vanguard to see the Army over bayou and swamp. I could have run to N—r

Town to make sure, but she was a big girl. She could fend for herself, couldn't she? My cotton sure couldn't.

The city was pandemonium on bark-juice. The New York regiment that Banks had assigned to provost duty was being mustered along the levee to evacuate. Those knickerbockers had done a fine job of keeping order and preventing arson-inclined jay-hawkers, former slaves, and gorillas from plying their friction matches, but now they were going. Women, children, dogs and old men were pouring into the streets wailing for protection from anyone in a blue coat. I had a blue coat but no inclination to help. I was on my way to the wharves to look up Captain Regan on the *Hannibal*.

There was considerable shipping along the levee. If Porter's fleet hadn't found salvation over Bailey's dams all of the steamboats present would have been lost. Now Porter's flotilla would shepherd them safe escort to what was left of Simmesport, and they could haul the Army's rations and fodder in the bargain.

"Got room for your twenty bales and a damn sight more, if you hurry," Regan growled with his thumbs hooked to his braces. "But you gotta hurry! And how in thunder will you get 'em past the provost?"

"The crushers are gone with the Army. If I hurry I can scrounge up some wagons. Lend me a half-dozen of your crew to do the bull work." I waved my plastered arm at him to show how helpless I was.

"You're on your own. If I let my crew off I'll never see the rascals again. They'll take to drink– or worse. We leave with the fleet." He squinted towards the city as a fire gong sounded in the distance. "Do your best and hurry your arse!"

And I did. It was only four blocks to 4th Street and the Baptist church where I had stashed my bales, but on the way I saw sights that did not bode well for the fair city of Alexandria. The New York infantry that had protected the city was gone, but they had been replaced by other Yankee troops. They were mounted infantry from

Whiskey Smith's gorillas– Sherman's men! They had burned Simmesport and Grand Ecore and Natchitoches and every hamlet and plantation in between. God help Alexandria!

I ran to my church, trusting that in the panic I could round up transport and labor to load my treasure. The streets were swarming with beasts, wagons and men with wild eyes. I'd offer 'em greenbacks and if that didn't work, gold. Fire bells gonged frantically from right and left. Smoke whiffed through the street, up my nose and into my eyes. The crowd that roared past in all directions was divided between desperate citizens, clutching at bundles and babes, seeking deliverance from evil, and drunken rioters, white and black, who sought to deliver that evil.

And then I saw men in Union blue, trotting at the double time, toting washtubs, buckets and great two-handled milk cans. They were shouldering mops and brooms like cadets with muskets. Salvation had arrived. The tubs and buckets were brimming, the mops were ready to drench any flame, and the devils of arson would be smothered before they could fly from hell.

Officers led them with pistols out at the ready. I almost shouted "hosanna", but then I heard a sergeant bellow, "Tis' war boys! Let 'em loose. Let them dogs o' war loose!"

"Burn the traitors out, sons! Not one brick left on the other!" crowed a trooper, face flushed with liquor and excitement.

"You there– ya silly sot!" the sergeant warned. "Keep your sleeve out a' the camphene or you'll burn like Lucifer. Dip your swab and mop it on that livery yonder. It'll go up like barns a' fire!"

He soaked his mop in the milk can and slapped it on the dry boards of the stable with a wet smack. Then he smeared it around like a boy white-washing a fence. The sergeant struck a match on his boot and in a rush and roar the side of the livery went up in flame.

Andy Jackson on a sled! It wasn't water in the tubs and this wasn't the fire brigade. It was camphene and turpentine in the milk cans and tubs. They were burning the city. And if I needed any further evidence, there was old Whiskey Smith himself on a fat horse trotting between the flames that were beginning to roar from both sides of the street.

"Hurrah, boys! This looks like war!" The bloodthirsty old bastard was red-faced with joy and heat. He waved his hat and spurred his mount into the next street. "Hurrah, this looks like war!"

And it did. The incendiaries were only two blocks from my church– from my cotton. I drew my Remington and sprinted to 4th Street. Kitty-corner across the way from *my* church was the Catholic Church. Before it, a dozen roughnecks had already gathered with buckets of turpentine. They sported mops and muskets with bayonets fixed on the long barrels. At the door of the church was a priest in full ecclesiastical fig, his gold vestments trailing to the ground. He wore one of those silly caps that papist padres sport, with a black pom-pom on top. He'd have looked a perfect fool if he wasn't standing in the classic en garde position and didn't have a silver rapier in hand. He was sideways to the squad of arsonists, thin as a rail beneath the thick gold embroidery, right slippered foot forward and left hand on hip. His elbow was bent just so, his blade straight out and he didn't seem ridiculous at all. Here's a cool customer, I reckoned and he proved it by addressing the incendiaries in a calm voice accented with French.

"Bless you my sons– bless you, but you shall die if you touch God's house with fire." He gave his rapier a slash that hissed in the air. "You, my son, with the mop and Lucifers– you shall die first– in nominee Patris, et Fîlii, et Spîritus Sancti!" And he whipped a cross in the air with his blade.

"You'll die too padre, if you'un don't step aside. This here's Army business!"

"And I, mon ami, am on the business of God. Va tén!"

The rowdies threatened him and swore and pointed muskets at his belly, but the priest stood his ground with a face like flint.34

"Va tén!" he said again, and they did.[r]

The men were set on arson and frolic but didn't have the stomach to gun down a priest. They turned with their torches toward me– and there *I* stood, another stalwart Christian guardian, before the door of *my* church, with a Remington in my good mitt and whiskers quivering with distress. I prayed they also wouldn't have the stomach to gun down a Union Colonel.

"This is a Baptist church, an' I'm a Baptist, an' a man o' God every bit as much as that papist pastor with a pig-sticker, an' a colonel, damn your eyes! I'll drill the first man to lay a mitt or a mop on God's house!"

Lord, the things I'll say to save a few bucks. I was willing to break the Third Commandment to save my cotton. I hoped these birds weren't willing to break the Sixth to burn it.[s]

"Va tén!" I blustered and waved my pistol in a sign of the cross.

They hooted me and threatened and cursed and I cursed them right back like a proper man o' God, and in the end my rank and my Remington turned them away. But I was shaking with palsy and sweating like field labor from the fright. The fires were closer. Smoke set my eyes to tear like a dowager's at a wedding, my thumb throbbed like a rotten tooth and I needed a drink. I forgot all about the spikes that should have been securing the church house door. I didn't think to fetch the claw hammer tucked under

---

[r] 'Va tén' means 'go away' in French.

[s] The Third Commandment is "Thou shall not take the name of the Lord your God in vain." The Sixth is "Thou shall not kill."

the step to yank them from the doorframe. I simply pushed open the door, stepped into the sanctuary and there, standing beside my wall of cotton, dressed modest as a schoolmarm, hands folded primly beneath her bosom was Hazel Brassard Ballentine.

* * *

She wasn't armed and I still had the pistol in my grip, but the sight of her brought a shout to my lips like I'd trodden on a serpent. Above the musty smell of the mildewed baseboards and the smoke drifting through the open door from the burning city, I smelled the stink of fear. Smelling fear is not just an expression. I've smelled fear, many times– usually my own. I was in desperate danger and not from the squads of arsonists ranging the town.

Hazel Ballentine was evil as an adder, game as a rat terrier and she sneered contempt at my Remington.

"Did you think I wouldn't find you?" Her elfin face literally glowed with triumph. "Your hours on earth were numbered from the moment you ran afoul of the family Brassard. You maimed my dear brother, you struck my noble father, you dishonored *me*! Cur! Your hour has come!"

She was tiny and unarmed, but as bold and sure as the Queen of Hell. I wasted the only seconds I was going to have wondering why. Then I felt my tunic bunch behind my shoulders and I rose from the floor as if I was weightless. A huge hand covered mine and the pistol was plucked from my fingers as easily as you would take a ginger snap from a toddler.

"Fee fi fo fum!" thundered in my ear and with a roar of laughter, Melrose Middlesex tossed me to the floor before Miss Hazel like a handful of rubbish. I tried to catch myself, but my cast slid on the rough planks, splinters dug into my knees and palm, and I crashed into a heap at Hazel's feet. She towered above me, all sixty inches of her, covering me with a pocket pistol that appeared in her claw like a conjuror's trick. I lay sprawling while they savored their hate and drank in their victory. From the city the clang of fire bells and church bells sounded hysterical alarms. An explosion close by set dust sifting down from the rafters and from the riverfront, steamboat whistles joined in the clamor. Out there the fleet was evacuating. Out there a city was dying. In here, so was I– but not yet. These villains wouldn't let me die yet.

Hazel gave me a kick in the ear with her tiny boot. It hurt like blazes, God help me if Middlesex kicked me.

"Take the cotton!" I begged. "There it is," and there it was, stacked in a neat row, four bales high along the wall. "It's fifteen thousand dollars– yours for the taking. Just let me go. I got a boat. I got a crew. It's yours. Let me go!"

"Where's my watch?"

Watch? What the dickens? This was all about his blasted pocket watch?

"I ain't got your watch, you bloated swine! Never had it. Missy Ruth has it. Take the cotton! Go away!"

Hazel kicked me in the face again for my troubles.

"I don't want your cheap pile of lint," Middlesex gloated. "I've got cotton piled in a king's ransom at Red House, up the Ouachita. It was bought and paid for in medicines and bullion. You made my business a sight more difficult with your cowardly assault on Colonel Brassard. He was my usual factor." The brute loomed above me, blotting out the wall of cotton behind him as I cringed on the floor. "You have interfered with my business for the last time!" Oh God in heaven, don't let him stomp me!

"I now deal through Mrs. Ballentine, a patriotic gentlewoman, Colonel Brassard's daughter. Opportunities blossom in wartime, especially Civil War! We would be daft not to pluck the blooms. The Brassards are my conduit to Southern cotton. I am their source of Northern medicaments and Nevada silver. How propinquitious that we find ourselves in Alexandria to settle new accounts. When we saw you on the levee we knew we could also settle old scores."

While he laughed and Hazel gave my poor head another kick, the back wall of the church exploded into fire. The rugged cross that sanctified the altar flamed like a holocaust. Those bastards with turpentine, mops and matches had skipped around the back to finish their work.

Middlesex laughed again. A great laugh that began deep in his vast belly and came out with a sound of undiluted evil.

"Shall we burn him, my dear? Shall we let him be roasted in the flames of his own fortune?"

"You kill my brother– assault my helpless father– drown me in pickles!" She was quite hysterical, skin stretched to the breaking point on her little skull and eyes reflecting flame as the fire reached the rafters and began eating away at the roof. "We will tie you to one of your own bales and let you burn. Burn like a runaway n—r! I will watch from the street and cheer while you scream in the flames!"

I tried to rise, but Middlesex pushed me back to the floor with his massive boot. "Tie him up? Now Mrs. Ballentine, we can do better than that. There is a hammer and some nails there, by the door. Let us nail Colonel Sawyer to the floor, shall we?"

She was triumphant! "Yes, yes! The Brassard family honor shall be avenged. Honor shall be served!"

Hammer! Nails! Nail me to the floor! By God, I'd burn, nailed to the planks like Christ crucified. Hazel hurried to the door to fetch the hammer and spikes right where Libby and I had always left them. Libby?

But then Middlesex was on me, straddling me with his huge weight crushing my hips. He pulled my left arm out to full stretch with his hand. I struggled with the strength of terror but I could no more resist his power than I could resist a landslide. Hazel squatted beside me with a fistful of spikes and handed the claw hammer to Middlesex.

"Hold that nail steady for me now, will you my dear?"

I clenched my hand into a fist to protect my palm, but the bitch stuck the point into the middle of my wrist and shoved until my skin popped and blood spurted.

I screamed my usual scream, "Aunt Pollllyy!" and Middlesex raised the terrible hammer to drive the nail through my wrist spiking it deep into the pine floor!

The pair of monsters glanced at each other with wicked joy as the hammer reached the top of its arc. Holy God, was this the last sight I would ever see, their faces lit with flame as the fire leapt from one rafter to the next with my wall of cotton beginning to smoke from the heat. The top bale rocked, Melrose Middlesex braced to deliver the blow, and then the bale tipped and toppled towards his fat head.

I screamed again, and with Middlesex's attention focused on hammer and nail, I managed to free my plastered right arm enough for a weak slap at Middlesex's ear. It stung him. It *only* stung him but he pulled his head away from the task at hand just as five hundred weight of Red River fiber crashed onto his head and shoulders. It would have killed any other man but it bounced off of him and tumbled into the piled-up pews with a splintering crash. But now he was hurt, not stung. He roared in hate, raised himself up on his knees and again raised the hammer high. He wasn't aiming it at a nail– now he was fixing to drive it through my skull.

At that instant, Hazel shouted a frantic warning, "Melrose, look sharp!" and another bale of cotton hit him across his shoulders.

Fire and flame were spreading closer, but above their roar I heard the sharp crack of a breaking bone. He was stunned like a poled ox, right shoulder sagging where the bale struck, but still straddling me, pinning me to the floor. I swung my plastered arm hard into his face. Fool–

his face is like a block of suet– can't hurt him there. I swung again and hit him flush on the crown of his head. His eyes crossed, he roared like a bull in pain and rage, and I hit him again on the left temple. The temple! That's where Missy Ruth told me the bone is the thinnest. If a fat whore could put out his lights with a sap above eye and ear, could I do less? But before I could strike again Hazel was on me in a frenzy.

"God damn you!" In the pandemonium of the brawl she quite forgot about her pistol but she drove the spike into my chest like a dagger. "Die you dog! Die you n—r lover!"

She pulled it out to stab me again, but from the gap left by the two cotton bales that had stunned Melrose, a colored drummer boy in Union blue jumped with both boots and a hoe handle straight onto Miss Hazel's back. She never saw it coming, and how could she? The five hundred pound cotton bales couldn't have just fallen by themselves, but who would suspect that a darkie lady, seven months gone with child, dressed as a Yankee drummer boy would be sulking behind the cotton with a four-foot lever of seasoned hickory?

I struck Melrose Middlesex in his temple again hard enough to crack the plaster.

"Libby, she has a pistol!" I shouted, but Miss Hazel was in no state to reach for anything. And fat Melrose was in a bad state too. His eyes were quite out of focus, blood was leaking from his left eye socket and I hit him again in the temple hard enough to shatter what was left of my cast and tumble him off of me onto the floor. He sprawled across both the hammer and Libby's hickory stick

I'm a quick study when I'm in a burning church with the back wall coming down in a crash of sparks and the flames racing for the only door. Libby was on her arse by the door, in one piece but with the oddest expression. Hazel was beside her, rolling from side to side, howling in agony from a broken rack of ribs where a drummer boy's boots served them harshly. Middlesex was struggling to his knees with the hoe handle tight in his fat fingers, my cast was shattered, my fists would make no impression and the pistol was nowhere to be seen, probably under a bale of cotton. I had no time to look. I had to keep the brute down, but how?

But I *am* a quick study. I ran behind the piled cotton. There was three feet betwixt the bales and the wall. Liberty must have grabbed up the hoe handle and scooted there the second my fine two fiends came to call. There were five bales in a line. They were piled four high, and except for where Libby had pushed down her two bales on Melrose's head they created a twelve-foot high wall of cotton. Libby had levered down one bale at a time, brave girl. She'd saved our lives. I'd bring down the whole wall like Joshua at Jericho. I wedged my shoulders between the wall studs and gave a mighty shove. The cotton moved a bit, but only a bit. I gritted my teeth and shoved with all my heart. It rocked outward six inches, but only that far.

By thunder, this wouldn't do. I put my back to the wall and my feet to the cotton and shoved. Six inches, no more! I had to go higher. I worked my way up to the third row of bales, wedged myself again and set to give it my all. The top row of bales burst into flame. By God the heat was set to cook me against the wall. Flames trickled down the wall of cotton like serpents on both sides of me. I was in a trap. I'd entered my own oven and it would bake me if I couldn't do what I came to do– and fast! I braced my back and pushed my haunches with all my might. The cotton shifted an inch. Flames dripped from above and sizzled into my jacket. I pushed until red filled my vision. My back popped, my knees were on fire.

From above the sound of flames Liberty's shout came to me. "He's movin', Mr. Colonel Sawyer, sir! The fat man, he gittin' up!"

If the flames didn't kill me, Middlesex would. I shoved like a man gone wild, and in a rush, the cotton came tumbling down. I was over the burning bales like a frog on a skillet. Middlesex was on his back with bales piled across his great belly two deep. His head and both arms were free but he was pushing at the weight with only one arm. Glory hallelujah, the crack I'd heard before was Libby's bale breaking his shoulder bone.

I wanted to gloat, Lord how I wanted to gloat, but the only part of the church not in flame was the floor we stood on and the threshold itself. The scalding air was making my hair stink like burning wool. I rushed to Libby who was still sitting like a fool.

"Let's go girl– let's go!" and I pulled her to her feet. Her pants were wet and steaming in the heat. Her boots were sopped. Poor thing must have peed herself in terror.

"Come on!"

Libby stood fast in the light of the flames. "No, Mr. Sawyer Sir," she panted. "We gotta take this one. Can't let her burn! Ain't right. We can't!"

She pointed at Hazel who was clutching her ribs and hissing hate at us through clenched teeth. It was at that second that the flames began to lick at Major Melrose Middlesex's head and shoulders. His thick hair, disciplined with greasy pomade, exploded into white flame. The fat man began to scream.

"Gotta go– gotta GO!" I ranted.

"No!" She held her place like a soldier in battle. "Tis murder! I'll not commit murder this day. I won't let her burn!"

Won't let her burn? I could let this bitch burn and toast my cheese on the fire. I pulled at Libby but she stood fast and suddenly doubled up with a spasm. This was no time to argue. With my good hand I grabbed Hazel by her hair and dragged. With my broken mitt under Liberty Smith's shoulders I lifted, pulling the two women through the door. I dumped Miss Hazel at the bottom of the step and good luck to her. Her ribs were stove in, her hems were smoking and her hair was a mess. But she was alive and that's more than her family wished for me. Like her brother and father before her she was finding out that Southern honor could have a high price.

*   *   *

A burning city is a sight to see. We couldn't have been in the church for ten minutes but in that time the entire town was blazing– except the Catholic Church where that frog priest still stood before the door with rapier presented like Napoleon's Imperial Guard. Roughnecks and incendiaries, white and black, in uniform and out, capered through the streets in all directions with flaming mops, brooms, and sacks full of loot. Women and children, choking and crying in the smoke and soot, staggered under whatever treasures they could salvage from their flaming homes. Nobody paid the slightest attention to a singed Union officer dragging a cursing lady from a flaming church. No one paid the slightest attention to the screams of Melrose Middlesex frying in his own fat as the roof collapsed on him in a roar of fire and sparks. And nobody paid the slightest attention to a singed and bloody Yankee Colonel hugging a tiny, trembling colored Union sergeant.

Then from the riverfront, sounding clearly above the din, was a whistle that could only have come from the *Hannibal*. TOOOOOOOOOT! TOOT TOOT TOOT! It was time to go.

"Come on Libby. That's our boat. We'll have to run!"

"I kain't run Mr. Colonel, sir. I kan't!"

Well she did look sickly and she did pee her britches and she did have some rough shocks, but we had to run.

"Pull up your socks, Sergeant Smith," I barked. "We've been through worse than this. You're a trooper in the 94th USCT. Don't forget it. Let's go, at the double time!"

"Colonel Ace of Spades, sir, I kain't go at the double time or any other way. I ain't a trooper in the 94th no more. I'm a woman. A woman havin' yo baby– an' I havin' it right now."

The Adventures of Sidney Sawyer
Missouri Yankees

Chapter 36

Putrification sets in quick if it's going to, and by evening the puncture from Miss Hazel's nail, an inch above my left nip didn't stink, so I didn't fret about lockjaw. But the blasted little hole stung to distraction. And my poor wrist where the bitch tried to crucify me to the floorboards throbbed almost as much as my thumb did when Captain Regan splinted it with a yard of muslin around a soup spoon. He must have known what he was about because in two weeks my thumb was as comfortable around a billiard cue as ever was. Oh, and I was the proud papa of a pickaninny named Edisto Alexandria Smith. That just goes to show what happens when you let darkies name their own brats, but Libby and Smitty set to call the boy Eddie Al, which ain't a bad tag. Sidney Junior would have suited the boy better.

I'm as gallant as the next singed, stabbed, pummeled and frightened fellow, but I had wanted Hazel Brassard Ballentine to fry in Middlesex's rendered lard. I was about to give Libby Smith a good scold on the folly of extending mercy to the merciless when she told me she was laboring her child. By grapes, that put a different spin on things, so being a gallant fellow I swept Libby up in my arms and set out to the boat at a trot. Thank Jupiter it was downhill to the levee. Expectant women pile on poundage like steers. No wonder Hazel's ribs came adrift when Libby landed on her with both boots. I was blowing like a knacker's yard nag by the time a trio of deck apes pulled us through a frantic press of refugees up the *Hannibal's* gangplank.

We had cut it damn close. Regan couldn't have waited ten minutes longer to skedaddle. The only reason he waited this long was he reckoned I be fetching wagons of cotton instead of a darkie drummer howling every two minutes in the labor of birthing a bastard. The riverfront was flaming along its length. Deck hands manned hoses that pumped sprays of water over the upper decks that steamed in the furnace of heat. The bow deck was packed with slaves escaping with the last of Marse Banks's Army. They scurried like chickens with sopped mops to smother burning embers that showered on the boat like deadly snow. Across the promenade the Icehouse Hotel, the pride of Alexandria that the locals bragged cost $100,000 dollars, was blowing flame and smoke from every window. Beyond it in the town, flames licked up the sides of steeples and the courthouse cupola to punctuate the disaster.

Deck hands, swearing and shouting, "Ship's business ye black bastards, make a hole, clear a path" kicked their way through the milling Africans to free up the bow lines, and with a screech of its whistle the *Hannibal's* side wheels backed the river into red foam. We left the levee as a mob of white women, dragging babes and pathetic bundles of what possessions they could salvage, dropped to their knees, arms outstretched to us for a mercy we couldn't give them. *Hannibal* was the last boat of the grand Red River Expedition to leave the dying city of Alexandria.

The boat boomed to catch up with the flotilla, and while I had a chat with Captain Regan, a toothless hag with a face as brown and pitted as a walnut took charge of Libby's birthing. Regan splinted my thumb and we plotted our plan. I wasn't worried about my little drummer boy any more. The old crone must have delivered half the brats born on half the plantations here 'round and knew more practical healing than a platoon of Army quacks. She certainly knew more about birthing babies. After my powwow with Regan I stood at the rail and smoked through a hatful of cheroots. Gerald D. P. Regan's Hibernian whiskey didn't tempt me. I'd need a clear head.

First, I knew why Napoleon P. Banks had a bee in his bonnet over me. It was Major Melrose Middlesex who'd put it there. Banks called me a duelist and a brawler who found his pleasures in the company of whores and drunkards. Of course that is true, but how could he have known? Middlesex told him, that's how. He was in Alexandria for the same reason he was on Morris Island with Gillmore, and with Dodge along the railroad from Decatur to Nashville. That was where the cotton was. He and his family of thieves, with their Massachusetts mills craved cotton like vampires craved blood.

I remembered what Bo'sun Jekyll Winchel told me about Red River cotton. There was plenty of it up and down the bayous and it could be gotten if you had something the Confederates wanted in barter. Middlesex had bullion and medicines, he'd told me so. And he needed an agent, a factor to see him and his loot through Rebel lines. He had the Brassards, father and daughter for that. Again, he'd told me so. Finally, he'd need transport to the Mississippi. Looking downriver from the railing of the *Hannibal's* Texas deck at the long line of steamboats whose only cargos were dwindling rations and deck-loads of runaway n—rs, he would have had the transport too. Yes, there was plenty of white gold left in Red River Country and I knew where Middlesex had stashed his. He'd told me that too.

And I knew how Melrose and Hazel smelled out my stash of cotton in the Baptist Church. Way back in South Carolina he'd told me so. The fat swine loved to brag at me and why not? He'd reckoned to see to my murder and a dead Sidney could tell no tales. His family had agents and spies up and down every river and railroad in the country. He spotted me on the levee while Porter ran his gunboats through the dams and he knew exactly why I was in town– for the same reason he was– cotton. I was a fool not to have taken precautions. Middlesex had probably ferreted out my church within the hour. He knew exactly when I would have to return to fetch it and was waiting for me like a bloated spider with the black widow Ballentine the queen of his web. That is why Libby was there. She also knew when I'd have to return to the church.

The city was being evacuated. Her pappy was with his regiment of pontoon engineers and would be gone with the vanguard. She needed me and knew just where to find me– with my cotton. *She* had pried the spikes from the door, set the hammer and nails in their place by the threshold and let herself in. She was watching for me as the city dissolved into chaos, poor thing. That's why she armed herself with the only weapon at hand, the hoe handle I had used to bull the bales of cotton. And who should stroll up to the door but the fat traitor from Morris Island and the tiny slut she had last seen arse-up in a Charleston pickle barrel. Behind the cotton was the only place to hide and I'm damn glad she took the hickory!

* * *

After its frantic retreat from Alexandria the flotilla was barely making steerage. The river below the rapids was flushed with backwater from the Mississippi so there was no danger of running up on mud bars or shoals. There was no danger from Confederates, either. We were loafing along to keep pace with the soldiers riding shanks mare along the river road. The gunboats protected the infantry from Taylor's Confederates and in turn the soldiers protected the Navy from any Rebel sharpshooters who tried to infest the riverbank.

I waited until the next afternoon to visit Libby. I made my way to the stern deck where Miss Liberty was basking in the company of a half-dozen darkie matrons, and took the acquaintance of my boy. In her day on the boat she had become a celebrity of sorts. It wasn't the baby, pickaninnies were a common breed, it was her queer manner of boarding the *Hannibal.* A pregnant colored girl in the uniform of a Yankee sergeant being hauled aboard in the arms of a bloodied Union colonel bellowing to the chief of the deck crew to take damn good care of 'Sergeant Smith' was *bound* to raise and eyebrow or two. She was glad to see me and I was glad to see her too with her bosoms presented to nurse the boy. He was as tiny as a bullfrog. I reckoned he was a month or two early, but he wasn't too dark which suited me. And he seemed healthy– at least the way he went after his marmee's nipples implied healthy appetites. I slipped a few greenbacks to the walnut faced midwife for services rendered, gave Libby a handful of bills in advance of her cotton commission, kissed little Eddie Al on the head and Libby on the lips. But I had places to go and opportunity was knocking on the Sawyer door.

I stood to attention and scandalized white crew and colored passengers both by saluting my little hero.

"Sergeant Liberty Smith, it has been an honor serving with you."

Libby straightened herself on her pallet, covered her tits, returned my salute and replied, "Mr. Colonel Sawyer, sir, the honor is mine."

I love to twist propriety by its pills when their ain't no chance my own petard will hoist me, and by that evening I was a hero to every black hide on the *Hannibal.*

* * *

The next morning Regan dropped me at the Marksville Ferry where I joined Banks's column of retreating infantry. In five minutes I was bareback on a scrawny mule, the Army was lousy with these broken down creatures, and I trotted past five miles of crawling wagons and infantry until I met up with a troop of Lee's cavalry. I took a spare mare from their string of remounts; a colonel has his privileges, and was up to Colonel Brant's

Colored 3rd Engineers by suppertime. I didn't bother with Brant– I wasn't interested in his damned pontoons. I was looking for Amos McCracken, not his red skinned boss. That paragon of the Seneca Nation would just poke a stick in my spokes.

Amos pounded my back and pumped my fin and was damned glad to see I was still alive and in marching order. He'd heard that I was with Lee at Sabine Crossroads. That was the *last* he had heard and feared the worst. He wanted me to gas about my adventures at the sharp end of the spear and then have his chance to brag on the Colored 3rd, but I brought him up short. I was there on business and I let poor simple Amos assume it was Army business. I was on my way up the Ouachita and needed a likely squad of soldiers, armed, square, and sharp to handle any Rebel mischief. I would have asked for a full platoon but didn't want any white officers along to ask awkward questions or make any embarrassing observations. I'd need Sergeant Major Smith, let him pick the men, and I'd have them back by evening rations tomorrow.

Smitty was damned happy to see me and even happier when I told him Libby was safe on the *Hannibal* and that he was a grandpappy.

His chest swelled like poultry, "Little Liberty's a mammy, don't dat just beat all? Edisto Alexandria…"

"Smith!" I interrupted. "You're gonna be more of a pappy to little Eddie Al than I'll be able to be. And Smith's as good a name as Sawyer any day. And the boy's likely to be a smithy like his grandpap, anyway, won't he? Oh, and by the way, you're rich. Liberty's my partner in the cotton business."

Smitty and I waited at the riverbank opposite the Ouachita with eleven likely darkie troops while the Army slouched past on the river road. Smitty knew how to pick 'em. They were big brutes, black as your boots and armed with rifle, pistol, and Dark Town stickers. They nudged each other and grinned like coons watching Smitty and the white colonel smoking delta stinkers and chatting like old chums as the flotilla steamed past. Maybe Miss Hazel Brassard Ballentine *was* right and I *was* a n—r lover.

I hailed the *Hannibal* as she came abreast at the tail end of the fleet. There was only a tinclad stern-wheeler behind her tending rearguard for the flotilla. *Hannibal* only drew two feet of water and Regan brought her close to the reeds for us to wade aboard, wet to our courting tackle. While the boat was heaved to, the tinclad passed us with a curse and a warning from her pilot to catch up with the flotilla and no nonsense. We'd catch up with the Navy, but only *after* our nonsense.

* * *

Red House Plantation was eight miles up the Ouachita on the starboard side. It was a substantial establishment with a wharf along its own levee, a warehouse up from the dock and the main house one hundred yards up a bending crushed stone driveway flanked by brick out buildings. The plantation house was a step above the usual run. It was two and a half stories of brick, painted a dazzling white with eight red brick pillars supporting a veranda that measured the length of the building. Shutters framed each window in the same shade as the brick, which must have given the plantation its name. The slave cabins were out of sight behind a swale but the arrival of a steamboat is an event. The *Hannibal's* whistle brought every darkie in the establishment running to see the sight. It also brought the proprietor of the plantation to the porch with his fouling piece, followed by a variety of females from sixteen to sixty, and a half-dozen brats of both sexes. There were no Confederate boats up the Ouachita this season so the whistle could not be bringing good news to mares and the mistress. And it didn't.

Before the deck apes had the mooring lines secured, Smitty and I had the squad swarming over the railings and up the dock. I roared to the old fool with the shotgun to lay it down, no use killing him in front of his womenfolk. Then the white family of Red House saw a horror they never hoped to see– n—r soldiers invading their kingdom. The black troops were grim, armed and under the no nonsense command of a black sergeant. And Smith was a sight to see, decked out in Yankee livery, with scarlet and gold chevrons covering his sleeves, Kelly green sash about his waist and Jeff Davis hat blocked and brushed with the badge of the engineers pinning the brim above his right ear. The white family on the veranda cringed. The black slaves milling on the lawn gaped. I held back grinning, and let Smitty do the honors.

He pulled my fiat from his sleeve, snapped it open and in his deep voice, half Missouri and half Africa, read, "By order of General Nathanial P. Banks, military governor of the District of the Gulf, all cotton, crops, produce, provisions, livestock, fodder and consumables are hereby forfeit and confiscated to the use of the Armies of the United States of America and declared and condemned as legitimate and true contraband of war."

By grapes and by golly I thought that sounded grand, even if I did just write it myself on our detour up the Ouachita. The old planter's knees almost buckled hearing his personal economy shattered, and from the big lips of a colored Yankee who could read as well as he could. Behind him the women of the plantation set up a keening, punctuated by curses you usually only hear from teamsters when their mules balk. Of course all their men folk were up the Red River with Taylor tormenting Banks and his defeated expedition. It must have been bitter that Taylor's victory wouldn't help them any more than it helped Natchitoches, Grand Ecore or Alexandria.

We found Melrose Middlesex's white gold in the warehouse by the levee. Lord, but I love it when villains brag. I remembered his gloat word for word, "I don't want your cheap pile of lint! I've got cotton piled in a king's ransom at Red House, up the Ouachita. It was bought and paid for in medicines and bullion." And he was right– there it was in a king's ransom. And Captain Regan knew just where Red House Plantation was. Every pilot worth his whisky knew every great plantation on every river. They had to! Each establishment was a kingdom of its own with lords and ladies and lackeys and slaves. They coopered their own barrels and tinkered their own pots, forged their own iron and tailored their own duds. Each plantation had its own wharf to import and export its treasure. In the memory of every pilot and notated on every river map, every dock was inscribed and engraved.

Heaven knows there were enough hands to load the cotton into every available space on the *Hannibal*. Smitty's squad stood guard as the darkies camped on the bow deck pitched in with a will. I was paying them twenty-five cents a man but they would have done the labor for free– I was their hero. I'm also a son of a bitch when provoked and the proprietor of Red House set about to provoke me. He was a ramrod straight old aristocrat with a great sweep of white hair, vast lip whiskers and a hate for all things Union and all things black.

"You n—r lovin' Yankee renegade. Turnin' your n—r rabble loose on the likes o' your own kind– Shame! Shame!"

The women folk keened behind him like a Greek Chorus, "N—r lover! Shame! Shame!"

"It's a new day, old timer. Make your peace with it. We'll be about our business and gone in an hour."

"You'll be in hell in an hour! General Taylor will kill you all, grind you up, slaughter you like hogs! Yankee trash!"

He was beginning to vex me.

"Sergeant Smith!" I bellowed. "If this man leaves his veranda, have the guard shoot him down."

Behind him the women folk and children set up a howl but the old fool recognized my Missouri accent.

"You are Southern! You are a Southern man, Missouri, most likely. You are a traitor, sir! You are a traitorous dog– a Missouri Yankee who turns on his own people in his lust after the Yankee dollar. You are here only to steal my cotton. You are here to steal the fruit of a better man's labor. All you Yankees hold sacred is the almighty dollar! I spit on you!"

And he did. The old bastard must have been chewing plug for fifty years and his aim was true. A long expectoration of brown slime exploded on my breast. The silence on the veranda was absolute until I realized that the vicious old Rebel was correct in every particular. I *was* a Missouri Yankee and I *did* lust after the Yankee dollar and I *was* here to steal his cotton.

"Sergeant Smith," I spoke over my shoulder in a tone of moderate conversation, "Double the stevedore's wages to fifty cents a man and spread the word that there is the same four bits for any negro of the Red House Plantation who will lend a hand. Inform them that they are free men and women and we will find space on the deck for all who wish to come."

I turned to the old Southern gentlemen while he was still wiping backy from his whiskers. "Imagine that! You woke up a rich man and you'll go to bed a beggar."

"Sergeant Major Smith!" I bellowed, "Clean out the smoke house and pantry– leave nothing that could be of use to the Rebellion. Send two good men to kill the livestock. Burn the barns and outbuildings. Private!" I pointed to the trooper that Smith detailed to guard the family on the porch. "Remember your orders. If any one, man or woman, leaves the veranda, shoot them down!"

The black soldier happily grinned with teeth white enough to startle, and leaned toward the white folks with bayonet threatening.

I shouldn't have hogged all the fun, but Regan and his crew were already being paid a fat percentage by the Temples, so I bulled through Red House's front door by myself and went on a scavenger hunt. They didn't have time to bury their silver and treasure in the flowerbed so the family plate was still in the dining parlor behind the glass of its fine cabinet. I slit two cushions on the davenport and turned the stuffing inside out. They made serviceable bags for swag. I smashed the glass doors of the cabinet with the barrel of my Remington and stuffed the cushions with a fine service for twelve including soupspoons and oyster forks. The big items like teapot and tureen I stomped flat and stuffed in with the spoons. Paintings of fat children and homely women spaced the walls of the dining room and parlor, but in the place of honor above the head of the table was a fine painting of the Madonna with the infant Christ smiling a shy blessing. I cut it from its frame, rolled it up and stuffed it down my britches. I still look at it every day above our hearth when Amy and I sip our port before the fire. Then it was upstairs to the feminine chambers where the real plunder would be found. In the big bedchamber I turned out a pillow and fed the old gent's cufflinks and the missus's broaches and flub dubs into the shimmy. Then it was down the hall in and out of each chamber with the sack getting heavier at each door.

And then I found the prize. In a bedroom with feminine traps scattered about the bed and bureau, in a mother-of-pearl case lined with velvet, was a gold tiara. It was studded pearls that shown in the light like quick silver. Its centerpiece was a square yellow stone surrounded by little white ones that I took to be diamonds. I made to crush it flat, the better to fit into my bag of swag, but at the last second had a notion that made me grin through my greed. I stuck it on my own head. It fit nicely beneath my Jeff Davis and I marched out of the front door feeling like Black Beard the Pirate King.

"An ounce of spit and bile never had a higher price, did it old timer?" I pointed at my breast, sticky with his plug. On either side of the big house fire was leaping from the windows and doors of the cookhouse, pantry and even the privies. I could hear the roar of flames from the barns behind the house and before the wharf the warehouse was blazing smoke and flame through its roof.

I snapped to the sentry who was grinning like a black Lucifer, "If he says another word, fire the house,"

I meant it too, but the old Confederate had the good sense to keep his trap shut. The only sound was the wailing of the women and the blubbering of the brats as the last of my black Yankee raiders, followed by the entire slave population of Red House, retreated to the *Hannibal,* lugging the heart and soul of the proud plantation with them.

I look back to the memory of my raid on Red House with nothing but satisfaction. The white-whiskered master of the house accused me of stealing the fruits of better men's labor. Maybe I did, but it wasn't the fruits of *his* labor. It was the fruits of the labor of generations of darkie slaves and I took all of them with me on the *Hannibal.* I'm sure that up the Ouachita in the Louisiana bayou country the Red House still stands, but it is surrounded by the gutted chimneys of its once proud prosperity and the fallow fields that have no labor to produce more crops of white gold. It has been fifty years and the old Rebel is dead now and bitching in heaven or hell about the Missouri Yankee that destroyed his civilization, but his women folk and brats who wailed in grief and outrage are probably still alive to remember. They should remember me in their prayers and thank their Almighty God that it was me who visited their world back in May of '64. They were committing treason with the likes of Melrose Middlesex and the Brassard clan. I left them their house standing. Sherman wouldn't have. Sheridan wouldn't have, and it's a damn cinch that Whiskey Smith and his Gorillas would have burned it to the foundation.

The Adventures of Sidney Sawyer
Missouri Yankees

Epilogue

On Wednesday we caught up with the flotilla at Yellow Bayou, five miles shy of Simmesport where the Atchafalaya joins the Red. The expedition had been held up all of Monday at Mansura just outside of Marksville where Taylor's Confederates tried to deny Banks the road. The cheeky dog lined up his artillery, the same guns he had captured from Commissary Banks at Sabine Crossroads, and opened fire. The battle was a frost. The ranges across a prairie as flat as a table were too great to draw much blood, but the delay did give me time to plunder Red House. Two days later Taylor tried again at Yellow Bayou. That little dust-up gave the *Hannibal* time to rejoin the flotilla and in the confusion of the waning battle nobody took notice that we had been gone and were back.[35]

There was a last panic, sopped in irony, when the Army reached the Atchafalaya River. It was usually a modest bayou, and once across it Banks and his raiders would be safe from Taylor and his Confederate pork butchers. The Federal flank would rest on the Mississippi where all the wealth and power of the Union would guarantee his security. But the spring rains that had refused to drench Red River country swelled the Atchafalaya to an ugly brown serpent over 600 yards wide. There was no way our pontoon trains could span the flood. If a month ago the gods of war had poured that water into the Red, the Army would be abiding in Shreveport and

Banks would be mantled in victory. We were stuck within sight of salvation with nothing to do but wait for the Atchafalaya to drop while the men nibbled through the last of their rations. If we ferried the troops over, Taylor, that audacious puppy, would wait until the Army was divided, half on each side of the flood and gobble up the Army of the Gulf piecemeal. That is when Colonel Joe Bailey of the Red River Dams had another epiphany.

Pontoons? The usual run of pontoons, the likes of which I had drifted down the Tennessee River past Moccasin Point in six months before, or ones the 3rd Louisiana Corps D' Afrique had dragged from Alexandria to Mansfield and back, were too small and too few. I'm West Point trained and a better engineer than most but all I could do was growl at the swollen Atchafalaya with the rest of the staff ninnies. I didn't have a solution in my head until Bailey pointed out the obvious.

Pontoons? Why the Army had more than enough pontoons– big ones, stern-wheelers, side-wheelers and even a couple of screw-driven pump boats. Feeling no end the fools for not thinking it up themselves, the pilots lost no time in lining their boats up in the sluggish current and anchoring them abreast of each other from bank to bank. It wasn't a proper bridge, but the gaps between boats were scabbed over with planks and timbers and before the last riverboat was anchored to the eastern bank the first regiments were marching across to safety. And the last boat in line was the *Hannibal,* looking like a snow mountain with her decks and railings lined with Melrose Middlesex's cotton.

On the way to our spot between a shabby commissary boat and the eastern riverbank we steamed past the *Neosho*. Her railings and woodwork, washed overboard in her nose-first plunge over the Bayou Rapides Dam, had been set to rights and her jolly boat and cutter gleamed with fresh varnish. The great guns bristled from her forward turret as if she was cleared for a fleet action. She sported the Red White and Blue from every mast, and her lines, fore and aft were garlanded with every signal flag in the locker. Her awnings, white enough to squint my eyes, were rigged against the Southern sun and for all her ugliness she was shipshape and grand. With Bailey's riverboat pontoon bridge spanning the Atchafalaya, the *Neosho's* crew knew that the campaign was over. To celebrate their deliverance Captain Howard had tarted her up like a New Orleans pimp at Mardi Gras. And there, amidships at her port rail, was my old pal in larceny, Bo'sun Jekyll Winchel. We saw each other at first glance and he stuck out his vast belly like a salute and lifted his mitt in a wave.

"Ahoy, Sawyer! Tis a grand war– I see you prosper."

He meant the cotton stacked on the decks, along the railings and bulging from the doors of the staterooms. How kind of him to notice.

"Aye, Bo'sun, if you're sharp for the main chance and gather your guts it *is* a grand war, ain't it just?" and I hooted like a loon as the *Neosho* steamed us out of hailing distance.

And I had a right to hoot! There were at least six hundred bales of Red River fiber packed into every cranny of the *Hannibal*. That was one hundred and fifty tons of treasure worth almost a half a million dollars. My ten percent share would fetch me forty five thousand dollars– fifty thousand if I was lucky. Christopher Columbus, but I was going to be as rich as Melrose Middlesex before he fed the church house fire with his four hundred weight of suet. And I had my bags of swag plundered from Red House Plantation stashed under a rubber sheet in the locker of my Missouri stateroom.[t] And don't forget that dandy tiara of gold and pearl and gems that I had stuffed under

---

[t] An American tradition on riverboats is to name each cabin after states, hence, staterooms. The biggest lounge or salon is called the Texas Deck after the biggest state.

my Jeff Davis bonnet. That vanity made me smile and besides, I had a special notion in mind for that flub-dub.

All the rest of that day, all through the night and into the next morning General Napoleon P. Banks's Army trooped across Bailey's bridge of boats with Porter's flotilla keeping any Rebel bush poppers at a respectful distance. The Army trudged up steep ramps and through the railings onto grand steamers, marched across their wide decks to slip down makeshift gangways to humble tugs and then on up whatever makeshift span that straddled to the next boat. The last in the long line was the bow deck of the *Hannibal*. We were three feet higher than the commissary boat to our starboard and four feet lower than the riverbank to our port. Hundreds of wagons driven by teamsters who swore their filthy oaths under their breaths so as not to startle their jaded mules to stumbling off the narrow gangways, rattled over and up onto the solid riverbank. Cannon and caissons pulled by thin horses with blankets snugged over their eyes to prevent spooking, lurched with their loads from one deck to the next, each team led by a sweating red strap. Lee's cavalry clattered across our deck, each dismounted trooper leading his nag. Thousands of infantry marched across by the regiment with heavy pack and muskets slung. And the colored cargo marched over our decks too. The thousands of Red River slaves, liberated by the Army from Grand Ecore to Simmesport, slouched across the Atchafalaya with the Army, including the *Hannibal's* own dusky cargo and three score Red House slaves. The only black hides left on the boat were Liberty Smith, Baby Eddie Al and our own half-dozen darkie deck apes. Every wagon and gun and beast and man crossed over a score of boats, each one cobbled to the next with whatever timber and gangways that came to hand. All through the night huge bonfires lined the shore and lit the way. With daylight, regimental bands struck up gay airs as the men scrambled ashore to a safety so secure that even the criminal foolishness of General Banks couldn't endanger them again. They sang and laughed and capered and on that morning of May 20th the grand Red River Campaign came to an end.

The *Hannibal* was the last boat in line. It would be the last boat of Bailey's grand pontoon bridge to kedge up its stern anchor and join the flotilla for the short run to the Mississippi and home. The commissary boat to our starboard pried up the timbered gangway securing it to our bow deck. As she drifted clear in the sluggish current, her whistle sounded and as her wheel churned the brown water both crews cheered three hurrahs and a happy voyage.

By God, it was over! I was alive and rich and safe. I was *safe*! Since that evil day when the Honorable Thomas Sawyer of the Nevada Territorial Legislature had darkened my door ten months ago, I had been at the mercy of maniacs like Stanton, Sherman, Grant and Dodge. I had been tossed into the soup by clowns like Gillmore, Hooker and Banks. I had been set upon by villains like King Wadmalaw, Poxy Opel, the father and daughter Brassard, and Melrose Middlesex. The *Hannibal* would fly me north to St. Petersburg and Auntie's home cookin'. I'd bounce little Ranty on my knee like a real daddy. I'd stuff myself at Ma Temple's table while Old Man Temple, Alfred and I divvied up our plunder of cotton like the river pirates that we were.

And Amy! I'd be in my Amy's arms again. Amy! Oh, I'd had other bounces since Stanton saddled me with the Colored 94th– a soldier leads a lonely life and certain itches must be scratched. There was fat Missy Ruth, Mrs. Newcastle and almost Poxy Opel. Of course little Liberty Smith was the prime piece, but that ended up with us prying Carolina swamp leeches from the cracks of each other's arses. No, Amy is my girl and I reminisced at the forward rail as the deck hands cleared away the rubbish from the passage of thirty thousand men, five thousand beasts and swarming mobs of liberated darkies. I was ready to fetch a pint, the better to daydream when I was interrupted. Interrupted hell– I was boarded and plundered.

Two-dozen Navy bluejackets thundered down the gang from the riverbank, armed like Jolly Roger with carbine and cutlass. At the head of the mob was Bo'sun Jekyll Winchel, vast gut wrapped in a scarlet cummerbund, massive shoulders squeezed in a scarlet monkey jacket embroidered with gold frogging, greasy hair tucked under a black silk bandana and sporting a cap and ball .36 caliber Navy Colt six shooter.

I stood at the rail like a sap as Captain Regan stormed down from the pilothouse at the intrusion. The bluejackets knew their business and with shouts, snarls and kicks Regan, his mates and the rest of the crew were shooed like chickens into the forward most cabins. The doors were slammed in their outraged faces and guards posted with orders to truck no nonsense from the prisoners. *Prisoners?*

At Red House I had reckoned that I felt like old Black Beard the pirate. Winchel actually *looked* like Black Beard, standing with one hand on his hip, pistol resting on his great belly and laughing as his old commissary boat, the *Lady Leavenworth* steamed beside us and made fast to the *Hannibal's* starboard rail. Work gangs of black stevedores swarmed aboard and began transferring the cotton– my cotton!

"See here, Winchel, you bastard! You have no business aboard this boat. *Hannibal's* a civilian craft with an honest cargo. Get your n—rs off the deck an' be quick about it! What's your game?"

"The same game as yours, Sawyer," and he threw my own words back at me. "If you're sharp for the main chance and gather your guts, it's a grand War." Then he leaned close enough for me to smell radishes and rum on his foul breath and whispered, "And I figured that if I'm gonna be a pirate I may as well dress for the occasion. How do I look?"

"You look like a Memphis brothel bully and that ain't Reb cotton your darkies are swipin'. It's mine an' I have the papers to prove it."

"Papers? Well, knock me down and steal my teeth! Papers?" and he gave a great laugh from his belly. "Them papers would be in your cabin, I reckon."

His laugh ended in a crafty sneer. He leveled his Colt at my face and ordered, "Show me!"

And I did. What could I do with a hog leg in my spine and a shellback gripping each elbow? He stationed his two crushers outside my stateroom door and pushed me in with his Colt.

"Show me your license, Colonel. You know, the one signed by the military governor of Baton Rouge to invoice your cotton– the ones that look just like the one I have here. The one you gave me."

"You can't do this, you swine! You'll never get away with it! It's robbery– it's larceny!" I was practically howling my righteous outrage. "It'll never wash– it'll never stand!"

But of course it did. My cotton license was valid. It was the best cotton license money could buy. It stated that Sidney Thomas Sawyer of St. Petersburg, Missouri was the legal factor for a cargo of 611 bales of perfectly legal and properly purchased cotton. Hadn't I bought a fistful of these licenses from the scoundrel that Napoleon P. Banks had installed to govern Baton Rouge? His signature was duly notarized and stamped. I didn't even have to bribe the notary, just the governor. I had enough of them that I didn't give it a thought when I gave one to Winchel to sweeten the deal when he moved my three hundred bales of pilfered Navy cotton to the church in Alexandria. And now this pirate was burning *my* license in the ashtray with my own cigar. While he covered me with his .36 he filled in his name and 611 bales on the proper lines, folded it neat as a napkin and stuffed it into his monkey jacket. Then he took a second look at the ashtray.

I had thought it a droll notion to use the Red House's sterling sugar bowl to butt my cigars. Winchel gave it a squint. His eyes darted to mine and like a ninny mine darted to the locker besides the bunk. In two strides he swung open the lid and there was my Red House swag. He left the silver, too bulky, and it was only worth a few hundred dollars. After all, he was a rich man now, wasn't he? He didn't notice the painting of the Madonna, just a roll of dirty canvas, but he positively giggled when he dumped the bag of feminine gee-gaws onto the bunk. A rich pirate could ignore the silver but the gee-gaws were prime plunder. There were broaches, rings, necklaces, gem-studded combs, two gold pendant watches, one crusted with emeralds and the other with pearls. There were delicate chains of silver and gold, pins, pearl buttons, barrettes, cufflinks, tie tacks and the master's watch.

"You've been busy, Colonel," the swine gloated. "Nine hundred bales of white gold ain't enough for you. Ya gotta swipe granny's wedding ring too. Haw-haw-haw! What would General Banks say?"

"Banks be damned! He was the biggest thief on the river until you came along."

"Mind your manners, Colonel. Banks is the only honest man on this river, more's the pity. He's simply an idiot."

With that he stuffed the booty back into the pillowcase, swung it over his shoulder like a satanic Santa Claus and was out the door with a slam.

It was another two hours before the *Lady L* untied from *Hannibal*. When Captain Regan's crew liberated me from my stateroom prison I raged and stomped and swore like an infant whose puppy licked his sweet-pop. I damned Regan for a fool and his crew for cowards and Libby on general principles. Winchel's pirates had thought to douse the boilers. By the time we could build up steam to pursue the *Lady Leavenworth* he'd be in Memphis selling my fortune to the highest bidder. The bastard! The swine! I'd hunt him down and shoot him like a dog. I'd wear his fat guts for garters … I'd … I'd …

*   *   *

I was going to give the tiara with the pearls and the big ugly yellow stone to Liberty. I really was. I knew she could never wear it. A colored girl sporting a golden crown wouldn't go unnoticed or be tolerated in Missouri, but what the hell– I reckoned it would be fun. After all, she was the marmee of my boy and we were partners. But my treasure was gone. I was still rich, but not as rich as I had reckoned. Libby did get her one percent of the three hundred bales she doctored in the church, but she never did get the tiara.

Thank God Bo'sun Jekyll Winchel didn't have the wit to check under my Jeff Davis bonnet. Amy wore that same tiara every night in the grand dining salon of the great ocean liner, *Olympic* as we steamed across the wide Atlantic in August of '14, fleeing the new Great War in Europe.

This concludes the fifth packet of the Memoirs of General Sidney Thomas Sawyer.

Appendix

1 The *Carondelet* was one of seven city class gunboats built at the beginning of the Civil War for service on the Western rivers. Built by James Eads and designed by Samuel Pook, (Hence the nickname 'Pook Turtles,') they were as ugly as Sawyer describes. These slope-sided gunboats were armored with timber and iron plate, and cut for eleven big guns. They were so alike that different colored bands were painted on their twin smokestacks for identification. The *Carondelet* served with valor throughout the war, being badly damaged at Fort Donelson and in her duel with the Confederate ironclad, Arkansas. She was decommissioned in 1865.

2. By World War I, the ugly doctrine of Social Darwinism was widely accepted. When Charles Darwin published *On the Origin of Species* in 1859 his concepts of natural selection and survival of the fittest were biological. Social Darwinism stretched the premise to include politics and economics. Nations and races competed for dominance and survival in a never-ending savage struggle. Before the First World War, this doctrine was used to scientifically support laissez-faire capitalism, eugenics, racism and imperialism. Leading up to World War II it justified fascism, Nazi ideology and genocide.

3. Sawyer's friend Jimmy *was* right. There *was* a lot more to it than just a dead archduke. A general European war had been brewing for a generation. Nationalism had become a stronger force than ever before. France lusted to revenge the humiliation of the Franco-Prussian War and a mighty, united German Empire upset the balance of power in Europe. To reset the balance, each country tangled itself in a web of alliances. If any one country went to war the entire continent would be dragged into the conflict. Small wars in the Balkans and vicious imperialistic rivalries balanced peace on a sword's edge as the powers scrambled for colonies in Africa, Asia and the Pacific. Unbridled militarism swelled armies to the millions, mobilization would bring in millions more reservists and war plans were finalized. Finally, the Kaiser was obnoxious, the Czar was a fool, the French were arrogant, the Italians opportunistic, the British were smug, the Austrians

were angry and no government was particularly afraid of the coming explosion.

4. The 1872 model Webley British Bull Dog pocket pistol was a .44 short, rim-fire weapon with a two and one half inch barrel that was as blunt as its namesake. It was popular, cheap (as little as $10) and deadly. It was the gun used to assassinate President James Garfield. Bull Dogs were widely copied and manufactured in several countries. It was in production up to the First World War.

5. The Society of Righteous and Harmonious Fists' (Boxers) answer to the Western imperialist dismemberment of China and the cultural disruptions caused by Christian missionaries was the Boxer Rebellion of 1900. It began as a popular uprising but was joined by the Imperial government of the Empress Dowager Cixi. In essence, China declared war on every great power on earth, including the United States and Japan. Its most dramatic event was the fifty-five day siege of the Legation Quarter in Peking (Beijing) by the Boxers and the Imperial Army. An eight-nation alliance broke the siege, scattered the Boxers, executed the ringleaders and humiliated China with a punitive treaty. China didn't win free of foreign exploitation until the Communist takeover in 1949.

6. The 54th Massachusetts Volunteer Infantry was one of the first and certainly the most famous of the Colored regiments of the Civil War. ('Colored' in this context is a correct and non-offensive term.) It mustered into service in March of 1863 after the Emancipation Proclamation. Most Colored troops in the Union Army were recent slaves but the 54th consisted manly of free Negroes and long established former slaves. Despite discrimination in pay and staffed only by white officers, it was a crack outfit. Its major battle was the unsuccessful assault on Battery Wagner on July 18, 1863. Almost half of the regiment was killed, wounded, captured or missing in the battle. Its commander, Col. Robert Gould Shaw was killed and the Confederates "buried him with his n—ers." The 1989 movie, *Glory*, staring Denzel Washington and Morgan Freeman memorialized the assault. The 54th Colored Infantry continued to serve through the April 18, 1865 Battle of Bykin's Mill, South Carolina, which took place six days after Lee's surrender at Appomattox.

7. The Civil War found Samuel Clemens navigating the Mississippi as a riverboat pilot. When war closed the river he briefly joined a Confederate militia but deserted to join his brother, Orion, in Nevada. It was in Virginia City that Mark Twain was created in February of 1863. Writing in the local newspaper and sending articles describing life in the silver boomtowns he perfected his humorous,

conversational style of writing. He also grew his iconic mustache. He stayed in Nevada for two years before moving on to San Francisco. It was during his time that the Nevada Territorial legislature actually did outlaw gambling.

8. In 1858 the Hardee Hat was adopted as standard headgear for the U.S. Army. It was named after the Commandant of Cadets at West Point, William Hardee, who resigned his commission in 1861 to serve the South. He became a corps commander and a lieutenant general. This headgear was also called a 'Jeff Davis' because the future Confederate president was the Secretary of War at the time. The hat was heavy, hot, and prone to dents so most soldiers instead wore the forage cap or 'kepi' for comfort. It was ideal, however for soldiers like Sidney Sawyer, who loved brass, braid, embroidery and plumes.

9. Secretary of War Edwin McMasters Stanton was President Lincoln's rock who "fights back the angry waters… Without him I should be destroyed." He was a happy Ohio lawyer until his daughter and wife died and his brother slit his own throat. These events turned him into the grim taskmaster who is known to history. He lusted with all his heart to be president and initially had nothing but contempt for the rail-splitter. Through the course of the Civil War, however, he came to love and revere Lincoln. His most famous quote was on Lincoln's assassination he prayed, "Now he belongs to the ages." He had well-founded contempt for President Andrew Johnson and was instrumental in his impeachment. President Grant appointed him to the Supreme Court in 1869 but Stanton died only four days after his confirmation. He is on the 1871 seven-cent stamp.

10. Model regiments like the 54th Massachusetts were not just fighting the Rebels, they were fighting to make a point. When they were paid three dollars less than White troops and had three dollars more deducted for clothing, they and other Colored outfits boycotted their pay. Colonel Robert Gould Shaw led the political movement to correct this injustice and when he was killed assaulting Fort Wagner other idealistic officers took his place. In June of 1864 Congress equalized the pay, but only for soldiers who were free before the War. This led to the "Quaker Oath." All Colored soldiers could swear in good conscience… "that you owed no man unrequited labor before April, 1861." Since abolitionists believed that no man *ever* owed unrequited labor to *any* man, the troops could so swear. In September of 1864, Congress corrected this injustice.

11. General Quincy Adams Gillmore graduated at the top of his West Point class in 1849. He instructed at the Military

Academy for four years, including Sidney Sawyer's plebe year. During the Civil War at Ft. Pulaski guarding Savannah, he made his reputation by pioneering the use of rifled artillery. The fort was destroyed demonstrating the obsolescence of all masonry forts. He also led the Army in the use of Colored soldiers as combat troops instead of simply a reservoir of manual labor. He was not a gifted tactician and despite awarding a medal to every soldier in the Department of the South (the Gillmore Medal) he was not loved by his troops. After the War he became an expert on cement.

12. In the 7th century the Byzantines developed a terrible and effective weapon– Greek fire. This liquid could be pressurized and squirted like a fire hose onto enemy ships or siege works where it ignited on contact and could not be extinguished with water. It was instrumental in saving Constantinople from early Muslim invasions. It was a closely guarded state secret and when the Empire fell the secret went with it. Subsequent incendiary weapons were called Greek fire, but they weren't. Not until WW I could fire be blasted on the enemy with a hose. In the Civil War the Berney incendiary shell was loaded with a mixture of petroleum, naphtha, beuzine and asphaltum and fitted with a fuse. There was only a 70% chance a Berney shell would work. In November of 1864 the Confederates tried to burn New York City using 'Greek fire' incendiary devices that were planted in hotels. Nineteen hotels were set ablaze in one night. Hardly anyone noticed.

13. In the wee hours of August 22 the Swamp Angel opened fire on Charleston. The first shell spread fire and panic in the sleeping city. General Gillmore did send an ultimatum to Fort Wagner, but it was not signed. The fastidious Confederates returned it without warning the city. Sixteen shells were fired the first night, ten of them loaded with 'Greek fire.' On August 24, the night Sawyer observed the battery, several of the incendiary shells exploded in the barrel. This dangerously weakened the gun by loosening the breech bands. Thirteen more shots were successfully fired, using a double length lanyard to fire the gun from a safe distance. As a show of bravado, the fourteenth round was fired by Lieutenant Sellmer standing beside the cannon. It blew up in spectacular fashion, slightly wounding Sellmer and three other men. The Swamp Angel's career was over after only thirty-six shots.

14. What was the South to do with captured colored Union troops? To treat them as soldiers taken in honorable combat would imply the humanity of the Negro and that would not do. Eight days before Emancipation Proclamation took effect Jefferson Davis issued his own proclamation. Captured Negroes would be killed or

enslaved and their White officers would be executed for inciting servile rebellion. Instead of being cowed, Negro units redoubled their determination, knowing the results of defeat. President Lincoln issued a counter order that for every soldier enslaved or officer killed the Union would retaliate in kind on a like number of Confederate prisoners. Rebel general Kirby Smith encouraged a no Colored prisoners policy, writing, "in this way we may be relieved from a disagreeable dilemma." Eventually Colored troops became common-place and captured Negro troops were treated pretty much the same way as White prisoners–wretchedly.

15. The Yankees didn't have the only navy that could build ironclads. In the spring of 1862 South Carolina began building two ironclad gunboats, the *Palmetto State* and *Chicora*. The *Palmetto State* was called the Ladies' Gunboat because it was partly funded by quilt sales and 'gunboat fairs.' They were underpowered steam rams, screw driven, rated at six knots, 150 feet long and mounting six guns. They had four inches of iron armor over two feet of oak with another two inches of iron extending for five feet below their waterlines. They were not black as Sawyer states but were painted 'blockade blue' in an early use of marine camouflage. Perhaps Sawyer was looking at the rust. They saw their only meaningful action on January 30, 1863 when they challenged the blockade squadron, capturing one Union ship and damaging another. However they were by far the most effective of Confederate ironclads. For three years they tied up the bulk of the Union ironclad fleet at Charleston and they kept the port open for blockade-runners, most of whom made it past the Union flotilla. After Sherman cut off Charleston from the rest of the Confederacy in February of '65 their crews blew them up to keep them out of Union hands.

16. The artist in Confederate uniform was almost certainly Sergeant Conrad Wise Chapman of Virginia. When the War began he was in Rome, Italy with his family, also artists. He returned to fight for the Confederacy and was wounded at Shiloh. (He accidentally shot himself in the head.) Transferred to Charleston with the 46th Virginia Infantry he was detailed to document the action in a series of paintings. General Henry Wise, a family friend and General Beauregard felt he would be of greater service to the Cause as an artist than as a soldier. At the end of the War he fled to Mexico and Europe rather than submit to the hated Yankees. He faithfully followed his art but alas, won little recognition until after his death. Returning to Virginia he died in 1910. Today 31 of his Charleston paintings are on display at the Museum of the Confederacy in Richmond, Virginia.

17. Thousands of women actively waged war during the Civil War but only 400 are documented as actually joining the ranks as soldiers. Most served as nurses, others as spies, and every bivouac had its 'camp followers,' (wives and lovers who followed their men to war and provided domestic labor around the camp.) Many others were 'Hooker's girls,' or prostitutes. Of the soldiers, Frances (Jack) Clatin is today the most well known. Her surviving 'male' and 'female' photographs are remarkable. She fought beside her husband, Elmer, at Stone River. When he was killed before her eyes, 'Jack' continued to advance with her company. One female soldier, Jennie Hodgers, claimed to see action in forty battles, received a military pension and continued her life as a man. She was found out in 1915 when geriatric medical procedures identified her true gender.

18. The Gullah or Geechee people, descendents of slaves, are today found in the low country and Sea Islands of Georgia and South Carolina. Their English-based language has vocabulary, grammar and sentence structure from African cultures stretching from the Guinea Coast to Angola. The Gullah are divided into Saltwater Geechee and Freshwater Geechee depending on their proximity to the coast. Gullah culture has its own unique cuisine, crafts and music. The larger American culture has adopted several Gullah words such as goober and gumbo, as well as folk tales such as "Bre'r Rabbit."

19. The tiny island of Edisto provided almost two hundred soldiers for the Civil War. According to *Edisto Island 1861–2006: Ruin Recovery and Rebirth*, by Charles Spencer, 110 Edisto white men joined the Confederate service. The plantations of the island were extremely prosperous and these men must have had a comfortable war. Only one is known to have died in combat. At least 70 Edisto Blacks volunteered for Union service, mostly with the 1st, 2nd and 3rd South Carolina Colored Infantry regiments. Liberty's recollection of the Seabrooks is accurate. Ten Seabrook men joined the Union Army, seven of them enlisting on the same day.

20. Edisto Island had a unique history during the Civil War. In November of 1861 the white population evacuated the island before the threat of the Union Navy. Sea island cotton had supported some of the grandest plantations in Carolina. At least 1000 slaves were abandoned to scavenge for themselves in the abandoned fields. They were joined by another 1000 runaways and together created a sort of independent Black republic. In 1862 the Union Army occupied the island, bringing with them missionaries, schools, and proper local government. By May there were over 10,000 Yankee troops on the island but they were called north to reinforce McClellan after his fiasco in the Peninsula Campaign. By July the last Union regiment, the 55th

Pennsylvania, was gone. Over 1600 freemen went with them. Sawyer arrived on the island over a year later and encountered the remnants of Edisto's free Black population.

21. Alfred Thayer Mahan was born at West Point in 1840, two years after Sidney Sawyer's birth. Against his father's wishes he attended the Naval Academy, graduating just in time for the Civil War. Mahan was a sailor who wasn't very good at sailing. His ships had a habit of running into things but his accomplishments were not at sea. In 1890 he wrote the world's most important book on naval strategy, *The Influence of Sea Power Upon History- 1660 – 1783*. His friend Theodore Roosevelt used it to justify the modernization and expansion of the U.S. Navy. Unfortunately, it was also used by the Germans and Japanese to justify their naval modernization and imperialist expansion. Mahan is memorialized at Annapolis with Mahan Hall, a building that looks like a Victorian wedding cake.

22. Frederick Douglass was born a slave in Maryland in 1818. His kindly mistress taught him to read but he endured all the degradations of slavery from lashings to family separations. At twenty he escaped, changed his name to Douglass, married a free woman of color and began his remarkable carrier as an author, speaker, preacher, and advocate for human freedom. To escape re-enslavement he traveled for a time to England, and with royalties from his autobiography purchased his legal freedom. He was one of the greatest orators in American history and spoke with passion for abolition, woman's rights and temperance. He was forty-five when he met Sawyer. His son, Charles, served in the 54th Massachusetts. In 1884, two years after his wife died he outraged the nation by marrying Helen Pitts, a white woman. They traveled the world as proponents of radical causes. In 1895 Douglass died after speaking at the National Council of Women.

23. George Henry Thomas was a slave-holding Virginia man who had all the credentials to be a great Confederate General; West Point (1840), Seminole and Mexican War hero, and friendships with Braxton Bragg and Robert E. Lee. However, when the Civil War began he stayed loyal to the Old Flag. His family turned his picture to the wall and never reconciled with him for his 'treason.' He had a reputation for cautious deliberation but he served in a dozen major battles and twice, at Missionary Ridge and Nashville, drove entrenched Confederate armies off in panicked routs. He is much less known than other Civil War generals because he never engaged in politics nor wrote his memoirs. To many historians he ranks in importance below only Grant and Sherman. Thomas is memorialized with Thomas Circle in Washington DC and in the 1890's his hairy face graced the five dollar bill.

24. Joseph Hooker had the usual resume for a Civil War general; Seminole and Mexican Wars and service in California. He was an enthusiastic braggart and gossip who undermined his superiors at every opportunity. His criticism of Burnside after Fredericksburg led Lincoln to give him a chance at the top command. He proved to be a very good military housekeeper, and with good food, decent camp hygiene and improved training he boosted the moral of the Army of the Potomac. His humiliation at Chancellorsville, however, showed he was unfit for independent command. He is best known for two reasons– his nom de guerre, 'Fighting Joe,' and the term 'hooker' for prostitutes. The first was the result of a misquoted dispatch during the Peninsula Campaign and had nothing to do with his combat prowess. The term 'hooker,' coined after a district in Manhattan where whores met ships, was used as early as the 1840's, but it fit in well with the casual lifestyle and habits followed at his headquarters. The men referred to camp followers as Hooker's girls or Hooker's Brigade.

25. Grenville Dodge was a railroad man. He is best known for his work on the Union Pacific Transcontinental Railroad. Educated as a civil engineer, he used his skills in a score of different tasks during the Civil War. He was wounded twice, including being shot in the head. He left the war as a major general. Under Grant he set up a vast spy network using prostitutes, slaves and deserters as agents. It was not as famous as Allan Pinkerton's intelligencers with the Army of the Potomac but that is why it was so much more effective. Immediately after the War he went west to fight the plains Indians and subsequently discovered a route for the Union Pacific RR through the Black Hills. Heading the Dodge Commission to investigate Army shenanigans in the Spanish American War, Dodge created many enemies, including General Sidney Sawyer. Dodge City, Kansas is his most famous legacy.

26. Thanks to survival skills taught to them by sympathetic Indians the Pilgrims survived their first year in the New World and celebrated with an autumn feast. During colonial times Thanksgiving became a common but never organized event. (The Pilgrims themselves skipped 1622) At various times the government, including the Continental Congress and George Washington, tried to unify the event but the celebration remained local. Southern colonies mostly ignored it. The hero of Thanksgiving was author, Sarah Josepha Hale who waged a thirty-six year campaign to make it an official holiday. At the height of the Civil War, Abraham Lincoln recognized its merit and made it official in his *second* most famous proclamation. During the Great Depression, Franklin Roosevelt tried to move it up a week to stimulate holiday shopping. This presumption was met with

such resistance that in 1941 Roosevelt relented and signed Thanksgiving into law as a legal holiday. There was no pumpkin pie at the first Thanksgiving. There was no grain to make piecrust.

27. Tom Sawyer was correct– the Red River Campaign was primarily a gigantic cotton raid, but there *were* other factors. Shreveport was a considerable manufacturing center that the Union wanted taken or destroyed. Also, western Louisiana was a strategic location to stage an invasion of Texas. The Confederates would oppose this at all costs, which would be a golden opportunity to destroy Kirby Smith's and Richard Taylor's Rebel forces. There were also political considerations. President Lincoln dearly wanted to use Louisiana as model for reconstruction. Indeed, Banks began his campaign late because he was holding an election for a reconstructed state government. When all was said and done however, Grant was correct that it was just a sideshow and, successful or not, it could have no effect on the outcome of the greater war. Without Nathanial Banks's ambition to become president it would never have occurred.

28. Almost 30,000 Native Americans from two-dozen tribes served in the Civil War– on both sides. Their dilemma was to choose the winning side. Most tribes chose the Union. The Cherokee, Choctaw and Chickasaw chose the Confederacy. The unlucky Creek tribe divided between North and South and fought bitter intertribal battles against each other. Most Indian service was in the trans Mississippi but the entire male population of the Catawba nation fought in South Carolina infantry with the Army of Northern Virginia. In the Union Army, many Indians fought in the U.S.C.T. Ely S. Parker, a Seneca from the Iroquois Nation, reached the rank of brigadier general and served on Grant's staff. He wrote the final copy of the Articles of Surrender (the one Lee and Grant actually signed) at Appomattox. One other Native American achieved the rank of general. This was Stand Watie, the principle chief of the Cherokee Nation. Two months after Lee, Watie was the last Confederate general to surrender to Union forces. Despite their honorable service during the War, the United States continued its harsh policies toward the Indian nations.

29. Ferdinand Maximilian was the younger brother of the Hapsburg Emperor of Austria. For a time he served as a naval officer but, as a Hapsburg, he was born to rule. In 1861, with the Monroe Doctrine temporally suspended by the Civil War, French Emperor, Napoleon III sent an army to occupy Mexico. To give an air of legitimacy to the invasion, the crown of Mexico was offered to Maximilian. In 1863, while still in Europe, he was proclaimed the Emperor of Mexico. His wife became Her Imperial Majesty Empress Carlota. He arrived in Mexico in 1864 to find the Mexican government

under President Benito Juarez was still a going concern and in active rebellion against the French. In 1865 the U.S. Civil War ended and U.S. support to Juarez increased. The next year Napoleon III evacuated his troops, ending the French adventure. In 1867 the luckless but gallant Maximilian's forces were defeated and he bravely faced his Mexican firing squad. The Juarez government was reestablished. Maximilian's wife lost her mind and is remembered to history as the Mad Empress Carlota.

30. The Battle of Mansfield or Sabine Crossroads was a Union humiliation. Banks's order of march made it impossible to present more than a fraction of his strength to confront General Richard Smith's Confederate Army. At the point of battle the Federals were outnumbered, 14,000 to 12,000. Sawyer's description of the action is accurate as far as it goes. After he absented himself from the field the Rebels routed a second Union line. The battle ended at dusk when Smith's assault on a third Union line several miles farther back was repulsed by stiffening Federal resistance. It was a small fight by the standards of many Civil War bloodbaths. 110 Northern troops were killed, 600 were wounded and 1400 were captured or missing. Confederates lost around 1000, killed and wounded. The Union cavalry lost every one of their poorly deployed wagons. They were all fully loaded and most still had their mules in harness. Commissary Banks, indeed!

31. Navy prize money was an institution dating back to the 17th century. It codified and legitimized plunder on the high seas. It also encouraged zeal in officers to strike at an enemy's commerce. An official prize court would evaluate a captured ship and its cargo. The booty would be divided into eights. One eighth went to the admiral. Two shares went to the captain, another would be divided between the lieutenants and the sailing master. Another eighth went to the wardroom officers, another to the midshipmen, warrant and petty officers. The final two eights was divided amongst the crew. Captains could become rich by taking even one fully loaded enemy ship. The last prize taken by an American ship was a month before Pearl Harbor when the USS Omaha captured a German blockade-runner. Raiding commerce without the mantle of codified prize money was piracy.

32. William C. Quantrill and William Anderson represented the very worst aspects of the Civil War. Quantrill, an Ohio schoolteacher with a mean streak and a propensity for larceny, led a makeshift Confederate guerrilla army using tactics learned from pro-Southern Cherokees. His most infamous outrage was the Lawrence Massacre in 1863 where he burnt the town and murdered 183 men and boys in front of their families. He did not surrender after the war and

was cornered and killed in Kentucky in 1865. Bloody Bill Anderson was worse. Anderson, a former horse thief, rode with Quantrill until they had a violent parting of ways. Anderson formed his own band, which included the likes of Frank and Jessie James. Fighting in Union uniforms stripped from murdered prisoners, they tortured, scalped, plundered and raped their way through Kansas and Missouri. To counter these raiders, Union forces established their own reign of terror, depopulating entire counties in Missouri. Anderson was killed in a skirmish in October of 1864.

33. Joseph Bailey was only one of 15 men voted the Thanks of Congress during the Civil War. He was a civil engineer and lumberman who knew that if wing dams could float logs over riffles back in Wisconsin they could float ironclads over rapids on the Red River. His dams were built as Sawyer describes and they saved the flotilla and army. His ingenious bridge of riverboats across the Atchafalaya River saved the expedition yet again. After the War he moved to Missouri and was elected county sheriff. In 1866 he was gunned down while arresting two brothers for stealing a hog. Bailey was posthumously promoted to Major General in 1867.

34. Sawyer's narration of the burning of Alexandria is correct but didn't go far enough in describing the full extent of the destruction. Flaming chickens flapped from coops, dogs snapped at burning tails, the entire population swarmed in panic to the levee fleeing the conflagration. A.J. Smith did indeed ride through the town cheering, "Hurrah, boys, this looks like war!" General Banks, watching from his boat ordered troops back to the city to halt the massive looting, (it was already too late to save the city itself) but it was a feeble attempt. All of the city's churches were burned except St. Francis Xavier Roman Catholic Church. Father J.B. Bellier, a former Lieutenant in the French Cavalry and an expert swordsman, stood off the mob with rapier in hand. Ironically the church burned down in 1895, but was immediately rebuilt in brick. In 1910, St. Francis Xavier's was elevated to Cathedral of the Diocese of Alexandria.

35. The Battle of Mansura (May 16, 1864) occurred much as Sawyer described it. General Richard Taylor deployed his forces across flat cotton fields to deny Banks's army the road to Simesport. The Confederates were greatly outnumbered, but with Banks's combat record Taylor calculated it was worth a try. After a long-range artillery duel, Union forces threatened to outflank the Rebels. Taylor withdrew to seek a better opportunity. The Battle of Yellow Bayou was fought two days later and was Taylor's last effort to prevent Banks and his Army of the Gulf from escaping across the Atchafalaya River. In a seesaw contest that ended when wildfires separated the combatants, A.J.

Smith's Gorillas held off Taylor's forces. In the last days of the War, Taylor was given command of the once mighty Confederate Army of the Tennessee. On May 4, 1865 he surrendered the last major Rebel force east of the Mississippi. In 1869, one week after publishing his memoirs, Taylor died of dropsy. After the War Nathanial Banks returned to the House of Representatives. He never did become president and died in 1894.

Acknowledgments

There are many people who made *The Adventures of Sidney Sawyer: Missouri Yankees* possible. Without their help and support I could not have completed this novel.

Most importantly is my wonderful and lovely wife, Nina. She has given me all the support and love I needed to complete this, the fifth book in *The Adventures of Sidney Sawyer* series. She took time away from her own passion for art to become my most important proofreader. Nina read to me aloud every word in each one of my books– twice. That is a lot of reading and a great testimony of love.

Also, without the support of my son Ted, it would have been impossible to complete this project. He polished my prose like it was the family silver. Ted, a classical violinist and violist, proofread each chapter correcting my hopeless punctuation and grammar. His efforts were a labor of love, and no father could be more proud of his son. After copyediting five novels, Nina and Ted have become experts in the difficult craft of editing and proofreading.

My inspiration for *The Adventures of Sidney Sawyer* was the *Flashman* series of novels by George MacDonald Fraser. In my opinion *Flashman* is one of the finest series of historical fiction ever written. What Fraser's Harry Flashman did for the history of the British Empire, I hope for Sidney Sawyer to do for American history.

Shelby Foote's three-volume history, *The Civil War: A Narrative* was my indispensable, (but by no means my only) source for this novel. (Random House, 1958) Shelby Foote passed away in 2005 but his *Narrative* has not been out of print since it was first published, and hopefully never will be.

Finally, thanks and blessings to Samuel Clemens, America's most beloved author who created the raw material for my series; Aunt Polly, Amy Lawrence, Alfred Temple, Ben Rogers, Becky Thatcher and her father the judge, Jim Watson and Lizabeth, Huckleberry Finn, Tom Sawyer and especially his nasty little brother Sidney.

ENJOY A SAMPLE OF

The Adventures of Sidney Sawyer

THE FATHER OF WATERS

A TALE OF HIGH ADVENTURE FROM THE PEN OF MASTER STORYTELLER

DAVID M. SMELTZ

It was moonless and black as your hat when the fleet of seven great ironclad gunboats sporting seventy-nine guns, a steam ram, and three transports bringing up the rear of the line, crept from the mouth of the Yazoo and into the Mississippi. We were hardly making steerage over the four-mile-an-hour current, and our machinery noise was muffled by the hay packed around the walking-beam housing. Stealth was the watchword. The plan was to sulk like chicken thieves past Young's Point and around the bend that would put us under the great guns of the Vicksburg batteries. If we were discovered, or more likely *when* we were discovered, steam was up and our cannon were shotted and primed. Then it would be Katie-bar-the-door and no place to hide except behind the hay. The gunboats were Navy, but the transports were manned by Army volunteers who were as giddy and full of bounce as schoolboys at the thought of the night's action– silly fools. The *Henry Clay* was second last in line. The only lights showing were dim, masked lanterns in the stern of each boat to guide the column. I was dying for a cheroot but I'd not have struck a Lucifer for my life. If I saw any trooper addle-brained enough to show a light I would have throttled the hound and heaved his arse into the wheel, but the men knew the risk and went about their duties like ghosts. It was quiet as the bottom of the pit and almost as dark. The boat before us couldn't have been more than fifty yards ahead but without the tiny prick of light from its stern-lantern it might not have been there. I took another pull from my pint and found a corner in the wet hay aft of the port wheel. If I was going into that black water I didn't want to be minced by the paddles.

From above there was a spate of nervous laughter and a low, sharp, "Belay that ,you web-foot son of a bitch. Quiet! There it 'tis."

And there it was. We followed the stern-light ahead around the great bend of Vicksburg Point, and there above us on the left loomed the bluff, with the lights of the city winking like fireflies in the blackness. In those still and awful seconds I was fool enough to say my prayers. Heaven knows what the Almighty thinks of me. He only hears from Sidney Sawyer when I'm in the soup. And here I was again, mumbling my childhood prayers and fumbling with the stopper of my flask with paws that felt as if I were wearing mittens. I dropped the cork with a curse and from the darkness a rough whisper hissed, "Shet-up there, you brim-pecker," and then all hell broke loose.

Pemberton was no fool and he had the river picketed with sentry bateaus. Even in the dark there was no missing the blunt bow of Porter's flagship the *Benton*. We were too far behind to hear the shouts and the crunch as the gunboat ran the bateau under, but the sentries got off a half-dozen shots of warning that we *did* hear. Then the line of ships went to full power with a throb of machinery that could be heard through the night like a landslide. Shouts came from ahead in the fleet, and more came from the shore on the Louisiana side, and in seconds the shore was lit with huge fires that the Rebels had primed with tar and oil. The flotilla was backlit like it was daylight. The Confederate guns opened with a smash that shook the night and blinding tongues of flame shot into the night like comets. The fleet answered with broadsides that actually shook the river itself as if the water was alive. The Reb gunners on the bluff had all winter to sight the batteries in on where the boats would have to be, and their high perch meant that their shot would slam smack into the armor and not bounce away. They couldn't miss and didn't. From my spot crouching behind the hay I could follow the fight by the continuous blasts of light from the heavy guns of the fleet. Shot after Confederate shot struck home, bashing at the ironclad armor like hammers at a forge in hell. And then a coal barge lashed to the port side of a Pook turtle in the center of the line broke loose and the gunboat slewed hard to starboard, got caught in the current and in seconds was steaming upstream dead back into the fleet. Boats scattered to the right and left, and for long minutes while fire thundered down on their decks, they steamed in great circles trying to come about and flee past the enemy guns. All the while they cannoned back with every gun they could bring to bear. As the *Clay* steamed into the melee the noise was enough to shatter the molars in your jaws. Then the ironclads at the front of the line were suddenly past the batteries and beyond the range of the grayback gunners. They ceased their fire and between the booms of the Confederate guns we could hear the cheers of the Navy crews. But now the hayclad *Clay* was finally in range and the bonfires on the far shore silhouetted us to the rebels on the bluffs.

It's a terrible and beautiful thing to be under fire from great cannon in the black of night. First you see from high up the white flash from the muzzle reaching into the dark as it blasts its missile into the air. The fuse burns a bright line of red fire, like a shooting star up into the sky, but instead of blinking out, it blinks faster and faster as the shell tumbles through the air. It comes down at you like a meteor, with the boom of the gun reaching you in the same instant as the evil shriek of the shell that rushes past you faster than light. The ball strikes the river just by the rail and the water gushes over you like a Niagara. And then, instead of one shooting star, it's three. As the lines of red arch out and down they are joined by five more, and then five more, and I'm out of the hay and gripping the sticky rail and damn the paint. The booms reach you all at once and there are screams and curses from the bow as the water cascades over you like a solid wave, and finally comes the terrible crash as the shot rips into the boat.

The guns on the bluff were huge smoothbore monsters that were meant to rip through the iron armor of the Navy. They tore through the flimsy *Henry Clay* as if it was gossamer, leaving ragged tears through the pine planking and scattering burning hay in clouds of flame. The crew didn't wait for disaster, clever lads. They swarmed up from the engine spaces like monkeys, seconds before heavy shot shattered the boilers with an explosion that lifted the deck sharp enough to buckle my knees. The port wheel was swept away as if by a great hand, taking the davits holding the port boat with it. As the *Clay* settled, the bum-boat launched itself and the crew swarmed aboard. I almost sobbed with fright. There was no way to reach the boat over the wreckage of the huge wheel. I turned to flee through the salon to the starboard side and salvation, but flames filled the cabin and the blast of heat drove me to the rail. Now the damned hay wasn't armor, it was death, catching fire with great whooshes of flame and driving me along the rail, closer to the stern. Another great shell swept through the woodwork with a swarm of splinters and I flipped backward into the dark River with water filling my boots, dragging me down. It happened so fast that even though the boilers were blown and the paddle wheels shattered, the *Clay* was still making way ahead of me as it sank. It went down like a brick with a great hissing of drowning flame.

Cavalry boots are not an asset in swift current and as I struggled to kick them off I gave my toe a good stubbing. I believe it was on one of the hogsheads of salt-horse that were sinking about me by the score. Other men would have drowned in panic. Other men would have flailed about in despair and fear, giving in to exhaustion, to sink and feed the catfish. But I didn't fear the Mississippi. I had prepared for this little swim all through childhood. As a child the River was my playground. All summer long, us boys of St. Petersburg, white and black, would race to the river, yanking our duds off all along the way, to be bare-naked by the time we jumped into the drink. We called it "river-balling" and it was great fun. Of course we didn't swim in the wee hours of the morning in the chill of March a half-mile out with heavy shot frothing the surface of the river, but at least Brother Tom wasn't dunking me while his gang hooted at me for being a crybaby. After my boots kicked free, I shed my jacket. I hated to flip my Adams revolver from the holster to let it sink it, but it was three pounds of iron. It was either the pistol on the river bottom or both of us. For the time being I kept my belt with the ten gold eagles. If I got too tired it would join the Adams, but for now I'd keep my coin.

I floated easy on my back looking up at the arching shells but the show was about over and after a two or three ragged shots it stopped. The night was again as black as the Earl of Hell's boots. In the sudden quiet I could hear Rebel pickets on the Louisiana side shouting over the water for the sentry bateaus to come sharp and fetch them before the Yankee patrols snapped them up. I could swim like an otter, but I was already shivering in the cold black water. The shore was too far away even for an old river-baller like me. There was nothing for it but to shout out to the Johnny picket boats for a rescue. The thought of spending the War in a Confederate prison camp set me to weeping at the injustice of it all. Wasn't I wounded? Well no, but three weeks ago I was, and didn't I deserve a pass from this folly? Why me Lord? Why me, and I began to mumble my childhood prayers. Of course the answer to the silly prayer "why me" always has the same answer– "why not?" And then I bumped into a great raft of wreckage from the old *Henry Clay* and swarmed up and out of the current. The Lord had answered my prayer and I answered back by cursing the loss of the Adams and my pint of sutler's brandy.

Why Huckleberry Finn and big black Jim remembered their drift down the Mississippi on a raft as a time of wonder and joy is beyond me. Other than freezing my courting package into a thimble, I was bored to distraction and I was only on that damn raft of wreckage for twelve hours. During the night I must have fallen into a doze because I woke with the low morning sun in my face, which was good, because I was past the high bluffs of Vicksburg with it's hellish guns, but bad because my raft was caught on a snag and I could see the Warrenton batteries across the river with the Stars and Bars flying over the works. I'd only drifted a mile or so during the night before my raft got tangled in the branches of a great tree that grounded itself in the shallow water of the Louisiana side. I was in clear view of any Johnny Reb lookouts, but it was a big river, and from a quarter mile my raft was just another bit of flotsam that fouled the River after the battle. It took an hour of shivering neck-deep in the branches to work my bit of the old *Henry Clay* free to take up its drift, and another three for the current to ghost me even with New Carthage. And hallelujah in a bandbox, there was the fleet, battered but afloat. Bluejackets swarmed over every inch of the gunboats repairing damage from the midnight run past the guns, and stretching away along the levee was McClernand's Corps in bivouac. The Navy was safe and by grapes, so was I, but this was too good a chance to let slip. I was only a pistol shot off the landing and … well … you know me.

"Ahoy Navy!" I shouted, standing on the rubbish with a dramatic fist upon my hip. Aye, I do like to strike a pose. I must have been the best show on the river because as I shouted, the racket of the repairs died to the odd clanging and all eyes were on me. "Ahoy buckos, ahoy! It was a grand show and damn good fun, whatdaya think?"

I was chilled to my marrow and my boots were gone, but I was still in my Union blues with my buff cumberbund about my belly and my colonel straps wide and gold on my broad cavalry shoulders. With my whiskers I must have looked like d'Artagnan on a platter. A wave of cheers came at me from the line of gunboats, so I figured what the dickens, I have an audience.

"Let's give our heroes three times three! Three cheers for Porter! Three cheers for Grant and three cheers and a bull-dog for the bluejackets of the Brown Water Navy!"

And then while a jolly boat shot out from the levee with a crew of hearties that stroked away like the Yale crew, the shore came alive with a roar that could be heard back in Vicksburg.

I do love to make an entrance, but it was almost ruined by that old maid Colonel John Rawlins. As I stepped off the boat to the backslaps of the jollies, General Grant himself met me at the landing. I had no notion what the deuce he was doing in New Carthage. Most of the Army was still back at Millikin's Bend, but there he slouched with Rawlins at his elbow glaring thunder.[o]

I stood to attention in my bare feet and snapped a salute.

"Sawyer!" Rawlings fussed, "Explain yourself, sir! You are a sight, sir. Where are your boots, man?"

Well this was raw. Grant wouldn't have met me if they hadn't heard the rumpus I had raised arriving on my raft of wreckage.

---

[o] Grant and his family watched the run past the batteries on the *Magnolia* from Young's Point. When the guns finally went silent he was so anxious over the fate of the fleet that he galloped all night on the new Roundaway Bayou Road, arriving in the late morning. Sawyer must have arrived shortly after the General.

"My boots, sir?" I drawled, cool as you like. I saw Grant's half grin beneath his face-hair so I dared to be fresh. "Why I kicked them off to stay afloat after the *Henry Clay* foundered. Wouldn't do the Army any good feeding the bull-heads, would I?"

"You were on the *Clay* because of your wounds, sir. You were all a' gimp. Where is your cane, sir?"

What could I say? "Colonel Rawlins, I am healed."

This silly statement brought Grant's eyes hard onto mine. He gave no truck for malingering fakers. He took a deep suck on his Havana stinker and asked in a cloud of smoke, "And just how could a body come to mend so quickly, Colonel Sawyer?"

My answer became a minor legend in the Western Army.

"General Grant, it's as simple as pudding. I soaked it in river water for twelve hours."

The Adventures of Sidney Sawyer
THE YEAR OF JUBILEE

Our hero battles through the second bloody summer of the Civil War– fighting rebel raiders, spying on Jeff Davis for Honest Abe, diddling vicious Confederate widows, racing for life on stolen locomotives, shepherding runaways north on the Underground Railroad, and surviving America's bloodiest day, only to face his archenemy in a duel to the death on the heights above Harpers Ferry. Master storyteller David M. Smeltz weaves his spell as President Lincoln proclaims "THE *YEAR OF JUBILEE*!"

The Adventures of Sidney Sawyer
THE FATHER OF WATERS

Ancient General Sawyer remembers the third terrible year of the Civil War. Trying to make a killing in Confederate cotton our man is captured by Reb raiders and joins the Johnny cavalry. Finding refuge driving slaves on a Yazoo cotton hell, he breaks for freedom with a train of runaways and the help of Ol' Uncle Remus. Rejoining the Union Army in time for the Battles for Vicksburg he sinks, swims, marches, rides, and shirks with Grant and Sherman, rogering beautiful but brutal Rebel spies and assaulting enemy works with Sergeant Huckleberry Finn. Captured, brutalized and hauled away for slaughter, Sidney has a deadly showdown on the heights above the Mississippi. Master Storyteller David M. Smeltz spins his web along *"THE FATHER OF WATERS!"*